BASIC BLACK

BASIC BLACK
TALES OF
APPROPRIATE FEAR

TERRY DOWLING

TICONDEROGA
PUBLICATIONS

for

Kerri Larkin and Bradley Wynne

As they say in all the best expatriate
Outback aviation classics:
Tag!

Basic Black: Tales of Appropriate Fear by Terry Dowling

Published by Ticonderoga Publications

First published by Cemetery Dance Publications, 2006

Designed and edited by Russell B. Farr
Typeset in Sabon and Century Gothic

National Library of Australia
Cataloguing-in-Publications entry

Dowling, Terry 1947–
Basic black: tales of appropriate fear

1st ed.
ISBN 9780980353198 (hc)
1. Short stories,
A813.54

  ISBN   978-0-9803531-9-8 (hardcover)
         978-0-9806288-2-1 (trade paperback)

Ticonderoga Publications
PO Box 29 Greenwood
Western Australia 6924

www.ticonderogapublications.com

10 9 8 7 6 5 4 3 2 1

ACKNOWLEDGEMENTS

The stories in this book span more than twenty years in a writing life. The author extends heartfelt thanks to: Leigh Blackmore, Simon Brown, Wolfgang Bylsma, Jeremy G. Byrne, Bill Congreve, Kate Cummings, Keith Curtis, Jack Dann, Ellen Datlow, Nick Dhamala, Harlan Ellison, Alan C. Elms, Russell B. Farr, Philip Gore, Carey Handfield, Kerrie Hanlon-Delas, Rob Hood, Van Ikin, Kohan Ikin, Kerri Larkin, Fritz Leiber, Neil Maloney, Sean McMullen, Peter McNamara, Mariann McNamara, Robert Morrish, Sergio Pinheiro, Jesse C. Polhemus, Russell Scott, Cat Sparks, Nick Stathopoulos, Grant Stone, Jonathan Strahan, Shaun Tan, Jack Vance, Norma Vance, Sean Williams and Bradley Wynne.

Contents

Appropriate Fears

Jonathan Strahan

This is the task of man always...not to illuminate the ancient truths, the ancient intimations of the unconscious, the ancient intimations of the soul, but...to make them immediate and contemporary, to give them meaning in the here and now

—CARL JUNG

THAT QUOTE FROM Carl Jung hangs above Terry Dowling's desk at Everard Street in Sydney's inner west where he has written the majority of his best and most important work, serving as both inspiration and challenge for more than twenty-five years. He has, referring to that quote, said that the task of the writer is "to restore numinosity to the human experience, to beguile readers into a confrontation with their own humanity." It's something that you can see clearly and perhaps most plainly in his science fiction, but is equally present in the darker tales collected in this, the eighth book of his short stories to be published.

Born in Sydney in the late 1940s, Terry grew up less than a mile from a mental hospital at Bedlam Point, and has lived less than a mile from a cemetery called the Fields of Mars. While there have been many other inspirations for his work, it's tempting to make a connection between the characters in his stories who experience some kind of altered state of mind, who profoundly doubt their own perceptions, and that young man growing up so close to Bedlam. Certainly, it seems to have had its clearest impact on Terry's Tom Rynosseros cycle of stories—collected in *Rynosseros, Blue Tyson,* and *Twilight Beach*—which are set in a far future Australia dominated by tribal forces and mostly told from the point of view of a man who has been released from a madhouse to chase an unlikely dream. Probably Terry's most personal work, it also plainly shows his other influences: the surrealists, the work of Dali and Delvaux, and equally the work of Bradbury, of Cordwainer Smith, Vance, Ballard, Dick, Leiber, Ellison, and so many more.

It's also tempting to look to the Fields of Mars for a connection that explains some of Terry's affinity for the wondrous, the numinous, and the darker side of our experience. From his early 'nature of reality' stories like "The Maze Man," "The Gully," and "The Bullet That Grows in the Gun," Terry has shown a keen understanding of how slightly twisting the reader's view of reality leads at first to a sense of discomfort, and ultimately to something deeply disturbing. And it is perhaps here that we should look to the term 'appropriate fear.' What fear is appropriate? Is it appropriate to fear some outlandish cartoon octopus with a polysyllabic name, or is it more appropriate to fear the world beginning to twist and distort, to feel an improbable but entirely appropriate chill when you realize that the gun you're holding continues to fire but never needs reloading, or to wonder exactly what is happening behind the curtains over there, and how are they shifting in a breeze that isn't there?

Terry devoted most of the late 1980s and early 1990s to writing science fiction—the stories of *Rynosseros* and the classic *Wormwood* story suite—only occasionally producing darker gems like "The Daemon-Street Ghost Trap" and "Scaring the Train" (both collected here). However in the mid-90s he began to turn his attention to darker fiction, and in 1996 wrote his finest work in that vein, the *Blackwater Days* story suite. Written in a red-hot burst of inspiration in mid-1996, the seven stories that make up the cycle are all in some way connected with a rural mental hospital in New

South Wales' Hunter Valley called Blackwater, and, with its chief psychiatrist, Dan Truswell, are alternately horrifying, disturbing and deeply creepy. Several of the stories in the book—"Jenny Come to Play," "Downloading," and "Beckoning Nightframe"—were published before *Blackwater Days* appeared, winning awards and confirming Terry's place in the pantheon of modern writers of the fantastic. The book itself appeared in 2000 and, along with the major remaining unpublished story, "The Saltimbanques," was nominated for the World Fantasy Award in 2001. It's a mother lode Terry has continued to mine, producing important stories like "One Thing About the Night," "The Bone Ship," and the two stories original to this book, "La Profonde" and "Cheat Light."

It is perhaps appropriate here to mention that I have some stake in all of this. I've been fortunate, since first meeting Terry in 1990, to serve as commissioning editor, first reader, and publisher of some of the stories in this book. We've become close friends and, as any reader knows, a favourite writer's stories become part of the story of your life. For example, I've been reading "The Quiet Redemption of Andy the House" for fifteen years now. A personal favourite, I missed it in *Australian Short Stories* when it first appeared, but not when it was reprinted in *Strange Plasma*. I read it again when it was reprinted in *An Intimate Knowledge Of The Night*, several times more preparing it for its republication in *Antique Futures: The Best of Terry Dowling,* and again just now for this book. Each time I am swept into the story, wrong footed by this disorienting tale of a young mental patient who dreams of blind gladiators, and of his calm, rational doctors in their island retreat, attempting to navigate his madness. Although not a horror story, or even a tale of fear, it is typical, brilliant Dowling. Why? The contrast between Andy's dreams and the doctors' rationality highlight the connection between the numinous and the explicable, making us re-consider how we see our world. It is, like "The Saltimbanques," like "One Thing About the Night" and "Jenny Come to Play," very special; I envy you encountering it, and the other seventeen stories collected here, for the first time.

And now, it's almost time for the stories themselves, but first an observation. I once heard it said, by someone who should have known better, that Australians couldn't write horror. From the barracks at Puckapunyal and the vineyards of the Hunter to the suburban streets of Sydney itself, the winds of Australia blow through each of these haunting tales, adding a scent of gum leaves here, a slant of light there and, always, very, very appropriate fear. Enjoy.

Jonathan Strahan
Perth, July 2009

TALES OF
APPROPRIATE FEAR

The Daemon Street

Ghost-Trap

I **FIRST HEARD** of the Daemon Street ghost-trap from Jarvis Henry on the day after he lost his aide of six years to an interstate posting.

I was doing my Honours year, and the retired academic had been giving some honorary lectures and a completely optional series of seminars on perceptual anomalies. I enjoyed the classes, participated readily in the discussions, and received an invitation to stay back after the three o'clock meeting on that momentous Friday. Jarvis Henry's words were gently spoken, but they exploded in my mind.

"Jack, I wonder if you would like to accompany me this evening to see a Renfeld ghost-trap in Daemon Street?"

We'd all heard the news of his assistant's departure, so I spent the next hour daring to hope I was being considered as a replacement for the job— the Sorcerer's Apprentice.

All through the class, I watched Jarvis (as he preferred to be known), his bushy eyebrows flicking about on that pink, scrubbed-looking teddy-bear face, studying the small blue eyes for some sign. But no. He seemed jovial, excited, and determined to leave me in suspense.

While he listened patiently to a question from Megan Hatford, I reviewed all I knew about the Sorcerer (our name for him), trying to distinguish fact from rumour.

This small neatly-scrubbed-looking man in a worn tan suit, for all his qualifications, had made a name for himself searching out ghost-traps and spirit-foils across the world. He'd already examined forty-seven, but as I was later to discover, the one in Daemon Street had always been the one he most wanted to see.

When the class finally ended I approached him.

"I'd love to—Jarvis," I said, as though the previous hour hadn't existed, only his invitation.

"Good man," he replied, then spent ten minutes with me talking about the visit.

All through the next lecture I thought about what Jarvis Henry had said relating to Daemon Street. I looked out of the window at the fading autumn light, hoping my friends wouldn't mind me cancelling our plans for the evening. As I tried to take notes, Jarvis's words kept coming back to me.

Daemon Street. What a name. What a rare joke.

For a start, he suspected it was a real ghost-trap, not just a foil for keeping ghosts away like the Baxter's staircase-to-nowhere, or the Talbot's Blank Door, the false Red Room at Cromer, the Rot Bottle or the Blackfriar's Eat-Yourself Spiral Maze. According to Jarvis's most reliable source, the Crane residence in Daemon Street probably had token versions of those too, but it was the doorless room in the centre of the ground floor that had Jarvis so excited. It was not a modification, Jarvis had said, not some afterthought added later, but part of the house's original design. Someone had set out to catch and hold something.

I marvelled at it too. It wasn't just that someone had had the determination and commitment to give over a dining-room-sized space to catching a family ghost. There was also the healthy respect that kept succeeding generations from breaking the thing open and putting it to more immediate use. As Jarvis said, it took a strong haunting tradition, recurring manifestations, to do that.

These people believed.

I arrived at Jarvis's office in the Whiting Building at six. It was a brightly lit room, with the same twinkling, neatly scrubbed quality that Jarvis had. Amid the drab functional greys of filing cabinets and bookshelves, there was a collection of small curios and talismans.

I took the sound equipment and cameras Jarvis handed me and we went down to his car in the staff carpark.

"I wish I had time to show you more of the Private Listings, Jack. The Bellerton and Dutton breakdown released last year, the Getier monograph. You only got to browse them in class and you would be interested. Oh, I am so excited!"

There was no need for the street directory. Jarvis had plotted the route in advance, had no doubt driven down Daemon Street many times just to look at the house. He put some of the heavier things on the back seat, gave me the Pentax to hold, and started the engine.

"It's a real one. Jack. I am convinced!" he said as we reversed out of the carpark.

"Are there many fakes, Jarvis?"

"Oh yes, Jack. It's like mazes and topiaries. You make their existence public and everyone wants to see them. They become tourist attractions, even status symbols. The fakes soon appear. It's understandable with the television shows and magazines paying so well for coverage."

While Jarvis discussed the next week's parking arrangements with a university security guard, I had time to savour what was happening, to glance at the traffic moving under a chill blue evening sky and know that this was a special time.

I was the Sorcerer's Apprentice. For tonight at least, I was it.

To my knowledge Jarvis had dealt with two recent fakes: the Garden Trap at Higgs, and the Wentletrap-in-a-Well at Barstow. Campus talk had it that he had exposed many others, always in the same urbane, thoroughly civilized way, always avoiding legal action with his celebrated and quite damning line: "There is nothing for me here."

"How did you persuade Mr Crane?" I asked, wondering why he had never been able to visit the Daemon Street site before now.

"Ah, Jack," Jarvis said, turning left and heading towards the city. "Ever since I heard about Tesserley Crane seventeen years ago I've been trying to get in to see it. Phone calls and letters every month for a while. Polite refusals every time. He's a widower, but one of his sons, Bradlan or young Roderick, or Tesserley himself, would point out that publicity wasn't wanted. I promised discretion but they refused. Every month became every other year. Now this phone call. The old man claims he has trapped a ghost—a Renfeld

Four—and apparently he's going to breach the room. He invited me to be there."

"A Four?" I said, deciding to show my ignorance up front.

"Yes, Jack. You've heard me mention Eugene Renfeld's *Ghostings: A Taxonomy* in class. Remind me to show you the extracts I have, if you like apprenticing for me."

And he winked. I definitely saw him wink.

"It's a limited edition, published in 1934. Very much a vanity press thing; none of the respectable publishers would touch it. The mutual friend who first told me about Crane's room also mentioned that Crane had a copy and, from what he says, probably believes in Renfeld's four types. This is a marvellous opportunity if this is the case."

I went to comment but Jarvis spoke first.

"Forgive me, Jack, if I leave it to Crane to tell you what the four kinds of ghosts are. I'm hoping to hear how the old man handles it, and your detachment may be useful. I'm even thinking he may have been a student of Renfeld at some time. But you may remember the concept of the Red Room. I mentioned it at our first class when I showed my slides of Cromer."

"Yes, I do," I said, trying to remember what I had heard in class, and what Jarvis had told me that afternoon.

"Well, Renfeld fixed on that as the best way to hold a ghost. I'm thinking that the room in Daemon Street is a Renfeld trap."

"A Red Room?"

"Yes."

We turned into Parkhill, then did a sharp left into Makinson.

"What's the reasoning there, Jarvis?"

"It's straightforward, Jack. Blood memory, I should think, though I prefer to leave that sort of theorizing to people like Renfeld. Honorary lectureships are worth a degree of circumspection. Off the record though" (and again there was a wink) "the ghost essence once occupied a living body. Whatever life is—or was—is drawn to that colour. Red and darkness. Renfeld gives ten cases in my extracts from *Ghostings* where Red Rooms attracted and neutralized Fours."

The car's headlights fell on a metal sign fixed to the brick wall of a corner terrace house: Daemon Street. I was startled by the archaic spelling.

The Crane house was halfway down the street. A large three-storeyed dwelling, it was set back behind some pin oaks, appearing smaller than it was because of even larger houses closely adjoining it on either side.

The evening had turned cold. The pin oaks shook in the sudden chill wind, and the warm light spilling out of the stained-glass fantail above the front door was a welcome sight. Through the ragged, autumn-stripped trees we could see more light falling from the long shades of the first-story windows.

A butler answered the door, a dour sallow-skinned elderly man in formal black who admitted us to a lit hallway. At the end of the hall, a stairway went up into darkness. The rest of the ground floor was in gloom.

"Mr Crane is upstairs, gentlemen, if you would be so kind. First door on the left. He is expecting you, of course. Dinner will be in twenty minutes."

Both Jarvis and I had been studying the panelled wall to the right of the staircase.

"That's it," the butler said, and moved off towards the kitchen at the back of the house.

We left our gear on a hall table and found Crane waiting for us at the door of an upstairs drawing room.

He was a tall, gaunt, bespectacled man in a mulberry-coloured lounge jacket and dark trousers, who was so pale and ancient that he made Jarvis seem robust and youthful by comparison.

Crane was in his early eighties, but even allowing for the rough usage of years his haggard appearance had to be the result of some affliction, though Jarvis clearly had no knowledge of it. He gave me a look of puzzled surprise as we were ushered into the large room which combined the functions of a study, library and dining room.

It was a splendid room, obviously loved and much lived in, occupying most of the second floor. Deep, comfortable armchairs were set before a crackling fire; high bookcases reached to the ceiling, holding thousands of volumes; a chandelier and fine crystal bent the firelight into sudden brilliant flecks and glimmers. To one side, a mahogany dining table was laid for three.

"This is very good of you, Mr Crane," Jarvis said when the introductions were completed.

"It's a pleasure, Dr Henry. Andrew and I keep to this part of the house when the boys are away."

He asked me to pour sherry while he and Jarvis discussed the house, which the Crane family had lived in for generations. I joined them by the fireside, waiting for Jarvis to steer the conversation onto the subject of the room.

It didn't happen, not then. Andrew called us to the table and served soup and croutons followed by a casserole. Crane ate sparingly, then settled back with his eyes closed as if he had fallen asleep. There was no sound other than the crackle of the fire and the tick-tick of our eating utensils.

Just when I felt that Jarvis would suggest we return another time, the old man's head came up and his eyes flashed with new life.

"I am doing the right thing!" he said. "The story bears telling and I've procrastinated long enough."

He then continued in a vigorous, forthright voice, as if the conversation had been proceeding all along. "I chose you, Dr Henry, because you make no coin out of this. Like me, you are the genuine article, and you remind me a little of Eugene Renfeld, as he's been described to me. Set your recorder going, Mr Obern."

Our things had been brought upstairs, so I placed the machine on the table and switched it on. Crane nodded with approval.

"I have trapped something, a ghost, a horrifying and utterly cruel Four, the very worst of them. Downstairs is a closed room. You passed it when you came in. Tonight, with your help, we shall breach the room. Then you will re-write the books, Dr Henry, should you have the courage. Or you will, Mr Obern, because it's a sensational new viewpoint. But, like poor Renfeld, and like my forebears, you will have the story and the truth, and that seems the very least I owe myself and my family and my faithful Andrew here."

Andrew created a silence by serving sherry, then went back to reading a book by the fire.

"Why are you doing it, Mr Crane?" Jarvis asked when the silence became unbearable. "Why you?"

The old man sipped his sherry, then cleared his throat. "Do you know of the Alderson house at Port Savine? Of Janie Alderson, the woman who for years added to her house, room by room, believing that so long as she kept adding new rooms, new corridors, that a ghost would not kill her? It's somewhat like that here. We have auspicious relatives all over the world, Dr Henry. In law, in politics, in commerce and the arts. We're well represented, quite wealthy, and long-lived.

"It fell to the Daemon Street Cranes to safeguard the rest, you see. Some forebear rightly divined that our family was especially prone to the destructive force of ghostings, so he established this house. At first, the occupancy was rotated among less accomplished, less promising cousins, for a handsome stipend and the privilege of living here rent-free. They had nothing whatever to do for it; they could just live their lives peaceably, so long as the room remained intact. It was a powerful family superstition. These are more enlightened times, but I suppose I'm still the poorer line of the family." He laughed.

"But it's coming to an end?" Jarvis said.

"Oh yes. It's time. The Cranes can fend for themselves."

"Your sons don't wish to keep up the tradition?" I said.

"Partly correct, Mr Obern. I live alone but for Andrew here." Crane gave an unreadable frown, one that might have hinted at recalcitrance and obduracy in Bradlan and his younger brother, Roderick, but which might have meant other things too.

"But it's more to do with something I have discovered, some researches I carried out on the Daemon Street Cranes."

"May I ask what that is?" Jarvis said.

"I wish to tell you. My father discovered that a great percentage of the Cranes who resided here in Daemon Street—men, women, young and old— all died of what is commonly diagnosed these days as carcinogens. Living here, they fell prey to cancer in all its hideous forms."

I could see why Bradlan and Roderick Crane had left. The rumour alone would be enough to set me packing.

"I had difficulty verifying much of this, of course. Cancer is very much a modern discovery by that name. But the coincidence was striking, especially in view of the Crane longevity elsewhere. Naturally my father suspected the ghost-trap downstairs, some deleterious by-product of its working through the years."

I glanced at Andrew sitting with his book by the fire, looked again at the ruined man at the head of the table, but could not bring myself to ask Crane if he were suffering from cancer.

Jarvis spoke carefully. "You suggest that such disease is ghost-related?"

"It's more than that." Crane poured us both more sherry and stood, indicating with a gesture that we should join him at the fire.

Jarvis and I sat in two of the deep armchairs, but Crane remained standing.

"It occurred to me shortly after my father's death that ghosts had to be homotropic in every sense. They only have half-life energy to draw on, sometimes very weak and fleeting, sometimes remarkably powerful and enduring. But it seemed natural then that the ghost would be directed to that end—which may account for conditions like possession and schizophrenia. Or, failing that, they would seek the strongest material things we ever own, houses, rooms, objects, as fixing points. But people first. They would try to get back to people first: relatives, friends, the impressionable young, unsuspecting tenants, doctors at the bedsides of dying patients."

"Hence your closed room," I said, welcoming the fire of the wine, relying on the act of drinking it to keep me from being too impatient.

Jarvis, however, seemed the very soul of patience, relaxing back in his chair, as if prepared to let Crane talk all evening.

I hadn't learnt the Sorcerer's ways yet. I was impatient to see the room, to break it open and look upon what Jarvis had probably seen many times.

Crane began to move slowly to and fro in front of the tall bookcases. He laid a finger on the spine of a red-bound volume.

"This is Renfeld. He classifies the ghosts as four types—according to power vectors and how they manifest the tropism. Do you know Renfeld, Dr Henry? Mr Obern?"

"Of him," Jarvis said. "Yes. I don't have my own copy, and I have never read it. Only extracts."

"This will be yours soon," Crane said. "I'll see to it. No! Here! Take it now." And he passed it over.

Jarvis accepted it, his mouth open in amazement at the unexpected generosity. Crane gave him no time to express his thanks.

"The Ones, Renfeld suggests, and I believe him, are the barest echoes, all non-specific residues. Premonitions and *frissons*. The conviction of something under the bed. The *déjà-vus* and *cauchemars*."

"*Cauchemars?*" I said, and instantly recalled the French word and regretted the interruption.

"The nightmare, Mr Obern. The ghost as nightmare. Intruding into our consciousness when the mind is at rest and vulnerable. Most spectres are Ones. Quite weak, ineffectual, diluted, just as many personalities are average, undynamic. Very tenuous life-echoes.

"The Twos are more powerful versions of these, still subjective experiences, private, solitary things, phenomenological rather than phenomenal, but more defined. With characteristics and features, identities, behaviour. You would agree, Dr Henry? Most ghostings, over ninety-five percent, are Ones and Twos. There is never anything to find; it all happens within the perceiver. Objectively, they do not harm us overly much."

Jarvis nodded, encouraging Crane with attentive silence.

"Exasperating for you two," Crane said, and smiled weakly. "The only haunted house is the self."

"The Bogeyman," I said, giving in to the flush of the sherry, needing to speak.

"The very worst of the Bogeymen, Jack," Jarvis said, and I appreciated his use of my name. "The ones children take with them when families move house."

"Absolutely," Crane said. "Renfeld's Threes, on the other hand, mark the cross-over. The subjective experience becomes the phenomenal one, measurable at last. External manifestations. Recordable bumpings and groanings. Visible signs and stigmata. Traceable energy surges. With enough power for the ghosting to sustain itself out-of-body, haunting a space, a locality, a house, a closet—"

"A sealed room?"

"No, Mr Obern. My sealed room is not where a ghost would ever *want* to be. It's where it is forced to be. By techniques which are not completely understood but which were discovered by chance and refined by repeated effective use. Cargo cult empiricism. A cause and effect."

"Mr Crane's point, Jack," Jarvis said, "is that with a Three, the ghost haunts the artifact rather than a person's unconscious, and different individuals will experience the ghost both subjectively *and* objectively, and with the same characteristics."

I didn't say anything. The wine was making me eager and I was coming over as foolish. Thankfully, Jarvis didn't seem to mind.

Crane continued. "The Four is the really dangerous one. It has enough power to haunt a house for many, many years, a whole town or neighbourhood, a lake, a beach, but it aims that power at a living person, directs all of its force to returning to an in-life state."

Jarvis leaned forward in his chair.

"What are you telling us, Mr Crane?"

Crane stopped pacing. "Just this, Doctor. The ghost-trap in this house has been catching ghosts since my great-grandfather's time."

And killing you with cancer, I thought. Jarvis too was busy trying to fathom what Crane had told us. The room downstairs was full of Fours?

"You are opening it tonight, Mr Crane," Jarvis said. "Tell us again why that is."

"I am dying, Doctor, as you guessed. I am riddled with cancers, and I know I have less than the few months the doctors have allowed. It will be sooner, I know. Much sooner.

"The Fours are not common, but statistically many exist. The Fours in our ghost-trap here at Daemon Street have all been focused there and neutralized long ago, 'consumed in the panelled darkness of the Red Room'. I love Renfeld's writing, don't you? Except for the one that arrived three nights ago and prompted my call to you, and the one I believe will appear tonight when the room is breached.

"I want to share my family's legacy now. People resist the idea of ghosts because they sense the harm; they seem to know intuitively that the ghostings accrue about the preoccupied and the sensitive among us. They come so quickly to any receptive person, bringing physical harm not just psychological. It takes courage to think of the discontinued identities trying to get back in, trying to be bodies again, trying to be people, trying to be what they cannot be. But they cannot stop.

"Tomorrow Andrew will deliver all my papers to your office at the university, Dr Henry. My other legacy to you; the legacy of the Daemon Street Cranes. We've done our share of ghost-hunting. Let the others try."

"Your sons will sell the house then?" Jarvis asked.

"My sons are abroad. Doctor. They want no part of this. And why should they? Why should anyone bring ghosts together, work at such a task, bear such a burden and die for it? It's better that we disregard these displaced forces, let them remain free radicals sullying our more susceptible moments. Acknowledging them focuses their energy, directs it. It is folly."

"Is your ghost-trap a Red Room, Mr Crane?"

The ruined old man smiled and moved away from the bookcases.

"Why don't I show you? Come, gentlemen. And Mr Obern, if you and Andrew would be so good as to bring those heavy crowbars by the hearth; we will need them. This is a momentous occasion."

We left the cosy room and went downstairs to the blind wall at the end of the entrance hall. Crane switched on the lights as we went, far more lights than were needed. The lower floor was ablaze with warm yellow light when we reached it. Then he began feeling the panelled walls, striking panels to find joists and sections.

"Some sealed rooms have spy-holes which, of course, render them useless," Crane told us. "Modern ones are totally sealed but have light-fittings and video cameras inside so the interior can be lit and observed. None of that foolishness here. This room has not seen light for one hundred and sixteen years. It is the no-place."

"Is it furnished?" Jarvis said.

"Oh yes. In a sense," Crane answered. "With enough people-things to draw the Threes and Fours."

The last words prompted a thought, one that suddenly grew to worry me in this overlit corridor.

"You said a Four arrived three nights ago, Mr Crane. Is it in there now then?"

Crane looked up at us again in a wholly unreadable way, giving a strange lopsided smile, his long hands planted on the panels like two parchment spiders. He reminded me of a creature about to spring, or a thief listening for the fall of tumblers in a hidden wall safe.

"The Four is in the trap, Mr Obern. But it will not harm you. It is otherwise engaged. Its days, too, are numbered. But another will come when the walls are broken. If this troubles either of you—"

"No, Mr Crane," Jarvis said. "Jack and I wouldn't miss this."

"Good. I doubt the exercise would be advisable for me. Or for Andrew. Mr Obern, if you would strike here, here and here,"—he indicated the spots with his white spider hands—"we can begin to make the breach."

I struck where he said, struck again and again until the panelling split and could be wrenched back, exposing joists which formed a door that had never been finished as one. Jarvis took some photographs.

"In the middle of the room, Dr Henry, there is a table. On it is a large porcelain bowl."

"A water-trap!" Jarvis cried. "Your ancestor used a water-trap?"

"Initially," the old man said. "It's basic and it works. Please, when the wall is sundered, shine that hand-light on the bowl immediately. Mr Obern can then bring those other lights in from the hall. The room must be lit."

Jarvis began taking photographs again while I pounded at the wood, shattering more of the panelling, ruining beautiful old timber that would have cost a fortune now. I had cleared the false door from this side. Only the inner panelling remained. I found I was trembling with anticipation and fear looking at it, aware only of the broken wood and the steady flash of Jarvis's Pentax.

Obviously the whole south wall had been fitted as a prefabricated section, with the outer panels added once the frame was bolted in place. It must have cost a great sum; the finishing was flawless, a true fourth wall, not just a partition.

"This is your moment, gentlemen," Crane said. "Andrew, goodnight to you. It's time you were out of this. I am in good hands."

Jarvis and I were surprised to see the men embrace, to see the tears of a painful and final farewell on their faces.

"Bless you, Mr Crane," the butler said. He made no further fuss, just nodded a goodnight to us, took up a small suitcase, and went out the front door.

It had a sense of unreality about it, how suddenly it happened. It seemed comical in its intensity and abruptness: the embrace, the door opening, the windy street beyond, the click of the lock.

Jarvis went to speak but did not.

"Let us continue," Crane said. "And thank you for forbearing with your questions. We can proceed."

I struck the inner panels a resounding blow, turning my anxiety into hard action. I struck and struck until the timber burst, and stale chill air engulfed me. I swooned a little at it, trying not to breathe, and kept up the blows, while Crane stood to my left and Jarvis took his pictures.

"Stop!" Crane hissed, and suddenly there was a parchment claw closing on my shoulder. I froze, stopped mid-strike, and lowered the crowbar.

"What is it, Mr Crane?" Jarvis said.

The hand relaxed its terrible grip.

"Not yet!" the old man said. "Proceed! Proceed!"

Again I put my fear into the blows. Like someone whistling past the graveyard or shouting at the devil, I made my big brash noises to hide the deathly silence, to distract me from the dread I felt growing within.

Splinters flew, whole sections of shattered oak fell inwards. I hit and pounded and poleaxed any part that resisted, until only the joists stood and the sealed room was no longer any part of that.

"Bring the lights!" Crane said, "Light everywhere!"

In my haste, I dropped the crowbar so it clanged against the wooden floor. Jarvis helped me set up the portable floodlights. We aimed them into the room and switched them on.

We saw striped wallpaper, polished wainscoting and panels, a featureless plastered ceiling. There was a wooden chair by one wall, a book resting on the chair. On the mantelpiece of the blind fireplace directly opposite was a clock with no hands. In the middle of the room was a narrow wooden table and on it a large bowl.

"It's not a Red Room!" Jarvis said, but the words were lost as Crane gasped, gave a soft cry of agony, and staggered against the wall. His face was a white mask, as if all the skin had yellowed cords underneath suddenly drawn tight. His hand was on his chest.

"Mr Crane!" Jarvis cried.

In a moment we had him, holding him steady between us, trying to ease him away from the trap to a chaise-lounge we saw near the front door.

"I can take it," he muttered, breathing deeply. "I can do it." Then: "It's all right now. Dr Henry, examine the room."

Jarvis did so, while I brought in yet another light. Crane sat in the hall while we moved about the panelled space.

"It's not a Red Room," Jarvis said to me. He moved to the bowl, empty of water for the best part of a century. "This is not painted red either."

Behind us, Crane had recovered and was climbing gingerly between the joists of the door frame, throwing long distorted shadows about the room as he came to us, crossing a floor unused before our intrusion.

"No, it isn't," he said, looking as if he would collapse at any moment. Jarvis steadied him.

"You said there was a Four here."

"There is. Now there is. And other ghostings. They know what I am doing. And they are vicious and blindly angry things. Powerful, vicious and quite desperate. They want to live again so much. A tropism—" The old man paused, grimaced.

We held him again. Jarvis got the room's wooden chair and we sat him in it. He nodded his thanks, then looked up at us.

"You know the story of Dorian Grey?" he said, panting, obviously in great pain. "The painting ages while the man lives on."

Jarvis nodded. "Of course."

"Yes," I said, seeking the connection.

Jarvis leaned in close. "Are you saying, Tesserley—?"

"Not Tesserley," Crane gasped. "Not Tesserley. I am Roderick, the youngest. I am thirty-two."

We stared at eighty-two, ninety, and more, at wasted, diseased parchment. At the mouth working to speak. At a dying man.

"Tesserley, Bradlan—died full of ghosts. Both filled up—choked with them. *We* are the ghost-traps! We never knew. The room only focuses them; they leak out into us. The Fours become living tissue. That is what cancer is, what ghosts become. So many of us—so full of ghosts. It happens more quickly once you know. You cannot stop thinking of it, drawing them to you..."

Jarvis stood wide-eyed beside me, saying nothing, but understanding as I was just beginning to.

"The room was never it at all," I said, marvelling and horrified at the same instant. Roderick Crane seemed not to hear.

"You only have to know, to think of them, to focus them somewhere." His voice was very soft, filled with his agony. "Then you cannot stop them." He gave a ratcheting, bleating laugh. "But the irony! We destroy them only by dying. And now I have Tesserley and Bradlan both. Now I have them."

"Here?" I cried, needing to be sure.

"Oh yes, I have them now," Crane said, at the edge of death, and jerked a thumb up to his chest. "In the Red Room!"

Downloading

WHEN SHADOWS MOVE in Casna Park and the wind is in the trees, I can't help but see it as the most terrifying place in the world.

It's brightly lit at night really, with more than enough lamp-posts throwing light along the intersecting paths, illuminating under the big trees, around the bandstand and war memorial. It's on the eastern side, the cemetery side of the park, that the darkness begins to take on its customary face, that the lamp-posts at one in twenty metres become one in fifty, then eighty, then infrequent enough for you to be in darkness, and light to be something over there, away from you, something to leave and reach again when you hurry along the paths.

And when the night wind comes to shiver the water of the pond and set the Moreton Bay figs tossing, shuddering, rushing like waves on an unexpected shore, then, then, it is a place to be away from.

I went there because *he* did. Went there (tracking it back) because a pattern emerged that showed he did, because he was one of those faceless people in a crowd who finally did get noticed, because I was asked to find patterns.

No, because I had a corner window looking along Bennett Street, *then* because of a conversation about patterns and how some things just don't get noticed till you look for them. Maybe because of the kind of cop Harry Badman was, that too, but for me it was the window, then the conversation, then the man, then the park.

I was still recovering from the car accident, and a left leg broken in two places, in the last week of being confined to a wheelchair I called Miss Nancy in my second-floor apartment above Bennett Street, looking forward to two or more months of brokering actual legwork to other PIs and the occasional errand 'boys' I could safely farm easier jobs out to. Paying the bills had always had a certain novelty aspect to it; now I had to be more creative than ever. Fortunately, Benny and Sue *could* be trusted; fortunately I had the phone and desk interview patter down well enough to make 'assigning operatives' sound like the very best personal service money could buy.

It was mainly that, in a region like the Hunter, people just didn't need PIs that much, let alone Jay Wendt Investigations.

Oh, and in case you're thinking that all this is too Sam Spade to be true, trust me, there really is a breed of private investigator who fits the Raymond Chandler model to the letter, just as there's a breed that never quite does but wants to really bad. Then there are those like me who, no matter how hard we try to avoid the stereotype and break it every chance we get, keep getting cast in the role by others so we're left grinning wryly at the irony, which somehow looks tough-guy knowing and cool too and just confirms all the clichés.

That's how it was with Harry Badman and me from Day One.

For a start, he didn't for a moment seem to read my agitation for what it was when he showed me his official ID. I'd seen him around a few times and my first thought was: *Shit, what have I done?!*

"So what can I do for you, detective?" I said, pulling back to let him in, doing my best professional roll away from the door.

"You're just like Jimmy Stewart in *Rear Window* up here, aren't you?" Harry Badman said, riding his own stereotype. At least he didn't say 'ain't ya?'

I guided my chair towards the window, glanced briefly out over Bennett Street then turned smartly. I'd practised that turn. "Or that TV series, *Ironside*. That had a wheelchair and Raymond Burr in it too, if you appreciate that sort of thing."

It was the one prepared tough-guy line I'd put together and, wouldn't you know, this time my delivery was perfect.

"Synchronicity," Harry Badman said, a word I'd never have expected from this particular balding, ageing, grey-suited cop, and broke his stereotype in one. "I'd like to think we can be as lucky."

We.

"How do you mean?"

Harry Badman sat in one of my old armchairs. "This isn't official business, Jay. At least not in the way you think. I want to *hire* your services."

"You do?"

It was slackwitted on my part, would've sounded lame and obvious to anyone else. Badman seemed to take it as cynical disbelief. Maybe there was a hearing problem. Tonal drop-outs. Maybe I reminded him of someone else.

"Look, Jay. Can I call you Jay? There are cases we've got that we just don't have time to do properly. Don't have the staff. Don't have the evidence and so the authorisation. Cases that don't catch the public eye. Little human interest. No-one cares."

"Go on." It must've sounded tough and considered.

"I'm a bit like you, I guess. I'm in it because, well..."

I was glad he hesitated. "You believe in justice," I said.

"Yep. In doing whatever we can."

He actually meant it. He really did, and in my profession, you quickly learn that truth is the first casualty of self-interest. This tired-looking police detective who sat in my living-room/office was a bona fide 'more than the job' type, and—by a quirk of circumstance, a blending of stereotypes and old movies—he was seeing me as one! I didn't dare snigger or flinch, just stared, aware of the traffic and people noise from Bennett Street. And, heaven help me, I replied with another of *those* lines.

"Where do I come in?" Which had me self-quipping: through the cliché door like everyone else. It really was one of those days.

"Hey, you're stuck up here convalescing. You're already doing what I can't get someone to do officially. Watching Bennett Street."

"And?" I decided to go with it, run the movies, trying not to spot the mannerisms.

Harry Badman took two disks from his jacket pocket. "What system you got?"

"Word 6. IBM compatible."

He handed me one, put the other away. "Run that when you get a chance."

"But you're going to tell me too." It was easy now.

Harry seemed to think a moment. "Let's just say that over the past eight years thirteen people have gone dangerously schizoid on that street down there."

I admit it threw me. I'd expected drug-deal surveillance of school kids, possible breaking and entering checkouts, confirming the presence of some major player hiding out in town, maybe even tracking the latest taggings by the Runalong graffiti raider everyone was upset about.

"Schizoid?" Bogart, Chandler and the rest went out that window. I just couldn't manage the poker-faced, four-beat, even gaze the occasion demanded. And I understood Harry Badman's problem: how could this possibly be a criminal matter, for heaven's sake? Unless...

I managed something of a recovery. "Dangerously schizoid? What exactly does that mean?"

"How about coffee while I talk?" he said, standing, then walked over to the kitchen area, switched on the kettle, found cups, waited till he'd made us both coffee and was seated again. Then he continued.

"I've spoken to experts over at Blackwater, so I'm pretty well up to speed on this. Dangerously schizoid means an unstable, disordered personality showing clear signs of dysfunctional or antisocial behaviour. Extreme anxiety and paranoia. Given to sudden outbursts."

"Violent behaviour"

"Quite often. They're the easy ones to spot."

"Surely your people would be involved then."

"Jay, there are thousands of locals using Bennett Street each week, but some of the thirteen were tourists, travellers passing through."

"Then how did you find out—?"

"It's on the disk. Doctor Dan and I got talking. He's in charge of the clinic over at Blackwater. Patient and next of kin questionnaires entered into the new DHP database showed the overlap. Eight cases who were okay before passing through Everton, who showed marked behavioural differences afterwards."

"That sort of data showed?"

"Over eight years it has. A lot of paranoid schizophrenics are happy enough to talk about their condition, when they first heard voices, had insights and convictions."

"But Bennett Street? So exact?"

"Jay, five of the thirteen occurred in the past fourteen months. They're becoming a lot more frequent."

"Or just the ones reported are."

Harry Badman regarded me over his coffee mug, nodded as he set it down. "Good point. That's exactly it. That's why I want someone watching. You're right here on the corner. You see it all."

"What part can Bennett Street play?"

"Exactly. What could possibly happen here? Down there?" He gestured towards the window. "But the questionnaires, Jay. Nine of the thirteen mentioned something here. They first had the feeling, heard the voices, saw themselves followed or watched, saw visions *here*!"

I truly didn't know what to think or say. Harry Badman probably saw that as considered resolve, matched it to some idea of appropriate response.

"It sounds way out, I know. You can see why there can't be an official investigation. Doctor Dan is really pushing for it though—we both are. It's—it's one of those demographics that, well, *shouldn't* be swept aside."

"Who are the five locals? I've read nothing."

"Why would you? They're borderline types. Jack Winters out Greta way. Mary Ash from Box Valley. Tom Coatley's youngest girl."

"Who?"

"Exactly. Just what I mean. No-one prominent. The media rarely reports on people going to hospital for this kind of observation. It's often gradual, inconclusive. Behavioural anomalies are seen as dietary, hormonal, some new spin-off of lead poisoning or attention deficit disorder. Victims are admitted to a psychiatric ward, then moved to the appropriate facility later when their conditions are diagnosed as chronic."

I actually rolled my chair over to the window, looked out at maybe fifty-two shops, the post office, the Imperial Hotel, at pedestrians, people going through their usual daily routines. I recognised faces, but not enough, nowhere near enough to make a difference.

"What do you want me to do, Harry?" The 'Harry and Jay' approach was just the way it was.

"Watch Bennett Street. Just watch the street. Log the flow. The constants. Build me a pattern. I'll come in, you explain it to me."

"A pattern?"

"You're in the trade, Jay. You know it all comes down to patterns. We get information but don't get enough to find a pattern. That's why this is so damn hard. Even though we refine the art of seeing."

I almost polly-parroted 'art of seeing' back at him but went cliché and just nodded. Harry was venting, probably had weeks and months of frustration pent up and flowing out.

And he was right. I did know all about patterns. I'd had to explain it at Neighbourhood Watch sessions often enough, remind folks how cops driving down a street saw everything in terms of stable patterns and what looked out of place: two people talking in a doorway who suddenly turn away, whose neck and shoulder muscles tense; how you learned to notice parked cars, what first-floor windows were left open, who was watching you in shop-window reflections. It's what you learned to do, I'd tell them, what we all needed to do. *Look* at what you see. Observe. Like doctors walking that same street seeing people in terms of nutrition, fitness, signs of fatigue.

"We've learned to allow for society's blind spots, Harry," I said.

"Exactly. And for predators scouting prey."

"Kills community, selling average folk that."

"Surely does. Or *builds* community. The commonweal in the real sense."

First synchronicity, now commonweal. I really had misjudged Harry Badman.

"Do this for me," he said. "I'll pay a third your standard rate."

"A third!"

"Hey, you're sitting here anyway. I'm paying this out of my wage."

"Then make it a quarter." Don't ask me why. I was sitting here anyway.

Harry nodded. "Thanks. I appreciate it."

"The disk has case profiles for all thirteen?"

"Correct. From Doctor Dan's enquiries. Do me a favour. Read it, return it when you're done. Don't copy it. It's supposed to be confidential."

"Understood." Yes, I was seeing Harry Badman differently now. Unofficial surveillance. Circulating confidential files. Risking all sorts of things probably—him and this Doctor Dan both.

The detective placed his card on the coffee table. "I'll drop by Friday unless I hear from you first. I'll bring a telescope if you don't have one, or a telephoto lens. Hey, and Jay, why the quarter standard?"

"Harry, I'll be candid. I'll need to slack off now and then. This stakeout stuff is eighty per cent of my business but it can send you crazy. Everything will start to look suspicious—patterns everywhere. I just need the downtime without the guilt, okay?"

"Sure." Then just to let me know we could both play the clichés. "Should've known it wasn't compassion."

"The moral high ground is for guys like you, Harry. I don't even try for it."

"You're helping. That puts you on the side of the angels."

"See you Friday."

So began my *Rear Window* period, right down to setting up my Pentax and telephoto lens on its tripod and snapping and developing shots of the street. It was like being a kid on a long country drive again, spotting a red car with a *J* and a *6* in the licence plate or a white Japanese import with two women in the front. I saw the shopping and sightseeing habits of thousands, saw the mosaic of parked cars form and change, saw good retail hours and bad for the local stores, who jaywalked, what age groups dominated what cafes, what bus seats, which times of day.

But I never let the window or the street or the patterns become a trap. I made snacks, left Miss Nancy and exercised as well as I could wearing a cast, re-read the case-histories from Doctor Dan, napped on the couch just as I always did, took phone calls from Benny and Sue and prospective clients, watched TV and read.

I was hoping I'd get detachment, objectivity, but the opposite happened. Being away from the view of Bennett Street only intensified the patterning when I went back to it. Everyone looked suspicious somehow. A quarter standard wasn't nearly enough.

The files made fascinating reading though, made it all worthwhile really, even without the 'he' in Case 11. Five locals, eight transients, people I might know or could've seen, all ages, but none younger than twenty or older than forty-six, both genders—seven women, six men. All displaying sudden and increasing disorientation, memory lapses, outbursts of irrational anger, an accelerating delusional state, paranoia, feelings of persecution and incredible anxiety, all markedly changed affects. When it became clear that all failed to respond acceptably to the standard medications like Prozac, Clozapine, Risperidone, all thirteen had been incarcerated at different institutions, were being steadily relocated to Blackwater as Dr Dan Truswell persuaded the respective authorities that the Everton concentration and common Bennett Street locus made it the best short-term strategy (made sure too that certain health subsidies were partly redirected in consideration of such reassignments).

Most of the thirteen had stabilized, remained afflicted by attacks of anxiety and paranoia, delusional lapses and occasional multiple personality 'manifestations', but were generally compliant, responsive to both medication and group therapy and capable of giving lucid if not always structured interviews.

It was only Case 11's allusion to a 'he' that gave the clue, lent an added edge of threat and danger to the whole thing. The transcript of the Susan Bellamy interview conducted by Dr Dan Truswell I read maybe a dozen times.

DT: Tell me about that day on Bennett Street.
SB: There's nothing there now.
DT: What was there that day?
SB: It isn't easy.
DT: I know, Susan. What was there that day?
SB: Nothing there. No more. Home now.
DT: In a while. You can go home in a while. What happened on Bennett Street, Susan?
SB: It was there. It was just there.
DT: Yes, but what was there? Susan, what was there on Bennett Street?
SB: [No answer]
DT: Susan, think hard. What was there? What was there on Bennett Street that day?
SB: It was there!
DT: What was there?
SB: It's just where he was, okay!

DT: Where who was, Susan? Where who was?
SB: [No answer]
DT: Where who was, Susan?
SB: [No answer]
DT: Susan, who was on Bennett Street that day?
SB: Nothing there. No more. Home now.
DT: In a while. Who was there?
SB: It was there. It was just there.
DT: Who was he? Susan, who was there?
SB: [No answer]

Each time I read it, I almost grasped something, possibly imagined some purpose, some deflected intent in the poor woman's words.

"Anything?" Harry Badman asked when he dropped by at 7.22 on the Friday evening. Bennett Street was set in a lustrous early autumn blue behind me, flecked with streetlights and traffic glitter. Familiar, comforting sounds drifted up through the open window. The curtains stirred in the balmy air.

"You could go mad doing this," I told him. "Everything becomes suspect."

"I'll tell Dan to save you a room over at Blackwater. Can you stay with it?"

I smiled, finding I was liking this unusual man more and more, his political incorrectness, his determination. "I should've sent Miss Nancy back a week ago, Harry. I'm cleared for crutches now. The cast comes off in a month. Then I'm walking-stick deadly. I can stay with it till then. Then it's back to ambulance chasing, I'm afraid."

"Slower ambulances anyway. I see you've got your camera set up. Why don't I bring in a camcorder? I can fast-forward through it in the evenings."

"You're not serious."

"I'm single at the moment."

"Tell Doctor Dan to book you in next to me. This isn't your usual stakeout."

"We're doing what we can, Jay. You saw the reports."

"Susan Bellamy's in particular."

"Exactly. We have a case demographic focused here no-one would usually buy. One but only one 'victim'—to use that term rather than 'subject'—suggests a perpetrator. Coincidence or paranoid delusion? Simple fact? No one else mentions anyone. You make a copy, Jay?"

"You said not to."

"Did you make a copy?"

"Would you want to know?"

"What, if you downloaded a copy or if I can trust you?"

"You said not to. I didn't."

"Hard copy?"

"Of course. That okay?"

"I guess. It's Doctor Dan I'm concerned for."

"Then you take it with you when we're done."

"Thanks. I'm not used to being this, well, extended."

"Compromised."

Harry nodded. "This whole thing bugs me."

"You plan to locate probable 'he's', take photos, show them to this Susan Bellamy, hope it loosens up something, right?"

"That's it. But not just 'he's', Jay. Could be a 'she' too. We need solo and crowd shots so we have a series for her to choose from."

"Harry, what can it possibly be? If the connection that seems to be there *is* there? I mean, we're talking varying degrees of improbable. Drug deals and—"

"Behaviour-affecting contact toxins." "Okay, at one extreme. Possession at the other. I don't buy the supernatural, I'm afraid."

Harry gazed out at the night for a moment. "Me neither, Jay. Dan says that hypnosis has been known to cause particularly dramatic reactions in latent schizophrenics. Perhaps it can actually trigger psychosis in certain types."

"That'd mean time was needed though, surely. A certain amount of willingness on the part of the victims."

"Maybe he does it over a cappuccino or on a bus seat or in a post office queue. Sitting on a bar stool at the Imperial. Tourists and locals could well do things like that. All we know for sure is that the change of affect seems too pathologically marked, too sudden and involuntary in every case."

"What does Dan think's behind it?"

"You think *we're* careful. His scepticism will make us look like foaming zealots."

"But?"

"He's building a theory even as we speak."

"What, that there are people who can catalyse virtually immediate and demonstrable madness in others?"

"Hey, Jay! Now you sound like the one who swallowed a textbook. I'm impressed."

"Don't go coy on me, Mr Synchronicity, Detective Sergeant Commonweal! You probably knew how I'd be with this. Dan must be asking how I took it."

"He is. But remember, Jay, he's not building a theory because he wants to. It's because he has to in view of case data. Can I leave you with this?"

"Sure. And bring a camcorder if you want. But I'll only use it on probables, okay? Anything I think you should see."

"You could miss it."

"I'll stay alert. Till I get to a walking-stick."

"Thanks, Jay. I'll drop in."

"Nah. Use the stairs. I need someone to remind me of what it was like."

Harry became busy with other duties and didn't get to drop by nearly as often as he wanted, which was just as well. I was two weeks off the crutches I called Long John Newton, out of my cast and well into my third week using a walking-stick (named Mr Falk—Post Who Walks), already making it downstairs and taking the occasional drives around town when it happened.

I'd given Harry shots and pattern profiles for a dozen candidates in that time, the most probable being the thin young man I called Scarecrow who lingered by the bargain book bins outside Crosley's Books; the little old lady with the handbag clutched to her front; and, most promising, Greenjacket, the short, grey-haired guy in his late fifties or early sixties in tan trousers and dark green jacket who just moved along the sidewalks, first one side then the other, repeating that, just walking, right hand in his jacket pocket, turning into shops in a way that made pretty fancy zig-zags when I schematised them during one of my final Long John hours.

Harry checked them all out as usual. Scarecrow was recently in from Raymond Terrace and staying with family; the CES placed him in a job the week I gave Harry the alert. Handbag turned out to be none other than Mrs Armstrong, my third grade teacher, a widow run seriously afoul of time and the hour. Greenjacket was a local accountant who'd retired early to take care of an ill wife, now recently deceased.

Harry turned up similar mundane explanations for the actions of my other likelies: Beanie, Jaywalk, Gruesome and Dreamer. I just added their portraits to my impressive folder of Local Character glossies and the assorted street shots I'd compiled with an eye to drumming up interest among the various local historical societies. Harry was already calling me the Charles Dickens and Mervyn Peake of Everton—allusions he had to explain to me (right before Philistine and Luddite).

It was a Saturday morning. Bennett Street was at its weekly busiest as usual. I'd been taking some routine streets shots, snatching bits of life, capturing forever an argument between two usually circumspect local politicians right outside Barnes Hardware, capturing the hearse and some of the thirty-two car cortege in the Giacomo funeral as it was held up at the post office crossing by a little boy dropping his ice-cream, capturing some of my latest 'planetary' constants in their usual Bennett Street orbits before dobbing them in for Harry's consideration

I had put down my copy of *Bleak House* (a gift from Harry) and was looking out, wondering yet again at the chances of Handbag and Greenjacket meeting and hitting it off—they'd come close so many times (when you're street-watching, you get off on these things). I'd seen people furtive, distracted, confused, seen arguments, irritable parents tired from long drives shouting at children, husbands promising just one drink at the pub and coming back after four, young people chatting up each other, individual jaywalking preferences, how people behaved when a police car appeared, how men did when Julie Cavendish walked by. I considered how easy it'd be to be an assassin hiding up here in roomshadow, how much of their lives people didn't think to notice, how aggressive they were at pressing the buttons for crossing lights; how they crossed the street to avoid meeting certain people. Patterns.

I was tracking Greenjacket through one of his pinball zig-zags, curb to shop, enter, miss one, enter, miss two, when I noticed him, almost occluded by Greenjacket's meanderings, a drab man on a bench outside the post office, right there near the crossing where people flowed, thoughts elsewhere.

Drab and forgettable, not characters like Scarecrow and Handbag, not an eye-catcher like Greenjacket with his amiable ramblings or Julie Cavendish with her striking feminine allure. Dickens, Peake and Shakespeare would have passed on this one. But gut-feeling grabbed and I felt a prickling of recognition, something.

Through the telephoto lens I snatched his image, learned him: balding, grey-haired, plain features, in nondescript thrift-shop jacket and pants, dull brown shoes. It was how he watched people, unobtrusively, just doing it from the eyes without turning the head, no sudden or big movements at all really, just being there, blending in.

It was during an intense close-up that I noticed his lips moving almost imperceptibly and felt an inexplicable chill. Sure, he might have been singing a song to himself but I doubted it, was certain he wasn't. It was so ordinary yet so bizarre, like something held carefully in control—like a mousetrap locked in its frozen moment, waiting. That's how it affected me, how much the streetwatching thing had wound me up. I took some video footage for Harry, then grabbed my folder of street photos and a reading glass, checked the bench back across the weeks and months. No sign of him. He was a new feature in the Bennett Street landscape.

Or an old feature back again.

Maybe it was the bright winter sunshine, the safety of people and traffic; maybe the Sam Spade / *Rear Window* routines I'd been following, maybe just more of Harry's commonweal pushing through, the looking out for others he seemed to set so much store by. I set the camcorder running, grabbed Mr Falk and set off downstairs as slowly—Sam Spading it—as a Zen soccer player, made it out onto Bennett Street and into the shot for once. I checked to see my subject was still there, then set off for the pedestrian crossing at my best speed.

Locals greeted me. From the door of the barber shop George Willis called out, "Comin' Mr Dillon!", which I figured for a line from some old TV show. I grinned at him as if I understood.

When I reached the crossing, I pretended to be waiting for someone and sat at the opposite end of the bench. I made like a guy kept waiting and did a watch check, then looked along the street as casually as I could so I could see his profile.

He was gazing ahead as before, just moving his eyes to track people coming and going, lips moving all the time like someone singing a song to himself. He seemed easy enough, relaxed, harmless, just watching and waiting. I behaved more or less the same way, watching people pass, checking my watch, not wanting to be too obvious.

When next I looked round to check on him, he'd turned his head and was gazing straight at me. At me and beyond me, his rain-coloured eyes looking on and past.

I felt a sense of utter dread, knew my eyes must've widened and my body tensed, but the man's eyes did seem focused beyond me, looking out there somewhere.

What to do? I had the gut feeling, more of the sudden certainty, watched the moving lips and terrible vacant gaze of those pale grey eyes.

I made myself stay calm. I'd been cooped up for far too long. I remembered how sure I'd been about Greenjacket and Scarecrow, Handbag and Dreamer. Without photographs, without confirmation from Susan Bellamy, I was being unfair, probably overreacting, being oversensitive and imagining more than there was. The man *could* be singing for all I knew, his rain-coloured eyes vacant only because he was in the reverie of where that song took him. Or he might even be a Blackwater inmate out on day leave. Or just another of those myriads of people I'd started to notice, someone whose wife might come for him at any moment and take home for a bowl of minestrone on a cold sunny afternoon.

But then, as if cued by my presence, the man rose and stepped onto the crossing, walked off down Bennett Street.

It was both an anticlimax and a relief. I hurried back to my office-apartment at my fastest limp ("See any white whales out there, Mr Ahab?" George Willis called, to which I answered: "Post Who Walks, never flies!", which left him frowning and bewildered), took a nip of brandy, then set about developing my 'Rain Eyes' black and whites in my makeshift dark-room/pantry, finally had a dozen, had Marty Done drop by for the colour rolls on his next lab run for the local realities, then phoned Harry.

By the time Harry arrived around 5:14, I had six colour enlargements, my own dozen shots laid out on the coffee table and the video footage ready to go.

"This smacks of overkill just a tad, Jay," Harry said, studying the photographs, "so I'm taking it as more than a hunch."

"Don't go cop on me, Harry. It was recognition. Something. Show them to Doctor Dan. Have him show them to Susan Bellamy. Do a series with her now. It can't hurt."

"That strong a feeling, huh?"

"You should've been there. Maybe it's just me, but it was strange. Suggest to Dan he present them in a series."

"I'll do that tonight, Jay."

"Can I come along?"

"I'd like you to. Say what you felt. We might need you there anyway if Susan Bellamy recognises him."

In the earlier days of the Harry and Jay Show, back when role-models seemed everything, Dr Dan Truswell would've made a perfect coroner at a crime scene, focused, good-looking, attentive, courtly in a truly natural and charming way, also weary from too much care and late-night concentration, so he looked older than his forty-eight years. The spectacles, the tweed jacket, the fly-away greying hair tipped him more towards psychiatrist academic/mad scientist than I'd expected, but he was a gracious and grateful man, and no doubt a solid and dependable part of Harry's commonweal.

"She may mis-identify, you realize," Dan said when the pleasantries were done and we were walking at my best Mr Falk speed to the interview room in Ward Four. It was 6:52 and late for interviews. Medication procedures had been delayed and modified. "But she's rested and alert and we should get a clear result either way."

"Mis-identify?" I said, even though I believed I understood well enough.

"Nature of the condition, Jay," Dan said. "Paranoid delusion. Misperception. Susan can re-build her world to accommodate strangers when required. Don't be fooled by a positive that's too definite. We'll rely on physiological response signs equally. Respiration. Pupil dilation and saccade activity. Hesitation. Tone. We'll naturally triangulate on the photo-identification, and often you can tell the difference between a convenient, associational blanket recognition and a genuine one. Paranoid schizophrenics want to find meaning and will seek objective correlatives. It can be immediate and alarming to see. A genuine recognition can possibly take longer, believe it or not—the subject rejecting confused, uncertain and projected memories, sorting false from real, actually remembering."

I couldn't help myself. I guess I needed to establish my own bona fides. "Unless trauma causes that delay, I imagine. Or the confusion is part of the individual's condition."

Doctor Dan cast a glance at Harry Badman and smiled. "Which is why this could take a while. As Harry would've told you, she gave no marked reactions at all to the shots of Scarecrow, Handbag or any of the others. No discernible traces of recognition at all. I emphasize 'discernible'. It's a deep pool in there."

Harry and I never met Susan Bellamy, of course. A familiar and 'neutral' base was needed, so we watched through the observation room one-way as Dan did the interview. Susan wore day-wear civvies and sat in a comfortable chair at a well-lit table, with an orderly waiting to one side. Dan sat opposite the woman, thanked her for doing this, and showed her the first of the six photos he'd selected. Rain Eyes was Number Three onwards.

"Nothing much tonight, Susan. Just a few pictures I'd like you to look at. Won't keep you long. Just say if you know any of these people."

Susan didn't touch the pictures, just looked down when Dan placed them before her, one atop the other. Pictures One and Two elicited no response. At Three, the woman reacted, first craned forward, then pulled back.

"What is it?" Doctor Dan asked, his voice low and gentle.

Susan Bellamy looked tense and disturbed. She started to make a long low humming sound.

"What is it, Susan? Do you know this man?"

The woman hummed, staring down at the picture.

"Susan, did you see this man on Bennett Street?"

She hummed a while longer, then spoke, not looking up.

"I mean it was where he was, wasn't it? Just where he was."

"Where who was, Susan?" Dan's voice remained gentle, firm and urging.

"What? What's that?"

"You once told me that's where he was. On Bennett Street. Was it this man you saw? Can you be sure?"

"Him. He came at me. He was there." Susan Bellamy's voice was breathy with emotion.

"But what happened there, Susan?"

"He was just there."

Dan tried a different tack. "Had you seen him before?"

"It's his place, isn't it? He was there."

"It's his place?"

"Yes. He was there."

"Yes, but had you seen him before?"

"He pushed me."

"Pushed you? You're sure? He pushed you?"

"He pushed me."

"You're sure? Could he have bumped into you by accident?"

"He touched me."

"Yes, Susan, but could it have been an accident?"

"He looked at me. He touched me."

"On Bennett Street? In front of everyone? He touched you?"

"Yes. He touched me. He knew."

"What did he know?"

"He was just there."

"What did he know?"

Susan frowned at the photo. Moving slowly, Dan spread the pictures out so the three Rain Eyes shots were showing.

"You're sure now? This is the man you saw?"

"He was just there."

"Have you ever seen him before?"

"He was there."

Dan poured her juice from a jug on the table, pushed the glass towards her right hand.

"Tell me about how you met him. Tell me about that day on Bennett Street."

"It can't be a good thing."

"Tell me about when he pushed you, Susan. On Bennett Street."

"What? What's that sound?" She looked up.

Dan did too, listening. "Just the air conditioning. What about him bumping into you?"

"No. That sound?"

Dan listened again. "I can't hear it. What's it like?"

Susan didn't answer, just frowned, looked down at the pictures.

"Is this the man who bumped into you?" Dan asked again.

"He didn't," she said.

"Who *pushed* you then."

"He was there for it. What's that sound?"

"It's the air conditioning, Susan. He was there for it. Tell me why he pushed you."

"It's not easy. It isn't ever easy."

"I know. But you do remember this man on Bennett Street. You're helping us by telling us about it. He pushed into you. He touched you. Why?"

"He knew."

"What did he know?"

"What it was. He knew."

Dan showed no impatience.

"What was he doing, Susan? Tell me what he was doing."

"Outside is easier."

"Why?"

"It all goes on. Outside. It all does."

"Susan, we're almost finished. Try to remember very carefully. Is this the man who bumped into you—who pushed you on Bennett Street?"

"I think so."

"Then think very carefully now. What happened that day? What do you remember?"

"He was there for it. He knew."

"What was he there for?"

"He was waiting for it."

"For what, Susan? What was he waiting for?"

"He was looking for me. Waiting. It isn't easy."

"What isn't easy?"

Susan didn't answer.

"Why was he waiting for you?"

But the woman was humming again and rocking just a little in her chair. Dan gathered up the pictures, smiled at her. "Thanks for your help, Susan. We'll try again tomorrow. Take her back now, Carla."

Dan walked us out to the car. "It's very promising," he said as we crossed the carpark. "But don't take it as reliable recognition yet. It could be projection from her, the need to anchor her experience on someone. We'll show her a larger series with a single shot of—what are you calling him, Jay?"

"Rain Eyes," I said.

"A shot of Rain Eyes at random in a run of ten, fifteen or so. See if we get significant repeated physiological reactions as well. ECG, EEG, optical, galvanic, things like that."

"You realize this guy's already here in town," I said.

Harry unlocked the car. "You may just be pattern sensitive, Jay. He might be in town every other day for all we know. We could just have blind spot. Despite the shots, you may have just noticed him today."

"I sat next to him on a bench, Harry. Where do you think I got the name Rain Eyes? There's something there. It seems. Seemed."

"Good recovery," Doctor Dan said, smiling, eyes twinkling. "We can't rush on this."

Harry got into the car. "There's probably never going to be a case either way. None of it can be remotely admissible. We three are legs on a pretty remarkable tripod."

"Doing my job, Harry," Dan said.

I waved to Doctor Dan. "Yeah, I'm being paid too."

Dan dropped me at Bennett Street after 9 pm and I hobbled upstairs, opened the window just a few inches, checked my phone and email messages, made coffee and settled on the sofa to re-read the twelve cases, keeping Susan Bellamy's till last.

At 10:55 the phone rang, startling me in the windy winter night. It was Harry.

"Jay, two things. Dan just called. You may be right about this guy you saw. It looks like there's another case. A Bob Reese was signed in at the hospital a few hours ago. A stock and station inspector from Morrisset. Stopped here on his way through around 5 o'clock. Had something like a fit at the Imperial and they brought him in for observation. The duty nurse called Dan. It's still too soon to say."

"And the other thing?"

"Apparently Susan Bellamy was being put to bed and began saying a name."

"What was it?"

"Rain Eyes."

There was a chilling silence between us. I was aware of the curtains stirring, of the night wind pushing along Bennett Street, of a few, just a few, traffic sounds.

"That can't be possible, Harry. We were never with her. It has to be coincidence."

"It's bloody disturbing is what it is, Jay. But that's what it sounded like. Dan says Carla seemed pretty certain. Susan said it three or four times."

"What do we do with this, Harry?"

"We wait. We find Rain Eyes and ask some questions. We wait and see what Doctor Dan gives us on Reese. We may have something."

"Yeah, well thanks for the nightcap."

"You deserved to know tonight, Jay."

"Yeah. You sleep well too."

"Can't. Got other cases to log time on. I'll keep you posted."

"I've got Mr Falk to keep me 'posted'. You keep me from going bankrupt."

"Mr Falk?"

"You ever read *Phantom* comics, Harry?"

"Never did."

"Then forget it. Sleep tight."

"I don't drink on duty, Jay."

And we laughed together and hung up, leaving a strange bleakness behind, an emptiness, something badly wrong and still unfinished.

I just sat there afterwards, watching the curtains, listening, trying to think of any way the name could have reached Susan Bellamy. Nothing on the backs of the photos. She'd never touched them anyway. I sat there trying for possible solutions: Harry or me mentioning it and forgetting we had, Carla somehow overhearing and telling Susan, things like that, taking it way beyond believability.

Coincidence. Spontaneous 'nomination'. A new term for Harry.

It just didn't work. Nothing did.

But I was probably tired. When next I looked it was 11:20 and the wind had turned chill. I went to close the window and glanced out on the empty street.

He was sitting on the bench by the post office.

I felt everything go cold, felt my legs weaken and my breath catch, instinctively stepped back into the room, did a twenty count (made myself do twenty not ten!) and switched off the lamp, stepped back to the window.

He was there. *Someone* was there. Something. I tried to allow for misperception, tried to figure what else it could be.

There was nothing else.

It was a person. It *was* him, I was certain. Same position, same end of the bench, right there on the empty wind-blown street where the white crossing lines lay like a fallen picket fence and the yellow crossing sign overhead winked on and off on its lines, making its pulsing heart rhythm.

He just sat there, night-darkened, shadowed, grey eyes probably peering out, mouth probably working in time with the hypnotic *Ham-Sa, Ham-Sa* breath rhythm of the crossing sign. Something from Chinese philosophical traditions. Something for Harry.

And as if cued by my light going off, by the darkness in *my* window, Rain Eyes stood and began walking off down Bennett Street.

What to do? Phone Harry, call Doctor Dan?

Because of what? A local who'd been dozing and missed the last bus, who'd woken at this late hour and was now heading home?

But we all need closure. Resolution. At the end of months of watching the street, never having had *this* feeling about anyone else, having seen Susan, heard her words, been told she'd said that name, something like it, I had to go. With Bob Reese today, I had to.

I tried Harry's mobile but got the engaged signal, so left a quick phone-mail message on his office line saying I'd be tracking Rain Eyes.

I grabbed Mr Falk and began my well-practised grab, hop and step downstairs, was finally out on Bennett Street in the close-to-midnight windy dark, aiming for the endless blink-blink of the crossing sign. A few cars came and went, faded as twin points of converging red, were soon gone altogether. The wind whistled about fences and the closed storefronts, fluttered canvas awnings, shuddered loose signs and rushed in the trees.

I thought I could see him ahead, crossing Bennett Street now, heading towards the darkened houses where the retail section of Everton became a sleep-darkened, residential part of town.

I was passing the Imperial Hotel, smelled stale beer, disinfectant, the barest hint of piss, smelled the land and dry crop smells lifting over fields and fences.

I felt I was gaining. Even with my leg and Mr Falk to slow me down, even starting after he had and from further away, I'd become quite adept at limping like this.

Or maybe Rain Eyes was lingering. Waiting. Preparing. Come on, Jay! Come get your madness!

But Rain Eyes was still a way off and there were streetlights.

Just see where he goes, where he lives, I told myself. That's all. Something for bright sunlight and a new day.

I tried Harry's number again, this time found myself automatically rerouted to his office voice mail. For all I knew he was out on a date; his 'duties' could mean he was with someone and had switched off his mobile.

I didn't have Dan's number and didn't have time to make other calls. Rain Eyes had reached Casna Park and had turned from my line of sight, was probably already crossing the park.

I slowed a bit, aware of my heart pounding, my breathing—*Ham-Sa, Ham-Sa*—matching the crossing sign back there, another part of the wind over all the safe, familiar places.

I'd driven down to this end of Bennett Street countless times but hadn't walked it in years. There was the church, the bridge, the river behind the willows. There were silos and the rail embankment all set in wind and darkness. And now the park, streaked with light and shadow, set with paths and lampposts, crowned with Moreton Bay figs, all rushing and flowing. But no sign of Rain Eyes.

Now was the time to go back. Leave it and retrace my steps—church, bridge, embankment—go past the shops and the Imperial again, back to the post office and the winking sign and the bench. Back to my window and the place where things like this were safely out there, at the end of telephone calls, the sort of things that happened to others.

Still no sign of him.

Was he behind a tree? Behind the bandstand or the war memorial or on the other side of the pond that I could see shivering with light? Beyond those long, lighted, forbidding paths, intersecting, crisscrossing, double-crossing?

I was aware of no conscious choice to go on through the stone pillars of the entrance, was just aware of the town changing as I moved away at an angle to it, darkened houses out there, the cemetery over there, the dark hills beyond, rolling under the cold wind.

With no sign of him.

I realised then why some people never go back, why they end up looking in darkened cellars and locked boxes, why they continue on like domestic cats following a python along a track, caught in a need-to-know suspension of smart and sensible, in a one-step-more of unconscious choosing.

The moment mattered. Primally and foolishly it did. Personally and vitally I had to resolve something for myself. Continuing was the only meaningful thing just then.

It was deserted all the way, just the trees and the wind and the shuddering light, no sign of Rain Eyes to be seen.

At last I reached the cemetery gates, found them closed but still unchained after the funeral earlier in the day, a minor oversight in a town like Everton.

Rain Eyes had vanished into the night, perhaps even this part of it, but I was on cat-after-the-snake automatic and actually walked among the graves, as cat-quiet as I could, followed the central path along to the Roman Catholic section, made out vaults and crypts I knew from boyhood games and teenage trysts, proceeded carefully and quietly, found the low Giacomo crypt.

He was stretched out on top of it.

I went no further. This wasn't one of those miniature house-style tombs; this was a waist-high, double-bed crypt for four, and he was laid out on top.

Murmuring, I knew. Staring upwards and murmuring at the night.

I backed away, turned and hurried. Stupid, stupid, stupid, I told myself.

Every far-off lamp-post beckoned, became sanctuary, priceless, wonderful, but I skirted them till I was in the park again, following the wind-blown path. Only then did I look behind me.

Rain Eyes was there, a hundred or so metres back, following, moving smoothly, silently, one moment lit, the next in tree-shadow.

Mr Falk made a dull staccato on the path as I hurried past the pond. It was shivering, riffling like softly gilded pages. I reached the cleated wooden drum of the bandstand, the statue of the war memorial, drummed my way on towards light and life and Bennett Street.

Rain Eyes followed on behind.

I thought of the Bible story of the man possessed by all those demons, of Christ driving them out into the herd of Gadarene swine. Thought of Reese being brought in, a new case, with the coincidence of Rain Eyes' appearance and the Giacomo funeral.

Though not Giacomo for Reese, of course. Someone else. He had Giacomo *now*.

Would he have to touch me, *bump* into me, *push* me as he'd done with Susan, possibly the others, or could he send it rushing along the path to strike home?

I could feel him behind me. Filled with his latest ghost. Waiting to download, give me someone to keep me company. A companion.

The understanding shocked me, but more that I felt so little surprise, that I had accepted something like this.

I glanced back again.

And he was right there, ten metres back now, like in a game where someone runs to catch up when you're not looking, then acts as if they've been walking normally all along. He was *too* close.

I could see his eyes staring. Could see his manic grin and the determined step. His mouth murmuring.

I couldn't outrun this. I turned, raised my only weapon. Mr Falk. Post Who Walks. Strikes.

But no. That would bring him too close. His eyes, his avid grin showed me that.

I raised my stick, threw it at seven metres, eight, whatever it was, struck him on the forehead it seemed, definitely on the face. Rain Eyes staggered, stumbled back, fell.

And I rushed on, my leg throbbing, aching, pounding down. Out of the park, along the street, the blinking *Ham-Sa, Ham-Sa* mocking, calling. I looked round once, twice, then pressed doggedly on.

I expected him on the bench, expected him in my room, expected some signature like my walking stick left on the bed, some obvious trick conclusion like you see in films. But no.

I tried Harry again, phoned Doctor Dan, expected busy signals as Rain Eyes came towards me along Bennett Street or worse, expected insanity on the other end of the phone, crazed laughter, but they were there, Harry awake, Dan crusty with sleep, and they said they'd be over immediately.

They were, in Harry's car fifteen minutes later, and we drove down to the park and found Rain Eyes lying on the path in the wind and the night, eyes open, staring upwards in a stupor but alive, lips no longer moving. At least that.

Dan used Harry's mobile, got an ambulance sent round, and Malcolm Jade—so his wallet ID said—was taken to hospital. My parting comment made Harry look at me long and hard.

"Doctor Dan, do me a favour and ride in front, will you?"

Dan nodded, probably just to humour me, perhaps because he sensed my fear.

"You're a mean shot with a walking-stick, Jay," Harry said as the ambulance disappeared from view.

"How're you going to report this?"

"Depends on how Malcolm Jade reports it I'd say. Looks to me like he was struck by a branch blown down from a tree. It's a windy night."

"Thanks, Harry."

"Thank me tomorrow."

The mind is an amazing thing as Doctor Dan will tell you. Both Harry and Dan let me run through it again over at Blackwater for the unofficial, inadmissible-evidence, legs-of-a-tripod record, then Dan stood with his back to the window, pure theatricality, and announced that Malcolm Jade was fine, doing well enough physiologically, but that he would have to remain at Blackwater, that when he wasn't raving incoherently, he was insisting that he was Mario Giacomo.

Malcolm Jade is gone, perhaps buried deep down. There's a new resident now, and there's a park I try to avoid and a walking-stick I'll never touch again. It's irrational, I know, but you know what they say about *The Phantom* and ghosts walking. They never die.

The Bullet That Grows in the Gun

THE SIX WORDS were all it took.

"Tell us about the Green Man."

And the five other people in Gustav Bremmer's eccentric wood-panelled office tensed, leaned forward in their chairs. The polite small talk was gone, as was the illusion of easy company.

"Not yet, Professor Bremmer, please!" Fair-minded, level-headed Harry Gellis made his usual plea for justice. "Mr and Mrs Tate have questions of their own first. They know nothing about the reason behind tonight's meeting. I didn't tell them."

Bremmer conceded the point, settled back in his chair and regarded his guests.

"Very well, Harry. But I would have thought that we could hear the Tates' account of this fabulous Green Man and not keep them."

"But I brought them along to illustrate Markham's point, Professor, not just to talk about their own experience. I want them to be here for the opening of the box. If you don't mind."

Gustav Bremmer leaned over to the gas-ring near the door and turned up the flame under the kettle, began to make the tea according to his ritual. Outside the leadlight casements, down in the quadrangle, night was falling. The small diamond panes were filling with an ever-deepening blue. An autumn chill was in the air, and the gas-ring warmed the room pleasantly.

"Ah, the grand opening of the box! No, I don't mind. But hardly impartial observers, Harry."

Harry pressed on. "Which is why Sally Radbrook and Charles Ross are here. They have no vested interests either way." He turned to the two students, gave each a smile of encouragement and silent gratitude. "All we need is Doctor Markham and we can begin."

Bremmer laughed indulgently and filled the cups. For the moment Harry thought he looked the kindly old gentleman, not the ruthless head of department who, through the years, had ultimately ruined the careers of Markham and possibly many others. Bremmer's ruthlessness was well known among his present staff—not just rumour, not just exaggeration.

"Good old Benjamin. Will he make it? With 'Form Follows Function' and all. Oh my! Can I stand it?"

"That's unfair, Professor," Harry said. "Doctor Markham was a devoted member of staff. He never falsified data and he believes in what we're doing. Meeting the Tates will be important for him."

"Yes, yes. Spare me, Harry. But I'd rather have a whisperer like you than a shouter like him any day. Attend closely, Miss Radbrook, Mr Ross! Tonight we see the folly of eight years laid to rest—the opening of the box! The famous Bremmer-Markham-Gellis box! Then we shall hear about the Green Man."

The undergrads exchanged glances. The Tates, a neat well-dressed couple in their early forties, did too. Harry suspected the Tates were feeling foolish, totally out of their depths. Mrs Tate reached for the walking stick beside her, gripped the curved handle.

When all of them had steaming cups from the famous Bremmer gas-ring, Harry made several polite attempts to chair proceedings, then gave up and sipped his tea. His watch said 6:25. Ben Markham would be here soon. Then Harry would have to keep control somehow, prevent this from becoming a contest of rivals postponed for eight years.

So far the tea ceremony had made his task easy. It always slowed things down. Bremmer was preoccupied with his ritual of making, pouring and now drinking tea, and Harry could therefore afford to let his mind wander, to relieve the tension he felt.

He recalled crossing the quadrangle earlier, after his late class, seeing the evening sky stretched like some lustrous blue canvas over a notched and ragged Gothic frame. Students had moved through the dimly lit cloisters and among the deep shadows across the grass as always, laughing and talking.

Harry had loved every step, the vistas he recognised and cherished. From one angle that piece of skyline was a blunt outcropping, a knob with no real shape to it. Another step or two and it sprang to life in silhouette, the sudden brutal shadow-play of a gargoyle.

And all across that placid, timeless backwater, Harry had been aware of the two keys in his jacket pocket. One for the closet, one for the box.

Then he had allowed himself his first direct glimpse of Bremmer's mezzanine 'garret,' that quirky afterthought of a room bullied out of a landing where two staircases met, never wanted really till Gustav Bremmer, all eccentricities and old-world charm anyway, had seized on it.

The Tates had been waiting for him on that side of the quad, near the only tree in the south-east corner, Marilyn Tate easily recognizable, as always, by her walking stick. It had been a short rise to Bremmer's office then; always deceptive that. You prepared yourself for a long climb, the full double-flight, and before you knew it, Bremmer's door was peeping out at you, dark shiny wood, on its mezzanine landing. Students would always overshoot that door, mindlessly climbing.

Footsteps on those stairs distracted him. Harry glanced at his watch. It was 6:32. There was a knock at the door.

Ben Markham had arrived.

Harry let the short middle-aged man in, introduced him and indicated a chair between Ross and himself.

Bremmer had the grace to turn up his gas-ring, though his "Nice to see you, Markham" was hollow. Harry could see he was enjoying himself immensely, suspected he had as much curiosity as the rest of them. After all, Bremmer too had lived with this for eight years. He had put up with the locked closet in his office and the locked box on the shelf behind the door, melodramatically hidden behind the bookcase.

Finally Markham's cup and the refills had been passed out and everyone was ready. The Tates and the students were looking from

Markham to Professor Bremmer to Harry Gellis, waiting for the proceedings to begin.

It was Bremmer who spoke. "Go ahead, Markham. Make your case."

"Let Harry tell it," Markham said, sipping his tea.

A wise move, Harry thought. Otherwise Bremmer would snort and guffaw all through the account. No. Better he present Ben Markham's case himself.

Now the eyes were on him exclusively.

Harry let a few moments pass, listened to the clock on the mantel above the closed-up fireplace, and drank the last of his tea. The room smelled of waxed wood, books and, faintly, of gas; but Harry had always loved it. It was the poet's garret his imagination had never needed when he was younger, an architectural marvel.

"Very well then, Mr and Mrs Tate, Charles, Sally," he said. And he began.

He told of how, nine years before, Ben Markham had started in the department as a senior tutor and part-time lecturer, an earnest, good-natured fellow doing doctoral research into the psychology of anomalous experience. Markham performed his duties well. He was popular with the students and with the staff, and he satisfied Professor Bremmer's requirements. At first. As the months passed, the events occurred that were to end Markham's teaching career in Bremmer's department. The first of these was an argument over Bremmer's pet theory of Psychic Stain, whose publication by this usually most cautious head of department had caused much comment.

Harry broached the subject carefully. He could not ridicule Markham (who, in the end, had thought enough of his own research to resign) and could not afford to alienate Professor Bremmer even slightly. It was a storyteller's nightmare.

"The most challenging and least extravagant theory about hauntings," Harry said, "is that when a person dies, their released personality, their vitality, actually 'stains' the room or locality in which that personality terminates. Like water-staining. Out goes the light of life—where does all that energy of self, of mind, go? Has it imploded, been sucked through some sink-hole, or has it leapt outwards as some measurable quantity? Professor Bremmer's view is that the liberated psyche does charge the surroundings, and continues in a much vitiated half-life state.

"The nature and degree of psychic staining determines the manifestations that other people later experience. Sometimes individuals react differently to these resonances and perceive different manifestations. It's uneven, of course. Some places are stained for decades, even centuries. Others only for minutes, hours, weeks, surfacing in premonitions and what we call *frissons*. At one extreme, some people see ghosts and hear voices; at the other there is just a feeling, uneasiness, *inquiétude*."

Harry glanced to see how Bremmer was reacting. The old man nodded.

There was no doubt that the Tates were engrossed by this. They were clearly looking for answers, watching Harry intently.

"Go on, Harry," Bremmer said.

"Doctor Markham here had another quite new approach. He was intrigued by the notion that houses are haunted because they try to grow their own people." He paused. "In itself, that view caused no great trouble; it's so hypothetical and intrinsically absurd."

Now Harry looked at Ben, but Markham showed no signs of disapproval. He understood Harry's position.

"But Doctor Markham was offering it as a topic for seminar discussion, a way for him to explore his views. For one of his tutorials he found a newspaper article listing how many people had been killed or wounded that year by supposedly unloaded guns. It was an incredibly high statistic, and, between considering that and the notion that houses could haunt themselves, he produced his own Form Follows Function theory."

Bremmer interrupted. "Don't call it a theory, Harry. It's an absurdity, a quantum leap in pure waffle! Theories have at least some empirical basis. Some semblance of feasibility. This notion of Markham's is the most dangerous form of claptrap. Guns growing their own bullets! Houses growing ghosts! Furniture growing people! I'm a lenient man and I approve of healthy speculation, but a line has to be drawn. This is abject nonsense! Lunacy!"

"Please continue, Harry," Markham said reasonably.

Harry swallowed. There was no way he could come out of this unscathed, he realised. He ignored the rivals and faced the other four.

"Doctor Markham's viewpoint is sensational and provocative to be sure, supported"—he put this in for Bremmer and his own future—"by no-one anywhere else in the academic world. His beliefs are his own, as revolutionary in terms of scientific thinking as the round-Earth theory or evolution ever were—"

"Wrong, Harry!" Bremmer said. "You give it the wrong emphasis—make it seem a truth whose time has yet to come. I don't know about the Tates here, but for the sake of Miss Radbrook and Mr Ross I'd prefer you say, like a flat-Earth theory or a creationist one."

"Thank you, Harry," Markham said. "I appreciate how difficult this is for you. But I am as fascinated now as I was then. A farmer in the Riverina shot by his father's unloaded rifle left in the attic. He'd cleaned it the year before, taken it down to show around and clean again. A policeman in Adelaide killed by an unloaded service revolver. Hunters. A soldier at Puckapunyal. All in a three-week period. Too much to ignore, to attribute to mere carelessness.

"Yes, for a gun a bullet is a causal proposition. It exists only to receive, hold and deal with a bullet. An irresistible purpose, an incontrovertible logic. And what about houses? Those with no deaths yet to stain the locale, but filled with a presence all the same. Not the restless spirits of the departed shot into the surroundings in death trauma, but probably the causal resonances of living people— induced by the presence of our psyches, our spirits, our personas, day after day. The magnetic fields of a person provide a template, a living by-product of our being. The used artifact is imprinted with it, saturated. Psychic stain, yes, but the stain of *living* forces not terminated ones. We impregnate our artifacts, load them with it. Any wonder there are ghosts, life echoes. It helps to account for the melancholy surrounding an armchair at a dump, a rusted bicycle in some dunes, ruins in the desert, derelict cars in a wrecker's yard. Closed factories, closed schools. The melancholy that De Chirico noticed, which could be simply the absence of people from their artifacts, but is possibly something more. It's residual 'vitality', or could be—let me finish, Gustav!—some outlandish cause and effect working at some level in inanimate things, at the level of design, of function, of intentions.

"*We* bestow the cause and effect. We must make allowances for our ability to haunt ourselves. Any bullet that forms in an unloaded gun represents the bridge between the levels of reality, the crossover point. Of course it sounds absurd, it must. We must be alert to that first and foremost, the inherent absurdity of any theorizing here at such a point.

"Professor Bremmer saw where my thinking was heading. He made it clear that if I continued with my line of research, it would affect my career opportunities within his department. No direct threats. Just reminders that he controlled funding and duty rosters, and made out the reports on faculty staff. So we came to the only sensible long-term solution. He supported my application for tenure at another university and, in return for my leaving the department, agreed to help me test my Form Follows Function *theory* to his satisfaction. That way he would be free of me and I would have a controlled test case."

Bremmer glared icily but said nothing.

"Eight years ago tonight, with Harry Gellis here as observer, we locked an unloaded—unloaded, mind you, we all checked it—.38 revolver in an iron deed box. Three locks, three keys, one for each of us, and locked that in the small walk-in closet that's now concealed behind that bookcase there. Again, three locks—Harry did the carpentry for us—and three keys. Gustav will presently allow us to move the bookcase, open the closet and the box, and inspect the gun. He is to put it to his head and squeeze the trigger six times. That was the arrangement."

Harry shuddered. Eight years ago it had been easy to agree to this. Now he wondered if Bremmer would do it, put the gun to his head, squeeze the trigger.

Harry thought about it for the hundredth, thousandth time, imagined the situation.

You know the gun in your hands is empty. You've checked it several times to be sure. You feel foolish, but you are compelled to check it again.

You lock the gun away—for eight years, for a few hours, it doesn't matter in the end. You know the gun is empty, but when you take it out again you are no longer sure. You want to check it again *just in case*! Even though you *know* it is empty. Know it!

You put it to your head, checked. And still you hesitate. You know, but you hesitate.

Then you feel a *frisson* of fear.

Harry could never do it. He wasn't sure he could let Bremmer do it.

"There is an armchair in there as well," Markham continued. "An old upholstered armchair, to test the other part of the experiment."

Bremmer placed his cup on the desk with deliberate force, catching everyone's attention. "In the hope, friends, that the gun has loaded itself and the chair has grown itself a person. Isn't that how it goes, Ben?"

"You know it is, Gustav. And I guess we're just pursuing a point to its natural end. Burying the crackpot. My position is untenable. I don't necessarily expect the gun to be loaded, or the chair to be occupied—that's too simplistic, too much how our universe of quantitative experience operates. But I expect—well, at least sensations. Feelings. Some signs at the threshold of perception."

Bremmer had to interrupt. "Oh, spare us, Markham, please! You're priming our audience. All of us are edgy and apprehensive. Even I, with all this confrontation, and I know the gun isn't loaded—"

"So you *will* hold it to your head and squeeze the trigger? We'll give you our keys and you can unlock the closet and bring out the box."

Harry had been watching the Tates, and now he interrupted.

"Hold it, Ben, Professor! Before we get to that I'd like the Tates to have their story told."

Bremmer seemed to remember that the Tates were not older students of his, but a couple from outside the university.

"Afterwards, eh, Harry?" he said. "Over more tea when this business is settled."

But Harry was committed to giving relief to Jeff and Marilyn Tate as much as he was to supporting Ben Markham through these final formalities.

"No. Please, Professor! It's hard enough for Mr and Mrs Tate to sit through this. And what they have to say will interest Ben."

"And flavour the whole thing further," Bremmer said.

Markham leaned forward. "How can it change anything, Gustav? The gun's either loaded or it isn't. No amount of talk will change that."

Bremmer noted the discomfiture of the Tates, saw their strange expressions. He observed too that he probably hadn't lost face in front of Sally Radbrook and Charles Ross, that he still controlled proceedings.

"Very well, Harry, Markham. Let us hear about your Green Man."

With careful bonhomie he leaned down and set the big kettle back on the gas ring, turned up the eternal flame of Bremmer hospitality.

Harry gathered up the cups and placed them on the table in what he hoped was a conciliatory act. Bremmer accepted the gesture with a nod. The tension lessened.

Behind them, Sally Radbrook tactfully murmured something about how intrigued she was. Charles Ross dutifully agreed.

Harry knew how engrossing the nature of the experiment being concluded here tonight was. Everyone at some time had felt compelled to investigate the allegedly unloaded gun, to feel the thrill of knowing that oblivion could be an instant away. It was like placing the tip of a knife into a power socket, the temptation to stand at the edge of a cliff and gaze down, knowing that one step would do it.

Yes, everyone in the room wanted that door opened, the gun brought from its box, the theory tested.

And four of the people wanted to see how Bremmer would handle it, this formidable man whose imagination had been pressed into the service of his ego only, never going beyond what ultimately served himself.

Harry had no difficulty accepting Ben's notions. When dealing with possibilities, didn't this Form Follows Function stand as one extreme on the scale to Psychic Stain, to be considered, if not equally, at least fairly?

No, there was a personal vendetta in this. Bremmer's resistance meant something else. Harry suspected that the older man was fascinated in spite of himself, that he may have even tested Ben Markham's theory privately and was now drawn to this moment as they all were.

Harry thought about it. That had to be true. Why else would he have sacrificed the closet, given excuses for its disuse to the few faculty members, University architects and engineers who knew of its existence and may have enquired?

Harry Gellis, trembling here on the verge of true sycophancy, between loyalty to an old friend and middle-aged fears for job security, was still able to pose the questions and see the answer.

Bremmer wanted part of the credit for what Markham had—no, not discovered, had suspected, intuitively; something that could amount to a revolutionary and dynamic approach to causality. Absurdity until proven logical!

Harry passed out the cups of tea, handed round the sugar bowl and the spoons.

Then, when there was silence, he took out his notebook with the names and dates he had collected and began.

He told of how, in the April of 1979, the Tates had leased a ten-room, two-storeyed house near where Jeff Tate worked. Their three children, Karen, Larry, and Jennifer, all liked the house—especially the attic bedroom, which led to many arguments about who would have it. The girls had won it with the toss of a coin. For the next seven weeks nothing unusual happened.

Then one Tuesday in June, Marilyn Tate returned home from the part-time job she had, to find that Larry had locked himself in the upstairs bathroom, hysterical. Larry was a pragmatic boy, rather stolid and not highly imaginative. Had it been one of the girls, Marilyn Tate would have been able to handle it better. But since it was Larry sobbing and shouting, "Is he still out there?" from the other side of the locked bathroom door, Marilyn Tate was immediately and deeply alarmed.

Harry paused in his account just long enough to see that he had every-one's attention, and that the Tates approved of how he was telling their story. By the desk, Bremmer was listening with professional, polite interest, keeping all of his options open, committing himself to nothing.

The clock ticked; the kettle simmered quietly over the low, comforting glow of the gas-ring. Outside, it was night now, and a wind was rattling the casements.

Harry continued. He told of how it had taken Marilyn twenty minutes to get her son to unlock the door, to persuade him that the figure he claimed he had seen was not there. When Larry emerged, Marilyn had recognised at once that the boy was in shock. She had called a doctor immediately. Larry was later sedated and taken to hospital with a detached right retina.

The specialists all insisted that the injury could not have been caused by shock, that Larry Tate must have fallen during his hysteria and no longer remembered. The boy kept to his story: that he had been in the upstairs bathroom when the figure of a tall man moved down the hall towards him. No details, no features, just a dark shape that moved oddly, strangely; a shape that terrified him. Larry Tate saw him directly for several seconds, in reasonably good light, but he could not describe him. He knew it was definitely a man, a man who frightened deeply, who brought on an awful fear— effects inconsistent with even the worst intruder-fear. Larry still called him The Frightener.

Two weeks later, the girls saw him. The Tates were awakened by their daughters, who said that a man had been sitting on the end of Karen's bed, watching them. A green man, though no questioning could reveal any more details about him. He was green, and he frightened them.

Later that week, the Tates found their daughters downstairs asleep on the living-room sofa. They'd seen nothing that time but insisted the Green Man had been there. They refused to sleep in the attic room again.

While the Tates were having dinner in the dining room the following Sunday evening, signs of poltergeist activity occurred. Some photos and vases on the mantelpiece in the living-room crashed to the floor. By the time the Tates entered, the mantel had been completely cleared; the objects were not just on the floor, but were on the floor in the *middle* of the room.

Nothing happened for two weeks. Then, during the night, Jeff and Marilyn were awakened by banging and stamping from the attic. Jeff Tate, a pragmatic man himself and still sceptical about what had happened, assumed some tramp was up there. He took a torch and a revolver he had borrowed following Larry's experience and went to investigate. The noise had stopped by the time he arrived.

This happened throughout several subsequent weeks, always with the same result—no intruder, no Green Man, no Frightener, just odd residual sensations at the threshold of perception: half-seen movements at the comer of the eye, small half-heard sounds, but very odd ones, a slightly bitter smell, not chemical but unpleasant and very fleeting.

Jeff Tate finally noticed the decals on a bookcase at one end of the attic— small stained-glass decals of sunbursts and pentagrams put there by previous tenants. They had been hard to remove and so were left. Larry had already shown these to his parents when the family first moved into the house.

Now Jeff had the idea that the room had once been used for some sabbat ritual, a meeting place for a neighbourhood coven. There were metal brackets fitted around the window seat, possibly for holding candles and turning it into a makeshift altar. What seemed to be the remains of a circle on the wooden floor, sanded back and varnished over, supported this idea. Rather than causing more concern, these suspicions actually alleviated the tension. There seemed to be an explanation, however trite. Subsequently, the manifestations had diminished.

Harry paused and regarded his audience once more. Bremmer was aloof, guarded. The Tates, Markham and the students were rapt. He returned to his notebook, very close now to his story's end.

He looked at the last entry and felt suddenly afraid. The wind played at the windows, the clock ticked, the silent plume of steam rose from the kettle. He returned to the account.

"Then in the last week of August 1979, Marilyn Tate stopped dusting her upstairs bedroom to investigate a slow steady pounding on the stairs. While she was there on the landing, looking down the empty staircase, the Green Man seized her from behind, lifted her and flung her down the stairs. Mrs Tate broke her back in two places, was hospitalized for six months and, to this day, as you can see, walks with a cane.

"And that's it. The Tates moved out while Mrs Tate was convalescing; the house was re-let to another couple, the Craigs, who later rang the Tates to ask if anything unusual had happened while they were living there. These manifestations for the Craigs, however, were short-lived because—"

"Because the Green Man came with us!" Marilyn Tate said. "Never as strong now we're away from Mercer Street, but still there occasionally as The Frightener."

Markham couldn't control his excitement. "You've all seen him?"

"The girls have. Larry and I have. Jeff hasn't. But always very quick flashes. Just enough to scare you. There and gone. Never threatening, as at Mercer Street."

Markham nodded thoughtfully.

Harry saw that Bremmer should be invited into the discussion now, his opinion sought in an appropriately deferential manner.

"Well, Professor," he said. "You've investigated anomalies like this. You can see why I felt the Tates would appreciate your views.

I think it's fair, too, to say that they have never recounted this story before they came to me. Not to Larry's doctor, not to the police, not to the specialists who treated Marilyn and insisted her injuries were more than those of just an accidental fall. A friend knew a little of it and referred them to us, but this is the first public telling. It hasn't been easy for them."

"Of course," Bremmer said. "I can appreciate that. And I'm intrigued, most intrigued. But first tell me, Harry, how you feel this story helps Ben's case? If anything, it would seem to be a rather nasty example of Psychic Stain, granting that it all happened as you describe."

"It did," Jeff Tate said. "Harry told it well."

Marilyn smiled slightly. "Yes."

Harry was grateful as he answered Bremmer's question. He could see Ben Markham was also curious.

"I'm suggesting that it supports Ben's approach because the Green Man appeared *not* because a house used for some fashionable supernatural meetings wanted to haunt itself—"

"Thank goodness for that!" Bremmer murmured.

"But because young Larry Tate, as down to earth as everyone says he is, *wanted* The Frightener to appear."

"What?" Jeff and Marilyn Tate said at once, their eyes wide.

"What's that you say?" Bremmer demanded.

The students and Ben Markham stared in amazement.

Harry held up a hand. "I asked to speak with the Tate children, and especially Larry Tate, soon after the Tates first told me their story. The boy and I had three meetings, and at the second of these I regressed him hypnotically back beyond the 1979 incident to his early childhood. Under hypnosis, Larry confessed to dreaming of The Frightener in some very vivid and quite atypical nightmares. I have the tapes from these sessions."

Markham leaned forward in his chair. "And you're saying that Larry willed the Green Man into existence, subconsciously, after he'd spotted the decals in the attic room?"

"Not necessarily the Green Man, Ben. But certainly an apparition called The Frightener. A very potent image which utilized forms and details from the minds of Jeff here or Marilyn, or any of the Tates."

Bremmer was shaking his head. The Tates were astonished, even a little angry at these new revelations. They were getting answers; it was just that they were so far beyond what had been expected.

Harry saw that Marilyn was trembling. Jeff had taken her hand and was patting it. Marilyn's other hand gripped her cane so tightly that her knuckles were white.

"Larry never mentioned hypnosis," Jeff Tate said.

"I'm not surprised, Jeff. He wasn't meant to remember it. He thinks we just talked."

"Well, I'm a little surprised at you, Harry," Bremmer said, annoyed. "You never mentioned this to me."

"It would have been premature, Professor. After all, I wasn't trying to prove any particular point of view at the time. It was a routine survey. I was examining confidentially a particularly vicious instance of anomalous behaviour."

Bremmer was hardly mollified, but could not object. "This is ludicrous! Soon you and Markham will say that cameras will start producing their own film—"

"Not that absurd, Gustav," Markham said. "I've documented four cases where cameras have taken their own pictures—shadowy exposures with almost-people shapes in them."

"I think this has gone far enough. Let Harry Gellis tell us how the Green Man is connected with your views."

Harry noted, with dismay, the use of his surname, but then made his closing remark.

"Simply this. Larry Tate brought The Frightener into the Tates' lives, powered it in a setting amenable to it. There is no proof but the facts in the Tates' story. No other proof, I repeat. The Green Man came from one of the parents—whom I haven't interviewed or regressed yet—because neither Karen nor Jennifer Tate revealed any such memories under hypnosis. As horrible as it sounds, I believe the Green Man was brought on by you, Marilyn, using your son's powerful summoning. I say you because Jeff never saw the thing."

Marilyn sat wide-eyed.

Bremmer raised both hands. "All right, Harry! All right! Are you saying that Mrs Tate carries the Green Man around with her?"

"That isn't clear. It's a matter of a suitable setting—their Mercer Street house—possibly unstained by death but primed, nonetheless, by efforts of will, possibly, from would-be satanists—and two quite vital power centres: Larry and Marilyn. This office is a suitable setting too; and the possible source, if not the carrier, of the Green Man is right here. You must draw your own conclusions."

Bremmer reached out for cups. "More tea, anyone?"

Pontius Pilate never gave a more eloquent dismissal.

Cups were passed in; the big kettle was hoisted to warm the pot. The wind rattled the panes, so many frosted diamonds in the unseasonable weather.

"Gentlemen," Bremmer said, while Sally Radbrook poured. "Your keys, if you please."

Ben handed his over and Harry did the same.

Bremmer held them up portentously. "For the record, ladies and gentlemen, I *am* fascinated with all that has been said here tonight, and I welcome Mr and Mrs Tate to phone me to arrange a time for further discussion of the Mercer Street visitation. I do believe, however, that much of what has been said has been disturbingly unscientific. We shall now finish with this. Markham! Harry! Will you move the bookcase aside please?"

Harry went to the far side of the room and helped Ben Markham clear some of the heavier volumes from the free-standing case. Then they heaved together, and slid it to one side to reveal the drab brown-painted door of the closet.

The teacups were being handed out again, full and steaming.

"Markham, you can have the honour of opening the door," Bremmer said. "And Harry can bring me the box. I suppose I should be the one to open that."

Markham returned to his chair, not even attempting to take the keys from Bremmer's outstretched hand.

"No, Gustav! You're the objective, trained, scientific mind. You should open the door, in case there is something, just a hint of something, in the chair. You won't believe me if I say I saw it."

Bremmer considered that a moment, then stood. "Very well, Markham. I take you point."

He took the three keys and approached the narrow wooden door. Though the lighting in the room was dim, they could all see their host as he inserted each key and, in a double-handed motion, turned them all.

There was a hush as he pulled the door towards him, a hush in which the clock's ticking, the hiss of the gas-ring and the sound of the wind at the panes were suddenly vivid.

"Empty," Bremmer announced, pulling the door back so that the closet's interior was dimly lit. The closet had its own light fitting but the bulb didn't work. When Bremmer reached to try the light switch, they could see an old armchair in the gloom, covered with a once-gaudy floral fabric.

"Not a thing!" Bremmer continued. "Just the chair, empty shelves, and this!"

He brought out the grey metal deed box and carried it to his desk, blowing dust from it.

"Stage one complete, Ben. No-one in the chair."

Everyone was looking at the metal box.

"Nothing visible," Charles Ross muttered, a comment meant for Sally Radbrook but overheard by Bremmer.

"Thank you, Mr Ross! Perhaps you would care to go and sit in the chair for us. Go ahead! It's perfectly comfortable. A little dusty perhaps!"

The student, looking abashed, said and did nothing.

Bremmer returned to the box, attempted to open the lid to show it was still locked.

"The three keys for the three locks," he said.

One by one they were inserted and turned, the lid opened.

Bremmer placed the deed box on the floor in front of him so that everyone could see.

"There is the gun," he said.

The tension was overwhelming now. Both Ben and Harry leaned forward nervously. The Tates sat very still, Marilyn Tate's knuckles white once again. Sally Radbrook and Charles Ross were like statues.

Bremmer lifted it out of the box, held it up for them all to see.

"How would you like me to do this, Markham? Just place it against my temple and pull the trigger—what is it?—six times?"

Markham's whole demeanour had changed. Till this moment he had been almost casual, fascinated by the Tates' story but detached. Now he was totally attentive, no longer just a thwarted rival but worried, even concerned, for his former colleague.

"Inspect it first, Gustav. Please. Very carefully."

The clock's ticking was very loud. The hiss of the gas flame was fierce. The wind clawed to get in.

Bremmer snorted in amusement, but everyone sensed that he welcomed Markham's suggestion.

He broke open the revolver, inspected the cartridge chambers, rotated the drum, peered down the barrel.

"Empty," he said, and went to hand it round.

"No!" Markham said, shocking them all. "Do it as we said!"

Bremmer looked a little stunned by the force of Markham's words.

"All right, Ben. All right. No need to get upset about it."

But Markham stared at him. "We're not playing here, Gustav. I'm saying the bullet could still be there. I don't want you killed."

Bremmer snapped the revolver shut, placed the barrel against his head.

"One," he said.

Click!

Breaths were released. The clock ticked. Outside, the wind slammed at the frosted panes.

"Two."

Click!

Six pairs of eyes watched the old man at the desk, never leaving him.

There was a sheen to his brow, the beginnings of a fear sweat. Night waited at the windows. The plume of steam rose from the kettle with an urgency, rising quickly, fanning out, gone.

"Three."

Click!

Harry swallowed, let himself blink, noticed Marilyn Tate's white knuckles, then it was back to the gun pressed to Bremmer's skull. A bead of sweat formed there now, though the voice remained level and calm.

"Four."

Click!

The clock pounded. Harry let himself notice the barely visible chair in the closet, the pool of shadow lodged there. Why hadn't someone closed the door? Closed it with the distinctive sound of the three locks Harry had fitted, a sound he would never forget.

"Five."

Click!

Harry found he was forgetting to breathe. Don't do it, don't do it, he kept thinking. The wind, the clock, the plume of steam, the glow of the gas-ring, the sweat on Bremmer's brow. The shadow in the chair was watching, watching.

Click!

"And six."

Bremmer put the gun on the desk, his hand trembling, then sat down.

"There, Markham. Satisfied?"

Ben Markham smiled oddly, as if he expected Gustav Bremmer's skull to burst open suddenly with a delayed impact. He rose.

"It'll do for now, Gustav. It'll do for now. Thank you for being patient with me. From the first, I only ever wanted to be indulged a little—to be allowed to take this most incredible of *What ifs?* as far as possible, to explore the statistical anomalies where no plausible scientific explanation was available. In a way, it's like locked-room murders. We need to know, but knowing is impossible. The bullet I expected to find in that gun is not just some phantom. It represents the corner that science hasn't gone into yet, because it cannot yet, because there is never any empirical evidence. It is the untenable fact, the chilling intuition-reality that we brush aside so that it won't leave us looking foolish. All I ask now is that, when I've gone, you have the chair removed at once and the gun taken as far away from here as possible. Let one of the students keep it till it can be disposed of. Or Harry, you take it. Please do it, Gustav! Please!"

Ben Markham then bid everyone goodnight, said: "See you, Harry. Call me," and left. They heard his footsteps descending the narrow wooden stairs, heard them for a moment as he crossed the quadrangle to catch a taxi.

In Bremmer's office there was a heavy silence.

Then, absurdly, Bremmer began to thank the Tates for coming. Harry heard himself thanked—thanked!—forgiven!—for putting up with Markham's imposition on his time and good nature, and for bringing the Tates to the department's notice. He also saw Bremmer shake the students' hands.

They were, all of them, being thank you'd out into the night.

Harry saw Marilyn Tate speak to her husband, saw Jeff Tate shake his head firmly and help her to the door.

"Shall we remove the chair and the gun, Professor, as Markham suggested?" Harry said.

Bremmer smiled. "Forget the chair, Harry. Forget the gun. Go home and rest. We have a faculty meeting tomorrow."

But Harry paused. "Should Ross and I move the bookcase back then?"

Bremmer laughed. "Whatever for, Harry? I have my closet back at last. Leave it." He gestured at the gun on the desk. "And that could well end up on my wall as a memorial to those who persist in staying on the idiot fringe. Go home and forget about it."

And again, absurdly, they were out on the tiny landing and Bremmer was closing the door in their faces. They were going down the steps, out into the windy darkness in the quad, crossing the path under a spread of chill autumn stars.

The students had already gone. Harry was walking with the Tates towards Parramatta Road. Looking back, he saw the cheerful yellow-lit windows of Bremmer's office, and wondered what Gustav Bremmer would be doing now.

He started when Marilyn Tate touched his arm.

"Harry? I told Jeff before and he said not to say any more, but I know the Green Man was in that room tonight."

"What!" Harry said. "What's that?"

"He's there," Jeff Tate answered. "Marilyn sensed he was there. The Frightener."

Harry stood a moment, watching the three lighted windows. Then he rushed ahead to the phone near the door of the Information Office.

He was almost there when he heard a single shot, echoing in the darkened quad, up among the gargoyles, out along the rooftops.

The Gully

Casting the Bodies Vest aside,
My Soul into the boughs does glide:
There like a Bird it sits, and sings,
Then whets, and combs its silver Wings;
And, till prepar'd for longer flight,
Waves in its Plumes the various Light.

—ANDREW MARVELL

THE GULLY WAS very quiet at noon. Not even a hundred metres, Ralph thought, most of it in sight of neighbouring houses, though the windows were usually blind at this hour on a Tuesday.

Not even a hundred metres.

But the shortcut between Tyagarah Street and Warner Street terrified him, filled him with the terrible anxiety again, in full light, *especially* in full light. That was part of it, the hot bright air.

Ralph's breathing was short and quick. He knew his pulse was racing. He stood in Tyagarah Street, a few paces from where the track began, studying the scene as he had on every other visit during the last two weeks.

There was Warner Street over there, on the other side of the gully, in full sunshine, ending where the gully continued on and fell away between some backyard fences and finally reached some playing fields down near the bay.

Ralph couldn't see anyone, but people were about. A sprinkler was going; curtains blew around the open windows of houses overlooking the gully on the Warner Street side.

Warner Street was so near. It could be reached only by using the diagonal track—down, curve, rise, out of sight, rise and safe. One and a half minutes. Two at the most.

Ralph looked down Tyagarah Street. It too continued on, parallel to the gully, pacing it, so that if the gully had not existed, it would have met Warner Street at right angles and probably been named Something Crescent. Then the whole problem would not have arisen, at least not here, not now, and Ralph wouldn't be waiting.

But the gully existed, choked with native bush and garden plants run wild, tangles of morning glory, stands of cannas and bamboo and a few ti-trees and eucalypts; and with the track a dusty brown thread straggling across the varying greens and summer browns and yellows (most of it in clear sight!) as if determined to link up with Warner Street and bring to pass what the gully had prevented.

A shortcut. A quick way home. Not quite a hundred metres by the track, much less if you stood at the end of Tyagarah Street and looked across.

The alternative was Potts Street and Weaver Street and an extra fifteen minutes.

Ralph had told no-one about his problem, not even Megan at school, though above her desk in the staff-room she had a small gift plaque—a picture of a field and some trees, with the legend: "Of magic doors there is this, you do not see them even as you are passing through."

On the strength of that, he had almost told her. Megan, help me! I'm haunted by a few acres of ground.

But he couldn't risk it. He couldn't let a wall plaque that spoke so urgently to him make him think Megan would understand. Or could. And it was school holidays; he didn't even have Megan's home number.

Ralph looked at the gully and the track and became angry again, hating the crisis, the foolishness, hating the embarrassment. He wished he hadn't moved into the area.

Don't think, Ames! Do it!

The anger surged up in him. He strode down the track, down to the bottom, the low-point—twelve metres in.

Then the fear stopped him, that and the way the landscape had changed, how it looked so different just by dropping four metres. Four metres. It couldn't be more.

Tyagarah Street was a flat deck, a green-limned edge with housetops visible, lifting out of it. Warner Street had disappeared altogether behind the bushes, though Ralph could hear the sprinkler working and could see the blowing curtains of one of the houses that looked out on the gully.

He stood at the low-point, before the track swung to the right and angled off to make its slow diagonal rise. He stood, twelve metres in and four metres down and listened to the silence, felt the heat, watched the uncanny stillness of everything.

An insect zipped past, not seen, just a quick buzzing that vanished in a second or two. Somewhere a lizard scurried through dry grass, a sudden rustle, part of the small sound to big sound conspiracy that was always there, a part of every previous visit.

Twelve metres in, four metres down.

Ralph darted glances about him—to the green lip of Tyagarah Street, to the bushes blocking the way ahead, to the hot sky and the blowing curtains of the Warner Street house on the gully's eastern side. He thought he heard a screen door close somewhere nearby— a good sound, a people sound, like the sprinkler, though he wished he could see a person to put with it.

That was part of the problem after all. He could hear everything to do with people, but down in the gully: no sign of anyone. Only detached sounds.

Ralph knew it mattered. He got the impression that if he had the courage to cry out, everything would go silent—the sprinkler, things like screen doors, even the far-off traffic noise from Victoria Road, far away over the rooftops.

His heart was pounding. It was too much to bear. Before he knew it, he was back on the edge, back in Tyagarah Street looking down to where he had been.

Twelve metres in. Twelve metres out.

Real courage. Thanks, Megan! So much for just the thought of you laughing at me.

Ralph needed a crossing. He stood there in the bright sunlight, tormented by the indecision, and felt keenly all the levels of his fear.

And there were levels. Fearing the gully: number one (and two and three and four, for that matter, because it was and wasn't that simple). And the others. Being a fool to himself. Being caught out as a fool, a teacher at the nearby primary school, a prize public fool. People could look out their windows and wonder. Worse, they might come out and enquire: "Why—Mr. Ames, isn't it?—what are you doing here?" Phone neighbours or the police.

God, that would do it! He ought to have more sense.

But school started next week, and so few of these quiet weekday noons were left. Next week he would be teaching and the gully would be lost to him, free to work its quiet acts, untested, unsuspected, until a weekend when too many people would be about. Or the Easter break. Or the July vacation, though it would be cooler then, different, the position of the sun, the quality of the light, all wrong.

No, he had put it off long enough. He needed a crossing now, to test his—calling it a theory was kind—his compulsion, his belief, now. It was crucial.

Ralph returned to his surveillance. The sprinkler threw a gleaming spray in the sunlight, making a cheerful rainbow, a glistening fan with a twist of light at its heart. The curtains beckoned.

Come over. Red Rover come over!

Ralph considered those words from the game he'd played as a boy, words suddenly so chilling. He tried to put them from his mind. His imagination would ruin everything, would beach him here, strand him. It happened every time. First the control, then the slow creeping fear, the sudden associations.

Red Rover come over!

He fought the words, but more words came.

Just a gully.

Just a track.

Just a green (something)

With a brown snake down its back.

A green what? A face? No, that wouldn't do. Not with the last line.

But why did he think of a face? Poetic license. Simple rhyme. Bad poetry. But why that?

Twelve metres in, twelve metres out. Four down.

The curtains were still now, with not even a hot useless breeze to stir them. Nothing moved in the heated silence but the sprinkler, a glass peacock forming and unforming, fanning itself in another world.

Ralph knew he was about to try again. He could feel resolve slipping in, the tension of it taking over his body.

Then movement caught his eye. Two young boys on their way to the local pool, leaving Warner Street, moving down into the gully from the end, the cut-off end (the dead end, yes) of Warner Street.

Ralph resisted the urge to cry out: "Go back! It's too close to the time. Don't spoil anything!"

He barely let himself blink, but fumbled for the stop-watch in his pocket, set it going, all without thinking, without taking his eyes from the boys. He watched the laughing, chattering figures follow the track down the slope, saw them vanish, appear, vanish and appear again among the taller bushes, heard their bright young voices. When they disappeared from view for ten, fifteen seconds, their voices told him where they were.

Ralph moved closer to the track.

Here they came, round the final turn, moving up the incline towards him, unharmed, oblivious.

"Hi, boys!" he called out, fearing they would be from his school, fearing (deeper down) that they would think he was someone out to molest them or something, or in case the neighbours did. Ralph tried to look as if he were waiting for someone, the only ploy he could think of.

"Hi, Mr Ames!" one of them said.

Ralph clicked off the stop-watch. The boys knew him. He knew them: Baxter and Grahame, in Megan's fifth grade.

He couldn't help himself.

"What was it like down there, boys?"

"What?" one youngster said. They were out of the gully now, passing him.

"Did you see anything odd down there? In the gully?"

"Nuh," said one.

"Nuh," said the other. "What sorta things, Mr Ames?"

The boys exchanged looks.

"Oh, nothing really," Ralph said. "Some kids said they saw someone lurking round down there and I'm checking it out. Keeping an eye on things in case."

The boys looked at him, both clearly impressed.

"Gee!" one said, looking back at the gully.

"We didn't see anything," the other added.

"Okay. Thanks, boys. See you next week."

"See ya, Mr Ames," they said, and kept walking, looking back several times as they headed for the pool.

Crazy man, they probably thought. Weirdo!

No, that wasn't fair. In their world he was Teacher. Capital T. And so he had reasons. Children granted reasons and purpose, trusted to wise motives. Teachers were still special cattle, sacrosanct. By the time school started, Mr Ames would be a hero, doing interesting and mysterious things even on holidays.

Ralph waited till they had moved out of sight into Potts Street, then turned his gaze back to the gully.

The curtains were blowing again. That bothered Ralph. And some of the bushes along the track were moving to a breeze—not blowing hard, just stirring as if from their centres, as if fists had closed on them and were shaking them ever so slightly. Higher, on the Warner Street level, the sprinkler fantailed and shone. He could hear insects, could see...

A green face.

The image came again, inappropriate and relentless. A stupid, annoying image. He had never had it before and it was a trigger. It made him recall what had scared him most on his other attempts.

Not a green face. Something that was no more than sun-dazzle above the hot track. No other name for it: sun-dazzle. Too much light. Corner-of-the-eye movement and flicker, and more. Something hanging above the trail.

Three desperate, frantic near-crossings (stop-watch running), and three times the burgeoning light, the dazzle caught up there amid the bushes, crazing the air.

Not a green face, though that image scared him more now than it had before. No threat from the houses with their blowing curtains and their lawn sprinklers. Just crazed air. Motes of spinning golden light coming together.

The boys were far off now, in another world too, safe and untouched.

Ralph wished he had asked them to take him across. Boys sense odd things but accept. They would have made it easy with their bright voices and healthy suspicion.

He had the pretext too. Let's check the gully out together, boys. It won't take a minute and it has Mr Ames' divine purpose behind it.

The gully waited. Twenty minutes past noon, though daylight saving made that a false noon and Ralph wanted the real one. That meant everything. The real noon lay ahead, and down in the gully time and light and summer silence were tangled together, woven, crouching.

Crouching? A green face, now crouching.

Shit! Ralph thought. My own imagination does it to me. Stop! Stop it now! Ralph thought of Megan's plaque ("Of magic doors there is this") and went back to his theorizing ("you do not see them"), to the conclusions and reassurances he had made so easily in the spacious sun-room of his new house and in the car ("even as you are passing through").

People disappear in gullies and such places, don't they? Lonely stretches of beach, forest glades, underground railway stations. They do; of course they do. Right. No big deal. They change places. When no-one's looking. Flick. Twist. The curtains claw you in; the bushes hide you. The sprinklers drown your cries. You go up or under or in; you slip away. No-one notices. The innocence of it is terrifying. It's just no big deal once you grant that unexplained disappearances do happen.

Circumstances create the juncture. Place, time, light, heat, opportunity. You bring the mind, the perception, the activating suspicion, perhaps, and the fear. Awareness does it, unlocks the secret, starts the process, reducing...

...everything that's made
To a Green Thought in a Green Shade.
A green face.

Ralph fought the intrusion, wondering where those lines had come from, realizing suddenly that they were from a poem he had studied at university, a poem by Andrew Marvell.

He pushed the words aside, collected his previous thoughts. He kept at it, trying to keep the logical flow of ideas he had brought with him.

This obsession, his madness, could be survival cunning, couldn't it? He was alert to subtleties here, nuances. Like so many unsuspected things, old houses, locked rooms, empty factories, lonely spits of land, the gully was a people-taker. He wasn't crazy, just alert, finely tuned.

Ralph thought of the boys, so immune. He thought of ladies with shopping bags and commuters returning home with their folded newspapers, emerging untouched in Warner Street.

Wrong time of day. Wrong time of year, wrong season. Wrong combination of things. Noon was it, summer was it, now, now was it. Ralph was certain. He read the gully. He could tell the signs.

Up here, nothing. Down there on the track would be the fractionating air, the flurry of light, the acute sensitivity to place and signs, the new truth. Down there the curtains clawed the hot air, the sprinklers began to murmur like conspirators, the insects threaded you in, sewed you up in a cat's cradle of change, of zip and slip, of flicker, flash, gone! Horror dealt in small dislocations. Horror didn't need midnight and howling wind.

The green face swallows you.

The crazed air follows you.

The gully borrows you!

Bad poetry. More terrible rhymes. Images feeding his terror. Making his terror, dammit!

Ralph recognised the obvious madness waiting in him, the recklessness and obsession. It always surprised him because madness was—well, inconclusive. There was no answer in madness, just the private problem, the solitary nightmare, a comfortable handle others could use. Madness was easy.

And it was all too easy to accept that he was paranoid, already crazy—much, much harder to believe in action and purpose regardless of what others, the experts, would say.

Ralph was terrified. He was anxious and embarrassed and close to nervous exhaustion, but he believed he was—even under those circumstances—still objective, exploring a truth from the heart of an honest conviction, a valid perception. A major intuition.

Now he was waiting for noon, for a noon crossing. He had never liked admitting his intention to himself, not ever, in case his imagination set to work too soon, too powerfully. As it had anyway. But for all his terror, that was why he was here yet again.

Ralph realised it and at the same time defended himself to himself with the usual rationale and fervour. He was a Teacher.

Not insane. Not schizoid and giving in to a solipsistic bugbear. Just sensitive. Just that one in a thousand, two thousand, ten or fifty, who intuitively knew, custodians of the outré and the absurd.

Twenty to real twelve.

Ralph smiled, feeling a little better to have faced his dilemma like this again, though it panicked him. He thought of the film *High Noon*, of Tex Ritter singing the title song. The waiting there too.

The air was hot and still. The rooftops of the houses, like the road surfaces, shimmered in the heat. A quiet filled the streets in spite of the small sounds he could hear. Traffic noises were far off. The bushes were unmoving once more and the curtains hung limp in the windows.

The gully waited, caught between the noons.

A quarter to.

And the breeze was back again, pushing around him, hot and no relief at all. It stirred the bushes, got in behind the little metal flaps in some of the letter-boxes in Tyagarah Street and set them swinging and ticking. It splayed out the fan of the sprinkler across the gully and teased the curtains out into strangely scalloped edges, like the sides of clam shells. Ralph watched them lift and settle, lift and settle, a lulling, slowing action.

Ten to real noon.

Now the breeze was gone, the gully's breath pent up and waiting. The easy familiar allusion came to Ralph, more bearable than some of the others.

He checked his watch, getting himself ready in all those little physical ways he didn't really care to notice.

Come on, noon! Come now while the imagination is slacking.

Ralph got ready, his heart pounding.

Suddenly there was a movement at the Warner Street end of the track. Not the boys—repeating their crossing in some time-loop replay—but a woman in a floral dress with a plastic carrying bag, moving down the dusty trail.

Damn! Ralph said to himself, unable to sound it aloud. Damn, damn, damn! Why now?

He checked his watch. Six to. Still enough time.

Come on! Ralph urged, not speaking, not saying a word.

The woman in the floral dress dropped from sight, appeared again, walking head down, not noticing the path she used, the crowding, saturated air, the blending of heat and sound and dislocation. She vanished once more behind the bushes.

The thought came then, a new thought, that this woman, so middle-aged, so innocent, might be the personification of the gully come to meet him, come to pass him on the track, suddenly turning on him, opening up, golden light springing forth, spilling out of her drab floral dress.

Ralph's hands were clenched. Come on!

But there was no sign of her. Not a trace. The new image firmed: she's waiting down there. And at another level was the fear that the gully had taken her.

Ralph checked his watch. It was over a minute. Easily more than a minute. He stood at the very edge of the gully, at his end of the track.

A breeze pushed by. The curtains stirred. The bushes in the gully moved again, lightly. Ralph heard the ticking of the letter-boxes, the sprinkler's steady rhythm.

Five and a half to.

No sign. Still no sign.

Damn the woman! Ralph fidgeted, unable to help himself. He stepped on to the track, began to move down it, two steps.

Then she appeared from behind the bushes, rummaging in her carry bag as she ambled along, checking for keys or something.

A ditherer! Oh God, a ditherer!

But Ralph edged back, went into his watch-checking, waiting-for-some-one routine all the same for when she looked up and saw him.

Come on!

The woman moved up the last twelve metres, noticed Ralph and smiled.

"A hot day." Ralph heard himself giving the words brightly enough, though he felt the tightness in his throat.

"I'll say. A real scorcher," the woman replied, already red-faced and puffing. She continued on her way up Tyagarah Street as his watch swept into three minutes to.

Ralph ignored the retreating back. He saw the whole gully, the whole demesne, vividly, as something made up of so many parts and levels—of real things like heat shimmer and dry grass smells, sprinklers and tick-ticking letter-box flaps in brick fences, curtains fanning out from open windows, the bright, unrelenting light. And equally as things of mind—a green face with nothing to support that notion, nothing, and, differently, the coiling air, the crowding light, the sun-dazzle above the trail, the gathering motes, the crazing.

Then it was Tex Ritter singing and one minute to go.

Red Rover come over!

It was so very still, an imagined calm beyond the ticking flaps and the cough and sigh of the sprinkler.

Thirty seconds.

Let's go, Ralph! Come on, Red Rover!

He stepped on to the track.

Twenty. Ten. Now.

Real noon.

Ralph moved down the track.

The breeze was suddenly there again, of course. The tick-ticking faded as Tyagarah Street became a green deck, the sound of the sprinkler too, as if it were something for up there, for the quiet ordinary streets. Ralph walked down his twelve metres into the changed world, sank four metres down among the cannas, the morning glory and the bamboo.

He saw the curtains blowing again. Of course they would be, soft fear-makers. Insect buzz. Yes, that too. One, then another unseen creature zipped past, stitching up the air.

Lizard rustle. Check.

Ralph watched the house where he thought the screen door had closed earlier. Its curtains stirred in the faint breeze, beckoned, relaxed, beckoned ever so languorously.

He walked round the turn of the trail, out of sight of Tyagarah Street.

He was committed. This was the stretch where you couldn't be seen clearly, he knew, where to look ahead and behind gave views of track and bush and only the house with the curtains to let you know you were in the midst of it.

He walked on.

Get ready, Ralph told himself. Soon now.

Thirty seconds in. Stop. Look back. Walk. Forty seconds. Look back.

Ralph couldn't be sure, but he thought he saw the sun-dazzle forming above the trail, hanging there, a coiling spring of light, a bright glimmering haze, spinning motes coming together, spiralling in. Ralph did see it. He was certain. He stood there and watched the light-trap forming. Was he going to vanish, would that be it? Would it change him? He thought of Megan's plaque. Goodbye, Megan. Goodbye, boys!

Maybe it wouldn't take him. Maybe it would give something back, unburden itself, leave him with all the poor souls it had ever taken, crowded into him. What if the gully was overloaded, waiting to discharge?

Or (not now!), his mind raced on, what if— No! Ralph fought against his mind. He stood in utter terror in the middle of the hardest and bravest thing he'd ever done and wiped his brow. Your turn, he said. Your turn! Here comes Red Rover.

And still in terror, Ralph turned his back on the heat-shimmer, the air devil or whatever it was forming around him, and moved along the track. Moved faster and faster, not looking to see what was happening.

His imagination fought back. A thought struck him as he walked on, a thought more terrifying in its simplicity than any fear of what might be at his heels following, spinning, twisting along behind.

The thought got to him because of Megan. He remembered a conversation he had had with Megan and Janice in the staff-room after his trip to the Flinders Ranges. They had agreed that places changed you, changed how you felt and behaved, how you saw things.

Places changed you, that was it.

The Warner Street he was going to need not be the safe, known Warner Street seen from the Tyagarah side. Being in the gully at noon could change that just as it could change him. Not just a people-taker or a people-changer but a place-changer. Ralph found his own word: an *outréfier*! Good theorizing, Mr Ames! Dazzle 'em with science. Dazzle them! Nothing would be quite the same again. Nothing.

Places could change you.

Or—you could change them!

Ralph ran. He fled up the track towards Warner Street because to go back meant more than facing the sun-dazzle at noon. It would mean not knowing and having to start again, and Ralph still had to know, whatever else.

He was almost there, almost out, twenty metres to go, when he felt the crazing at his shoulders, the boiling light, the settling cat's cradle of heated air.

"No!" he yelled, and ran.

And he burst up into Warner Street, exploded into the sudden quiet. Behind him, the curtains settled, the zip-dart-dash of insect noise faded, the tide of dazzling spinning light fell back. The tick-ticking came to him again. The sprinkler on the front lawn of Number 34 chattered busily, folding and unfolding rainbows at its heart.

Ralph skidded on gravel where the street itself started, and came to a stop. He was laughing, bent over, hands on knees where he stood, panting and laughing, sucking in mouthfuls of air.

Then he realised he had an audience. That was natural too, completely proper, a good sign. An old man had been gardening near his sprinkler at Number 34. Ralph wondered how he could have missed him. He was standing now, watching Ralph. There were two old ladies talking at the front fence of Number 33. Another, younger woman had come out to her front porch to see what the disturbance was.

Ralph knew how completely absurd he appeared, so he waved, trying to create a picture of a man who had raced through a gully, timing himself, reliving younger days in a simple exuberant act.

"Why, Mr Ames, isn't it?" said one of the older women, and to her friend: "That's Mr Ames, my grandson's teacher."

Ralph moved towards the two women but suddenly stopped.

He backed away from what he saw, went to cross to the old man at Number 34 and again froze in his tracks.

He moaned in terror, a low defeated sound.

People-taker, place-changer. People-changer.

He stepped back towards the gully, retreated towards it, though he feared it greatly and knew it was no answer, not now, not with the trap sprung and locked.

The woman on the porch looked normal, seemed to be showing equal parts of alarm and concern.

"Why, Mr Ames..." she said, recognizing him too.

Ralph stumbled to her gate, staggered towards the porch. But then he saw that the shadows there only concealed what he had seen in the others.

He had brought it with him.

"Are you all right?" the woman said, with the real concern of someone whose back door slams and whose curtains move lazily in the breeze of a hot summer's day.

But Ralph was beyond answering. The gully had him and he could only stare at the unmistakable twisting sun-dazzle in her eyes.

And the green face that was not a face but was.

The Bone Ship

WHEN MRS DAVINON brought in the tea and the plate of dark coconut-frosted cakes, Paul Rodan lost his concentration all over again. He had hoped he could manage the old traveller's trick: half closing his eyes and imagining where else he could be. In England, certainly, that went without saying, inside like this where it was cool enough. Somewhere in the United States, San Francisco in the summer, yes. In Africa perhaps, Johannesburg or Tangiers, even parts of Asia, but in the highlands there, out of the terrible humidity.

It was a favourite game, and it had only just started to work when Mrs Davinon arrived with the tea and the cakes and ruined what was possibly his final chance for now. The ceilings of her house were high enough, this spacious parlour large enough, cool enough, tastefully furnished enough, and the ceiling fan gave it the right cosmopolitan touch (India was there then; India, or it might have been Singapore, Shanghai or Hong Kong), but the woman's alarming accent and the plate of wretched coconut and chocolate sponge cakes brought him back to the parlour of a two-storey Victorian (one-time) mansion in Parkes, in central-western New South Wales, in Australia of all places. In Australia! The Gautier-Davinon search had led to Australia. Who would have thought?

"How do you take your tea, Mr Roddin—is it Roddin?" the woman asked, looking to Paul like failed gentry in some period film—wearing a neat, once stylish grey dress, flat shoes, closely coiffed hair still brown enough amid the grey, a good face with sharp dark eyes. She had to be in her sixties, either that or life in this God-forsaken town had been especially cruel. A doctor's wife, going by the dull bronze plaque beside the front door: *Dr C. Davinon*, and widowed by all counts, judging by no mention of a husband in their phone call, and no sign of one since he'd arrived. Or even a doctor herself, though probably too old (and too old-fashioned) to be practising any longer. It explained the house: once stately but now almost beyond her, both woman and house hopelessly *déclassé*.

"Rodan, Mrs Davinon. Rodan. Like the flying creature in that Japanese monster movie, if you know it."

(Japan, yes! A stretch, but he might have been in some old embassy building in Kyoto or Osaka, and wished that he was, that the search had led there. There were some good bone ships in Japan. But not the Gautier ship. Not the *Felice*.)

"I can't say I do, Mr Ro-dan," she said, pronouncing it out with too much inflection, too much emphasis, letting him know she was a dutiful study. "I don't keep up with the latest films any more." She offered him the cakes and he took one. "But like I say, I only hope I'm not wasting your time. There must be other Davinons."

Oh there were, there were, as he knew only too well—in Montreal and Ontario and in Marsala on Sicily. In Madrid, Trieste and Buenos Aires. Hundreds in Paris, thousands all over France. But the research and the search had led here, to Parkes in this horrid, blazing, Australian summer.

He wiped crumbs away carefully. "The facts are quite conclusive, Madame," he said, realizing he sounded frightfully formal. Something about the old house, about this quaint, premature relic of a country doctor's wife, seemed to make it appropriate. "As I said when I phoned, all the evidence points to the Davinons in Parkes. I am very hopeful."

More than hopeful. That was why it had been a phone call from Sydney, no letters of introduction, none of the usual polite enquiries. He was sure of his facts and he was on a time. Others were on the same trail.

"Well, we're the only Davinons in Parkes. The family has been in this house since 1845." She pronounced it as 'Davinnens' as if to rhyme with 'paraffin', one more vile atonal anglicisation Paul had lived with for so long. It was Paul's single rebellion: keeping to the French 'Duh-vin-non', with its stress on the second 'n'.

And now the woman was frowning with polite concern. "When I said on the phone that my great-to-the-fourth-grandfather-in-law brought his father's things from Paris, I tried to make it clear that they've been looked over again and again."

Paul made himself conceal the excitement he felt, the very real wave of— yes—agitation that came over him. So near, so very near. It was such an intimate, urgent feeling.

"But they took nothing away you said, Mrs Davinon. You said they looked through the papers but you and your husband allowed nothing to be taken."

"That's right. Charles was very strict about it." She leaned over and poured him more tea. "Apart from the historical society people, everything has been kept in the attic untouched for sixty years. But looked over again and again before that."

"So you were with them while they made this recent examination?"

"Of course." Again Mrs Davinon frowned, and Paul cautioned himself. Too keen. He was being too forward, too keen. "But, then again, Mr Rodan, we did not search them at the door."

Paul made himself smile and nod, taking the rebuke. "I am deeply sorry, Mrs Davinon. I meant no offence. I have come a long way in the hope of at last settling this mystery in my family's history. A long way in time—the years spent making such a search—and now in space, travelling here to your wonderful country. I apologize again if I seem—too eager."

His hostess seemed mollified. She gave a smile and a nod of her own; it was all so courtly between them. "There are no valuables. Charles and I checked. Everyone has checked. Just papers and a few oddments."

Oddments, Paul almost parroted, but was able to stop himself. He nodded again, showing interested respect while his thoughts raced. So near, so near. Bettelmann and Lucas were half a world away, chasing their leads, quizzing other Davinons in other lands, sending out their letters and interminable emails, making their phone calls. He could take enough time. And he could use force if necessary. That was why he hadn't registered at a motel in town yet; this way there would be no trace. Just the hire car paid for in cash, using the false ID, the false name. Easy to fob off. He was a museum acquisitions expert by profession, he would say. Discretion was always essential. There were reasons.

So he sat sipping the awful tea, nibbling one of the—what were the horrid things called: lillingtons? livingstons? Then, judging his time, he continued. "It is nothing valuable in the monetary sense, Mrs Davinon. It is information, documentary proof about the fate of a model of a ship. More clues perhaps. My own great-to-the-fifth-uncle was involved with your husband's ancestor in connection with it."

"And it's to do with this ship?" Mrs Davinon said.

"Model ship. Exactly."

"Then what are you looking for? You must explain it, Mr Rodan. I'm sure I present as a country doctor's wife and must strike you as very provincial by your practised European standards, but I assure you I am a sharp customer by my own lights and I love history. That's part of why Charles held on to his father's things. They've been passed down. I belong to the local historical society here. Some of our meetings are held in this very room. I may not have all of your conservationist's gloss, but I am active enough."

My, isn't that wonderful, Paul would have said ten minutes, five minutes earlier, but now she had cautioned him with her boast of being a 'sharp customer', and the glint in her eye warned of a native cunning. As dangerous as intelligent people were, Paul had found those who thought themselves intelligent often presented a much greater danger. They were obdurate, more wilful by far, usually less tractable.

Instead, Paul nodded as if to a peer. "May I just say as one sharp customer to another that it is a relief to be with a woman who understands the absolute importance of custodial care, Madame. You are being most kind." He deliberately laid on the continental charm, though in subtleties, he liked to think, not broad strokes. It had always worked for him before. He wanted coffee and pâté, but now, smiling wonderfully, he held out his cup for more tea as if it were ambrosia, and took another of the wretched lillington things. He was Paul Louis Rodan, *former* museum acquisitions agent, now freelance raider of history and resolute builder of a history of his own, and he was very close to owning the Gautier ship, the *Felice*. Bettelmann and Lucas be damned!

"Now I must have the story you have only hinted at, Mr Rodan," Mrs Davinon said, and reached down and brought up a small tape recorder. "If you have no objections, I will tape what you tell me. For my own records."

"Not at all, Madame." (If it came to force, that could easily be disposed of.)

Paul waited till she had set it next to the tea service on the table between them and switched it on. There was none of the 'Testing, testing' that amateurs so often went on with. Mrs Davinon had already practised with it. It made Paul even more circumspect. She was indeed a sharp customer.

"Madame, are you familiar with what are called Prisoner of War Models— models of sailing ships built by prisoners interned during the Napoleonic Wars?"

"Only in the most cursory fashion. I know there is some mention of it in the papers upstairs. Or, rather, a model ship is mentioned. It is made of bone."

"Exactly. Between 1793 and 1815, the English were constantly at war with the French. During this great struggle, as you may be aware, Dartmoor Prison was built to house over eight thousand French prisoners of war. Americans, too, fighting on the French side. Other prisons were used, Bideford, Norman's Cross and the like, even old castles and the hulks on the Thames mudflats, but my husband's ancestor, Giles Gautier, and yours were interned in Dartmoor in May 1807."

Paul made an appropriate hesitation at that point, hinting ever so slightly at an emotional stake in what he was saying.

"Go on, please, Mr Ro-dan."

"Many French sailors were conscripts, so you had bakers, tailors, farmers and skilled artisans imprisoned side by side with experienced seamen. It wasn't long before the more enterprising of these found they could augment their rations and earn money by making toys and selling them first to the trusties, then to the English officers and gentry who learned about them. These toys soon led to more desirable objects like model sailing ships, miniature replicas of specific vessels currently engaged in the fighting. If only you could see the beautiful model of the 120-gun *Brittania* at the Maritime Museum in Dartmouth, fifty-one inches long, or the *Ocean* in the Science Museum in London, or the 52-gun *L'Amatone* in the South Shields Museum—"

"I'm sure. Please continue, Mr Ro-dan." Only the accent ruined her queenliness, that and her insufferable, almost wilful mispronunciation of his name.

"Some of these models were made of ivory and tortoise shell, sometimes mahogany, but a great number were made from bone."

"But not human bone!"

"No, Madame. Sometimes whalebone, but mutton bone mostly, salvaged from refuse bins or the cookhouse, sometimes bought from the prison market if there was one. The sailors and shipwrights provided details to the jewellers and other craftsmen who then did most of the work, and they divided the profits. It became quite a cottage industry, quite a production line: some hands carving the planks, others doing the finework using nails shaped into chisels, others preparing the rigging with threads from their garments or their own hair. The English commissioned models of particular ships, and helped provide brass rivets and fine woods for the detailing. There are supposedly several here in Australia. I know one very fine bone model belongs to the Moxon family in Brisbane, recently restored by your own Australian master model ship-builder, John Larkin. The largest, in the Waterman's Hall, London, is said to be seven feet long, and—"

"And where do Giles Gautier and Phillip Davinon come into this?"

It brought Paul up short. My, but the woman was quick. There they were: the names of both their respective ancestors.

"Dartmoor was terribly overcrowded. While many of the model-makers lived very well indeed, other prisoners suffered in absolute squalor. They were meant to be maintained by their respective governments, but this simply didn't happen. Many human skeletons were found when the camp at Bideford was excavated for the new gas works."

Mrs Davinon looked suitably aghast. "So human bones *were* used?"

It hadn't been what Paul was going to say at all. He'd just meant to illustrate the range of conditions at the POW prisons in preparation to explaining the Gautier/Davinon connection, working round to what was done way back in 1807 in that dismal overcrowded cellblock the poor unfortunates had christened the Oubliette.

"Not at first. But there were factions, you understand. Arrangements between model-making groups and particular trusties, favours and preferential treatment. Dartmoor was terribly overcrowded. Giles and Phillip were both on the *Felice* when she was taken. They were with thirty-six other prisoners added to a prison block called the Oubliette. It was already filled to capacity; people sleeping on the floor, fighting over scraps of food. But Giles was a watchmaker, and your great ancestor, Phillip, a master mariner, and they began work on a model of the *Felice*, reinventing the wheel as new model-makers often had to do, scrounging whatever they could, but in the most horrendous circumstances. The Oubliette was full of troublemakers— hence the name: a place to put people and forget them. Giles and Phillip were accused of trying to be better than the rest and were both beaten for it. Their first model was wrecked during an incident, possibly an attempted escape. Whatever actually happened, rations were reduced as general punishment. No longer were even mutton bones allowed for their use. No metal pins and fittings. Nothing."

"How did they manage?"

"Other fine bone ships were made under similar trying conditions. The schooner *Alyson*, the sloop *Deirdre*—using bone pins and glues—"

"But the bone, Mr Ro-dan! The bone!"

She *did* have a bone ship here. Paul was sure of it. This rush of emotion gave her away: her very real concern that a prized heirloom was made from the bones of humans.

"As you suspect, Madame. They used human bone. It was all they had. On burial detail, they would retrieve bones from the lime pits, whatever they could get."

"And the result, Mr Ro-dan? The outcome?"

"Is what I am hoping you can verify for me, Mrs Davinon. My sources say that a second model was begun but not completed: a thirty-five inch model of the *Felice*, just the hull and main deck and very little else. The footings for the masts were barely started. Apparently my distant uncle and your husband's ancestor had a falling out, or they were separated to other cellblocks. Stories differ. Some say disease took them, some say they died during repatriation back to France, though in 1807, I don't see how that could be. It's far too early. At any rate, both men perished; at least their names were dropped from prison records. There were no homecomings recorded after the war. All we know for certain is that the unfinished hull of the *Felice* was given over to your husband's family in Paris, and that—so far as my sources show—it was brought here to Australia. I am hoping I am not mistaken, and that you have it in safekeeping here and are simply being appropriately cautious with a stranger."

Mrs Davinon gave what looked to be a sympathetic smile. "Such a thing would not be for sale, Mr Ro-dan."

"I accept that, Madame. I do assure you of it. I am a *former* acquisitions agent, as I said. No longer a collector of anything more than the history of the Prisoner of War Models as they relate to the Gautiers and the Rodans."

"And the Davinons."

Paul didn't miss a beat. "And the Davinons, most assuredly. The names are inseparable. I meant only that it is my own family search that brought me here. I can only hope that you might let me see it and photograph it and publish its history, both for its own sake and as part of our shared family histories. It would mean a great deal."

Mrs Davinon put one slender hand to her throat and looked off across the parlour, as if surrendering to her own run of emotions: thoughts of a model made of *human* bone, recollections of her lifetime with Charles, of her father-in-law's stories of old and precious things, of the trap of years that had left her here now in this particular lacuna of time.

Paul set his cup down as gently as he could, but the smallest 'chink' doing so brought her back in an instant.

"More tea, Mr Ro-dan?"

"Only if you will have some too, Mrs Davinon. As I say, in both senses, it has been a long journey. Your hospitality is wonderful."

"Perhaps you would prefer coffee instead?"

Hah! A truce. Paul seized at it. Coffee, at last. But better yet, a chance to be alone while she went to make it, a chance to rally and consider his best options, to give her time to consider his requests.

"I'd be most grateful. A Frenchman—you understand how it is with coffee."

Mrs Davinon rose. "Of course. Excuse me a moment."

Paul rose, being his most chivalrous, the cavalier, the attentive and gracious guest, but Mrs Davinon beat him to the tray and carried it off to the kitchen.

He sat down again, listened to the deep ticking of the clock on the mantel and the distant sounds of her moving about in the kitchen. Somewhere in this house, no doubt up in the dim stuffy attic, sat the model of the *Felice*, probably locked away in a trunk, the stark white hull wrapped in packing, nothing much to show anyone, but real. No longer just the rumour, no longer just the tantalizing listings in old editions of Filiger's.

The smell of brewed coffee came to him through the hall. Avignon, Paul told himself, his favourite little café, or André's in Marseilles, though too many of his competitors went there now, and lately to keep an eye on him. They knew how accomplished he was. But brewed coffee. It would do. In Parkes, in a blazing Australian summer, it would do.

Finally Mrs Davinon returned with the tray and set it down between them. On it were fresh cups, a teapot and a glass plunger of coffee. He waited for her to settle, waited during the pouring and serving, paced himself with quick thoughts of Amsterdam and Berlin, Prague and Istanbul. The coffee smelled wonderful. He made sure he sipped as she did, mirroring her body language, being *with* her, courteous guest, completely in her hands and at her pleasure. He made a single sound of appreciation—totally genuine— and tried to seem relaxed.

"I have the story a little differently," Mrs Davinon said, surprising him.

"Pardon, Madame?"

"From what Charles's father had passed on to him, it was Phillip who was the watchmaker, and your Giles Gautier the mariner who provided the specifications."

"What's that?" Again Paul was thrown, but at least it was all coming out now. He leaned forward, composing his face to show quiet interest, not the genuine startlement he felt.

"And you are correct: the two men were not repatriated. As my father-in-law explained it, they were being transferred to a prison hulk on the Thames—it often happened with recalcitrants—and the prisoners managed to take over the prison barge. They almost succeeded in making their escape, and were out in the Channel when the pursuit ship *Llewelyn* fired on them."

"I am fascinated by this," Paul managed to say. "I knew nothing of it."

"But *before* that happened, Mr Ro-dan, our ancestors were both *thrown* over the side by the other prisoners. My husband's ancestor perished. Yours was rescued, it seems, and lived long enough to tell of his experience of looking up and seeing the hull of the prison barge overhead as he swam up towards the light."

"That's where my accounts resume, Mrs Davinon. The hull reminded him of the *Felice*—or, rather, of the model sitting on the window ledge they used as their work bench. In his oxygen-deprived state, Giles felt he was swimming back to the real *Felice*, reprieved, born again. I knew nothing of them being tossed overboard. It is incredible."

"What else you may not know, Mr Ro-dan, is that when they were cast over the side, they were tied together at the waist and told that only one would be allowed back on board. Only one, you understand?"

"Surely not, Madame—"

"I can forgive it. It was long ago. Perhaps they were never friends, just two men trying to do a model ship and stay alive. The survivors from the barge picked up by the *Llewelyn* said it was what had happened. They let the one who killed the other back on board."

"I'm shocked. I had no idea. I'm so sorry, Mrs Davinon—" Paul didn't know what else to say. All this had thrown him. The fatigue from his drive down from Sydney, from his flight from Paris, was finally catching up with him, the lack of sleep, the determination to keep ahead of the others. Suddenly he was exhausted.

"Please, Mr Ro-dan. I didn't mean to upset you. Each would have been desperate to kill the other. People do these things to live. But we can make a truce between our families now, can't we?"

"But of course, Madame. *Merci, merci mille fois!* I don't know what to say." The sudden weariness was confusing him. All this way, all this effort, and now this. His search was over.

Mrs Davinon rose from her chair. "You look tired, Mr Ro-dan. So at least let me show you the hull that was never finished, that was passed on to Charles's ancestors by a kindly ship's officer aided by a sympathetic trusty. You can come back and look over the papers another time."

"Yes, yes. That would be splendid." Paul set his cup on the table and stood, steadying himself on the arms of the chair, then followed the woman towards the dark-timbered double sliding doors at the far end of the parlour. He felt odd, leaden was the word, definitely strange. It was as if he were weighed down.

"I keep the *Felice* in here."

In here. Not up in the attic then, not wrapped up and tucked away. She had the ship down here.

Mrs Davinon slid back the doors to reveal what had once been a dining room with double sliding doors at each end. No doubt the kitchen lay beyond the second pair; it made sense. What made no sense, what startled Paul in his growing stupor, was the stark white hull of *Felice* atop a narrow, six-foot wooden pedestal of the same dark timber as the doors. It stood in the very centre of the room, in a room whose walls were painted the deep rich red of old blood. Dark timber, dark red walls, the almost glowing, bleached white of the *Felice*.

But it couldn't be the *Felice*. Paul fought to make sense of it. This wasn't thirty-five inches. This was sixty plus inches, five feet long or more, a huge impossible version.

"As you can see, I've made modifications," Mrs Davinon said. "It always seemed so small before."

Paul stumbled, actually fell to one knee. He was seriously unwell, all the stress, all the travel. All the years of searching.

"I'm ill," he managed to say, but even as he forced the words he saw the truth. Not ill; he was drugged. The coffee had been drugged.

He fell to the floor. He couldn't prevent it. He lay looking up at the monstrous white hull, seeing it like—like—why, like Giles Gautier must have seen it swimming up after killing Phillip Davinon so long ago, imagining it to be the *Felice*.

"But why?" The words came out slurred and wrong, but Mrs Davinon understood. Of course she understood. Through shifting, blurring light he saw her go past the great white hull of the ship to the other set of double doors and slide them back.

There, in a glance, he saw the operating table pushed back against a far wall, in a horrid, few seconds saw the two figures strapped, propped up in wheelchairs, two men, both securely gagged with white surgical tape, with their legs and arms missing and their eyes wide with drug-numbed terror. Bettelmann and Lucas.

"This—can't just—be—revenge." He dragged out the words.

"Of course not, Mr Ro-dan," Mrs Davinon said, just a blur and a voice now. "It's completion and closure, with those who know the worth of it assisting. The ship will be finished!"

Paul tried to fight the deadness but was being swallowed by the depths of the blood-red room, so that all he could do was lay looking up at the bleached white hull of the *Felice*, as if looking at it from beneath the surface of the ocean.

"Masts and spars, Mr Ro-dan," he was sure he heard the voice say. "I must have my masts and spars!"

Beckoning Nightframe

CORINNE KESTER HAD once been described as a knife. Hard, sharp, bright, relentless, yes, and penetrating, that's what George Faye had said, both in his review of her first book and on some TV talk show.

It had brought her a certain cachet at the time, had led in fact to her latest project and George being one of the twenty-two guests at her combined launch and thank-you party. Had led too to Corinne's renewed determination never to let their one-time attraction for each other have any kind of resolution—a sort of revenge by nostalgia and lost opportunity.

Perhaps George had reached the stage where he wanted more, could even deliver more, but there'd been too many years where it was obvious he was just trying to ground her mystique, to satisfy his curiosity and be gone. So now he would die wondering. She would remain shiny bright, hard and, yes, penetrating.

That's what Corinne Kester was thinking when she first noticed the curtains beckoning to her.

All twenty-two guests were out on the terrace—the six psychiatrists who'd helped her profile the Harbourside Killer, and their respective wives, husbands and partners, several of the editorial people, several publicists, some closer friends. George, of course, careening from one to the next like some lonely planet. Planet and knife. It seemed apt.

It was a mild autumn evening, darkening quickly after a splendid sunset and a successful *al fresco* dinner, certainly warm enough to use the spacious deck, though a cool breeze had come up and they would go inside soon. Her apartment in the four-storeyed, tiered apartment building was higher than the houses across Victoria Place. There was a view of the bay across low rooftops, framed at the top by a rich lapis blue, at the sides by black tree silhouette and adjacent apartment buildings, at the bottom by the white house with its warm lighted windows and the path leading down its north-western side to what looked like a semi-detached shed with its long window of two square panes.

Curtained, never lighted that she could remember. House, shed, long window, all noticed a thousand times, part of the view, the nightframe.

And now that frame was beckoning. True, standing there with Doctors Michael Castley, Samantha Crewe and Dan Truswell, listening to Dan speak of some recent developments in the Hunter, she just looked casually, contentedly out at the night, had her eye caught by the lights across the bay, by the boats moored there, the merging blues, then by the black sideframe of trees, down to the bottom frame edge of house, warm lights, path, long window, to where the dull white curtains were, yes, beckoning to her.

Someone who lived there had opened the top-hinged casement window a bit, pushed it out so wind sliding under a door formed a draught, causing the curtains to belly out, to ripple and lift, to make swift scalloping edges of darkness under the dull white.

It was just something you noticed when it wasn't your turn in conversation, then noticed again, then kept noticing, a visual refrain to the evening, a flicker of movement in the splendid stillness, soothing, relaxing in a way.

Checking on other guests, pouring drinks, letting Max Jobarth take some final publicity shots with her advisory 'team' of experts, took her away from it for awhile, but the beckoning effect was there when she stepped back onto the deck twenty minutes later, just keeping an eye on things.

The whole scene was darker, of course. Little of the blue was left in the sky; now it was a starfield above and intense blacks all around, distant light-points, barest hints of boats, cables slapping masts and, there at the bottom, like peering down a tunnel of flaring, hooding trees (one on the street, one in the front yard of the house), focused by a security light on that side path, was the long double-paned window still raised, the curtains still rippling, scalloping, offering hints of darkness beyond.

No longer soothing or relaxing, Corinne found. Mesmerizing, an unexpectedly dramatic centrepiece to the night now that the sky had gone dark, withdrawn the last of its sunset glory. Hypnotic, those edges rippling at her.

"Corinne?"

It was George Faye, the planet on its sad orbit, hunting, reaching out, expecting nothing.

"George. Hi."

"Wondered where you were."

"It's a nice night."

"It's a good party. Interesting party, with your hand-picked boffins in there. Everyone's sure they're coming over as prats." George was 'eroded' English. His language sometimes gave it away.

"As what?" Corinne said, though she'd heard well enough.

"Spill a drink, stand a certain way and you feel those psychiatrists of yours taking you apart."

"Like novelists and journalists. Everything is grist."

"Then I've been through the mill twice over. Castley and Crewe just put hands to their chins and nod at whatever I say. I feel I'm being dissected."

"They were essential for the book, George. Gave it respectability."

"Doubled the advance too, I bet."

"Something like that. I don't think I betrayed their trust."

"I'm sure."

Corinne saw he was going to stay around, was about to say "Better join the others" when he noticed the curtains too.

"Now that's weird."

"What is?"

"That house across the street down there. That window down the side. The way the curtains are moving."

"It's just the wind."

"Yeah, but eerie, you know. Like they're reaching out."

Beckoning. Reaching out. It didn't help Corinne's mood. She resented George being part of it, finding her out at something that had found a place in her mind. It was one more unwanted intimacy. After the months of research and writing, the endless interview transcripts, revisions, proofing and editing galleys, the media gauntlet, she was in shut-down mode, ready for private head space, solitary moments, everyone to be gone. Curtains reaching out! It was George reaching out, needful as ever, trying to connect. She resented it with a vehemence that surprised her.

"We should go in."

"Corinne?"

"George, I'm host. Let's go."

The night wound down from there—probably inevitable with her panel of experts lending an air of implied scrutiny to everything, as George said, giving even the smallest lapse or gaffe a curious weight of significance. It remained a fascinating party but not an altogether comfortable one. By the time the first guests began leaving at 9.45, Corinne had decided she'd never try it again.

George Faye posed his usual problem, tried to linger, but one of the psychiatrists read the situation for what it was and stayed to lend an avuncular hand.

"Corinne," Dan Truswell said in George's hearing. "You still want to go over those latest interview briefs? If you're too tired…"

"No, let's get it over and done with. Then I'm turning in."

George took the hint and left with good grace, promised he'd call.

Corinne didn't mention the curtains to Dan, the oddly compelling signature they made on the night. "Thanks for that, Dan."

"He looked needy. You didn't."

"Yeah, well. I invited him."

"Going for closure, I'd say. He's been part of your professional life."

"Where I have to keep him, Dan. Not too vindictive, I hope."

"We ritualize our lives according to our needs, Corinne. I imagine you know that better than anyone after the Harbourside business."

"We did good, Dan."

"You've done an excellent job."

"You truly don't mind staying on for the interviews?"

Dan Truswell smiled. "We've been through this, what, four times now? I'll see you Tuesday at 11 am, then Friday at 10. You've got my mobile number."

"I appreciate it. Rebecca says it really will help sales. Lend respectability."

"Of course it will. We've discussed this, Corinne. The level of responsibility you showed makes it a pleasure to help. See you Tuesday."

When she had her apartment to herself at last, Corinne didn't go out on the deck. She understood the sequencing of pathological behaviour so much better after reconstructing a putative mindset for the Harbourside Killer, knew the difference between psychotic and psychopathic conduct, how a rather routine MO could be so bizarrely anchored yet not be a psychotic disorder, rather the fruits of dissociation and childhood conditioning fraught with trauma resulting in compensation exactly as Dan had said. The rituals.

Time to let it go, she resolved, though she ran the sequence in her mind: casual preoccupation to fixation to neurosis, obsession and monomania, the *idée fixe* becoming everything.

So, none of the casual checking to see if the front door was locked (she'd locked it after Dan), to check her alarm was set (she'd set it before the guests arrived), to see if she'd put detergent in the dishwasher (she had), none of those things people do, a lack of focusing on the moment producing the first glimmers of anxiety. She spent forty minutes cleaning up, then went to bed.

And woke at 3:40, lay blinking in semi-darkness, watching tree-shadow on the ceiling, running through the Harbourside MO as she had so many other nights: the painstaking, incredible things Jenko had done to those fourteen people. She got up for a glass of water to wake herself enough to push those thoughts aside, stood looking out her window as she drank it, and saw the curtains again. Rippling at her. Swelling out, waving. Hi, Hi!

She smiled, laughed out loud once.

"No you don't," she said, closed the blinds and returned to bed, took some time sleeping but managed.

The window was closed on Sunday and Monday nights. On Tuesday and Wednesday it was open but there wasn't enough wind. The curtains hung off-white and unmoving in the tunnel of the night, set about and around with twinkling streetlight, flaring house-light, distant and near—like a kaleidoscope fixed on a still image but whose sides were bright, fractionated and changing. Yes, a peripheral kaleidoscope focused on a set, intriguingly still centre:

a window one and a half metres long, fifty centimetres or so deep, top-hinged, with twin square panes and dull white curtains. The heart of a kaleidoscope of night.

Or better yet, like the dioramas she'd made as a girl. A peephole in a shoebox, giving a view of a tiny room or a single image made compelling and dynamic by the false perspectives, miniature light sources and intense focus. Its framing effect.

Just a chance arrangement of things. A nightframe, yes. With that diorama, kaleidoscope sort of intensity.

On Thursday it was closed again, which reinforced the idea that the shed was a sleepout for someone, though Corinne had never seen a light behind the window that she could remember.

On the Friday night it was open, and the chill southerly that came up around 7:15 had the curtains rippling and fluttering at her. When she got back from dinner with Paul and Chloe after 11, the window was closed, just part of the larger world again, and though it again suggested habitation, she had never seen a light and still felt it was deserted.

On the Saturday afternoon, the window was open, the curtains bellying slightly in a mild breeze. When she saw the elderly couple who lived there getting into a cab shortly after 1:15 pm, she realised two things: that this was her chance to go down and see it all up close and that the whole thing was a lot more important to her than she wanted to admit.

She stood deciding. It was a warm quiet Saturday afternoon; the couple had gone out; the house seemed deserted; the gate, the side path, the shed were all in sunlight.

She'd say she was looking for a missing cat, knock on the front door first, say a few 'kitty kitty's' in case anyone was looking, make it all seem casual.

Within minutes she was out in bright sunshine, walking round the front of her large apartment block, crossing Victoria Place to the white house. She began her 'kitty kitty' routine almost immediately, though no-one seemed to be watching.

Soon she was on the sidewalk before the low cast-iron gate with one of the 'frame' trees at her back, looking down the path as if for a lost pet, but really noting the window and the curtains as they stirred gently, ever so slightly. Then she was at the front door, ringing the bell. She waited an appropriate few minutes, then walked around the side.

The curtains stirred lazily, languidly, bellied at her just enough behind the two square panes.

"Pablo! Here kitty! Here kitty!" she said, and kept walking, reached where the path turned left towards the back door, dog-legged right. She followed it, saw the deserted backyard, lawn, bushes, fences, and moved down the long front of the shed.

The brown wooden door was closed. Whatever breeze moved the curtains was slipping in underneath or perhaps just lifting in under the panes.

But locked? She had to try.

Maybe her cat had been locked in by mistake—that would be her excuse.

Acting concerned, she turned the knob, pushed the door back on a cluttered interior, a dusty gloom dispelled as she opened the door wider, then stepped inside. The curtains bellied away from her in the sudden draught, pushed and curled against the panes, flared briefly and settled back.

Corinne saw boxes and tools, a lawn-mower, an old bicycle, what was possibly covered furniture. No bed, no signs that it was used as a flat. Just a shed. A storage shed.

She moved to the window, felt the curtains, lifted the unlined fabric between her fingers, moved it, felt its texture, let it fall back.

There, she thought, smiling. Done.

Corinne felt so much better. She stepped out into the yard, pulled the door closed behind her, then moved back up the path to the street.

Done. Done. Done.

Back in her apartment, she set the kettle going, made coffee, then, only then, went out on the deck to look down at where she'd been—at the quiet house, the sunny path, the shed with its barely moving curtains. She imagined herself there and how she would have looked, going to the front door, moving down the side, disappearing to the left. The few minutes in the shed.

Then Corinne noticed it. There was hardly any wind, barely a breeze, but now at one corner of the window there was a solitary spot of darkness, as if the curtain were hitched up there, caught on something or—yes—as if someone had lifted it to peek out, and was now watching her.

Corinne stared in dread at that point of darkness, saw it vanish as the curtains bellied and shifted.

Just a corner hitched up. Just a coincidence.

But it was so silly, so amusing to the rational part of her, yet at the same time so, what?—potent, vividly disturbing—that she told Dan Truswell about it over coffee when he dropped by the next day, keeping it light, simple, not mentioning the visit. She just sketched it in as something noticed, something intriguing, even compelling, intruding now and then but hardly a serious preoccupation.

Dan listened, smiled, nodded, finally said exactly what she expected. "You of all people, Corinne, understand how profound things can be at the level of perception."

It was such a relief to hear it said she found she wanted to say more, take it further.

"It doesn't feel like misperception, Dan."

"I didn't say *mis*perception. Don't twist my words. The individual is the only reality. Whatever is, is. For you it may be a feeling of uncommon sensitivity, even intense focus, but an important stimulus nonetheless, even profound recognition. You may feel the anxiety of not being able to convey to another what you've *recognised*. I'm saying I accept your reaction to this stimulus, your response to it as a psychoactive agent. How could it be misperception?"

"You see it as a clinical condition?"

Dan smiled. "Only inasmuch as it's my profession to process experience this way. It can be reported on this way. We're a consensus society. You know me well enough to know I accept the normality of the subjective truth while advocating consensus. My appropriate reaction is to accept what you're telling me at face value, match it with cause and effect, then be a fair observer."

"It's not enough."

"Of course not. I'm agreeing totally. I see the window and the curtains, but *I* don't feel the stimulus or have the recognition; therefore it's hearsay, reported phenomena. Because I'm cast as a champion of consensus, I comment on you, not it. How could I comment on it? I'm not qualified."

"It seems to be real."

"That 'seems' is important. But see it as hypersensitivity, a kind of hyperaesthetic reaction, a glitch in perception. My first concern is that you allow a false recognition, a miscuing of perceptual functions."

"Like *déjà-vu*."

"Just like *déjà-vu*. And *ideès fixes* are like that. Why don't you go visit the residents. Ask to see the inside of the shed. Say you're—"

"I've done that." Corinne felt a rush of guilt.

"And?"

"It's just a storage shed. Tools, furniture, boxes and stuff. Not a flat or anything. No-one lives there."

"Good. That was probably hard to do. What did they say?"

"I didn't get permission."

"Oh."

"I've only ever seen an older couple, a guy and his wife. Yesterday I waited till they'd gone out and went over. Pretended I was looking for a missing cat. Just went down the side."

"Okay. The window was up?"

"Yes. But there was hardly any wind. The curtains weren't moving much."

"The door was open?"

"No. But it wasn't locked. I looked inside."

"You went inside?"

"Yes. I touched the curtains. Dusty unlined cotton. Just ordinary curtains. I looked round a bit then went back out, kept up my 'kitty kitty' routine till I was back here."

"How do you feel?"

"Better. Better now I've done it. Know the mechanism involved."

"Mechanism?"

"Yeah. That it's wind under the shed door helping make the draught. That it's just boxes and stuff in there. Dan, it was like a visual thing, you know? You look at something a thousand times, then suddenly it resolves into something distinctive you haven't noticed before and now can't help noticing. Like those paranoiac-critical paintings Dali did—*The Invisible Man* and that one with the bust of Voltaire. When you see the hidden images or they're pointed out to you then it's all you see. Like those tests you use in perception testing. Those Rorschach inkblots."

"You feel you're going to be okay with this?"

"Sure. What do you think?"

"I think you've been through a lot. For the better part of a year you've been involved in the profiling of a dangerous psychopath.

You've followed the trial, had access to transcripts and case details that are, well, harrowing to say the least. We're in a society just coming to grips with things like postnatal depression and attention deficit disorder, all kinds of compensation and denial behaviour. I don't have to tell you. Of course we can allow severance phenomena."

"That's what you call it? Severance phenomena?"

"That what I'm calling it here today, Corinne, yes. It's up there with recently bereaved people seeing deceased loved ones, all manner of anomalous perceptions that are part of normal life. Just do what you need to and put it behind you as soon as you can."

And they spoke of other things. Corinne very carefully made sure they did so.

She knew it was full-blown obsession, sweet monomania, a week or so later, the night she arrived home from a publicity dinner organised by Dennis and Gillian, stepped out onto the deck just to look at the night (of course) and saw the security light wasn't on across the street. There was only blackness at the side of the house, an unseen tunnel of darkness, a black hole in the night she couldn't see but knew was there, pulling at her.

With dismay she realised she wasn't able to see the nightframe as complete without it. Most of it was there—the twinkling lights in the lustrous blue-black expanse, the deeper framing blackness of the trees and roofline silhouette. But it was incomplete; worse, it was as if the long window, the curtains, sat in darkness like something watching again. It was what you did to watch someone, wasn't it? Switched off lights and stood back in darkness to look out?

But she didn't think of the double window-panes as eyes, no, not even as a spider waiting or fingers beckoning, not even as some sinister, snaring flower. Deadly nightshade. Such a term. Deadly nightframe. No anthropomorphising at all. She saw it (some detached, clinical part of her realised) as the curtains she had *touched*. Cued. Given *her* scent to.

And being locked into obsession, being so irrationally focused and finding it so suddenly rational, eloquent unto itself, she had to know what was down that unseen flue of darkness. Window open or closed? Curtains blowing or still? There was wind. But enough wind? There'd been wind on so many other occasions and the curtains had hung unmoving behind the open panes.

Corinne laughed at the recollection—the distant, observing part of her did. God, I'm losing it and here I am pondering weather anomalies and microclimates.

She had to know. The cat routine would probably cover it, but she did have to know. Like someone checking that the car headlights were switched off for the second or third time, that the alarm was set, that a fax had gone through, she had to go down and see. Just did.

She put on casual clothes, got the torch from the kitchen drawer, let herself out into the windy darkness, went round the side of the apartment block into Victoria Place, crossed to the white house, passed under parts of the nightframe, again passed *into* it, she noted, stepped under the tree, stood on the sidewalk with the tree behind her right shoulder and the slough of darkness right there leading down.

There was a glitter of glass. Nightsighted, nightframed, she could make out the twin panes glinting in hints of streetlight. She stepped over the low gate, getting ready to call "Here, kitty kitty!" if an automatic security light came on, though she doubted it would. There hadn't been a night she'd looked out and not seen the light on and the double panes and the curtains clearly. The globe had gone. Or they'd forgotten to turn it on. Deliberately hadn't?

But she was ready with her alibi call as she moved down past the front windows, raising her torch, finger on the switch. It wasn't a long walk, eight, ten metres at the most, and she was darksighted enough to see familiar detail, to almost see enough.

Still, she had to know.

She flicked on the torch, saw the curtains bellying, scalloping, rippling at her, right there, the wind getting in under the door, draughting up, saw them so much closer, so urgently working their window dance in the thin light, in the thick dark, saw in the small lunate flickers, in the parings of darkness flutter the curtains made at her, something standing back, staring back, the sense of something, someone, an immanence in those flecks and spatterings of deeper black.

She turned and ran, must have cried out because the front houselights came on as she leapt the iron gate and turned to the left, slipped beyond the tree, hurried beyond the street. By the time she was staring down through her own dark window, the side light was on too, the nightframe intact again, restored to its full configuration. When the bedroom lights went off, Corinne went to bed with a strange sense of peace, of having won some kind of test. And though she woke at least twice, she didn't get up to check. She could hear the wind and see the tree-shadow on her ceiling and knew that down there the light was on and she was safe, everything in its place, no matter how the curtains might beckon during the long night.

"I'm well into it," she told Dr Dan when he dropped by the next day and they were chatting over coffee again. He was down in Sydney on business, he said, but she felt it was probably his way of keeping an eye on her too.

"Tell me."

"Started out keeping it to myself. Only told you the other day, no-one else. But I'd ask people about fixations they might have. Building a normality horizon."

Dan smiled kindly. "We hate to be alone. Did many admit to having some?"

"Only a few. Most of us keep our rituals secret. We don't like to say we recite a lucky word or touch a jade Buddha or avoid a particular street or colour. What's that Asian concept: public face, private face, secret face?"

"Add day face and night face. Japanese, I think. Some societies don't even have the concepts."

"That's it, Dan. That's exactly it. We do need terms like that French one for thinking of what to say too late."

"*L'esprit d'escalier*?"

"I think that's it. We need terms for the moment when we're talking with someone and we know *they* know we're lying."

"Or we know, incontrovertibly, that a relationship, a marriage, is over. Yes. Do you have such a term for me, Corinne?"

And there she was—exposed at the very point she sought the term for.

"Yes. Or rather no, not a single term. But I feel anchored, you know? Right here and rational. Sane and focused. Yet it's the moment nothing I say can win back your belief that I'm wholly sane. I've passed into clinical for you. Convictions, anxieties are now being read as part of a pathology. I can sense you tracking me, regarding me differently, storing your perceptions differently."

"I disagree. I'd say it's the moment you *fear* that has happened. We're friends, Corinne. You're a smart, gifted lady coming out of an intense period in your life, an overloaded, supersaturated period, if you like. The difference is that you're admitting to something others can regard as obsessive—"

"Aberrant."

"—ritualised behaviour, to use that valuable term. Aberrant doesn't cover it."

"But it is morbid fascination."

"You haven't hallucinated, have you? You don't hear voices?"

She shook her head.

"You don't seem to be displaying undue paranoia or loss of self-control, just reasonable concern. I don't see much evidence of flattened or inappropriate affect."

"Dan—"

"Corinne, you must know why we avoid using clinical terminology with 95% of our subjects. People imagine things while they're under incredible stress. Seize on terms *they* think account for their condition. It's the worst trap. We carefully avoid talking about mental 'disease'. People resist the idea of the brain being ill like any other organ, susceptible to disease. We say disorder. We're well beyond the days of tidying it all up into neat categories like hebephrenia and catatonia and prescribing pherothiazine. Just look what you've been through with the book, steeped in the deeds of a late-onset schizophrenic who displayed little of the usual disorganised behaviour. You learned the facts. You were locked up with theories and terminology and an intense and informed scrutiny. Of course there might be a residual hyper-awareness. We all need to be de-briefed after this sort of thing. Barbara, Mark and Jay have to talk me down all the time. It's part of it. I could give you dozens of cases from psychotherapy and forensic psychiatry where gifted and experienced professionals have been harmed by the nature of the task. If you're not prepared to go on a holiday or re-locate for awhile, I suggest you enjoy the curtains while you can. Take a mild sedative at bedtime and consider yourself lucky it hasn't been worse. I'll monitor your conduct; you just let me know about anything else."

"If I hallucinate or hear directives from the soul."

"Correct."

"Dan, this has the intensity of hallucination."

"Yes, but pull over and turn off your car engine in a forest glade and a natural silence will seem preternatural, even uncanny. I was studying those slate tiles out on your deck last week and saw a fossilized fern leaf, realised it was, what, 140 million years old. That made me notice every damn tile there. Little packages of frozen time. I didn't mention it but it was profound. Humans move through this sort of stuff all the time, trivialising the living of life which is both intrinsically so marvellous yet so natural and mundane.

Corinne laughed, was so glad to laugh, to have Dan's words, his humanity. "So just go with it, you reckon?"

Dan laughed too. "Just go with it. We desensitise so quickly, so damn quickly."

"Come on, curtains! Do your stuff!"

"Indeed. And keep me away from those deck tiles for awhile! Get 'em back to mundane as soon as possible, thank you very much!"

Dan's words helped. His easy encompassing wisdom, born of grief and suffering, of witnessing worlds breaking down and reality re-made, gave her a handle on it, let her go out on the deck in bright sunlight and study the bits of what she could see—the so much larger, infinitely extended dayframe. The window, the curtains, didn't intrude. It was all to do with visual effect after all, and there were so many windows, so many things vying for consideration. The curtains hung white and still and didn't stand a chance.

Journeys in light, she remembered someone saying, perhaps Jenko, the Harbourside Killer. We are designed for journeys in light.

So she sat through the late afternoon doing an outline for an article, making and taking phone calls, even told Dan what she was doing when he phoned. She watched the gradual darkening of the land around 4:30, saw the nightframe shadowing into being: a lessening of light in the space between two apartment blocks, the gloom forming in that backyard as bush- and fence-shadow lengthened, stole definition, stole the light, just wore it away.

She had it all in its increments and installments, how bits of night slipped in, so much of it unnoticed—one minute: dayframe, the next time she looked, something else, some interstitial wearing down of light, darkness glooming up. It was marvellous and relentless; natural, mundane and utterly terrifying. She laughed in unexpected wonder and fear and relief.

Then at 5:30, when the streetlights came on, it was almost fully in place, needing only a deepening of colours already there, needing only subtleties of wind and the security light to be added.

When Dan phoned again at 6:30 (granting the importance of her ritual), she had a question.

"Dan, what if the brain *likes* the effect of something more than it should? More than *I* am aware? What if it notices phenomenal elements and, independently of what I consciously know, chooses to find significance?"

"It's still you," Dan said.

"I know it is. Of course it is. But it's also aesthetics, isn't it? Like a piece of art? We're predisposed to things. To natural things meaning something. Do you allow that the mind can find something profoundly beautiful, compelling, and important that the conscious self doesn't know about, doesn't have a conscious grasp of?"

Dan barely hesitated. "Of course. It has to be how it is. We said it the other day. Any human society is just consensus reality. We withhold things. Conceal things. Orthodoxy is just generally sanctioned consensus reality."

"So it has to do with paradigms. Patterns. How we *agree* to model what we perceive."

Again Dan hesitated, reading beyond her words. "Ultimately that's all it is, yes."

"Like the Japanese notion of *tenko*. A government fiat decreeing how the populace is to regard something. Determined consensual reality."

"Controlled paradigms, yes. Quite a crime against humanity. But it goes deeper. Corinne, look—"

"It's what I'm saying, Dan. I rationally accept what I'm responding to. It's just that I'm allowing that some part of *me* has identified something meaningful, and is trying to place it in a consensus paradigm that doesn't altogether work. Bits are left hanging out. My question is should I be dishonest about a felt imperative just because an arbitrary, conventionalised thing called 'normal reality' doesn't have room for it? Or because it might be seen as clinically suspect?"

And with a stab of alarm, Corinne heard how she sounded, what she was saying, heard Dan's silence.

"Sorry," she said. "I'm just waxing lyrical, Dan."

Dan Truswell's tone had shifted to the careful, considered timbre she'd heard in his Jenko interview tapes, every word measured for ambiguity and its ability to be evaded.

"You are and I'm agreeing. There's not one of us hasn't got alarming, astonishing secrets, yearnings, convictions. It is what we do, just as we do match the *idios kosmos* of the self with the shared *koinos kosmos* of consensus society and use that as a standard for regulating conduct and expectations. We can talk paradigms any time you want, Corinne, and I'll be right there listening to you and agreeing. We did it with Jenko, saw how a fundamental paradigm shift and some powerful ritualised and subjective reality patterning led to those terrible deaths. What I'm hearing, and what you're now hearing me responding to in my best professional tone, is someone behaving in an anxious, overstimulated way, yes, with obsessive, stressed and fixated responses. Any disordering I hear from you is only in degree, in the extent to which it troubles you and obsesses you. In other words, this matters and I care. I take my first position as your friend, my second as a caring professional who has given most of his life to allowing for vital alternative paradigms in others as the result of illness and injury, not automatically as this intense existentialist package you're experiencing. It's the difference between Jenko and Sartre. Charles Manson and Picasso."

"What should I do?"

"You've said no to a holiday and re-locating, so go where it takes you. But listen, Corinne, just let me know if you hallucinate."

Corinne laughed. "Because I won't let you know if I feel paranoid delusions or follow inner voices, will I?"

And Dan's voice warmed. "Remember that old saying: be careful what you resemble. I'll be phoning in."

"Monitoring my affect. I'll have to be good, won't I?"

"I've known you long enough to know."

"Lines like that kill conversation."

"So do lines like that. Speak to you soon, okay?"

She did well for awhile, but it *was* as if part of her knew something the rest of her didn't. She found herself checking on the curtains—in between publicity outings and signings, while working on various freelance articles, planning follow-up projects to capitalise on her current high profile.

It was a holding pattern in a sense, a kind of status quo. In the mornings the light was wrong; rather that there was just too much light. In the afternoon it began happening, the consolidation, the languid building of the frame. It got so she scheduled appointments elsewhere for the mornings, had people visit her at her apartment after mid-day rather than going out, tried not to miss the last few hours of daylight. There were evenings with friends, a few dates—though now she finally had time for them she found herself disinclined, distracted, yes, preoccupied. She did good saves: she was still coming up out of a major project, still putting together a viable social life not made up of medical and publicity professionals.

She told herself she just liked being around the apartment. So, her mind might be sorting through a perceptual something, trying to find homeostasis—psychostasis?—but on the surface (how it was with so much life, consensus or private) she didn't check the window too often, wasn't constantly jumping up from her desk or her deck-chair to see if the curtains were blowing. She just let it be, let it complete whatever it was, wherever it was happening in her, submitted to Dan's phone calls and occasional visits with composure and pleasure.

The Monday phone call marked the change.

"How am I doing?" she asked for the fiftieth, probably the hundredth time.

"Fine as always," Dan said. "A darn sight better than your old admirer, George."

"George Faye? What's happened?"

"I saw him last week, just by chance. He looked terrible. Haggard. Wasn't sleeping. Couldn't seem to concentrate on things. I recommended him to someone local."

Corinne wasn't aware she'd left a silence till Dan said her name.

"Corinne?"

"You're going to hate this, Dan."

"Speak."

"That night of the launch celebration. He was there, remember?"

"Of course. We worked as a team to save your honour."

"Yeah, well he came out on the deck. Saw me watching the curtains."

"And? Don't go careful on me, Corinne. Just say it."

"He commented on them too. Said they looked weird."

"And your perception is?" (Dan never said, "What's your point?")

"Remember with Jenko, one of the hardest things the authorities faced was predicting methodology. One time the blue paint, the next time the melted coins, then the soft toy stuffing. We did finally allow what was obvious all along, that particular things were psychoactive for him—just randomly affecting. Can this be psychoactive, Dan? Can it? I've seen it. George saw it."

"I've seen it too, Corinne. Lots of your guests have."

"So it's not automatically psychoactive. Some people respond, others don't."

Dan made a thoughtful sound. "I'm resisting this."

"*I'm* resisting this! Neither of us can afford to though. Do you think I like going on like this at you? *George* mentioned it! *He* remarked on it! Now you say he's showing signs."

"Professionally he'd already lost it, Corinne. Apparently drinking too much. Missing deadlines."

"This is different."

"Not part of something already happening?"

"You saw how he was. You're the one who spoke to him. Would you say altered affect?"

Dan hesitated, tellingly, damningly. "Yes. But Corinne—"

"Dan, I can't possibly convey something that's personally, dynamically psychoactive to someone who hasn't felt the imperative."

"Corinne—"

"You've got to speak to George! Ask him about dreams, preoccupations. See if anything matches."

"If he thinks of the curtains, you mean. Has dreams. Senses something."

"Dan, why not? I may be wrong, sure, but this takes it beyond me. You must allow how important this is for me."

"He may not remember. Like you say, a wholly unconscious thing."

"It takes it beyond me, Dan! Either way I'd be grateful."

"I'll see what I can do."

And when Dan had rung off, for the first time she felt she'd been pretending, feigning much more control than she really had. But the important thing was that he'd gone, left her with the news of George, lonely planet spinning away, deflected, wobbling towards ruin.

She could deal with Dan. She'd maintain her calm demeanour, urge him to consider the possibility of what, psychoactive loci? Chance alignment of objects, arrangements of line, light and angle? Get him to experience the assembly of its parts, perhaps the delivery of some super-rational agenda.

God, these terms. Where were they coming from?

But no hallucinations. No inner directives. Not yet.

No new legacies from interviewing Jenko or too much time spent considering psychopathology.

It had been weeks, carefully negotiated days. She'd maintained homeostasis, a psychostasis. She'd passed Dan's assessment of her or he'd be phoning, pounding on her door.

Dear deflected Dan. (No, that was George Faye. Deflected George.)

Part of her rallied, some part made for reason and orthodoxy; she calmed herself.

Dan would call. Good.

She'd display for him, show she could connect.

And she'd also keep an open mind: accept the possibility of something given, recognised only for its possibility, but working in her mind and following, what, its template, agenda, super-rational logic? Whatever.

The options? Without Dan, despite Dan, Corinne considered some. This chance directive fading, the agenda working itself away, eroded by orthodoxy. Or would it catalyse? Volatise? Commandeer more of her mind?

Well, Dan would be watching, keeping an eye on her. Being a lifeline.

And it was natural, not supernatural. Preternatural maybe, by its nature. Hyperaesthesia. Intense seeing. Intense focus. A chance triggering that was surely ghosting away even now, worn down by too much else.

Corinne put it aside, went back to her article.

The trap was sprung that night.

Corinne had enjoyed a pleasant, comfortable, safely ordinary dinner with a publicist, Tony Ashcroft, had flirted just enough to keep him interested, and was back at her apartment at 11:15. She got ready for bed, then stepped out on the deck to check the nightframe.

Street. House. Bay. Boats and twinkling streetlight, all there in a glance. Then, taking it slowly: blue-black night and starpoint, down to the bay, hints of boats, the streetlight beyond standing reflected on the water, then the black trees stirring in the night wind and, across Victoria Place, the house, its side security light on at this hour, the window sitting at the end of its channel of light, window open but the curtains not moving.

Corinne went to bed, read awhile, slept.

Woke at 12:40 to tree-shadow on the ceiling, found herself wondering, went to the window, saw that the curtains were rippling at her, blowing out, half-moons of utter black in the scalloping white, fluttering at her. Hello. Hello. Awake now.

It was eerie but something known, familiar and mundane, part of orthodoxy, just chance elements, suggestions.

Corinne smiled and went back to bed.

Woke at 1:50, sighed to find it becoming such a long night. Looked out the window again, saw the security light was off. The window had vanished in a mass of darkness. She imagined it there, couched in black, curtains fluttering at her, watching.

No you don't. Oh no. We've done this before.

Corinne made herself go back to bed, even slept for awhile, but woke at 2:14, went to the window, needing to see.

It was hard to know what she expected. The streetlights off ? Everything dark and focused on that black rippling centre?

The security light was on again, and though there was wind, a strong and cool southerly, and though the window was definitely open, the curtains hung still behind the twin, angled panes.

She knew she had to go down there. Find out why.

The security light was on. No torch was needed, though when she'd dressed, she grabbed it just in case.

Once again she went round the front of her apartment building down to Victoria Place, crossed the street, stood on the sidewalk at the top of the path looking down at rest of the tableau.

Wind blew around her, had the trees churning and heaving. The curtains hung still.

Corinne stepped over the low iron gate, began down the path.

Was there movement? Had the curtain on the left twitched at her, stirred slightly?

She strained to see, *did* see a movement there. A bellying out, a settling back.

Perhaps it had been there all along. She just hadn't see it, had imagined the stillness.

Another few steps. Again they bellied towards her. And again, though this time the edge scalloped once, showed a black edge, quickly gone.

Microclimates. Anomalies of airflow. A draught getting in. Just ordinary things. Orthodoxy.

Two more steps. Then she paused, waited.

Your turn. Your turn.

Sure enough, the curtains bellied, scalloped, beckoned twice this time, cautioning, two vents of darkness, offered, stolen away.

Your turn.

Corinne took her step, waited.

Nothing. The dead hang of fabric. Nothing.

Another step.

The curtains bellied, flared out in a sudden shuddering ripple, a gust of wind, gave four, six black hearts or more, settled back.

Corinne smiled. She hadn't screamed, hadn't cried out. The window had done its best, screamed at her silently, but she had managed.

So close now. She took two more steps. Three.

They bellied, heaved, showed a solitary twist of black and settled.

Corinne smiled. She had won.

She reached the window, could have touched the twin panes, with another step could have felt the curtains, but turned aside instead, left then right, moved down to the door of the shed.

Would it be occupied? she wondered. Decided no. Just knew.

She grabbed the knob, opened the door, shone her torch into the gloom. Saw the same clutter as before, and the curtains hanging. Just boxes and junk and, yes, a view of her apartment if she cared to look back up the tunnel of light, back through the nightframe. Line of sight. Line of night. The other part of it.

She'd have that view, she decided, would look out, complete the equation, perhaps even see herself gazing down, waving, beckoning, an absurdity, a fancy.

Corinne went to the window, pushed the curtains aside and looked out, felt them struggle around her as the wind surged in through the open door and the security light went out. She was inside the frame.

And as the edges settled, folded, sank in and the warmth flowed, Corinne knew that behind the shock, the panic, the terrible dread, what she really felt was incredible relief, and that though her final word was "No!", what she was saying with every part of her being was "Yes!"

Stitch

SOON BELLA WOULD find the nerve to go upstairs. Soon she would be able to excuse herself from her uncle and aunt and climb the familiar old stairs, counting every one, enter the toilet in the alcove of the upstairs bathroom, and confront Mr Stitch.

She couldn't leave without seeing him. Not this time. It was Auntie Inga's birthday, occasion enough, yes, but this time Mr Stitch *was* the reason for being here. Bella had always tried to see him once or twice a year, just to make sure he was still there, shut tight behind the glass, locked in his frame. This time it had to be more.

"Your boyfriend couldn't make it, Bel?" Auntie Inga asked, but gently, in case there was a point of delicacy involved.

"Roger? No. He had to work, like I said." Bella knew she had said. It had been the third or fourth line out of her mouth when she arrived. "Sends his best wishes though. 'Manniest happiest returns'—quote, unquote. His exact words." What he would have said anyway. "He has to work every second Saturday."

Bluff and hearty as ever, but it's what you often had to do where Roger was concerned. Maybe it would have been better if he *were* here. Having someone to be with her through it. Through this. Bella couldn't remember feeling such dread.

But this time she had to be alone. This time she wanted more.

"This photo of your mum was always my favourite," Auntie Inga said, returning to the page in the old album, going through them as she always did when Bella visited. Possibly when anyone visited.

Bella ignored the mention of her mother, concentrated instead on what Uncle Sal was doing. He smiled kindly at them both and poured more coffee. Bella couldn't remember him any other way. It was as if at some point in his life he had discovered the word 'avuncular' and had resolved to be precisely that for the rest of his days. With Mr Stitch upstairs, it made him seem positively sinister, a gleefully distracting conspirator. An avuncular usher, Bella thought, then was reminded of the old witch in the story of Hansel and Gretel. And witch rhymed with stitch, so back she went, into the panic loop again, with both hands steadying her coffee cup, her heart hammering and her feet flexing inside her shoes, itching to run. If only Roger *could* have been here, could have at least made an effort to understand what this meant. Stayed close. That would have made all the difference.

Though alone, alone. Some things had to be done alone. And today had to be different. Today she had to change it all.

"Auntie Inga, do you still have that old sampler on the wall in the upstairs toilet? The one with the two Dutch children in the street?" Bright voice. Light voice. Smiling all the while. No big deal. As if she hadn't been up there in years, hadn't *made* herself go up and see it on each and every one of those terrifying visits.

"What's that dear?" Auntie Inga said. "Dutch children?"

Summoned by name, the rosy-cheeked sixty-seven-year-old came tracking across the years from where the photographs had taken her. Smile for smile, here she was: Auntie Inga, always Hansel and Gretel witch (stitch!) friendly. She'd never been any different. But forgetful today. Mentioning her mother.

What *was* the female form of avuncular?, Bella wondered. Because here it was, tidied up, presented and displayed: more in terms of velour and Hush Puppies than gingham and gingerbread, but just as real.

"The sampler?" her aunt added, as if only a few words ever got through at a time, drip-feed fashion. "That old thing! Of course. Been there forever."

This was the moment. "Of all your cross-stitch pieces, that's my favourite." Bold and direct. Tell a big enough lie and people will believe. Could she pull it off?

"Really, Bel? I would have done that when I was thirty-one. Just before you were born. Landscapes. Street scenes. I suppose they are Dutch children when I think of it. I did so many. Gave them as gifts too." She considered the framed pieces on the walls of the cosy living-room. "I did a lot of these pieces then."

Bella dutifully let herself be seen to be admiring the embroideries. Yes, and both you and Uncle Sal are so like the smarmy, neighbourly, *avuncular* people in them. Made up of so many tiny squares, a neat and orderly mosaic. Four stitches in the aida backing to give a really good square. Four to make each black square of Mr Stitch. But, yes, neat and tidy like that, Inga and Sal. Chock full of smarm. Terminal avuncular.

Though one of the cliched pieces did charm Bella, she had to admit: the road leading off from the open door towards a sunset, with words set in the doorway, picked out vividly against the light.

Westering home,
And a song in the air,
Light in the eye,
And it's good-bye to care;
Laughter o'Love,
And a welcoming there;
Isle of my heart,
My own one!

The door, the setting sun, the sentiments, the sheer belonging: such precious things. It brought her parents' faces, always did, but she was skilled at pushing those aside. She'd dealt with that, and so could almost let herself go there, through that door. But no bidding care good-bye today. And that door, pulled right back, inviting in, inviting out, showing the road and the setting sun, was the absolute opposite of her own dark green front door, always locked these past ten, fifteen years. Double locked. Triple locked. Because of Stitch. Mr Stitch. Because of all that her life had ended up being.

Even as Bella pulled back, accepting how the world was, there was Auntie Inga. A new thought, *that* thought, had occurred to her.

"Funny that you like it now. You were frightened of it as a girl."

Frightened. An understatement in the ratio of Hitler being misguided, or the atomic bomb at Hiroshima causing collateral damage.

"Oh?" Said calmly enough. Interested. This was the part Bella had to get through.

Auntie Inga was looking off up the stairs, as if a part of herself had been sent off to check the piece or, better yet, was running replays of a tinier, younger Bella Dillon sobbing, yelling, refusing to use *that* bathroom, *that* toilet. "You hated going into that bathroom. Lise—your mother—we always noticed it. That cross-stitch upset you. Two little kids in a street and you'd run away screaming."

Her mother again. Aunt Inga *was* forgetting.

Can't stop. Can't stop. Can't stop now. Bella pretended to be easy. Pretended to remember. "They were facing away, looking off up the street," Bella said, feet wanting to run. *Don't mention Mr Stitch.*

"It wasn't that I couldn't do faces," Auntie Inga insisted, some old point of pique and a welcome show of larger humanity, a blemish on the sugar rose. "It's how the picture came in the kit. I liked doing faces. Look at *The Man in the Golden Helmet* there."

Bella glanced briefly, dutifully, but stayed on track. "Well, I'm very fond of it now. Just being sentimental, I guess. That one in the bathroom." Bella added the last remark to keep Auntie Inga on the piece upstairs. Even Uncle Sal stayed with her. He was nodding: Uncle Sal on Avuncular Setting #3.

"You're welcome to go up and see," he said. "It's still there."

At one level, Bella would never need to see it again. She knew it intimately. Two children holding hands seen from behind, looking off up a street. The boy in long-sleeved blue top and white pants, long brown hair, a brown Dutch or Flemish hat—soft, shaped like a bucket, definitely a hat worn by boys from another time and place; the little girl in a dark red dress with a white lace collar, long blonde hair. Two houses foreshortened, leading off up the street, then a wall and a tree beyond; an old-style lamp-post in the middle distance on the footpath just at the edge of the road.

And the face of a woman, probably their mother, looking down at them from a partly opened leadlight window as if reminding them what to get at the village shop, possibly warning them to beware of strangers.

And that had been the crux of it.

For along that foreshortened street, off in its tidy, converging cross-stitch distances near where the wall met the tree, was just such a stranger. A pedestrian on the sidewalk, stylized, minimalist, no doubt meant to be a token figure to fill out the scene, sketched in, stitched in with exactly seventy and a half black cross-stitch squares. Small, yet large enough, exactly seventy and a half squares big in fact, each set of four making a bold black larger square, squares set oddly so he was jagged and jigsawed down one side. A jigsaw man.

Bella could never forget that figure beyond the lamp-post, beyond the houses, small and sketchy, jagged with distance. Give her a pen and she could draw him, could tell his bits like marking squares in a hopscotch rhyme. It had been the mantra of her years.

Four in a true square
Then eight more in two lines
Four in another square
And four for shoulders fine
Six in a body line
Then six to get it right
Five more make it odd one out
Like someone took a bite.
Six more in a body line
Then six to keep it strong
Five again is odd one out
Like someone got it wrong
Three begins to give him legs
Then three and a half—it's true!
Four in a line is almost there
But not like me and you.
One and a half—space—a half and one
Now Mr Stitch can run run run!

It was all in *how* they were set together. A man in a thick-brimmed black hat (or with a hideously deformed head), with two bites out of his left side, ruining his body, a third snipped out of his legs. A lopsided, jigsaw man.

And here was Bella about to confront him again. The figure who stood behind her days, who determined things like the extra locks on her big green front door, on the inner doors as well, the green Keep Away doors, because she'd read somewhere that dark green kept demons and devils at bay.

"I will go up and take a look, if you don't mind," Bella said. "Guess I'm sentimental like you, Aunty Inga."

"Sentimental is good, dear," her aunt said. "Too much nastiness in the world. Too many bad people. Old values are best."

"Why don't I keep you company, Bel?" Uncle Sal said, totally unexpected. "I have to get something upstairs. Inga, we could sure use some of that new Darjeeling you bought. I'm sure Bella would."

Bella was surprised, pleased, shocked all in an instant. When had Uncle Sal ever initiated anything? When had he shown such strategic thinking too, any kind of thinking that put him at odds with the Inga and Sal show?

There had to be a reason.

And before Inga could veto it, ask him to help with the tea—it was her birthday, after all—Sal was out of his chair and leading the way.

Another first.

Bella was after him in a flash, ready for that climb to that landing and that bathroom. But there had to be a reason.

"Uncle Sal," she said at the foot of the stairs. "You really don't have to."

"Nonsense, Bel. When do I ever get to do anything for myself ?"

Again he'd surprised her. So why now? Why this? Bella decided to be direct.

"So why this time?" Sharp and hard, considering, and he blinked at her as she took the first few steps ahead of him.

"Just wanted to see you were okay," he said, following her up the staircase. "That cross-stitch bothers me too."

Bella could have stumbled and fallen in amazement. What had he said?

"What's that, Uncle Sal?" She heard the tremble in her voice.

"Bothers me. Bothers you," he said from behind. "Always hated it. Figure in the distance. Small and wrong."

Exactly! Exactly that! Small and wrong. Jagged and incomplete.

They were halfway to the landing when Bella slowed, hearing his breathing, laboured, agitated somehow.

For it had dawned on her.

He's serving me up. Making sure I get there. They're in collusion.

Bella stopped on the stairs.

It made terrible sense. The *new* Uncle Sal, the odd behaviour. *Bring her to me!*

Bella turned, pressed her back hard against the wall.

"Don't think I will," she said.

"What, Bel? What is it?"

"This." *You.* "I can't do this today." *You're different.*

"Bel, I'm being brave. I'm doing it right. Should have done it years ago."

"What?" She gasped the word and so said it again. "What?"

"Should have told you. Said something about Benny."

"Benny? What's Benny got to do with anything?"

But it was all there in the instant. Benny in his stupid blue plaid shirt. Benny eight years older, surprising her in the bathroom. In the toilet. Benny and Stitch.

Time was frozen on the stairs: Bella against the wall, Uncle Sal two steps lower, back to the rail, Aunt Inga lost in the impossibly far reaches of the kitchen.

"We know what he did, Bel. Your aunt won't have it. A mother can't. But we know. I know."

Part of Bella stayed on the old safe track.

What's he going on about? They haven't seen Benny in years. Benny went from their lives. Upped and went, just like that. Just like anyone can.

Part of Bella was in the other fork of that eternal moment. Benny against her. The smell of his blue plaid shirt. The hand over her mouth. And Stitch. Mr Stitch urging him on. Stitch behind it all, looming on the wall, waiting off along the street, there but not all there. Jagged. Dark man-thing in a funny thick hat or with a big cross-shaped hammer head. Benny breathing hard. "My word against yours! No-one believes a kid!" Hard against her. Then inspired, worried, improvising. "That's Stitch! Mr Stitch! He'll get you. It was his idea. He's coming for you, see! He'll get you if you tell!"

Both tracks running, playing out on the stairs, Uncle Sal's eyes catching hers at last, pulling her back, but the walls pounding, drumming, thundering with the mighty secret heartbeat of the house.

"You're safe now, Bel. We're all safe. You can go see."

Bella was back with him, five steps from the top. Blue-plaid Benny was gone and Uncle Sal was here and Bella was back and doing what she still had to do, always had to do.

"Thanks for knowing," she said.

"You can't go home again. Had to be said."

"I can do it alone."

"Never doubted it. I'll be outside."

"Th-Thanks."

And into the bathroom she went. The door to the toilet was ajar. She couldn't see the back wall, of course, just the strip of dim blue wall through the crack. *You can't go home again.* The truth in those words. *But I keep trying. Keep coming here.* She couldn't see the back wall, or the frame, or the children. A warning to the Dutch children. *You can't go home again! You'll never see your mother!*

That word. Bella had closed the bathroom door behind her. Old habit. But she hadn't locked it. Hadn't locked it then, hadn't now.

Put on your blue-plaid shirt, Sal, and bring her to me!

But she could lock the toilet door. Lock it this time. Just in case. Though that would be locking her in. And Benny, something of Benny, might be off in the cross-stitch distance. Two of them now, along that terrible, too tidy street.

She had to know. Had to act. Now or never.

She grabbed the door-knob and pushed back the door.

There was the old patterned lino, so well known, the old toilet and cistern, the air freshener in its container, the two frosted window panes on the right, the pale blue walls. There—letting her gaze move up—was the frame, brown wood, the neatly braided world forming, the children and the street, the lamp-post in the middle distance, the wall and the tree.

The black ragged form.

Hello, Bella.

"Bastard!" She said it quietly.

Sal's putting on his blue-plaid shirt.

"Bastard! Bastard!"

Like father, like son. He's bigger. Older but bigger.

"Bastard! Bastard! Bastard!"

Put your hands on the cistern like before. There's a good girl.

"Bastard! Bastard! Bastard!"

You could ask for me. Take me home. Get me through your Green Door.

Reading her mind. "Bastard!"

Language, Bel. Get a needle and thread then. Make me complete.

Tears were hot and brimming, running down her cheeks.

"Bastard! Bastard!"

Mr Stitch was moving in her tears. Her tears were making him run.

You like me jagged. Ragged. Here I come!

Bella wiped her eyes with the back of her hand, freed herself from him.

Steadied herself. Her hands were on the cistern. "Bastard! Bastard!" She snatched them away.

You want it! You were ready!

"No! No! Bastard!"

Scaredy cat! Ready cat!

"Bastard!"

And Sal was pushing at the toilet door. "Bella! What's wrong? What is it?"

She hadn't locked it! Meant to. Thought to. Hadn't.

Says it all, Bel!

Stitch was running in her tears. Jigging. Jagging. Running.

"Bel, what's wrong?"

Sal pushing at the door. Stitch running.

One hand was on the cistern, but to steady her, so she could turn. Nothing like before. "You bastard!"

"What, Bel? What is it?" Sal's voice. And the door was finally open far enough and Sal was there and no blue-plaid shirt.

Bella stole a final glance. Stitch was back along the street, back by the wall and the tree. The children were safe. *All* the children were safe.

"Oh, Uncle Sal! I thought—for a moment, I just thought—it's all right.

It's fine now!"

"What happened?"

"You know. Old memories. Dealing with old memories. Would Aunt Inga let me have this?"

Yes! Take me home!

Sal, bless him, understood.

"Bel, just take it. Sneak it out. I'll distract her."

It was beyond all expectation, Uncle Sal saying this.

"But—"

"You mightn't have noticed, but your aunt—she's getting forgetful. Repeating herself, things like that. We can say she gave it to you. I'll put another one in here. She won't remember, won't—be certain."

"Uncle Sal, it's not—you know?"

"Can't be sure yet. But Alzheimer's is a possibility, the doctor says. The thing is, she doesn't come in here much. She uses the en suite. So take it. She's got so many. It's never been a favourite."

Yes! Bella thought, so relieved, so grateful, then hesitated.

Too easy. Too easy. What if Sal were an accomplice after all?

Get me through the Green Door, Stitch had said.

And was quiet now, down by the tree all jagged and waiting. With not a word.

It was what she wanted too—crazily, what they both wanted. Unless this impulse came from Stitch via her mind, via Sal's. Stitch using them all.

He never said a word. Just stood off in the real, never-real, cross-stitch world, just seventy and a half stitches himself, but trying to be more, embroidering back.

How could she know? How could she be sure of anything now?

"Probably shouldn't," she said.

"Your choice, hon," Sal said.

They stood in the bathroom, Bella staring in at the piece in its frame, waiting for some reply. Stitch would be thwarted if she went without him. Furious. Bella laughed at the word-play. *Cross* Stitch. But he would still be *here*, in this blue-plaid, hands-on-the-cistern place. And she'd be back again and again because of it.

Her need was as great as his, that's what it came down to. And this was her chance to be free of it. To move it along. Stop it being something here and now. Now and then.

"Sal, why don't you bring it over tomorrow? Tell Aunty Inga she promised it. See if she goes along with it."

"Bel, one more thing."

"Yes?"

"You mum and dad—"

"Uncle Sal, let it go, please!"

"Has to be said, darlin'. Now that we're talking, just let me—"

"No!"

"Bel, you've managed this much. Go the rest of the way. They weren't to blame. They couldn't protect you—"

"Listen, Uncle Sal—"

"It wasn't their fault. None of it. What happened on *Sea Spray*. The explosion. Of course you feel responsible—"

No! No! No! No! No!

Bella actually had her hands over her ears. "Uncle Sal!"

"It was an accident! If we'd found their bodies, maybe that would've made a difference. They didn't leave you with this! Didn't desert you!"

Stitch hadn't said a word.

"You promised, Uncle Sal! You promised!"

Stitch was out there, up there, back there, listening.

"Okay. Okay. Enough. But it had to be said. I'm sorry!"

Bastard, bastard, Uncle Sal.

Or Stitch was putting his words in Sal's mouth. Had a thin, jagged, cross-stitch arm up Sal's back, working Sal's jaws.

But Bella saw the resignation in the eyes, the strain on the old face.

This wasn't Stitch. This was Sal, torn loose from avuncular, reinventing himself second by second for this desperate task, with only a few known aces up his sleeve. Known cards every one.

"I'm sorry, Uncle Sal," she said into the silence, the terrible end-time silence of these haunted upstairs.

Stitch was nowhere to be found. Back on the wall. Back in his frame. Seventy and a half meagre twists of black. Barely made.

"It's just—hon, you couldn't do anything. They didn't fail you."

Again. Bella added the word. *Get it right, Uncle Sal. You meant to say didn't fail me again.*

"We'll play it your way," Sal said then, saving what he could. "We'll come over tomorrow. I'll tell your aunt we promised. We'll bring the cross-stitch."

Better. Much better.

"Can't guarantee that your aunt—you know—won't mention certain things. Won't—"

"Listen, Uncle Sal, let's take it over now! You said Auntie Inga forgets things. Let's just do it! Tell her we arranged it. A special outing for her birthday. It's a surprise! I'll take you over in my car, bring you back. You said Auntie Inga's always wanted to see— mum's place again. What I've done with it. This is her birthday treat!"

"I don't know, hon. It's so sudden. Your aunt—"

"I'll have you back inside the hour, two at the most. Say it's important to me. Important that she sees where I'm going to hang it! We can do it, Sal!"

Panic was driving her, determination to do it before her courage failed, before Stitch came back.

"I'll go see, okay?" Sal turned towards the stairs.

"We can do it, Uncle Sal. It'll really help."

He looked back, smiled his old safe smile. "Anything for closure, they say."

Stitch was too quiet. It had been too long.

"Anything. Look, I'll come down with you now. Tell her I've got a birthday cake or something. We can get one on the way."

Pride, vanity and panic of another kind helped. Auntie Inga wasn't about to admit that she had forgotten their outing, or that she couldn't remember promising the cross-stitch. Bella felt a stab of guilt and shame at the duplicity, using such a desperate condition against the person suffering from it, but her own need was greater. Having the person who had created Stitch carry him across the threshold, through the green door; now that was perfect. Suddenly important. Closure, Sal had said. This would do it.

They left the pot of new Darjeeling cooling on the kitchen bench. While Bella jollied Aunt Inga along, helped her into the front passenger seat of the Lexus, got the seatbelt done up, Sal fetched Stitch, brought him down swathed in an old towel and put him in the back.

Bella could never have done it. She felt a giddiness, an intense, irrational joy, a sudden certainty. This was right in every sense. Inga doing the honours. Inga bringing Stitch. All so perfect.

Bella couldn't remember what she said as she drove, just that she was babbling happily all the while, going on about a special birthday treat and how important it all was. Aunt Inga blossomed under the attention. This was her day, her outing. Bella was being, well, avuncular.

Stitch never said a word.

He was there in the back next to Sal, hidden under his towel. This was what he wanted too, no doubt, staying close like this, but at least he was out of the upstairs bathroom, *that* place.

They stopped for a birthday cake as Sal and she had agreed: a store-bought mudcake with *Happy Birthday* in white looping letters. Then, in another two minutes, they were at Eltham Street, tree-lined and shady, and there was the big white house with the green door.

"It looks wonderful, dear," Aunt Inga said. "Your mother liked the white with the green trimming. It's nice that you've kept it. She'd be very proud, Bel."

Bella endured it, forced herself to say thanks, again half-expecting a refrain from Stitch: *She'd be very proud*. But nothing came. Again nothing. Perhaps he thought he could still win. Perhaps he was saving his best till last. Perhaps—it suddenly occurred to her—being out in a *real* day on a *real* street was simply too much. Either way, she'd prepared. She was ready for him.

Bella swung into the sheltered driveway, opened the garage with the remote and drove in. A wink and a smile at Sal in the rear-view mirror, then more fussing over Auntie Inga, helping her out, drawing her attention to the marigolds and geraniums in the big planters while Sal hauled Stitch out after him. Who would have thought that it could go so smoothly?

Then they were through the first green door and in the hall, then through the second and in the sitting room at last.

Inga and Sal never expected it. Even as their noses twitched at the odd smell, even as their eyes widened, making sense of what they saw, Bella had the stiletto off the sideboard and into Inga's throat. Had it in before her aunt knew it had happened, before her little shard of a scream died in a gurgle. Then Bella had the blade out and into Sal's neck at the exact moment he dropped the shrouded frame and managed: "Bella, what on earth—?"

But he saw what it was and had to know. His eyes were wide as they glazed, as the light in them died. He'd know. He had seen the figures— Bella's mother and father, and Benny and Roger—sitting upright in their chairs, had seen them totally stitched over with black, head to toe, every surface covered with precious dark thread, protected forever from the jagged man.

Bella closed and locked the door, old instinct, old habit, then reached down and removed the towel from the frame with its broken glass and tiny helpless figure. She wiped the stiletto clean, then sat cross-legged on the floor and began the unpicking. Seventy and a half stitches, then they would be safe. All the children.

La Profonde

THERE WAS NO mistaking how surprised Derwent was when he saw Jay walking along the railway tracks towards him. Jay's one-time business partner was wearing sunglasses, so his eyes were hidden, but his mouth actually fell open. Then, in true Derwent fashion, his surprise and fear turned immediately to anger.

"Fuck, Jay, what is all this?" he shouted. "This 'meet me at the station' stuff?"

Jay just smiled and waved, then waited till he'd reached the end of the otherwise deserted platform, and Derwent was glowering down at him over the safety rail.

"Tell me, Dee"—Jay deliberately used the unwelcome nickname—"Do you know what a *profonde* is?"

But Derwent wasn't up for any of Jay's smart-ass questions. He was hot and sweating, clearly upset. Though only thirty-seven, two years younger than Jay, red-faced and agitated like this he looked ten years older. One well-timed email had turned Derwent's world upside-down.

> *Dee, we need to talk. I have documented proof of what you and Cally did to Edilo Ltd. Take the 12:55 to Morley Station on Sunday for a 1:30 pm meeting. You won't tell the others and you will come alone. This is your one chance.*

Jay couldn't see Derwent's eyes, but he could easily picture the determination he'd find in them amid the rage and desperation. Dee had been threatened with having his scam exposed, the dangerous emails he'd thought he'd purged from the office systems while he and Cally were plundering Edilo in true insider fashion. Three years of enjoying the spoils; now this summons to a deserted suburban railway station on a hot Sunday afternoon. He'd had enough.

Jay hauled himself up onto the platform. Morley Station was almost as new as the housing estates going up all about them beyond the cutting, just a stretch of hot concrete between two sets of tracks, with nothing more than a modest double-sided passenger shelter, two lamp-posts with signs attached saying *Morley*, and a set of iron steps at one end leading up to a deserted bus-stop and a car-park, both as deserted as the station at this time of day. "A *profonde*, Derwent? Ever hear of one?"

But for Derwent there was only one issue. His sunglasses might be hiding his eyes but his other features showed the full extent of his emotion. "Three fucking years, Jay. What do you want?" Not, Jay noticed, how the hell did you find out?

Jay grinned and gestured down the platform to where the rails stretched off in the afternoon glare. "I want you to take a walk with me, Dee, that's all."

"Christine and the kids know where I am, Jay."

Jay doubted that, but ultimately it didn't matter. "So what's the harm in taking a walk so we can talk about this?"

"Talk about it here. What do you want?" It was the old Derwent, the pre-scam Derwent showing through, but it truly was a mere shadowplay of how Dee had been three years before, a bravura display from a broken puppet.

Jay squinted in the glare. He glanced up and down the quiet platform in its lonely cutting. No sunglasses for him. Never. He listened to the hot breeze pushing through the grass on the embankments, then glanced at this watch. "Derwent, I'm going to start walking north along the tracks now. If you've got any sense, any interest in saving your fat ass, you'll take that walk with me. It's up to you, buddy."

And, true to his word, Jay turned and began heading along the platform.

Derwent swore, called after him, shouted abuse, even the beginnings of threats—just the beginnings—but Jay kept walking. When he reached the end of the concrete deck he crouched and jumped down onto the rail-bed, then began moving north along the tracks.

There were more angry shouts from the platform behind him, but Jay didn't stop. He kept walking, smiling into the day, relishing the warm breeze on his face and the realisation that this could indeed be done exactly as he had planned it.

Back at that hot quiet station Derwent would be running through his options, railing at the universe, at the insufferable turn of events. Sooner rather than later, he would accept that there was nothing else he could do but follow. He'd been caught out. He could only try to survive this. Maybe he'd blame Cally, say that *she* had persuaded *him*. That was likely.

Finally Jay heard, "Well hold on then!" But, of course, Jay didn't slow his pace. Couldn't. He'd checked his watch and it truly could remain a matter of timing. Let Derwent shed some of those happy fat-cat pounds he'd been putting on during the past three years.

It was easy to tell when Dee was gaining by the laboured breathing getting nearer, the growing thud of footsteps out of time with Jay's own. It was like someone imitating an old-style steam locomotive, exactly that.

Then Derwent was there, staggering, straining, hauling in big ragged breaths. When he could get words out, they were the expected things.

"Wasn't personal—Jay. Never—personal. Un'erstan'?" It seemed like all he could manage.

"Glad to hear it, Dee." Jay didn't look at him, just kept watching the way ahead, reading every detail of the route between the two sets of tracks. "But how exactly do you mean that? Never personal?"

Derwent stumbled along, still trying to catch his breath but probably exaggerating that, giving himself time to gather his thoughts and, hardest of all, hold back his anger. Would he blame Cally, take the easy out and blame it all on her? Difficulties for him later, certainly, but a solution now.

Jay savoured the breeze on his brow and wondered what line the other man would take. However it went, Derwent would be sensing there was hope, would believe he knew exactly how he had to play this. Maybe he'd be thinking he really could reach some private settlement here, buy himself out of trouble.

Derwent finally answered. "You were just someone, okay?" More ragged breathing. "Could've been anyone." Another pause, laboured. He truly did seem to be judging every word. "You un'erstand? It was just—the situation. An opportunity. It's not like we ever—signed on to get *you*." Derwent emphasised the last word.

Finally Jay did look across at the man trudging with him between the two sets of tracks. "Who's we?"

"Aw, hell, Jay. What does it matter? It was just something that came along, you know? Never thought about it too much."

"Enough to get away with it for a while. Ruin the company. I trusted you."

"Yeah, well, some of us aren't as trusting as you, okay? We don't light up as bright. We try, but it doesn't always happen. You made it easy."

"There was Cally. Who else?"

"Hell, Jay. It's been three years! Why this now?"

"Brian had to be in on it. Those emails make that pretty clear. And Mark, doing the accounts. You needed him. Barbara, Ashley and Hiro were mentioned."

"Christine knows where I am, Jay."

"I grew up on a railway line, did you know that, Dee?"

"How the hell would I know that?" Derwent said, thrown by the change of subject and forgetting for a moment how this had to be played.

"That was out in Leederville. As kids, friends and I would walk the tracks between Leederville and Quinton, just exploring, you know. Always loved what we found along railway lines."

"Is that right?"

"Nothing forces patterns on a landscape more than a railway. All those lines and curves. No barriers. Hills cut away, fields divided. Rivers hardly stand a chance. It's all so precise, so artificial. Then it changes. It doesn't stay like that. It's almost as if the intrusion is resented, worn away."

"Resented? That's a bit much."

"Not at all. It's the elevator effect. People get in an elevator. It's really just a little room that moves up and down over a tremendous drop and takes them to where they're going. Most people don't think of using an elevator in terms of shafts and counterweights and terrible drops. It's just a room that moves and does a job. Same with railways. People notice the trains, sure, maybe the tracks while a train is on them, but what about when a train isn't passing? The tracks are overlooked, forgotten. All that precision, that regimentation gets blurred, roughed up. Pretty soon those railside corridors become wilderness, bits of a rogue landscape. People looking out train windows always look *beyond* the corridor, have you noticed?"

"No, I haven't. Listen, Jay, this is interesting but I don't see what it has to do with our situation."

"Love that word, Dee. Situation. Tidies it up so nicely, don't you think? That's why names are so important. Finding the right handles."

"What can we do about this, Jay?"

"One thing at a time. You never answered my question."

"What question?"

"When we first met back at the station. First thing I said."

"A question? What question? Hey, look, Jay, I've had a lot on my mind. You really can't expect—"

"I would've been in your thoughts though. You would have been very much aware of me. You wouldn't have given me a thought in years, but when my email arrived the other day, ever since Thursday, I would've been in your thoughts surely."

"Well, yeah, but—I mean, I was pretty mad. Worried and all. You have to allow that—"

"You were right, what you said before about destroying Edilo. It really wasn't personal, was it?"

"That's right. That's right, Jay! It just happened."

"No, I mean in the sense that I never got to *be* a person to you with a life and interests, plans and hopes. Never got on your radar."

"Well, you were the boss. Always so earnest, you know? So remote. It just never—"

"Right. But if I'd been a *person* enough, mattered more, you wouldn't have pulled something like that. You'd have picked somebody else. If you'd liked me at all, thought I was *worth* liking, worth respecting at least, you wouldn't have used me like a mark and taken advantage."

Derwent's eyes were hidden by his sunglasses, but the way he suddenly went quiet, suddenly became fixed in his gaze while walking, let Jay know that there would be a very different look in them now.

Jay smiled and glanced at his watch again. It was 1:42 and here it was at last: the *You're a wacko!* look tucked away behind black Raybans.

"Where are we going, Jay?"

"Just to the next station. You ever take this line?"

"You kidding? I'm a city boy. I never get out this far."

"Right. Well, Greenwood's just another little station like Morley back there. Brand new. They all are once you get past Belmont. Just a platform, a shelter, some steps up to a bus-stop for a feeder bus line that doesn't seem to be operating yet, not much else. Not much of a train service on a Sunday out here, not yet anyway. What's that term they use a lot nowadays: abandoned in place?"

Derwent nodded and uh-huh'd. He'd adjusted again, had worked out a new strategy, all predictable really. "You did this as a kid?" His tone was pitched to invite sharing.

"It's where we played a lot. I still love walking the tracks."

Derwent knew his cue. "We never knew stuff like that, Jay. That you had a thing for trains—"

"Not so much the trains, Dee. More the landscape you find around railway lines, the narrow strip of land they run through. Even out here where it's not too built up yet you get the same no-man's-land corridor you find in cities and the inner suburbs. The moment a line is opened up, there they are: the same lines of fences and plantings, the same cuttings, power poles, the chain-link barriers and supply sheds. Look at all this! Grass, bushes, mounds of soil. Rails and sleepers for repair work, future track development. Today I've seen an old tanker bogey left on a spur not even joined to the main track. Not even joined! Then half a dozen cattle trucks, just left out here. Go figure. That's all part of it."

Derwent didn't miss a beat. "So how far have you walked today, Jay?"

Jay knew exactly how far to the precise mile and yard, the exact meter, but he pretended to think. "Let's see. I drove out early and parked at Silverton, then caught the 9:40 back to Belmont. Now I'm walking back to the car. That's five stations so far. One more to go: Greenwood, then it's Silverton again."

"I caught the train out like you said. I'll need to get back."

Jay nodded. "I can give you a lift. I can drop you off once we settle this."

That clearly made Derwent feel better. "And just how do we settle this? Like I said, Jay. It wasn't personal. I can pay you back something if—"

"It can't be about money now, Dee," Jay said, and looked at his watch again. There was a double coming up, he was sure of it.

"Hey, you're counting!" Derwent said. He'd only just noticed.

"I am," Jay answered. "Ten more paces and I'll show you something really interesting. Here we go: six, seven, eight, nine, ten. Look over there now! Where that stanchion meets the embankment. Near that pile of earth."

"What? What am I looking at?"

"You don't see it?"

"See what?"

"To the left of the stanchion. That shimmer of light on the soil. See the light near the top? It's a hot-spot. Unfinished, but what's called a double."

"Jay, it's a hot day. Of course there's going to be heat shimmer."

"Not this. This is different. It's a double."

Derwent would have that look in his eyes again. "Okay. Then it must be something *you* can see."

"Guess so."

"Walking those tracks back then, you probably learned to notice lots of things other people don't."

"Quite likely." Jay almost made it sound sad the way he said it.

Derwent reacted to the tone. He had to be figuring that every step took them closer to Greenwood. "What about the other kids you played with back then? Did any of them see these—these doubles?"

"Sometimes. Not often. Jenny Attard did for a while. Jeff Callan did a few times, but we disagreed over details. We both wanted to name them, but we always disagreed over the names."

"Are there that many?" Derwent seemed genuinely interested, though doubtless he figured this was the best way to play it. Either way they were on the same page of the script.

"You'd be surprised. You see them more easily as kids. If you work at it, you keep the skill."

"Does this other kid—Jeff ?—does he still have the skill?"

"Can't say. Haven't seen Jeff since we were kids. Guess you lose it if you don't keep at it. I put in a lot of time. Only stands to reason that I've kept the knack."

Derwent didn't overdo it, didn't say something like: "There's more to you than we ever knew, Jay", or "If only we'd known..." He kept it simple, kept the focus on more immediate things.

"That was a double back there, you said. Okay, tell me some other names."

"I'll point them out as we come to them. There's a clearback up on the embankment, but it's very faint and the grass is hiding it."

Derwent looked to where Jay was pointing, even removed his sunglasses to squint through the heat. "A clearback. Okay. Can't see anything." He replaced his Raybans.

"You won't. I barely can. Clearbacks are common, but they come and go. There should be another one soon."

"Is there a particular one I'll be able to see, do you think?"

"That's what I'm hoping to show you before we reach Greenwood. *If* it's there. Sometimes they come and go. That's why I'm counting. This one's called a *profonde* and it's a bit of a test really. If you can see it and describe it to me, I'll forget the whole Edilo business."

"But, Jay, you said it yourself. Most people don't have the skill."

"Turn back any time you like, Dee. No-one's forcing you. I tell you when we're near a *profonde*. You try to see it and describe it to me. That's the deal."

Derwent stopped walking, put his hands on his hips. "I have to describe something that no-one else can see but you! That I only have your word exists in the first place! You're crazy!"

Jay didn't stop. "You should be able to manage it. It's one of the more noticeable ones."

Derwent started walking again. "Oh, fine, Jay! Just one of the more noticeable among invisible things! Great!"

"Greenwood is about ten minutes around that next bend. You'll just have to master the skill. If it's any help, there's a rather special *servante* over there to the left of that bush. Nowhere near as common. There's a prime *antesammis* near that fence there."

"You know, I was just going to say that, Jay. Yessir. That's a prime antipasto over there, whatever!"

Jay ignored the barb, just breathed in the smells of hot steel tracks, the dry grass and the heated eucalyptus beyond the embankments. "There's usually at least one *profonde* before we reach Greenwood."

"And you reckon I'll see it."

"If you take off those sunglasses you might."

Derwent did so, putting them in his shirt pocket. He squinted in the glare again. "Fine. Just say when."

They walked without speaking for a while, following the lines as they began to curve through another cutting. The breeze followed them. Dry grass rustled on the embankments.

The quiet was too much for Derwent. "So we're just walking through these things right now?" he said.

"Not right here," Jay told him. "But the one we want is very close. It's usually—No, there it is! Get ready, Dee. It's not even fifteen yards away, exactly in front of us. Describe what you see!"

"What I see! I can't see anything!"

"We're heading right for it. Ten yards now, right in front. Try looking from the side. Turn your head a little."

Derwent did so. "Is it still there?"

"Right there. Two yards now. Opening and closing along its seeking edge. It's got quite a rhythm going." Jay steadied himself on the stones underfoot.

"I can't see anything, Jay. What's it like exactly? How big is it?"

"Both big *and* small. That's why it's called that. A *profonde* is a word that conjurers use."

"Conjurers? Do they?" Derwent was peering into the emptiness ahead.

"It's what magicians call the long pockets in the tails of their coats. The ones they use for making things disappear."

"Okay, so how—"

It was all he managed because Jay had pushed him hard from behind. There was a single yell, more like a squawk that ended almost as it began, and it was done. There was just the heat shimmer above the tracks, the sound of the breeze rushing in the dry grass.

Jay glanced at his watch, then stepped around the hot-spot in case it was still active, and continued walking. Another hundred yards and he rounded the final curve of the tracks and saw the small Greenwood platform in the bright afternoon light. And there was Cally, exactly on time.

Jay quickened his pace and was soon looking up at the last person on his list.

"Hey, Cally," he called, pleasantly enough. "Do you know what an *oubliette* is?"

The Saltimbanques

FOR DANNY TRUSWELL, his world changed forever that day in 1962 exactly one week before he turned fourteen, a hot dusty day in Reardon, one of those blistering Australian summer days just after Christmas when the air shimmers into haze in every direction and the trees hang and it seems no-one is out on the streets.

He followed his usual summer holiday routine, got his chores done early, then planned ways to lie low till about 4 pm when the sun was far enough down the sky for life to ease back towards normal.

'Normal' was hardly the right term with Danny's Dad taking a rig across the top of Australia and not due back for six days, and his Mum away in Dubbo visiting a sick sister. Danny was having his meals with Kenny's folks and sleeping over.

'Lying low' was hardly the right term either, for Danny and Kenny (and sometimes Annie), like most other kids, rarely managed to do the sensible thing. It was summer holidays, after all. And Danny liked to think they had something of an advantage over the others. They had the chart.

When you saw Reardon from the air with its dozen streets and eighty or so houses (population 434), its two pubs, two churches, community hall, school and library, the co-op up by the railhead near the railway station, the sheds and silos, the clumps of trees following a creek pretty well dry for a half of any year, it looked like so many clustered flecks of grey and silver set in a large, mottled, red tile, with a splotchy line of dullest green winding across it (the creek with its eucalypts) and a thinner silver hairline dividing the top third (the railway line).

That was the view framed on the office wall of Hendist's Stock and Station Agents. An even larger version, two yards on a side, hung over the saloon bar of the Stockman Hotel, the red sweeping out as if Reardon was a colony on the planet Mars.

But a third such aerial shot, left over from the same 1956 International Geophysical Year shoot, tattered, faded and almost forgotten, was pinned to the wall of a deserted shed at the back of the Woke property, and that's where Kenny Woke, Danny Truswell and 'Sometimes' Annie Hendist had their clubhouse and planned which properties to visit, which parts of the creek to try. It gave them an overview, a sense of the town as finite and just *a* place on the land, not *the* place. Horizontal vistas somehow locked you in too much, were too real, too irresistible to allow that other kind of perspective.

The Reardon Rangers, as they called themselves, were lucky. There'd been six of them in the group originally, but Cathy's folks had moved the family down to Dubbo, and Billy Mack and Keith Spicer, just a year before, had gotten too grown up, they reckoned, for that sort of clubhouse stuff.

Annie Hendist, curiously, had stayed around though. She was already fourteen, a long-legged brunette, disturbingly female, and while her mind often seemed on other things, she'd surprise the boys by dropping in and tagging along just as it used to be. Sometimes it'd be for cricket or soccer with other kids, sometimes on one of their Ranger expeditions.

That was how it came to be three, not two, on that momentous Thursday. The boys were so glad to see her again (awkward as well, they were at *that* age) when she appeared in the doorway in her shorts, striped tee-shirt and old sandshoes. She looked so grown-up and knowing that they made it her turn, let her point to a destination on their aerial 'chart'.

Barrack Creek. Dusty and dry until five weeks after the rains in the north, when with all the impact of a miracle, it flooded just like that. But mostly dry and dead, just seeming cool because of the river gums and occasional scrappy willows, because there was shade that wasn't made by blazing, overheated iron and canvas and old boards.

She pointed to a spot close to where the creek, the train tracks and the dirt highway almost came together, creek and road curving in and curving away again, the tracks dividing them.

"How about there?" she said in that calculatedly artless way that had Danny and Kenny swapping looks.

"Roger that," Kenny said, as he so often did, a misuse of old World War 2 lingo.

Danny grabbed his Dad's army surplus canteen. "Fine with me."

If it had just been the two of them, Danny and Kenny would've been laughing and joking, pushing and shoving, saying goofy things, making a big deal of it. With Annie along they kept it simple, sensing that there was something fragile, special and fleeting in Annie being there. You couldn't talk it, could barely even grasp what it was, but they all knew, which had made Mr Jarvie's words at school for the past two years so much more thrilling and embarrassing.

"Here's Kenny and Danny. Now where is Annie?" Mr Jarvie would say. And when Dan retorted (fairly, he'd thought) that Annie was only with them sometimes, that naturally became part of the refrain. "Here's Kenny and Danny and Sometimes Annie," he'd say when they came in, which had the other kids sniggering and sing-songing it too. Kids can be cruel, but how often their cues came from adults enjoying a different kind of humour.

Sometimes Annie it was from then on. In fact Kenny even said, "Roger that!" the very first day, because he figured everyone had to have a nickname.

They were a good mile from town when they realised they probably should've picked somewhere closer. The heat was relentless. The land shimmered in every direction; the railway tracks blazed up at the sun as if just freshly poured and still molten; the highway stretched off into the burring of haze, a crusty deserted ribbon. The trees along Barrack Creek danced as if they might vanish at any moment.

When they finally did reach the bank, they found the scant shade barely helped. Leaning against the trunks of the larger river gums, they looked out at the flat stretch of creek-bed, rippling with heat, set with the shifting, black and grey shapes of old tree trunks left by past flash-flooding, set to the mindless sawing of insects, then began moving along to where the trees were thickest.

That's when they saw that someone had set up camp right near the creek. Three drab buses were parked under the thickest stand of river gums, all with roof-racks packed high with bundles and boxes lashed down every which way. No cars were visible, just three old buses, one with its dusty windows catching bits of sun, the second with the windows of the back half painted over, the third all riveted metal with no windows at all that they could tell, just the front windscreen glinting dully.

"Who's that, y'reckon?" Kenny asked, and got no answer. It was so quiet that his words seemed way too loud. Danny and Annie didn't want to speak.

They moved closer, edging along the opposite side to the visitors, slipping from tree to tree.

No-one was about. The buses had to be like ovens inside, especially the third one, but Danny couldn't see anyone lying underneath them or leaning against tree trunks. The occupants were in town or off somewhere else, visiting one of the properties maybe. *Inside* only if they were crazy.

There wasn't a lot of mystery in Reardon, so sometimes you made it up. You told other kids stories about the bunyip that lived in Barrack Creek (you knew someone who knew someone who'd actually *seen* it), or the 'bore' woman who appeared around the clanking windmills and poisoned the water and sometimes stole children to drown in one of the artesian dams, or the *min-min* lights you saw flickering over the railway tracks after midnight, sometimes dancing along the creek. But this was the real thing, a real mystery, nothing like the box Mr Jarvie had put on his desk and asked them to write about, what it might contain. Here were three genuine 'mystery boxes', made only more mysterious by the faded letters Danny could make out on the sides of at least two of the vehicles.

"There are words," he said.

Kenny agreed. "Roger that."

Annie turned on him. "Enough of the 'Roger that', will you, Kenny?"

Kenny blinked at her. "Roger. Right. But there *are* words. Can you read 'em?"

None of them could. The buses were angled wrong and too dusty. They discussed moving closer, trying to make out what the words said, but even sneaking out to hide behind one of the bigger logs left by past floodwater still meant crossing the creek-bed in plain view, and, though they didn't say it, none of them wanted to do that right then.

It was just so quiet, so eerie, with insects sawing away in the scraps of grass, the tides of heat rolling along the creek and those dark windows glinting.

If only there was movement, someone visible, maybe a dog about. But it was all heat shimmer and unexpected strangeness.

"Know what?" Kenny said. "We oughta come back later an' spy on 'em. What d'you say? Come back after tea?"

Dan and Annie agreed to it, then all gladly turned and headed back towards the shimmering spill of dirty quicksilver that was Reardon.

It took no effort for Kenny to get his Mum to serve them all an early tea. Monday's leftovers made it easy. The three of them were back at the clubhouse soon after six, killing time till it got darker by testing their flashlights and locating the little caravan of buses on the chart.

"Right here, I reckon," Danny said.

Kenny leaned in close. "Roger that. Er, sorry, Annie."

"It's okay, Ken," Annie said, leaning in to see as well, which had Dan suddenly, totally aware of her, of her dark hair and how much her skin smelled of heat and summer. He could've gone crazy on it right then, but just kept pointing at the map, trying to ignore her arm pressing on his, most of all the alarming stirring in his loins, suddenly there, determined not to goof off like Kenny did whenever Annie Hendist came too close. He wanted her to like him. He liked her being close.

Then, when the air had cooled by twenty degrees and the sky was a rich, deepening blue, with stars pushing through and a scrap of a moon showing, they set off again, striking out pretty well in a straight line to where they figured the camp ought to be.

This time there were people. The kids smelled the smoke from a cookfire and heard voices well before they could make out the welcoming flicker of the fire itself and see the cheery, calmer points of hurricane lanterns. There were tents set up now too, two of them, large and square, and four people at least, then five, laughing and joking just like people anywhere. Six, Dan counted, when someone else stepped from one of the buses: four men, two women.

Without discussing it, Annie moved down onto the creek. The boys followed, moved out to halfway where she was hiding behind an old log and hunkered down next to her.

In a whisper, Annie spelled out the words on the side of the bus nearest the fire. "S-A-L-T-I-M-B-A-N—now what's that? Oh yeah—Q-U-E-S. There's a 'The.' The Saltimbanques, it seems like."

"The Salt in Banks?" Danny said, even as Kenny spoke too.

"Salting Banks? What's that?"

"The name of our carnival," a man's voice answered, right near them.

Kenny yipped in fright. Danny's heart caught in his throat. Someone was there on the creek-bed close by.

"It's French," the voice continued. "I'm Berty Green. Why don't you come over an' say hello?"

The fire, the lanterns, the fact that there were two women, more importantly that Berty, whoever he was, had started walking on ahead, made it seem okay. They were just carny folk camping along the road, tired from driving in the heat.

"Let's go," Kenny said.

Dan and Annie exchanged a half-seen glittering glance, and the three of them followed Berty up into the camp.

Framed above and around by flickering tree-forms in the firelight, warmly lit by yellow lamplight and walled in by the sides of one bus and one of the tents, to Dan it was like walking onto the stage of the Community Hall back in town to do a play, or peering through the eye-hole of a diorama at some painting by that guy Mr Jarvie liked, Breughal. Updated, sure. Australianised, yes, but just odd and interesting people caught in the middle of being easy among themselves. Yet not altogether *his* people.

And there was Berty, fully visible now and quite a sight himself, a short dusty-looking man with a sharp face, his chin and forehead pulling back from his nose like some cartoon figure who'd stood too long in a scorching westerly.

But there was hardly time to take it all in properly because Berty Green was introducing them.

"Some kids from town dropped by to pay their respects. Don't reckon I caught your names, kids."

"Danny."

"Kenny."

"Annie."

Berty gave a deep bow, then gestured at his companions. "Right you are. And here we have Jeffrey, Gwen, Walter, Haunted Jack, May and Robert."

There were nods, smiles, salutes, quick looks at the boys, longer looks at Annie from all of them, not just the men. Danny couldn't be sure who was who, but it didn't seem important just then.

"Take a seat! Take a seat!" Berty cried. "Gwen, pour our guests some tea, will you? Later we'll take you in to see Mr Hasso."

"Mr who?" Kenny asked.

Berty grinned. "Mr Hasso. Our ringmaster, our maitre'd. The boss. He's been shut away all day doin' his calculations."

"All day?" Danny said. "Not in the bus without windows?"

"Oh, not in there," Berty answered. "That's our darkwagon. We only go in there on special occasions. His office is in the back o' that one." He pointed to the one with the closed off back half. The painted-over panes glowed with dim yellow light.

"All day?" Kenny echoed. "He would've fried to a crisp in there today."

Berty laughed. "You'n me maybe. Not our Mr Hasso. He's a bit of a lizard that way. Likes it warm."

Gwen handed them tin cups of steaming billy tea, sweetened with condensed milk, stirred with a eucalypt twig.

"What are Saltimbanques?" Annie asked, blowing and sipping.

"That depends," Berty replied. "Going traditional now, we're showfolk, mountebanks, jugglers, acrobats, harlequins, ballerinas and buffoons."

"Clowns?" Kenny asked, missing some of the words.

"Inevitably, Kenny," Berty said. "Ask any juggler who drops his balls."

"Or any ballerina past the point of doing point," one of the others said, laughing. Walter, Danny thought it was.

"We're all just clowns if the figures aren't right," Gwen said, sitting by the fire again. "How's the tea?"

"Great."

"Beaut."

"Terrific, thank you."

Berty got up. "How 'bout you set your cups down awhile and we'll pay a call on Mr Hasso?"

Danny was glad to, if only to get away from the indulgent gaze of the others around the fire. He didn't much like adults having jokes at his expense. Mr Jarvie was bad enough.

Berty led them between the tents towards the middle bus. There was only the dull yellow glow from the back section, but Berty switched on a front cabin light as they climbed in, illuminating bench seats, a fixed table, some fitted cupboards. A door in the wall halfway down its length had a plaque with the name *Bernard Hasso* on it.

"There. Let's see if he's taking visitors." And Berty winked at them as if they knew a lot more about Bernard Hasso's ways than they let on.

He knocked lightly at the door. "Mr Hasso? We've some young visitors from town come callin'."

There was no reply that Danny could hear, but Berty smiled at them and turned the handle, opening the door on an office that took up the whole back half of the bus.

There were bookshelves and charts along the walls, all aglow in the light of two parafin lamps, and a big desk at the far end littered with papers, maps, lists of calculations. Bernard Hasso sat grinning at them with a pen in his hand, a large blacksmith of a man in a grimy sweat-stained shirt and dark pants. Where Berty Green had sharp features, Bernard Hasso had craggy ones, his eyes set deep under heavy black brows and above a full black mustache. It was as if a gypsy and lion-tamer had been blended with one of those dark mysterious Egyptians from either version of *The Mummy*—the 1932 original or the recent 1959 remake Hank Burgess had shown as a midnight double at the Lyceum in town only a month back (surely one of the weirdest choices for a double-feature ever). The smile was amiable enough, but his eyes glittered approvingly at Annie in a way Danny didn't like, the same way the others had looked at her, all except Berty. Hanging on the plywood wall behind the man's chair was a framed picture—a painting of circus figures caught while performing or rehearsing.

"So, kids. What's the verdict? What d'you think of us so far?"

"We haven't seen much yet, Mr Hasso," Kenny said, eager as a puppy.

Bernard Hasso nodded and set down his pen. "Not much to see yet, I'm afraid. "We don't play many towns during the summer."

"Don't see any animals," Kenny rattled on, clearly on automatic.

"Oh, animals come and go. We don't go in for animal acts too much. Not too much."

And Berty Green sniggered.

"You're Saltimbanques," Annie said, as if identifying a rare breed.

"Why yes, Miss—er?"

"Annie. This is Kenny and Danny."

"Miss Annie, yes." He gave glancing nods at the boys, turned his deep-set, black eyes on her again. "That's exactly what we are. Not your usual troupe of wandering players certainly. Saltimbanques every one!" He indicated the framed print on the wall behind him. "Picasso, 1905. *Family of Saltimbanques*. From his pink or rose period. The name is from the Italian *saltimbanco*— coined in 1646 from *saltare*, to leap, *in*, on, *banco*, bench. Leap-on-benches, yessir. Mountebanks, yes, charlatans and quacksalvers—another marvellous word—from the Dutch *kwakzalver*. Ignorant pretenders. Quacks. That's us."

"Do you do magic?" Kenny asked.

Berty Green sniggered again and sat on a bench seat near the door.

"Why yes, Master Kenny. Sometimes we do." Bernard Hasso patted the papers on his desk. "When the planets are right and the wind blows a certain way. Sometimes it just flows out of the land. Real magic, yessir. A fickle thing though sometimes, just like the favours of pretty young ladies."

"You sure made yourselves disappear today," Annie said, with more pluck, Dan thought, than this Mr Hasso expected. There was something going on that Dan didn't entirely understand.

Bernard Hasso frowned, even as his eyes widened and his big smile came back. "Ah, Berty, hear that? Our young friends called earlier. We were remiss."

"Couldn't see anyone," Dan said, feeling both annoyed yet curious. Something *was* going on. Adult stuff, but not like with Mr Jarvie.

The ringmaster nodded. "Off getting supplies probably."

"Sometimes there's a bunyip here in Barrack Creek," Kenny said, determined not to be left out.

"That so, Master Kenny? What sort?"

"I dunno. You got bunyips?"

"Sometimes. Bunyips are easy." Bernard Hasso's dark eyes twinkled and glittered under his heavy brows, and Kenny looked puzzled, as if not sure if the man were making fun of him or not.

"We should be going, Mr Hasso," Annie said, and it struck Dan that she needed to be the one to say it, that he had just been sort of drifting there in this stuffy, closed part of the bus while some other level of exchange had been going on. He wished he could've re-run everything they'd said, but it was too late now.

"Yeah, we should," he heard himself say, just to be out of there.

Dan wasn't really sure why he had to go back that night. A lot of it had to do with Annie, with how Mr Hasso and the troupe had looked at her, with wanting to both keep her safe and impress her. It was just something he had to do.

He didn't stay at Kenny's long. He told Mrs Woke that there were some chores he'd forgotten to get done like he'd promised but that he'd be back later, that Kenny should expect him in their front verandah sleepout as usual. At 10:12 pm he was pedalling out of town on his bike, riding without a light, using what moonlight there was, heading to where the creek and the highway bowed together, the silver tracks cutting between.

Dan figured he didn't have to tell anyone he'd done it, maybe Annie later on. He hurried along under a vast field of stars, watching austrolites streaking down, now and then looking back at Reardon where it made its neat huddle of yellow light in the greater darkness.

Reaching the closest point to the creek, he left his bike just off the road and moved carefully across to where he figured the buses were. The camp was quiet, with a lantern burning and the fire low. The two tents were dark amid the long hulks of the buses. The only other light came from the back of the second bus where Mr Hasso was probably still working on his mysterious calculations.

The odd thing was that no-one slept in the open as you'd expect on such a mild night, arranged about the fire like you did when you camped out. Maybe they were in the third bus—the closed-up one Berty had called the 'darkwagon', sleeping or practising tricks away from prying eyes.

Dan had intended just to look them over again from the safety of darkness, to maybe eavesdrop on conversations and gather more information about the group, but mainly to just get a better feel of the whole thing, to make up for being so out of it in Mr Hasso's office.

It was seeing the dim yellow glow from the second bus that made him cross the creek-bed and go among the darkened shapes. He'd say he'd lost a ring or something if anyone caught him, say he'd come back looking for it, though that would mean he'd have to be using the torch he had in his back pocket, the last thing he wanted to do.

He made it to the second bus, stood beneath the yellow panes, heard the muffled murmur of voices within. But the windows were closed and Danny couldn't make out words. It was infuriating.

Then the office door opened and Bernard Hasso and Berty Green emerged into the front of the bus.

"I want it brought up first thing," Mr Hasso was saying. "Take Walter and Jack. We've got a little over eighteen hours. Mr Atterling's party will be here at 7 o'clock."

"Right," Berty said (Dan almost expected him to say 'Roger that!').

"And I've reconsidered. Tomorrow you will take the mantacycle into town, drum up some local business. We might as well be seen to be earning our way in case folks get to talking."

"Right you are, Mr Hasso. Good night."

"Good night, Berty."

Bernard Hasso went back into his office and closed the door. Berty clambered out of the second bus and headed for the darkwagon.

Danny stood as motionless as possible, vividly aware of his heart pounding, of the torch stuck in his back pocket, of a stone in his left shoe, of how perspiration had to be making his forehead shine in the moonlight through the trees. But Berty passed obliviously by, climbed into the closed-in bus and shut the door behind him. Only then did Danny cross the intervening space and stand beside that third dark vehicle with its faded legend: *The Saltimbanques*, snaking in the darkness—an incantation to the night and all its silence.

It was *too* quiet. There were insect sounds, the usual clicks and chirrups, but absolute silence from the bus, no footsteps, no voices. But it didn't *feel* like the silence of seven sleeping people, rather more like the silence of people standing, waiting inside till he had gone away so they could resume what they'd been doing before. He imagined them there, eyes wide but catching no light whatsoever, the sighted but unseeing eyes of the living trapped in caves, buried in tombs, caught in air pockets in the holds of sunken ships.

Danny moved away as silently as he could, crept back across the creek, taking care to avoid any logs, reached his bike and hurried back to town, finally joining Kenny in their sleepout.

"You sure took your time," Kenny said drowsily as Danny climbed into bed.

"You know what it's like, Kenny. Sometimes you just get caught up."

"Roger that," Kenny said, and slipped off into sleep again.

Danny lay staring at the night, watching the stars move round the sky. When he slept at last, he dreamt he was being chased by a terrible creature called a mantacycle with Berty Green perched on its back. Bernard Hasso sat to one side working on his calculations.

Danny had meant to wake early to go spy on the camp and see what it was Berty and the others had to bring up for Mr Hasso first thing, but when Kenny roused him at 8:06, he knew it would be too late for that.

But Annie called by the clubhouse at 9 o'clock and Dan made sure the three of them were at the northwestern end of town, maybe two hundred yards out, when Berty Green came pedalling in from the direction of the creek.

The mantacycle was quite a sight, a tall four-wheeled contraption at least six feet high and six feet square at the base and tapering in, as rusty and weird-looking as an old torture machine, with arms and overhangs and a dozen flags snaking out from as many flagpoles set into the tube-metal frame, all long, faded pennons: blue, orange, red and purple, curling out behind. The whole thing was like the skeleton of a pyramid hauled up from the bottom of the ocean, and Berty was as extraordinary a sight, bent over the pedals on a small saddle seat, elbows out, legs pumping furiously in the early heat, his long, tattered dustcoat flaring behind him. He was wearing a wide-brimmed hat set with corks on strings, no, not corks—set with dancing, swinging, bleached-white things, bird skulls, Danny saw when the man-tacycle got closer.

Seeing what they were, Danny realised the little man's name was probably Birdy Green, not Berty. Somehow it just tipped everything further over into strange.

"Mornin' to you, kids!" he called when he recognised them, breathing hard and letting the tall vehicle roll to a stop, its four pumped-up tires making their gritty tearing sound on the hot road surface. "You were a big hit with Mr Hasso last night, I have to tell ya. He figured, what the hell, let's put on a show anyway! Seven o'clock tonight. Five bob admission. Go tell your friends!"

"Roger that!" Kenny cried, as Berty—Birdy!—set to pedalling again, and ran off to follow the machine into town, as if there was anything else happening in Reardon this Friday night that might stop folks being available.

In a strange way, standing there in the road with the dust settling around them was the first time Dan had ever felt truly alone with Annie. They watched Birdy ride off with Kenny scrambling back and forth like some native runner in a Jungle Jim movie and the silence just grew up around them, the sense of being together.

"I went back there last night, Annie," he said, expecting her to act annoyed and disappointed.

"So did I," she said.

You could have knocked Danny over. "You what? When? What did you see?" So much for protecting her.

"I went real late. Around midnight, I guess. That Mr Hasso was so creepy, Dan. I just wanted to see the place again."

"See anything?"

"Nope. When did you go?"

Danny told her, describing what he'd heard and felt, growing more and more uneasy at the thought of Annie crouching there in the dark watching the buses and the tents. "What do we do?" he said finally.

Annie shrugged. "I'm just really glad you're here, Dan."

"Me too," Danny said. "That you're here, I mean." And they started walking back towards town.

Birdy Green and his 'Frying' Machine, as townsfolk cheerfully called it (it was 10 am and already 93°), was a definite hit. Locals bought him beers, shouted him an early lunch, offered to give him a tow back. By the time he was pedalling out of town at 11:48, he had two dozen kids straggling along behind like he was some latter-day Pied Piper doing a practice run. Kenny was one of them.

The kids straggled back ten minutes later, dusty and exhausted, and the day settled into its most terrible phase, the heat lending everything its dreamlike shimmer for what Hank Burgess called the 'wait-out'.

"Whatcha doin' after wait-out?" Hank would say from behind the bar at the Stockman Hotel, asking any number of patrons staring up at the big aerial shot of the town as if expecting some trace of Birdy's carnival to suddenly appear like stigmata or a face on a shroud.

"Dunno," most said as usual, though more and more added, "Might give the circus a look-see" and "Yeah, might give the circus a go".

Pete Byles would invariably correct whoever said it. "Ain't a circus, you blokes."

"Must be," someone would invariably answer. "Seen one clown already."

And round it would go, all through the blazing afternoon.

Annie's mum ran the pub's kitchen, so Danny heard part of it when the three Rangers dropped by so Annie could get permission to go see the show. You always remembered to check in when money was involved.

Now that they had a legitimate reason to visit the carnival (and since Kenny was seeing himself as something of a self-appointed sidekick to Birdy Green), the three Rangers went out to the campsite around 6 pm, this time riding their bikes along the highway and leaving them by the road near where it bowed in to meet the railway line.

They were rather surprised to see two tents set up on the flat hard ground this side of the creek, both warmly lit, one quite large and unusually long, the other smaller and square and placed a few feet away from the bigger one like an afterthought.

No-one was about so they looked into the large one first, saw twenty hurricane lamps set on as many supports, warm and welcoming, and lots of benches set up down the far end. All it was really was a large empty space. There was no bunting or posters, no attempt at decoration at all. When they peered into the smaller tent, they saw nothing but one of the bigger, darker logs from the creek. It seemed to swallow the light from the eight lanterns hanging on the uprights. Maybe that's what Birdy had had to carry up.

"Hey, they've got a chain on it!" Kenny said, and laughed. "Maybe they're worried someone'll steal it."

Kenny was right. Around one gnarled length of snapped-off root was an iron ring, with a short chain leading to a spike driven into the hard ground.

"Maybe they're going to turn it into an elephant!" Dan said, more to ease his nerves, he realised, than because he thought it was funny.

Kenny laughed though. "Roger that! Sorry, Annie. Say, why don't we go find Birdy?"

It wasn't a bad idea, Dan thought, given the little man's good humour towards them earlier in the day, and it gave them a reason to cross the creek-bed and go among the buses again, which Danny found was what he wanted to do.

But when they reached the camp, Birdy was nowhere to be seen, which made Danny think of the closed darkwagon and the silence there. The only sign of life was Mr Hasso sitting on the doorsill of the second bus puffing on a pipe.

"Right on time," he said, knocking the pipe against the lowest step to empty it, then getting up. "Come on in awhile. It's almost showtime."

Dan had reservations about going into Mr Hasso's office again, but at the same time wanted to test himself after what had happened the previous night. He followed Annie and Kenny and was soon standing before the ring-master's big desk, littered as before with charts and pages of figures.

But now there was a different picture on the plywood wall behind where Bernard Hasso was once again seated. Smaller than the Picasso, almost a foot on a side, it showed a washed-out grey landscape under a lowering sky, with shapes like polished river pebbles scattered about, dull and metallic-looking, some set on their ends, some more geometric than others, those in the foreground rising up in columns like those limestone shapes you read about, stalagmites. Among the clustering and spill of grey and white forms were a few touches of colour, here a drab yellow stone, there an ochre one, there a pale red trapezoidal shape, but there was only one distinctive focus in the whole moody scene, a rectangular patch of red on the left side, like a window or door or even a mirror in a worn, rolled, leaden frame.

Dan was about the mention it when Mr Hasso clapped his big hands together and grinned at them, his eyes flashing under dark brows.

"Now you see us at our best!" he said. "This is our emergent phase."

Their what? Danny didn't understand what that could mean.

"And the tents over there?" Annie asked. "All part of your calculations?"

"Exactly so, Annie. Position is crucial. Always crucial. What do they say: time, place and identity, that's what it's all about. You kids won't know it but the layout of Reardon configures to the sacred geometry of the Vesica, quite by accident, mind you, purest chance, sweetest serendipity. A circle, a square, a triangle, a rhombus, a hexagram and polygons all tipped in together."

"Is that good?" Kenny asked.

"Oh surely it is, Kenny. Very much so. And just there where the road bends in to the creek with the tracks between, we have a most wonderful confirmation of Bruno Taut's *Stadtkrone*, can you believe it? If only I could convey even a fraction of what it means to us—the theosophical blend of ley-line traditions and geomantic corridors with the *axis urbis* of imperial Rome. The cityline. Cities built along lines of force. The ancient scemb lines. No wonder all these crackpot doctrines sprang up, spring up and will forever do so. How else to interpret the truth. But I do forget myself, going on like this. Kenny, Birdy says you were a great help today. How would you like to assist him with his final preparations now?"

"That'd be great! We didn't see him round though."

"Oh, you'll find him, I'm sure. Off you go. You'll see your friends again when the show starts."

"Hey, roger that!" Kenny cried as he left the office. "See ya!"

Danny heard him clamber out of the bus, heard a dwindling, somehow disturbing: "Hey, Birdy! Hey, Birdy, wait up!"

Now Mr Hasso's smile changed, or rather changed at the eyes, which glittered full of unreadable emotion.

"You changed the picture," Danny said, partly to relieve the tension, the dreadful awkwardness he felt, partly out of determination to stay with it this time no matter what happened.

"I did. We always do. Yves Tanguy, 1954. *The Saltimbanques*. What do you think of it, Danny?"

"It's strange. I prefer the other one."

"The Picasso. You do? Tell me what you see in this one."

Danny studied the strangely lit plain, the clustered eroded shapes and spires in the foreground, the scattered ones farther out, the dramatic patch of red in its frame.

"It's like things waiting for other things to arrive."

"And when they do?" Mr Hasso's voice was rich, his words lulling, soothing. Danny concentrated on the shapes, partly wishing Annie would chip in, partly wanting to impress her and hide the fact that he was truly and deeply afraid.

"I don't know. They change. They grow."

"I see. And the patch of red?"

Danny knew he'd be asked that. "Energy. Force. Or something has scratched through the surface. Made a door maybe. Something showing through under the grey. Peeking through."

"Mr Jarvie never knew what a smart student he had, did he, Dan? Now tell me. Did you find your ring?"

"My what?"

"Last night when you came back to pay us a visit. Did you find your ring?"

Danny felt the clutch of panic, pulled back from the picture, from Mr Hasso's incredible voice and eyes and saw that Annie wasn't standing next to him.

"Where's Annie?" he cried. "What have you done with Annie?"

"You didn't hear her? She said she had to—you know—use our convenience."

Danny didn't believe him for a moment. "And where's that?"

Bernard Hasso gestured casually. "Back over there a ways. She'll only be a minute."

"Mr Hasso, what's going on?"

"What do you feel is happening, Danny Truswell?"

"I didn't tell you my last name!"

"Birdy picked it up in town." An answer for everything.

Did not, Danny wanted to shout right into his face, tried to recollect what else he had to remember, something Mr Hasso had just now said. He was forgetting again. Forgetting to notice things. Like Annie going off, leaving the office. She couldn't have. Wouldn't have. Then how—?

"I asked what you feel is happening, Dan," Mr Hasso said, snaring him again with that way he had, killing thoughts by imposing others.

"Something's pushing through," Danny answered.

"Almost right. Almost got it. Now forget the red bit."

How could he? Danny stared at the picture, just couldn't help it.

"Something's getting nearer."

"Now that's really got it!" Bernard Hasso said, seeming genuinely pleased. "Slouching towards Reardon to be born. Something very pure. A network of energy, Dan. Moving across the land, travelling in lines. Lines of force. Spotlights of magic. Some of us know how to plot 'em, track 'em, use 'em. We travel the grid. Sometimes we follow, sometimes we wait for them to catch us up. It's what gives history its buzz and fizz, Danny, me pure boy! Shamans and wizards! Smart old codgers figurin' out the conjunctions. Merlin having a good day. Sacerdotes and mages, seers, sibyls and sorcerers all waiting for auspicious windows of opportunity, knowing how to play the game. Oh, it's an art, I tell ya!"

Dan tried to imagine lines of force, thought of moving spotlights of magic, and something else.

I didn't tell him my last name.

"It's supernatural then!" he managed to say.

"No, it's not! That's precisely *not* what it is. Once your so-called supernatural manifests itself then it's *natural*, don't you see? *Part* of nature. This isn't nonsense about mummies responding to ancient curses. This is things happening as they always happen whether we notice them or not. It's like forgetting to notice gravity because it's always there, or what the Moon's tidal pull does to your body, or negative ions from thunderstorms. This isn't quackery, Dan. Not this! We travel the grid, flexing muscles most of us never get to try, meeting lots of different people, looking for those who think the same way we do, keeping an eye out for apprentices, too, though we're very picky there. Taking turns in trying to pass it on."

Dan was hearing yet not hearing, snared by the smooth round stones, the shadowy sky, the clustering shapes.

"Now Mr Atterling is a politician, see, and this show's really being put on for him. He's one of those secret-handshake Freemason mystic types too, you see, Danny, but he doesn't know how to use it. So it'll do us all good to keep him careful and in his place, in awe of the way it is. Make 'im think it's us. Pay to get bits of it. But for us, for me, it has to be pure, Danny, you do understand that. It's important you do."

Danny understood stones and sky and a shadowy distance, disturbing weights, curves and edges, a comforting patch of red. Though he did hear, part of him did.

"Whatever happens, Dan," Mr Hasso was saying, kindly enough it seemed, "it's all for a good cause. Now you run along and find your friends."

Danny stumbled from the office, blinking, shaking his head, trying to fathom what it had all been, nearly fell out of the bus.

Spotlights of magic. Moving. Getting closer.

The carnival following them.

These Saltimbanques.

The spotlights.

The lanterns. Dan noticed the lamps hanging in the trees, hanging from the buses, lighting the tents across the way, noticed how the words on the long bus sides seemed brighter, richer, firmer. So magical.

The Saltimbanques.

Performing in spotlights. Moving about. What *had* Mr Hasso said?

Kenny was there then, grinning, excited, seeming too young all of a sudden, just too too young.

"Danny, hi!"

"You seen Annie, Ken?"

Kenny shrugged and grinned. "Think I saw her over at the big tent. Lots of people are arrivin'. You're getting sweet on her, Dan!"

"Hey, she's a Ranger too! Just want to know where she is."

Kenny's grin became a leer. "Whatever you say. But ain't that closed-up bus weird?"

"Sure is. Why, do you reckon?"

Again Kenny shrugged. "Dunno. Just don't like goin' near it. It's real quiet. Spooky."

Like someone's waiting in there, Danny thought. Listening. "You keep clear of it, Kenny, okay?"

"Don't have to tell me. See you at the show."

"See you."

By the time Danny reached the big tent, there were well over two hundred people either crowded on the makeshift benches at the far end or standing along the sides, talking and laughing, poking good-natured fun at the modest set-up. Dan hurried to join them, unable to see Annie in the crowd but sure she'd be there waiting for the show to get underway. After what Kenny had said, he was sort of glad she didn't come over to join him, though another part of him wished she would.

He'd just squeezed in between two kids he knew on one of the front benches when he noticed the four serious-looking men in crumpled dark suits seated further along the row: no doubt Mr Atterling and his party. They were definitely from out of town and were clearly impatient; one of the men kept looking at his watch and muttering to his companions.

When Bernard Hasso entered the tent, it was without a fanfare of any kind. He just strode in looking appropriately splendid in black tails and top-hat, carrying a glossy ebony cane with a silver ferrule at one end, a faceted crystal knob at the other. It glittered and shone in the lamplight.

The chatter subsided immediately. People were grinning. This was more like it.

There ought to be a spotlight, Danny thought, seeing the ringmaster standing before them all. He looks good but he should be standing in a spotlight.

"Ladies and gentlemen, boys and girls," Bernard Hasso said in his rich and wonderful voice. "Welcome, one and all! We are The Saltimbanques. Nature's clowns and mountebanks. We have travelled the highways and byways of Australia to be here tonight, to offer an entertainment to the good folk of Reardon. The time is right for magic and merriment once again!"

And he held his arms wide, the crystal knob of his cane twinkling with lamplight. There was no fanfare, but there was a sense of one as the performers ran into the tent: Walter, Haunted Jack and Gwen to the left, Robert, May and Jeffrey to the right, all wearing loose, brightly coloured bodysuits, stitched all over with shapes and signs like Danny drew with his compass set at school, arcs intersected by straight lines.

All but Mr Hasso himself ran down the length of the tent to shake hands with members of the audience, then, after pinching cheeks and tweaking noses and pulling coloured kerchiefs from the pockets of some of the children, they all rushed back to form up around Bernard Hasso near the entrance.

"Here it comes!" the ringmaster cried, and began twirling his cane, making a Catherine Wheel of flashing light as his troupe began making a human pyramid to one side, Haunted Jack supporting the other six as they climbed aloft to compose themselves in a very impressive display.

Something was wrong about it though, Danny realised. He had done a bit of balancing at school, and this looked like it should topple over any second. But there was Haunted Jack holding them all, and now raising his left leg, supporting the whole thing, *and* going up on his toes.

And—was Dan really seeing it?—now raising his right leg, so the whole pattern of human forms was just hanging in the air, all strobed by the dazzling twirl of Mr Hasso's cane.

It couldn't be.

Everyone was leaning forward trying to be sure of what they were seeing.

That's when Danny noticed how close and warm it was, and that the air smelled of woodsmoke and resin and something else. He kept blinking and sniffing to make sure of what was going on.

These hardly appeared to be the same people as the night before. They all seemed taller, stronger, not so much younger as more, well, in control, focused, powerful. They radiated confidence and energy.

And just how had the hovering pyramid been dismantled? For now Haunted Jack balanced Walter and an improbably nimble and alluring Gwen more skillfully than he'd seemed capable of sitting around the campfire that first night. Robert was juggling twenty balls with casual recklessness, an almost disdainful smirk on his face. May and Jeffrey strode about on stilts, seemed to fall, would catch one another, then go teetering and tottering towards those standing along the sides at that end of the tent before steadying themselves and staggering back the other way. Now Birdy made his appearance, running about in his long coat and bird-skull hat and flinging buckets of confetti over the laughing onlookers.

At first glance, apart from the opening pyramid, the acts weren't anything special, though if you did look close, you started to notice things, how every now and then May and Jeffrey would lean too far over on their stilts yet not fall, or how one of Robert's hands would lift to wave at someone in the crowd or mop his brow without disturbing the steady flow of the balls. Even when Birdy substituted warm perfumed water for the confetti, the audience responded with delight.

There was a drunkenness, a euphoria surrounding everything. The air became heavier, smokier, dimmer. The lanterns had haloes. The resin smell was stronger than ever. People were still blinking and squinting to be sure of what was going on, but no-one complained, no little kids cried, no-one got up to leave. It was as if they were in the presence of magic and knew it, and all wanted part of it.

And the players came ever closer as the evening progressed, moving from the far end of the tent towards the benches.

Spotlights of magic.

Danny found himself remembering bits of what Mr Hasso had said. Something about moving points of energy.

The performers were getting nearer. Soon they'd be clambering over the benches.

No, Danny realised. The show would end first. The smaller tent was next-door—*in a straight line to this one!*

What was it Mr Hasso had said about ley-lines and the *urbis axis*? Cities built in lines.

More to the point, why would he have told him?

There was no time to consider it further, for once again Mr Hasso had his arms raised, and his voice was rumbling in the silence.

"Our final treat, ladies and gentlemen, boys and girls, is in the tent next door. Yes, the Barrack Creek Bunyip itself ! But it's one at a time, I'm afraid, bunyips being nocturnal and shy creatures when a crowd's around."

Muttering and exchanging uncertain smiles, the townsfolk filed out of the long tent and formed a queue outside the smaller one. Just as

Mr Hasso had stipulated, one person was allowed in at a time, to emerge a short while later blinking, with looks of puzzlement on their faces as if not quite sure what they'd seen.

"Keep it short, folks!" Robert kept saying from his place by the entrance. "There's lots of people so keep it short!"

"What did you see? What did you see?" younger kids were calling, eager for their turns, but it was clear that those who'd been inside didn't know what to say and just went off looking bewildered and smiling sheepishly to join relatives and friends.

Danny held back, hoping to see Annie, to share as much of the experience together as Robert made possible.

"You there! Danny!" Robert called. "You wanna see the bunyip or not? You'll need to be quick. Show's over in a few minutes."

Danny pushed into the tent, smelled resin almost immediately, saw the lamps had haloes, saw the log over by the tent's far wall. Someone had moved it; the chain was stretched at full length. That was all.

"Too bad, kiddo," Robert said, right behind him. "Too late, I reckon. Maybe next time."

Danny was glad to be out of there, was relieved to see Kenny right in front of him, a few feet away, noticed too over near the large tent, Mr Hasso shaking hands with the men in Mr Atterling's party. They no longer looked bored or impatient but were smiling and nodding as they started walking back towards their car.

"Did you see it, Danny?" Kenny asked. "The bunyip, did ya?"

"I missed it. What did you see?"

Kenny frowned and got a silly grin on his face. "I dunno. Hard to describe it really. But it was real neat."

That's when Mr Hasso came over. "Right then, Dan. Thought Kenny might like to help Birdy and the others strike the tents while you and me walk a bit and continue our discussion from before."

And before Kenny could express his pleasure at being a carny roustabout, Danny got in with it first. "Roger that!"

Kenny stared at him in amazement, unable to believe what he'd heard.

Mr Hasso slapped Dan on the shoulder. "That's the way! Never know when you can use twice the pure!"

Danny looked straight at Kenny. "Roger that, too, Mr Hasso!"

And they walked off, leaving Kenny Woke staring after them in confusion and disbelief.

Moments later, Mr Hasso and Danny had left the others and were moving along the creek-bed. Almost all the townsfolk had gone, walking or driving back to town. A few headlights could still be seen heading off to distant properties, and if anyone noticed three bikes left by the highway they would've paid no mind. It was summer holidays, barely 10 pm, and with the days so hot, kids stayed up till all hours.

All Danny could hear apart from their footsteps and the occasional insect sound were members of the troupe calling to one another as they brought down the tents. The voices faded with distance.

"Twice the pure, Dan," Bernard Hasso said, guiding him with a hand on his shoulder. "That's the way. Still workin' on that part of it—why that kind of sacrifice is the best way to go, why sacrifice is necessary at all really. Like to think it's like the Indians killing a buffalo, you know, making an offering to the Buffalo Spirit. Then there's the alchemical angle, reconciling the opposites, and the geomantic tradition. There's just so much to know. But, hey, so long as it works, I say. What d'you reckon, Dan? Ah, but here we are."

Another tent stood in the middle of the creek, square and dark in the thin moonlight.

"In you go, boy," Mr Hasso said. "Don't keep her waiting." And he lit the single hurricane lamp hanging on its wire hook, illuminating the only two things inside.

One of them was Annie Hendist, sitting in the middle of the dirt floor, bound hand and foot, a hankie tied in her mouth. The other was a large black tree-trunk, hooked and broken, shaped by some past flooding, just lying there. The tent had been set up around it.

In line with the other tents, Danny knew.

He hurried across to Annie, pulled the hankie from between her teeth and started freeing her while Mr Hasso took the lantern outside with him and began lacing the tent flaps together behind him. "Won't keep you long," he said, then the lamp was extinguished, plunging them into darkness, and Dan heard footsteps moving away.

"Oh, Dan!" Annie said, grabbing his arm, standing close. "I've been so scared!"

"What happened?" Dan was vividly aware of her.

"I—I'm not sure. One moment I was in the bus with you and Mr Hasso. Then they'd brought me here. I was so terrified, Dan. They just left me here. I didn't know what they'd do."

"It's okay, Annie. You're safe now. It's okay now." *So aware of her.*

She continued gripping his arm. He could feel her breath on his cheek. "Do you know what's goin' on, Dan?" she asked.

He didn't. He did. He tried to think back, almost had it. It was gone, then bits slipped back again.

"It's something about spotlights of energy. Moving in lines. They follow them." He was surprised to hear himself saying it. "Go from place to place, keeping up. They use it, Annie."

"For what?"

"Everything. Their performance. They were so different, so— changed. And that long tent, remember? Everyone was down one end. Their performance got closer and closer. Then it moved to the bunyip tent."

"The what tent?"

"The smaller tent. The one with the log chained down." And Danny went silent a moment. "Like this one."

Annie's eyes twinkled in the dimness. "This one isn't chained."

"I know."

They peered off to where the hooked, torn silhouette of the old log showed against the moonlit east side of the tent.

"How long we got?" Annie asked him.

"I lose track of time whenever I'm with Hasso. An hour or two. I don't know how long it takes. Let's try to get out of here."

The sturdy canvas walls had been spiked through brass eyelets on the ground outside; the lacing on the flaps was knotted outside as well. The central and corner uprights were simply too thick and too well planted to break or dislodge, and repeated running against the tent's sides seemed to have no effect at all.

They were standing by the entrance, trying to work the lacing rope so the knot was nearer, when they heard it.

Barely heard it, for it was the softest wrenching, the slightest sound of twisting.

They stared at each other, then at the shape.

And saw one of the snapped-off roots at the top move, twist.

The log was alive.

They could hear it creaking as it lifted slightly, testing the life it had, then heard a scrape, and another. There were a few pounding heartbeats of silence, then a third scrape, this time louder, harsher as it gouged the ground where it lay, made with the determination of something *discovering* itself alive, filled with the desperate chance to live again as something so new.

Annie grabbed Danny by both arms this time.

"You believing all this, Dan?" she said. Such an odd question now.

"Of course."

"He wants us 'cause we're pure, Danny. That's what he told me. You know what that means?"

"Yeah. Sure. Course I do."

"And are you?"

"What? Me? Yes. Of course. You?" He would never have dreamed of asking it. That sort of directness was four, six, ten years in his future at least.

"You know it. Quickly. Take off your shorts!"

Perhaps it was what they did then, perhaps it was Kenny arriving in time, perhaps the enlivening energy simply moved on, but Kenny Woke *was* suddenly there, stirred from his hero-worship of Birdy Green by Danny using *his* signature line like that—a sailor's SOS, a flyer's Mayday, a carny's Hey Rube!—fumbling at the tent rope, undoing the flaps, never noticing how Danny and Annie checked their clothing as they left the tent.

It all remained so dreamlike and uncertain, what happened in those few days, what Mr Jarvie later described as "smoke and mirrors" when school started back, just "so much hypnosis and hallucination".

The heat and the sameness of the days soon wore it down all the more. Blokes at the bar of the Stockman Hotel stopped peering into the aerial shot of Reardon, began looking at their beers again as they talked, and when Danny reminded people (even Kenny) about the carnival that had played out near Barrack Creek, they said, "Oh yeah", as if it had happened years ago not weeks, but sure, of course they remembered it. But what else could you expect in a land where the heat doomed normal folk to the limbo of wait-out, blurred grain trucks and silos into dragons, burred every lonely windmill into Don Quixote tilting at himself ?

And just like that, Annie went off to stay with her aunt in Mildura for a while, which was no big deal, she'd done it often enough before, but she didn't say goodbye and it just pushed the whole thing further across into unreality and lack of proper consequence.

Then Mr Hasso's letter came.

> *Dear Daniel,*
>
> *We pay our price too. Forfeit things like families. Something to do with the energy, May says, probably where the notion of changelings comes from down through the ages. But no Dannys, Kennys or Annies for The Saltimbanques unless we borrow, find apprentices however we can. Where else do you think we come from? It's the other thing we do. You didn't disappoint us, Dan. The magic passed through you. The child will always be drawn to magic. For that, our heartfelt thanks.*
>
> *Bernard Hasso*
>
> *PS: The 'bunyip' was just to motivate, you understand. Excuse the theatrics.*

For a moment Danny actually thought the 'child' reference was to him, but the postscript stole that in an instant. There was only one thought then, a question, desperate, bittersweet and somehow extending his whole life out into something infinitely, ultimately beyond Reardon.

Had she known all along?

In the space it took to read the few dozen words, Danny learned two crucial things, vital to learn at any age but so powerful to have at fourteen, that you always had to grant unlimited possibility, and that happy endings were as fleeting as you let them be. If not protected, they vanished out of lives like the bunyips along Barrack Creek.

They Found The Angry Moon

THE ANGRY MOON was not where old Tanner had said it would be. It was seven streets due east of his given location, and if Andy Lynch and Pete had followed the old man's hastily scrawled map they would never have found it.

"Y'see, Petey," seasoned thief, thug, hitman Andy Lynch explained to his accomplice as they entered Carlotta Lane, walking because there was nowhere to park in these dark and narrow streets so close to the harbour (nowhere safe from others like Andy Lynch and Pete Dudley, if the truth be told). "Old Tanner knew we was gonna do 'im. He reckoned on that, figured it 'cos of the types we were. He read us as types even before we killed his dog like that."

"Yeah," Pete said, remembering the poor dog. *We* killed it. Whatever you say, Andy. And Pete, only two months younger than Andy, but a thousand years younger really when it came to being street-wise, hard-edged, a survivor; caught between an unthinking, all-accepting eagerness and a dread of all the things it meant, found himself wishing, wishing, wishing he were away from all this, that he'd never taken on the job.

But assured, accomplished Andy Lynch always knew how to coax Pete into a "quick evenin's work," knew the exact way, the precise touch-points of Pete Dudley's soul. It had been like that for twenty years, ever since primary school. Pete had always been in Andy's gang (and Andy had always had a gang), the gopher, the volunteer, the eternal legman. Andy had always squeezed his soul, right from the start, known the ways—when to caress, when to hit hard, when to hurt him, shame him, build him up.

And Pete knew it, but was helpless in the face of it.

"Y'see, Petey m'boy," Andy continued (Pete hated that more than Petey), "we is known types. Remember I said it. Everythin' about us shows what we are. But what ol' Tanner didn't reckon on was we saw 'im as a type too. Stubborn. We got to 'is daughter and granddaughter first."

"They'd be dead by now, wouldn't they, Andy?"

"Sure as anythin', mate. Maybe if they were conscious in time. Maybe if the cement was still too wet. But don't fret yourself, Petey. You were outside. I'm t'blame, remember? You weren't really there."

"I was there," Pete said. "I was there for the dog too."

"Okay," Andy said, changing tactics. "But you came through, right? When I needed you, you came through. An' I'm not forgettin' it. No sir. You got a full share comin' this time."

"Sure." Pete muttered the word, wishing again, wishing for the hundredth, thousandth, ten-thousandth time that he could slip, run, jump free of Andy Lynch, that he had the pluck, the courage, the simple human decency to refuse, to lose the only person who had ever even pretended to be his friend.

Better the gopher, the volunteer, the eternal legman, than to be alone, Pete knew. Better the 'quick evenin's work' when it came, the sly coaxing and the rough cruel camaraderie of Andy Lynch, than the dingy second-storey bedsitter, the TV, the porno magazines, the numbing cycle of the evenings, those tiresome empty evenings at the end of empty days, the loneliness without end.

At least Andy never called him Stinky or Roach or Ugly Dudley. At least that. Not since primary school anyway. Twenty years of small mercies there in one hit. Reason enough right there to owe Andy Lynch.

"There it is," Andy said, touching him on the arm, actually touching him, the only person ever to do that as well. "Has to be. Carlotta's what the granddaughter said."

The tavern was hardly a hospitable sight, Pete saw, stuck back out of the main street like that. The dim light above the wooden door threw yellow slashes across the wet cobbles, sent fans of sickly light up the rime-covered walls of the harbour warehouses to either side. A forbidding place.

There was a faded wooden sign facing out at them on an iron frame, a square of wood with a barely visible orange circle and some words painted on it. Even from the end of the street they could see the curve of a grin on the circle, like a badly faded Smiley Face, Pete thought.

"Doesn't look too angry as moons go," Andy said as they moved in closer. "Not sleepy, not sad or reflective. What d'ya think, Petey? Not even pensive, as your scholars would say. Not even a pensive moon, Petey."

Pete swore, but swallowed the word as he always did when he cursed Andy Lynch. Andy went on like this all the time, using odd words and phrases, showing off how he read books. Well, Pete had read books too. Real books. Quite a few over the years.

But Andy kept on. "I'd say this is a Happy Moon, Petey. Nothin' we can't handle."

Pete thought it looked downright sinister, too much out of place with the surroundings and all. No place to put a tavern. But, relentless as ever, Andy led them towards it, straight over the cobbles until the weak yellow light set its sickly pallor on them as well and they could read the three words above the Smiley Face.

"Hah!" Andy said, scanning the words and laughing. "*The Happy Sun*! What d'ya make of that, Petey?"

"It's the wrong place," Pete said, looking up at the image, the cracked and faded picture of a very happy sun—what he could see of it through the grime—with full cheeks, a wide grin, and eyes nearly shut with mirth; the face framed with small curling licks of fire, the whole thing beaming forth at them cheerfully.

"Rubbish it is!" Andy said. "It's the opposite, y'see? Just an opposite. One of Tanner's jokes, disguisin' the name. They play tricks like that all the time in old maps, reversin' things, giving cryptic clues."

"This is weird, Andy. It's as if—"

"C'mon, Petey!"

"But, Andy—"

"Hey, don't make me sorry I brought you along, okay?"

Pete felt the sudden stab of alarm. Don't push it, don't push it, he told himself.

And reading that alarm for exactly what it was, Andy became easy again, friendly and concerned.

"Is it the poem in Tanner's book? Is that what's goosin' ya? The Waiting Room?"

"I dunno," Pete said, trying to relax. He was usually happy to let Andy soothe him. He looked forward to it, deliberately feigning funk sometimes, but only so far, never overdoing it. It was part of an unspoken arrangement. This time was different though. Andy saw that.

"Like I said, mate. Tanner was a type. He had the money stashed where the daughter said it would be; he had the book like she said. The rest of the stash is in here. That's where Tanner's strongbox is."

And as if that answered even a part of what Pete felt, Andy laid his hand on the door handle and let them into the tavern.

The common room was quiet and dimly lit. And strange, Pete thought. Decidedly queer. Above the bar were gourd masks, very Polynesian-looking, but with a curious glazed finish—"lacquer of hearts," the notion came, from where Pete had no idea. Probably Andy-talk filtering back, or something he'd read himself. There were some tall pewter beer steins lined up too, but all with long doleful faces on them, so that they glowered and gloomed like mournful coffee-pots. Very odd.

The queerest thing, Pete decided, was the light. What there was of it in this old inn, this "place of careful, controlled shadows" (more sudden information in Pete's mind; it terrified him), seemed to get in behind the lines of bottles on the shelves and glow at him as emeralds and rubies and amethysts, as softly-glowing topaz and tiger's eye. The common room glowed from the walls as if with hidden lighting.

What was it the poem said in the front of Tanner's book, the words he had tried to say before he died?

The Waiting Room at The Angry Moon
Is lit with a baleful glow...

Andy must have recalled the poem too. He grunted.

"Hm. Look at these," he said, indicating the displays on the side walls next to the bar—some large copper plates, again showing what looked like faces but with whole pie-slices missing, like unfinished zodiacs or those pie-graphs economists use. Pete had seen plenty of those in newspapers.

On some of the simple wooden tables there were displays as well: here a puzzle-box of interleaved metal shapes, a hopeless tangle; there, near it, a compressed block arrangement—a shape made up of fitted metal segments. And there, incredibly, a human heart in a jar of formaldehyde, and at a table over there a small stoppered bottle resting on a velvet cushion, held upright by a four-legged metal retort bolted to the table and giving off a dusty yellow light from within, as if a candle flickered there behind the grime of years. Other things as well, off in the gloom.

There were no customers, which was understandable, Pete thought, with surroundings like these. The centre of town had shifted long ago, away from this part of the harbour, out near the airport and the container terminals. No proprietor either...

"Can I help you, gentlemen?"

The dark man was there, squeezed out of a corner behind the bar where the strange light didn't quite reach. A wizened ancient man, a narrow band of shadow precisely suited to such a peculiar domain.

Andy Lynch had something he could deal with.

"Ah, yes. Good evenin' to you, innkeeper. It's Mr..."

"Crick."

"Crick, isn't it? M'mate and I are friends of Bert Tanner's. He sent us over to pick up—ah—let me get this right—some merchandise. A box. Pretty valuable, he said. Gave us a poem from his book to establish our bona fides."

"Did he?" Crick said, moving along behind the bar from his tight dark comer, gliding along like token night before a coloured line of days (more bizarre associations flashing through Pete's mind—where did these queer thoughts come from?).

"Yes, sir," Andy said, smiling. "Said you might show us around a bit too. Show us more of the Waiting Room here."

"Oh. The Waiting Room. Bert said I might, did he?"

"That's right. If it's no trouble."

"Hm. Well, maybe," old Crick said, rubbing his sharp grizzled chin with one hand. "Since Bert mentioned the Waiting Room and told you the poem."

Andy reached for the pocket of his jacket. "Do you want me to read it—?"

"Not yet," Crick said. "Have a drink first. I've got one or two things to see to."

"Sure," Andy said, grinning. "Why not? Petey and me could stand a hit. We've had a busy evenin'."

Crick nodded, still behind the bar. "No doubt. What will you take?"

Andy looked up at the shelves and chuckled, and Pete immediately understood Andy's line of thought. Too obvious, too obvious, Andy, but Andy could judge such things better than Pete could.

"A scotch on the rocks for me," Andy said brightly. "Pete here will have a beer."

Crick shook his sharp narrow head. "Sorry. We don't get many customers in, so we don't keep the usual trade lines anymore. There's just our own night wine, the Harsh Black and the Spangle, or our cellar brew, but I can't vouch for that."

"Harsh Black," Pete said.

"The Spangle," said Andy Lynch.

Crick turned back to the shelves. "Take a seat. Any table you like."

And he began gliding before the bottles again, with the same smooth uncanny motion.

Pete opened his mouth to say something about it to Andy, but thought better of it.

"We'll be over here," Andy called to old Crick. "With the fireflies."

"The what?" Pete said, following Andy but with his mind still on the old man.

"The fireflies! The bug-bottle," Andy said, moving to one particular table, taking a seat before the small flickering bottle held upright on its worn cushion by the metal retort. He tapped the grimy yellow-lit glass with a dirty fingernail, making the candle or whatever it was—fireflies!—dance within. He peered in close, trying to see what caused the light, then gave up and sat back.

"Do y'see those pie-slice plates on the wall, Petey? Silver, I'm bettin'. The weird coffee pots too. Tanner was right. Y'got his poem?"

"Sure," Pete said, and dug out the scrap of paper, glad to be free of it.

Andy took it from him, unable to resist making a small grimace of distaste because it had come from Pete's pocket—one of Andy's ways of never letting Pete forget how it really was.

Andy opened the paper out and read the words aloud.

"The Waiting Room at The Angry Moon
Is lit with a baleful glow,
Down the corridor to the curving floor
Is where the damned ones go.
A soul comes in, a soul goes out
With burning gold between,
A burning gold, an ancient gold
With edges very keen."

Pete followed the words for a while, but a part of his mind stayed with the figure across the room, now opening bottles, old dark bottles, now pouring, now sealing them again and placing them back on the shelves where they shone dully once more.

Then Crick was appearing round from behind the bar, and for an instant, the barest, most vivid split-second, Pete had double-vision. He saw a normal old man emerge, a drink in either hand, knees slightly bent, but at the same time there was something horrific underlying that: a figure without legs at all, a torso with hip stumps set into a tall tube frame on castors, impossible to balance really with the centre of gravity so high, but Pete thought he saw it all the same, and it chilled him to his heart.

The weird light again, Pete told himself. Playing tricks. Don't trouble Andy. Lots of people have that underwater gliding motion—ballroom dancers, mimes…dancers. All sorts of people.

"One Harsh Black, one Spangle," old Crick said, placing the glasses on the table. He stood there then, rubbing his grizzled chin again. "So Bert trusts you?"

"Sure, Mr Crick," Andy said, his voice confident and easy. "We used to do errands for his daughter. She put in a word for us, recommended us. Bert had no complaints. He said to bring you the poem and collect his box. Something like that. You probably know what 'e means. He said we'd be interested in seeing the Waiting Room too."

Crick looked about him, studied the dimly glowing walls.

"I'll get the box," he said. "I'll just be a moment."

He left them, moved behind the bar and vanished into the shadowed alcove there.

Andy and Pete sat sipping their night wine, thinking their separate thoughts.

Pete tried to relax, but the room had him—the whole tavern-dockside world had him, had him drawn as tight as a bowstring.

When he thought about it, he realised he knew quite a bit about strange things. He'd watched *Great Mysteries of the World* on TV. He'd seen specials about the Bermuda Triangle and people taken up by UFOs, skimmed books about the Mayans, Easter Island and the Pyramids, Nostradamus, things like that, and this place was strange, dangerously strange.

He couldn't get used to it, no matter how he tried. Look around, and there was always something—a pie-slice plate leering at you, maimed and frightening, or the metal puzzle-box, drawn-in and knotted, swallowing itself like that, or the steel segmented block thing, all squashed and sealed, making Pete feel—what?—a terrible pressure, a weird constriction in his throat like it was making him forget to breathe.

Pete gulped the last of his drink, intently studying the different table displays. The jar with the heart floating in it sent a chill through him. Not only because of the grisly object within, but because the shape of the jar reminded him of the bottle of sleeping pills he'd nearly taken that stupid, achingly lonely night when Andy hadn't showed up when he'd promised.

The heart seemed to glow, but that was probably the pearly embalming fluid twisting the light from the walls. Come to think of it, the squashed segmented block two tables away also had a sheen to it, as if lit from within its cold blue steel parts, light sealed in under pressure. And Pete found himself mesmerised in turn by the hour-glass tube thing with the dark oil coiling through it; the oil pooled blackly in the bottom cup, and—yes—there too was lodged a bead of the deepest green light, like a lonely torch shining up from the bottom of some ocean.

Why didn't Andy feel it? Pete wondered. Andy sat there watching the curtained alcove where Crick had vanished, sipping his drink now and then and idly tap-tap-tapping the flickering bottle before them.

The curtain stirred, and Crick appeared holding a steel box. He came towards them around the bar, and once again Pete caught a glimpse of Crick-on-wheels. It sent a thrill of terror up his spine, tingled and tightened the skin at his temples, even gripped his balls.

The drink, he told himself. This bloody wine Crick served us!

Andy! What do you see, Andy?!

Crick came up, rolled up, walked up, smiling, holding the box out for Andy to take.

"Here it is," the old man said. "Since you have the poem. If you'd be so good as to take it back to Bert for me."

"Glad to, Mr Crick," Andy said, taking the box and setting it down before him. "But shouldn't we be checking the contents together and issuing bona fides t'each other?" He tried the lid, found it locked.

Crick reacted at the suggestion, but it was so hard to read the emotions that passed across the sharp lined face that Pete couldn't tell what that reaction was.

"Very well," Crick said. "Why not?"

"We'll need the key then," Andy said, trying the lid again, using his best candy-from-babies voice, wearing the same winning smile he'd worn when Tanner had died, when he was smoothing the cement over the buried women in the kiln in Tanner's basement.

Crick chuckled, muttering to himself. "The box is its own key."

"What's that?" Andy said, still fiddling with the lid.

Crick gave his odd smile, and repeated his words, though this time, Pete was certain, one word was different. "The box has its own key. You'll get the knack of it."

Andy looked across at Pete, and Pete knew this was the moment.

"Go check the street, Petey," Andy said, right on cue. "We wouldn't want someone comin' in while we're doin' this."

And he gave Pete a wink, the same wink he'd given just before Bert Tanner had let them in.

Pete rose and headed for the door, happy to leave Andy to deal with Crick, to handle the bad stuff as usual, knowing too that now Andy could pocket any special items from the haul.

Pete didn't care about that. He never cared. At least Andy would give him something.

Pete opened the heavy door, stepped out, and closed it behind him, to stand looking down the deserted laneway, noticing the wetly glistening cobbles, hearing the drip of water somewhere, a far-off harbour bell chiming forlornly through the mist.

It was cold now, and Pete slapped his arms and sides for warmth. He glanced around him, then looked up at the sign fitted in its frame above the door, and for the first time saw that there was a reverse side to it, a side facing in to the wall. Barely visible on that hidden other side was the smiling sun image again, with the same words: *The Happy Sun*, but upside-down this time, all upside-down.

Pete was puzzled by that, then noted the central pin on the side of the frame, and a movable holding flange at the bottom, then saw the extent to which the sign frame protruded from the wall above the tavern door.

The sign rotates! he realised. I'm seeing the first side turned over!

Pete ventured out on the street a few steps, knowing what he'd see when he looked up.

It was a moon. A grizzled sharp scowling crescent of a moon in profile, painted in drab silver on black, with a grim down-turned mouth, one closed eye under a threatening furrowed brow, and underneath, three words in faded yellow script: *The Angry Moon*.

"Andy!" Pete yelled, not sure why; they'd already known this was the place, but he was filled with dread. The changed sign, the deception, mattered, signified something important.

Pete grabbed the door handle, pushed back into the bar-room.

There was no Andy Lynch. Just the box, still closed. Or closed again. And Crick remained at the table where Andy had been, his long narrow face lit by the dancing flicker of the bug-bottle, the walls of the Waiting Room glowing all about him, the light seeming more intense now, infused with new life, though that was probably because Pete had just been peering into darkness. Or was it? The coffee pots seemed to scowl with malevolent new knowledge, the plates with their missing wedges, forever short of being whole, were evil-looking, watching.

"Where's Andy?" Pete demanded, trying to sound threatening and tough.

Crick smiled. "He opened the box," he said, as if that explained it.

"So where is he?" There was more than a touch of hysteria in Pete's voice.

"Come and see," Crick said, and indicated the box, as if to say: Your turn—you have no choice.

Pete moved to the table, unable to stop himself, watching the narrow face in the bug-bottle light. The walls, the shelves, seemed duller all of a sudden.

As Pete reached to lift the lid, the bug-bottle flickered frantically, a warning, but then it was all light and pressure and sucking, and a sudden crushing surrender.

And Pete fell, tumbled, and looked up into a glaring, yellow room, with round walls bulging outward and a floor curved like a dish, and overhead a dark blackened chimney rising like a throat into who knew what?

And there, spinning, struggling, burning on a cord, hanging down from the chimney into the central space was Andy Lynch, what was left of him, a screaming charred consumed-but-not-consumed Andy, hooked, blazing and kicking.

Pete couldn't bear to look. He turned away, pushed his face into his hands against the smooth curving wall. And saw beyond— through his fingers, through the wall of dirty glass—the vast staring fish-eyed face of Crick leaning down, leaning in to cradle the bottle that stood before him.

All these things filled with light, Pete realised. With strange light, decanted souls! *This* is the Waiting Room. One of them. The bug-bottle. Next stop, Hell!

"My turn, Andy!" Pete screamed, needing to save his friend, the only bit of a friend he had. He managed to stand, to rush forward at the blazing torch of Andy Lynch. "You can go on through!"

And stumbling and giggling, his arms across his face, he lunged up at the shape on the cord, to stop it swinging and spinning like that, to extinguish it, he wasn't sure.

But never made it.

When he took his arms away, he found he was in the lane again, with his back to the closed door of the tavern, staring down the empty dark distances towards the harbour. He staggered out from the door, one step, two, three, and took the time to glance up at the sign, to see that it was turned over again, that now it said: *The Happy Sun.*

"My luck!" he cried, giggling with relief. "The sign changed! I scored the Sun. I don't get damned, Andy! I don't get a hell!"

But he was halfway down Carlotta Lane, with lonely empty night on all sides and no Andy Lynch, when he realised just how wrong he was.

Clownette

I'VE ALWAYS HAD a love-hate relationship with Macklin's. When the place is full, when there are conventions or tour groups booked in, then relatives, friends and discount regulars like me get offered the Clownette. There's no other choice.

Not that it's a bad room. There are darker, meaner rooms at Macklin's, many with brick wall views. The Clownette opens onto a back lane, true, but it's on the top floor and there's sky and light. That's the upside. That's by day. At night—well, it changes.

And this time, for maybe the eighteenth, nineteenth time in six years, it was house full and the Clownette or nothing.

No big deal, never a big deal. But there's always ten, twenty seconds or so when it almost matters a lot. I could trek over to Wright's or the Walden; they have budget plans as well, not that that's any kind of issue with my Hopeton's expense account. But, taking the good with the bad, there's something about the Clownette. Once those ten, twenty seconds are done, you see it as clear as day. You get the sky and the light—at least until nightfall. You get to check out the latest additions to the décor. You get to see the face, the "Motley", the Macklin Hotel's very own Shroud of Turin right there in the wall.

Dry-staining as art. A platter-sized discoloration that spoils the room, does so crucially for some. And it does look like a clown in a sketchy man-in-the-moon fashion, with blotchy there-but-never-quite-there features. Paint it over as often as you like, the Motley creeps back, pushing through bit by bit, first as the barest hint of shadow, then as a chain of dusky fractals linking up. And once they connect: hey presto! Peekaboo! Bozo in the wall!

I took the house full news with passable grace, expecting one of Gordon's usual quips. "Off to see the Wizard again, I'm afraid, Mr J." Or "Tell me again, Mr J., how you always wanted to join a circus as a kid!" Or, perfectly po-faced, as if taking the straight part in our long-standing, front-desk, double act: "So he misses you, Mr J. 'You see the kid,' he says, 'you send him right up.'"

Six years of staying at Macklin's and to Gordon—and the Motley, to hear Gordon tell it—I'm still the kid!

None of that today. Maybe there were things on his mind. Maybe he'd had bad news. He just gave me a warm-up smile straight out of Hospitality 101 and handed me a new-style magnetic key.

"Made some changes since your last visit, Mr Jackson," he said.

There it was again, the Mr Jackson! I'd thought it had been a natural-enough slip when he'd said it the first time, some automatic holdover from dealing with too many new guests at once.

Thrown by how correct he was being, I was an extra second or two answering. "Don't tell me it's gone!"

"No, sir. I meant the key. The wall's been painted again since your last visit, but you know how it is."

Sir? Mr Jackson, now *sir!*

"Wouldn't be the same without it, Gordon," I said, to keep the patter going, trying for a handle on what was amiss here. These Gordon glitches overshadowed getting the Clownette, stopped me switching modes and welcoming the news that my special contingency plan for this particular "Meet the Motley" visit could be put into effect after all. Maybe the staff were being assessed. Maybe there were new owners, time and motion people on the premises, efficiency appraisals and staff cutbacks looming, even video surveillance right now. I'd seen it in so many other places: three-star establishments trying for four-star status. I forced myself not to look for cameras.

"Guess I'm off to see the Wizard then!" I said, making one last attempt to rebuild the old Gordon Maher and Bob Jackson bridges, and the smile did widen a bit, though a wink would have helped enormously.

I'd ask about it later. Now I reached for my bag.

"Let me get someone to help with—"

"Gordon, how many years have I been coming here?"

"A lot, Mr Jackson."

"Then you know the drill. This front desk is yours. This bag is mine. Want to swap?"

The silly Gordon grin switched up a notch, seemed almost normal now. Much better. *Call me Mr J.! Just once! Call me the kid!*

"No, Mr Jackson."

Damn! One more try. "You still sleep over on-shift?"

"Sometimes."

"Then how about we swap digs? *You* can have the Clownette?"

"Never again, Mr Jackson!" Gordon was really grinning now, as if finally braving the old Jackson-Maher routines in spite of himself.

"Then off I go."

Let the unseen time and motion gremlins add compassion and humour to their ticket and we might save Macklin's yet, keep it a strictly three-star haven in a cold and busy world.

I took my bag across to the elevators, rode one to the fifth floor, then followed the long, softly lit corridor towards the rear of the hotel and Room 516.

Other hotels had trained me well. I swiped the card in the new magnetic lock and pushed back the familiar old door.

And there it was.

Both parts of the 516 experience for me. First, the "Rush of Weird," as I called it, the deep-anxiety, almost-dread stab of whatever it was I felt whenever I first opened the door on any visit. More than the Motley itself, it was *that* feeling that struck the brain, poleaxed the spirit, made me want to turn and run. It only happened on that first opening of the door during any stay.

Then there was the face.

Beyond the old queen-sized bed I knew so well, left of the same curtained triple windows, it blossomed against the load-bearing wall that somehow kept bringing damp up from the core of the old building, one and a half metres above the floor on the only wall not papered over, *never* papered over.

The Motley. Seven main blotches, enough of a man-in-the-moon soot-smudge face, but nothing that definite, just a grey-scale glitch in the latest colour field.

They'd tried covering it with paintings, mirrors, other decorative features, but that's where things became truly wacky. It wasn't that screws and bolts gave, nothing as simple and conclusive as that, or that the damp leached out to create penicillin fields. It wasn't that furnishings placed in front soon had sprung backs and internal mould. This was *dry* staining—*dry* to the touch, no damp smell at all.

The Motley moved.

Put something in front, a painting, a cupboard, and within the week, sometimes overnight, Bozo would be starting to peer over the top or around the sides. A few more days and it was out of hiding altogether. Remove the obstacle and gradually, over days, nights, a week or two, back it went to its original position—but without any sign of a re-location trail. That was the real wonder of the thing for me.

Experts spoke of micro-climates, of internal convection variables in the space between the stain and whatever fronted it, re-routing the damp-track, some central core problem, whatever. No rising damp anywhere else in the building. No explaining the lack of residual staining left behind when it did re-locate. It just—moved.

Make it a discount room, they said, or a freebie. *Not* a storeroom. Keep it open and airy. Count your losses. One room out of nearly sixty wasn't bad considering.

Which is what Macklin's was given in lieu of any kind of adequate scientific explanation.

There'd been a fleeting Indian summer of notoriety: a month or two of minor tabloid features, even a guest spot on Ross Haslan's *Mysterious Houses*. But that kind of publicity drew the weirdos, management quickly discovered. They issued a press statement saying that modern damp-proofing techniques had fixed the problem. When journalists phoned and the weirdos enquired, they were told the face was gone.

But here it was in all its dusky, smudgy, chimney-soot glory. And, oddly enough, management had found a winner with the latest colour scheme. They'd painted the wall a soft tan, quite a nice contrast to the three papered walls with their familiar, muted yellow and white pattern. The blotches were less intense, less ominous somehow. I'd been here for olive, russet, even for an overkill chocolate brown. But darker colours had made the blemish seem more intense—another trick of the staining, the lighting, Room 516's Turin Effect, as if the Motley was determined to secure its place in the world.

My thoughts were definitely elsewhere, so the knock at the door startled me.

I hurried to answer it, first peering through the spy-hole to see who it was. When no-one was visible, I just assumed there would be fresh towels left on the floor, or a fruit bowl, something that hadn't needed personal attention.

But when I opened the door, there was nothing. *Seemed* to be nothing, for when I glanced down the hall towards the lifts, there was Gordon standing right there, a few steps back from the doorway.

"Shit!" I cried, badly startled. Then I saw the bottle of wine he was holding out for me to take, and immediately flashed the best smile I could manage.

"Look—er—Mr. J.," Gordon said. "About before. I'm sorry. I just wanted to give you this. With my compliments."

"Gordon, what's going on? Are they doing staff evaluations? You were so formal down there."

"That's it." He cast a quick glance back along the corridor. He was still edgy.

"Is your job at risk?"

"Maybe. Not sure. Something's happening, Mr J. They won't tell us. We just need to be careful. I—wanted you to know."

"Well, hey, thanks, Gordon. I was worried. Hope it goes okay for you."

"Thanks. Thanks, Mr J. You want anything, you just call down to the desk."

"Will do. Thanks for this."

He smiled, nodded, then turned and headed for the lifts.

I locked the door and went back to laying out my things. I felt a lot better about the business at the front desk now, though something still felt wrong. But what? What?

Then I knew.

Gordon hadn't wanted to be in line of sight of the open door. He was scared of the Motley!

I could hardly blame him. Some people flatly refused to stay in 516. With its Rush of Weird and its "what-do-you-see-in-this-picture" Rorschach feature to grab your attention, the room had a survival potential of five guests in ten. Gordon had given me the statistic on my third visit. Once the stain was seen as a face, he'd said, five out of ten first-time occupants refused to stay. I just hadn't for a moment considered that Gordon might be one of those who found it too much.

Who could blame him, any of them for that matter? In daylight the Motley was fine. Once your eye had resolved it as a face, it was a bit like having one of those cardboard cut-outs of cops used as thief deterrents in stores constantly staring at you. But at night—a few of the more forthcoming refugees from 516 had admitted—especially once the lights were out, it just became too much. *Knowing* it was there, leering in the dark, big blotchy grin twitching up, smudge eyes staring.

The remaining five guests in ten did better apparently, and I was a borderline member of that line-up. We endured it, were either too drunk, too stolid or too budget-conscious. The last two probably did apply to me, but only if you added curious to the mix. With my plan for this latest stay, I was probably closer to the journalist/ weirdo margin than I cared to admit.

The Motley fascinated me. I'd balked at the front desk, sure, hesitated that ten to twenty seconds, but that was because of the anticipation, the weird feeling I knew I'd have when I first opened the door. That was because of—something. It didn't last more than a few seconds, otherwise no cut-rate plan on earth would have made me keep taking the Clownette. It was the love-hate, yes-no of it for me, the whole complex mix of "What's going on here?" / "You won't get me this time!" bravado and determination.

I smiled at how intense I was being. These were pretty much my usual daytime observations for 516 anyway, the ones I always had after I'd first felt the Rush of Weird again, but the business with Gordon—parts one *and* two!—had thrown me.

I checked my watch by the digital clock alongside the bed. Three forty-five on a bright sunny afternoon. The Motley was in its day phase, its blotches so ordinary, so formless, like any of the other countless stains in countless second-rate hotel rooms across the country, across the world.

I smiled at a word-play that was suddenly there, paraphrasing the famous movie line.

Of all the grin-joints in all the world, why did you have to walk into this one?

There was nothing like a face now, certainly no more than in any other set of stains in any other place. The day was too sunny, too bright.

And, to be fair, the features probably didn't get any more definite after dark. Not really. It was more to do with the ambient lighting, how the shift to evening let the room's lighting focus the observer's eye differently.

With the Rush of Weird behind me, I could deal with all that. I shifted my bag to the stand beside the bed and went to say hello.

"Tonight, Mr Motley," I said, running my hand over the sooty spread of blotches as I always did, "we're going to try happy trails together. See if we can make you move a bit!"

There. Intentions declared. Our latest meeting formalised, everything stated up front. I sat on the edge of the bed then, studying how the smudges sat in the tan. Just an overnight stay, but somehow I felt this visit would be the one!

I *wanted* the Motley to move, wanted to be the one to make it move—see what Gordon and other hotel staff said happened.

"Guess we're just at that stage in our relationship, Mr M.," I said, then went down to the bar to get a drink.

The sunlight was well and truly gone from the back lane when I returned at 5:30, and the Motley had fallen into shadow with the rest of the room's features. No face. Nothing like a face yet.

But I knew only too well how to hasten Bozo on his way, knew from experience to draw the curtains and switch on both bedside lamps to compensate.

The result was instantaneous and surprising, even reassuring in a way. The fall of artificial light in the room was such that the main features were evident almost immediately, first as the eyes and browline, then, bit by smudgy bit, the grin, which always surprised me by how wide it actually was, how completely it had been there all along, waiting to be stitched up by just one more blotch resolving. Slowly, finally, the nose and cheeks emerged, cohered—there were no other words for it. It probably had more to do with an observer's brain providing whatever "nosing" and "cheeking" was needed, a few key bits of recognition cuing the rest.

Again I had to smile at what a good job we did when it came to haunting ourselves.

On other visits, I'd switched off the bedside lights, gone out to a movie or a restaurant, taken my time, then returned close to bedtime and slept through. I was still deciding how to fill this particular evening, but first there was work to do.

I set about moving the television cabinet out from the wall, disconnected the antenna cable and power lead, and dragged the unit across the carpet until it was in front of the stain. During my last stay in 516, I'd worked out that the cabinet with the black Akai television itself wasn't large enough to hide the Motley. But replacing the television with the large square painting above the bed would do the job nicely.

Unlike many of the more modern hotels and motels, Macklin's didn't bolt their prints to the walls. The copy of Van Gogh's *Sunflowers* hung by wire on a wall stud in the traditional manner, so it took surprisingly little time. I set the television on the floor, then placed the framed print on top of the cabinet so it was facing the wall. It covered the Motley completely.

Operation Happy Trails had begun. On the one hand I knew that nothing could come of it in the time available. I could hardly expect it. But on the other, there was a strange feeling that anything could happen. At least I was giving it a try, taking my relationship with Bozo to a new level.

I took the reports for the next day's sales meeting from my briefcase, called "Lazarus, come forth!" to my hidden room-mate, then set off for Saffron's. No movie tonight. I'd read the Deane and the Warnock proposals again over dinner, have a few drinks, and turn in early.

I bid Gordon goodnight as I crossed the lobby. He flashed his smile, waved, and called, "Have a pleasant evening, Mr Jackson!"

I smiled back. We were doing well. We were fellow conspirators now. Maybe we'd get a chance to laugh about it over a drink in some safe, three-star, Macklin's tomorrow.

I was relieved to find Carmen at the front desk when I returned around ten. It had always been "Mr Jackson" with her, so when she wished me a pleasant evening the world felt back on track again. I was surprised at how much I needed it right then.

My room was as I'd left it, of course, which suddenly made me wonder what other guests got up to in their rooms. I had plenty of horror stories from other establishments, and Gordon had shared some of Macklin's with me: about guests painting the walls with their faeces, jumping into completely filled bath-tubs, playing autoerotic hanging games from the pelmets and light fittings. Bob Jackson rearranging a few pieces of furniture was rather small-time in that larger scheme of things.

With the television cabinet borrowed for other duties, I had no choice but to turn in, though falling asleep took some doing. It only served me right, of course. Try as I might, I kept thinking of the Motley there in the darkness, grinning away. It'd been—what?—at least seven hours now, probably more. In a single night I could hardly expect anything. But what if there *was* a trace, some sign?

I switched on the bedside lamp. There was nothing visible around the edges of the painting that I could tell, but there simply wasn't enough light to be sure.

I reached along the headboard and switched on the main room lights. Nothing. The Motley was still in hiding.

I was tempted to leave a light on, but there was my nine-thirty sales meeting to consider. This would have to be just a rehearsal for the Happy Trails outing I'd originally planned. I'd try the whole thing again when I was in town for more than an overnighter.

I felt much better once that was decided. I switched off the lights and actually managed to doze for a few hours.

But just a few hours.

Something woke me at 1:47, a sound, a movement, I couldn't be sure.

The sense of the Motley's presence was stronger than ever. All imagined, no doubt, but such a thing had never happened before.

I didn't turn on the light this time, just lay in the dark thinking. The whole thing with Gordon had me again. There'd been something about him, the intensity. I couldn't shake it. It wasn't the "Mr Jackson" or the "sir" business. That was easy enough to understand once staff appraisals were factored in, or the possibility of some influential guest complaining about too much familiarity among the staff.

It was *how* he was when he'd given me the wine. It should have made things better—that was clearly the intention—but it hadn't. It was like being with someone who thanked you too much or apologised too many times, or asked too often if there was anything he could do once. It was overreaction.

That was part of it, most of it! Just a few words out in the hall and he'd said Mr J.—what?—three, four times? As if overcompensating. As if he'd remembered to do it all of a sudden.

And there was something else, a body language thing. Aside from the edginess, the anxiety, there'd been something about his eyeline. His gaze had been wrong. What had those sales training videos said? True friendly gaze went from the eyes in a triangle *down* to the smile. Formal business gaze went *up* from the eyes to a point on the forehead.

Hard to be sure now, but maybe that was it. Gordon may have been genuinely worried, but something had made him seem detached as well. Not sorry at all. It had happened all too quickly.

Another thought struck me then. Gordon had been standing to the side of the door, hadn't wanted to look in and see the Motley. What had he told me down at the front desk when I suggested he take 516? "Never again, Mr Jackson!" That word! *Again!* Had he recently spent a night in the room? Had 516 done something to his memory, his way of looking at things? His personality?

Ludicrous, ridiculous, but the craziest things made sense in the small hours. And such late-night thoughts always seemed to drag their own wacky logic along with them. It worried me. Too much fear could trigger—what were the terms?—a behavioural shutdown or a post-traumatic adjustment of affect, a way of dealing with severe personal crisis. I'd read about that somewhere. Maybe this was something like that.

I smiled at myself in the darkness. I was haunting myself, using 516 and the Motley to do it.

Still, at 1:53 in the small hours, with newly limbered night at the windows, it did make sense. Provoking the Motley no longer seemed such a good idea.

I was half-asleep, being irrational, but enough was enough. I switched on the bedside light, got out of bed, crossed to the painting, hefted it and prepared to set it on the floor. Before I could do that I dropped it in astonishment.

The Motley wasn't there!

I stood staring at where it had been, *should* have been, *had* to be! Then I broke free, stumbled across the room, switched on the main lights and rushed back to the wall.

Not a trace. Not a sign.

It was gone!

Which wasn't possible. Not like that. Not after so little time.

It was 2:09, but I did the only sensible thing. I took a shower, turned it to cold at the end so I was completely awake. Then I made coffee, strong and black, and sat on the edge of the bed sipping it, re-learning the room and trying to eliminate the things that almost make sense at that hour, can make too much sense if you're not careful.

"Serves you right, Jackson," I said, as much to hear a voice as anything. "Now you either go join the refugee queue down in the foyer or you work through this like an adult!"

I set my cup on the bedside table, went over to the television stand and pulled it out from the wall.

Nothing. Not a smudge, not a hint that I could see. The tan was unblemished.

Which was impossible.

Maybe it was me. A vision thing. But after ten minutes of sightings from various points in the room, I was back sitting on the bed staring at the blank wall.

What to do? I could phone Rhonda or Bruce or Katie half a continent away, have friends talk me through this. Better yet, phone down to Carmen at the front desk, get her up here, let her be a witness to the whole thing.

I didn't, couldn't. Not yet.

What if the Motley re-appeared just before she arrived? That's how these things happened, didn't they?

It was that certainty—absurd, laughable, vivid at this hour—that stopped me. Not because I truly believed it would or *could* happen, but because the certainty itself felt so real, had me so completely.

I couldn't help it. What if Carmen came up and the smudges *did* re-form just as she knocked at the door?

It took me back to my thoughts about Gordon staying the night in 516, being changed by the Motley. Maybe it adjusted your mind, how you saw things. That was it! The Motley was still there, had worked its special Bozo magic and done something to my ability to see it!

I grinned, laughed, was still able to, thank God, tracking my growing fear with an equally impressive detachment. I needed to act, do something.

"Clever, Mr M.," I told the blank wall. "Seems this round might go to you unless a little Jackson finessing can save the day."

Save the day? I immediately corrected myself. *Save the night!* That was more like it, but definitely the wrong thought right then.

I grabbed the phone handset from the cradle by the bed and pressed the key for the front desk.

After a ten-second delay, Carmen answered. "Reception?"

"Carmen, it's Bob Jackson in 516."

"We don't talk to you."

I froze where I stood.

"What? What did you say?"

"I said: Yes, Mr Jackson? How can I help?"

"No, what did you just say before that?"

"I said 'Yes, Mr Jackson?' Is there something wrong?"

Sure is, kiddo. I've spooked myself good!

But no point pushing it. *It adjusts your mind.* "Ah—look, I know it's late, Carmen, but I'm really not sleeping too well. Would you have any sleeping pills down there?"

"Of course, Mr Jackson. I can't leave the desk—"

"That's okay. That's fine. I'll be right down. Thanks, Carmen."

I fumbled getting the handset back into its cradle, fumbled pulling on my clothes.

What had she said? That other comment? So odd, so truly strange.

And now there was the prospect of actually leaving the room. Everything could change. Most certainly would, I was certain. That's how these things worked. I'd go down, get the pills, and the Motley would be back on the wall when I returned, grinning at me, its own Happy Trails manoeuvre wonderfully complete. *Not a bad trick, hey, Mr J.? Motley one, Bob Jackson nil.*

I had to take charge, go down, anchor myself in the ordered, everyday world.

I grabbed the magnetic key from the night-stand and stepped out into the hall, waited till the door clicked shut behind me then headed for the lifts.

And discovered Motley's next piece of trickery!

The corridor seemed longer, impossibly extended.

Adjusts your mind! How you see things.

My night logic snatched at it. Not surprising, not so strange, I told myself, dragged from sleep like this, primed with weird thoughts. Just another optical trick.

The setting encouraged it. By their very nature, hotel corridors existed in a state of timelessness. Day or night, the lights were always on. The carpeting stole sound. Every footstep was snatched away the moment you made it. You passed other rooms as if you never existed. And the doors! Blind, replicated, one after the other, just their vacant spy-holes tracking you sightlessly like the eyes of figures in portraits.

Another key factor right there.

No portraits in hotel rooms or hotel corridors. Always landscapes, abstracts, vistas, safe impressionistic pieces. No-one wanted eyes watching them in hotel rooms or down those long hallway approaches. Which explained 516's five refugees in ten, why the Motley had the impact it did. Of course! The portrait effect!

Almost at the lifts, I noticed Room 502 with its double spy-hole: one at the usual eye-level, one lower down for guests in wheelchairs, children, shorter people.

My rational mind understood, but the night terrors had me.

Being watched by something doubled over, folded in on itself.

I laughed—my struggling, rational self did—and laughed again. I was imagining a third spy-hole way down at floor level. For the snake, I thought. Or Randion the Living Torso from that old Tod Browning movie!

Crazy. All crazy. But what you did to cope. To turn it and make it right again.

Then I was safely past. I pressed the elevator call button, heard one, possibly both of the carriages responding, climbing the long dark throats of the old building.

One car signalled its arrival with a soft chime, a sound quickly snatched away by the carpeting. The doors slid back. I stepped into the plush interior and descended to the lobby, which seemed stark and overlit after the dim infinite corridor up there.

"Mr Jackson," Carmen said from behind the reception desk. "Sorry you're having trouble sleeping. This should help."

She handed me a sleeping pill in its foil wrapping.

"Thanks, Carmen. I'm probably just overstressed. Got a big meeting tomorrow." *What was it you said before? What?*

"What time did you want to be woken? Just in case?"

"Good point. Make it 7 am, okay?"

"Seven it is. Goodnight, Mr Jackson."

"Goodnight, Carmen. Thanks."

It was easier going back, riding the lift up into the night, reaching the quiet fifth-floor elevator lobby, finding the hallway its normal self again. It was as if everything had been re-set.

Not completely re-set, thank goodness. When I swiped my card in the lock and pushed back the door, there was no Rush of Weird.

But the Motley was back on the wall!

Of course it was, back where it should have been, no doubt had been all along.

No more games. No more tricks. I re-hung the Van Gogh print above the bed, moved the television cabinet back to its original place, re-connected the leads.

"You win this round, Mr M.," I said, feeling exhausted, beaten and yet strangely elated by the whole thing. Collateral damage, I told myself. Waking like this. Being primed. Seeing things.

I probably didn't need the sleeping pill, but when I was back in bed, ready to settle again, I popped it from its foil and swallowed it just the same. I was asleep in minutes.

And awake again at 3:17. The Motley woke me.

It was leering, shimmering on the wall, having itself a merry time! But glowing! Shining somehow!

Never knew I could be a night light, did you, Mr J.?

I lurched from bed, leaden, dizzy, but driven, and lunged at the wall.

Wrong way! Wrong thing to do, I knew, even as I did it. Should have turned on the light first! Should have kept away!

But it was panic. What passed for it in my drugged, terrified state. I went reeling, fell at the wall, with arms raised to stop myself.

But it wasn't there.

Now everything is different, of course. Not just because it's the view I've never had—looking *out* from the wall. It's because there are so many of us in here, crowding behind, all in our turn, so needy, so frantic to look out again. It's knowing that the next too-curious guest will force me back into that darkness, that *all* the Clownette's guests checked out, and that out there in the world is a brand-new Bob Jackson farewelling a brand-new Gordon and whatever other bits of itself this dark place has managed to squeeze through.

I'm beyond the revulsion and panic, the rage and disbelief. It adjusts your mind. Now there's just the numbness and despair, the agony of waiting. Feeling them crowding in behind, touching, snatching, muttering.

At least now I know what the sensation was whenever I first opened the door to 516—all that's left of a scream from a place where screams can no longer be heard.

Housemaid or guest, housemaid or guest—that's all that matters now, knowing that the day will come when Macklin's has a full house again and the scream is mine.

The Ichneumon and the

Dormeuse

THIS TIME WAS different. This time on his way past the tombs, Beni turned left, ignored the guard Stones of the nearer mounds and headed down the path through the trees to the wide low tumulus where her tomb was.

He granted that the Stones had him, though nothing showed it. The tumulus was quiet under the hot afternoon sun, the trees, the grass barely stirred, the fields stretched away to meet the sky. The only movement was the heat shimmer on the other tomb mounds and the endless pull of the sentry Stones.

The Nothing Stones were neither stones nor quite filled with nothing, though that was the sense they gave, all sixteen of them, low basaltic pillars two metres high, as wide as his shoulders, as deep as his thigh, standing in the usual henge circle around the foot of the tumulus itself.

Their onyx-black, outward-facing sides were filled with stars, converging points of light, and while Beni would not look into those glossy midnight fields, he knew that if he remained, if they didn't have him already, the darkling, star-ridden massebots would solve his mysteries, totes and sly conditionings and come to snatch him away, pulling, pulling, grabbing at sight and mind, close obsidian in the hot afternoon.

Always assume the Stones have you, Ramirez had said, told him now in memory, the greatest tomb-robber of them all, and Beni did so, leaving it to his autonomic tote systems to sort out. If they had him in a trance loop, he'd probably soon know. He continued through the perimeter henge, leaving the deadly megaliths at his back, and headed down the access ramp to the black gulf of the doorway.

Doorway not door. None of the old tumulus tombs had ever had doors. Beni stood before the quiet, porcelain-smooth, darkened throat in the side of its vast, low hill and called out.

"Dormeuse! Dormeuse! You have a visitor!"

The words echoed against the ceramic, died. There was only stillness, silence again, smooth cool midnight before him, daylight and blazing summer behind.

Beni, tech'd and toted, wearing a flamer he'd been told he probably wouldn't use, carrying a meter-long touchpole over his back as nearly all tomb-robbers did, just in case, now brought up his wrist display, saw what the optics gave.

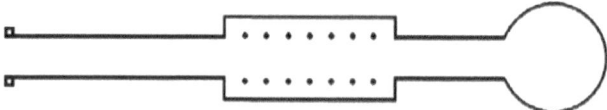

Classic plan clear and sure. Free of the Stones too, if he could trust the readings. It was the standard schema confirmed by all the survivors (most of all by Ramirez himself, one of the very few to make it back totally unharmed) as the basic Tastan design: stretch of corridor, peristyle hall, corridor, burial chamber.

Simple. Direct. Two hundred metres, fifteen, another hundred, then the ten-metre circular chamber: the classic Tastan biocromlech. Simple. Linear. Very deadly.

For there would be traps, illusions, sensory and neural tricks. Standing there, Beni ran the latest figures again, unchanged, of course, since the last postings, but you never knew when new data might be collated and added— the town's comp systems were constantly at it. Outright death with bodies recovered still stayed at 12% of annual penalties, selective maiming and stigma—the 'souvenirs', 14% (but at least you returned), failure to return at all was still 63% (up 2% on last year's average—things did change), failure to enter the tomb but believing so, 11%.

Beni cleared that, studied the simplified plan again—spinal access corridor (axial, porcelain-smooth), vertebrate peristyle (handsomely corbelled, and otherwise featureless but for the fourteen columns, seven to a side, and the intaglio relief on each of the back walls), more corridor, finally the central tholos, the skull chamber: unavoidable analogy and another of Ramirez's terms, just as he had been the one to revive the old names: tholoi, tumuli, henge megaliths, cromlechs, dolmens, going through the old databases, going on about Celts, Myceneans, Etruscans, whoever they were, much older peoples than the Tastans.

Beni flicked random selections, chance plan superimpositions, hoping to trick any tomb override. The defences were clever but they were old.

No change. The classic plan remained. No *apparent* change.

What would Ramirez do now?, Beni wondered again, again, again, putting it off, avoiding. And, finding that he was doing so, made himself take the first step, found the others easier, was soon leaving the square of warm daylight far behind. His cap-light struck out ahead, illuminating the corridor, the smooth and off-white walls; his footsteps echoed off the cool ceramic, carrying him into night, into the underworld of the vast low funerary hill.

"Dormeuse?" he called. "You have company, Dormeuse!" Called it over and over, as Ramirez suggested he do.

"Not so loud," a voice finally said, and a host flashed on beside him, a startling mummiform of light, gaining resolution, female distinction. "I'm trying to sleep."

She was lovely, as perfectly formed, idealised, as Ramirez had said she would be, the tall glowing enantios intercept of an auburn-haired woman in middle-age or backtracked to about 45, with an open, pretty if not wholly beautiful face and eyes like blackest glass, but a gentle gaze all the same, with nothing like the cold arrogant manner of intercepts the grim-faced 'souvenired' veterans back in town had told him about.

Beni glanced down at his scanner, glad to see the basic plan confirmed, even if not to be trusted, never to be trusted, and kept on walking. The intercept 'walked' with him, fully formed now, smiling like a curious servant, which is exactly what she was. It was. She.

"Someone has been talking to you," she said. "You're too confident."

"But new to this all the same. I need as much help as I can get."

"I have much more experience. Listen. Turn round now. I'll let you go. Promise."

Beni smiled. Even without the advice he'd been given, he would have found the offer unacceptable, though it actually did happen now and then. Sometimes did. Justified the old saying that even the tombs had a bad day now and then.

"Don't believe you. Won't do it. Thanks."

The display flickered but held, his reader sorting, sorting, seeking any other valid plan, if only as a split-second glimpse.

"Last chance," she said. "Keep going and I'll have you."

"You probably already do," Beni said, heart pounding, afraid and exhilarated, entranced by the image, forcing himself to talk down at his scanner display, avoiding the eyes. "The Stones'll have me if they don't already."

"Do you know what souvenir I have planned for you?"

"Please, Dormeuse. Do what you must, but enough of these threats."

And sure enough, the intercept changed tack.

"You see no ethical problem with this, do you?"

Beni smiled at the shift, gave the rote answer. "There has never been a time where one age and culture hasn't plundered the remains of another."

"But why? There's no wealth here. Nothing you can use. No gold, jewels or funerary possessions. Forget the rumours. Not enough precious materials in the circuitry and hardware. Certainly nothing accessible to you. No meaningful tech knowledge."

"I know."

"So why? Why do you use the term 'tomb-robbers' if—?"

"I prefer the 'reasonable' to the 'threat' mode, but could you bring on the next phase? I do need to concentrate."

The phantom hovered, seemed to walk. "Such an arrogant young man. Someone has been talking to you. But I'd really like to know."

Arrogant? Beni stared down at the display and considered it. Overconfident perhaps. Optimistic. Determined to be among the best. But hardly arrogant. "What have others said? Ramirez managed it. What did he say?"

"He was courteous but wouldn't talk to me as freely as you seem prepared to. He probably suspected a voice trap, some trance dislocation induced by word pattern, tone and timbre. You don't seem to fear that."

"There were others though, Dormeuse." The maimed ones, he didn't add. Barlow, Deckley, Kylow, Soont, the others, all skilled men and women, all souvenired. "What did they say?"

"Again, not too much," the phantom answered. "Concentration does that, I suppose. And fear. I gather it is some emblematic thing, using the term 'tomb-robber' and all. You're stealing the chance to do it, aren't you? Stealing the privilege. The mystery of another age. Some said it's rites of passage. The tombs are here, they said. Intact. Penetrable yet at the same time impenetrable ultimately. One age scorning another."

"Scorning? They said that?" Beni found it hard to imagine any of those bluff or dour survivors back in town saying that. He was impressed anew. "But, Dormeuse, you're the one who must feel something like that surely. Scorn."

"A sentry profile can't. I'm just a print of my original; my job is to represent my occupant's self. Keep her safe. Or me, depending on how you view architectural psychonics."

"But no body, I'm told. Just the stored personality index."

"Ah, little hunter. I recognise a question when I hear it. One age does plunder another. You, too, would have my secrets. Perhaps that is what you come for, the chance to steal knowledge of my day, get the old sentry intercepts talking. Yet such a risk. Death and injury on the chance of just a little something more about the Tastan past."

A stab of youthful defiance surged up, made Beni want to stay silent then, but, like countless others before him, he did want to know. He had to ask. "Your body is here?"

"Curious and stubborn, like all who come calling. Why should I tell? Perhaps the people of my day did preserve the body as well. Or the head. Who knows? We may have had cryonics long before we could code personality. The others you spoke to said what?"

"Dormeuse, I'm new to this. A lot of the veterans in town won't talk to me. They only sell what they know. I can't afford them."

"But, little one, you're in this far. I know you won't believe me but you're past the Stones. You're very well prepared tech-wise, my systems show. You've accessed a third-level intercept response from me. I frankly didn't expect that. You have to have the advice of others."

Beni felt his heart pounding. Could it be true? In this far! Free of the Stones. Could it?

"Ramirez," he said, deciding she'd probably guessed it already. "One day he stopped on the way past my family's farm. I was in the orchard. I reminded him of a son he'd lost, he said. He told me things about the tombs. About your tomb. He was giving it up at last, he said, going away. But he told me of you, Dormeuse. Of all the tombs yours was the one, he said. He was an eidetic, as you probably guessed. Perfect recall. Helped him with variants in the tomb plans when there were some, but more with the characteristics of the intercepts, their features and mode changes. He drew your likeness for me. Your image's likeness."

"Why, Beni. Don't tell me you're infatuated? In love?"

"It's not that! It's complex. I was without a father. He was without a son. We just talked."

"Oh stop! Stop! Don't tell me. And I became mother and wife! I love it. Midwife to hunters."

Beni clenched his jaws in anger. They walked in silence a while, down the ceramic corridor, him concentrating on his plan readings, glancing up at the passage ahead, glancing back down, up, down, she flowing beside him, a spindle of light with eyes like onyx.

"You said it was complex," she said after a time, coaxing, sounding just contrite enough. Perhaps he had accessed a new mode from her.

"Then I don't know why I'm here. All my life it was what the best of us did. The tombs were something you couldn't ignore, how's that? I've walked past yours probably a thousand times. More than a thousand over the years. Yesterday I finally decided to try. Today I came out here again."

"Your point, little hunter?"

"Our own culture formed around the leavings of yours, Dormeuse, but yours keeps intruding. Your language has virtually replaced ours. Do you know how insufferable something like that is? Can you imagine how it's become for us? Competing with our past?"

"You're telling me, little one. I'm sure it's happened before. I seem to recall something about the European Renaissance being in effect a rediscovery of the wisdoms of earlier civilisations in Greece and Egypt. Though I believe that was a very positive thing, probably nothing as desperate as this."

Despite her disparaging words, Beni preferred this mode, this kind of directness. Ramirez had told him to push for it, that the host would treat him differently once he accessed it.

"My father died over in 37. Left our orchard one day, just upped and turned tomb-robber, tomb-visitor, whatever term covers it. It's what more and more of us do. Spent all we had on maps, comp and the best sentry tech he could get. I didn't find out till later! A neighbour came over and told me he hadn't come out of 37. I didn't even know he'd gone in, been planning it all those years. So I ask you: why would he do that? Why do any of us?"

"But I'm asking you that, little hunter."

"Don't call me that. I'm Beni."

"Beni. So as well as being in love you're in hate and loss. Potent mixture. Think of it though. I'm five hundred years in your past, yet held accountable, made responsible somehow for a boy losing his father centuries later. And, marvellous paradox, without me, without the loss and envy, it seems your life, all your lives, would be lacking in purpose."

"That's not it."

"Would be meaningless."

"That's not it!" The cry was swallowed in the ebbing, flowing, warm ceramic night. The thief had stopped walking at last, stood grimly silent. The ghost hovered, drifted, spoke.

"Maybe not. But perhaps you fear so. All your people. So you come here and test yourselves, steep yourselves in the mystery, could that be it? Plunder us from time to time. Carry out acts of astonishing vandalism."

"I haven't done that." Beni started walking again, drew the phantom along with him.

"No, Beni. You haven't yet. Thank you."

"Ramirez didn't."

"No. I agree," she said. "A lot don't. You're different than most. Ramirez was, both of you are, that curious blend of romantic and"—she said it very gently—"innocent. After something else."

Doesn't mean I won't though, he almost said, felt he should say it, a young man scared and confused. But didn't. "So what are we after then, Dormeuse?"

"Back to that, are we? Both wanting the same question answered."

"I'm afraid so." He continued walking, watching the scanner.

"All right. I allow you're motivated by the quest, by envy and reprisals against the past, the need both to have the past mysterious yet know it. I allow disenchantment, rites of passage, because it's there, all that. But we're generalising. It doesn't tell me why you're here, does it? Why Beni is here as an individual."

Because I want to win, he could have said. Be up there among the greatest of them all: Ramirez, Callido, Asparan. But again didn't, feared sounding arrogant, brash, deluded like so many who came here. He *was* after something more. He was.

"You're being gentle with me, Dormeuse, so I'll try to find an answer. A real answer."

"Please do. And my name is Arasty. 'Dormeuse' means 'sleeping woman' in an ancient language. Which is what I am, just as you are ichneumon."

"I'm what?"

"Ichneumon. Another very old word. Means 'hunter' or 'tracker'. A small animal that used to hunt along river banks. Ate the eggs of crocodiles."

"Of what?"

"No matter. Beni and Arasty. We're here now and, yes, I'm being gentle because you are."

"But it's a mode as well. Tactical."

"Yes. It is." The black eyes glittered.

"You could stop me?"

"I'm sure I can." Glittered.

"Yet the fact is you want us here."

"Oh, tell me why."

"Not yet."

"I'm curious. Tell me why."

"I need to concentrate."

For ahead, his cap-light's glow fell on something different at last, caught in strange verticals, made new shadows for his eyes and tech to fathom.

He had reached the peristyle hall.

Beni had expected it to be little more than a widening of the axial corridor, with the seven pillars on either side keeping the passageway's alignment from entranceway to central tholos. But when he entered, he found it went back even deeper behind the smooth featureless columns than his stylized display suggested, just as the corridors were so very much longer than the plan showed. The walls shone with the same vitreous pallor as the corridor, but opposite each other in the centre of each back wall was the circular intaglio motif Ramirez had told him of.

The intercept appeared beside him while he stood exploring one of the grooved mandalas with a finger.

"Know what that is?"

"Ramirez told me. It's a maze. The classic seven-ring design. The archetypal unicursal maze built round a cross and four points. Used by lots of ancient peoples, the Romans, the Cretans and Syrians, the Irish, the medieval Christians—"

"Yes, yes. So what is its significance? Did Ramirez tell you?"

Beni smiled. "A unicursal maze has a single path from the entrance to the centre. It looks complex but is really very direct."

"Why it appealed to the Tastans too."

"I'm sure."

"Beni, I fear you're an optimist."

"What do you mean?"

"You see it as something complex being ultimately very simple. Like your comp reading there."

"So?"

"Why not a simple path made difficult. Look at your comp now."

Beni glanced down, saw with a stab of alarm, panic, sudden terror, a new reading. He keyed randoms, saw only the new double-peristyle configuration.

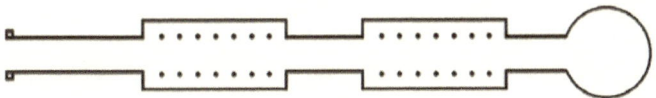

"This does get interesting," she said. "Oh, by the way, 'ichneumon' also refers to a parasitic, hymenopterous insect that lays its eggs on another's larvae, using it as food for its own young as they hatch. Nice thought, yes? Little hunter." And she vanished.

Beni had been told this would probably happen, the host's hunt-mode surfacing, solicitous, caring, then cold, callous, vindictive, seeking to undermine any sense of hope.

He strode on, left the columned hall, plunged into the next length of corridor, just the tiniest dagger edge of doubt pushing through the confidence Ramirez had given him. What if there were a second peristyle hall? What if the tomb plan actually shifted, shunted him from one course to another, on and on? The mound was large enough.

Ramirez had spoken of it. It was a doubt he could still push aside. The tholos, the skull chamber, would be ahead. Not far.

The yellow cone pushing ahead became brighter, strengthening, whitening, as the host flashed in.

"Can we resume, Beni? You said that we want you here. Tell me why?"

Beni did not look at the intercept. He walked on, glancing at his display, then ahead, corridor, display, repeating that. He might have stayed silent, punished her for the trickery with the plan. But he sensed, just as Ramirez had told him, that it would probably be the worst thing to do. The tomb profiles liked to talk.

"It occurs to me, Arasty, that a sentry program would want visitors to test itself against, that the self whose tomb this is would have designed the tomb so its sentry profile would be exercised, challenged, kept entertained and satisfied. It's what I'd do."

"That's a very smart observation. What made you think of it all of a sudden? Or was it also something—"

"I asked Ramirez about it that day in the orchard. Mentioned it before he did. We talked about what the tombs really were. He told me that your intercept, Dormeuse—Arasty—would appear at various times, run different modes—"

"And walk with you like this?"

"Not necessarily. Some intercepts did, he said. He also told me that whoever could code personalities and structure reality perception would not bother with ancient mortuary forms— corridors, burial chambers and such like—unless they were playing at something, *wanted* to invite plunderers."

"Again, very shrewd. He didn't say much when he was here but I miss this Ramirez. You're both right. We do want you here. We give each other purpose."

Beni watched his display for the slightest flicker, let his peripheral vision guide him. "We are your future. We let you exist in time."

"Empowering each other. Yes, Beni. I like that. Like the fish and the fisher. Here for each other."

"So let me get on with it, Arasty. You try to stop me. I try to reach the core chamber."

"And what? Put your name up there with Ramirez's. Scrawl it on the watch screen and hurry out again? Did he tell you he did that?"

"I don't believe you."

"Did he tell you what else he did? Everything he did? You said Ramirez drew my face. Did he love me too, do you think? This image from an ancient age?"

Which part to answer? She was distracting him with her intriguing remarks, possibly giving deliberate untruths to unnerve him. "I'm not sure what he felt. Fascination. Determination to see you as the person who made this. Set this up for the future. It makes for a sort of intimacy. Something very powerful."

"Intimacy. I'm flattered. I never expected this sort of—well—kinship across centuries."

But Beni had stopped.

"What is it?" the phantom asked. "Worried that there's no core chamber? No second peristyle?"

"I should have reached it. Show me the plan. The real one."

"You've already seen it. Look."

Again there was the alarm, the panic, terror surging up.

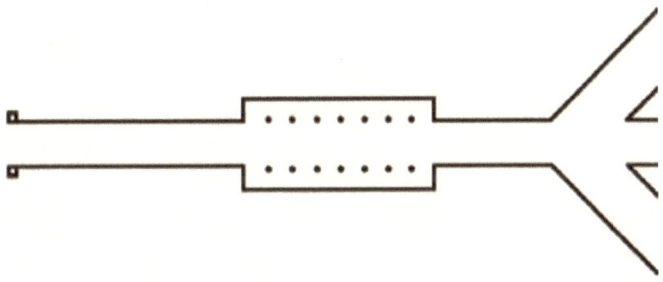

"You continue to make it more interesting."

"It's all I have, like you say. The chance to challenge, be entertained."

Beni needed to talk it through. "One of the few things we learned from you Tastans was sealed comp technology." He touched his scanner. "This can't be tampered with, so you've interfered with my perceptual processes."

He pressed a contact, randomised the grabs, sent surges through both equipment and self. He had practised this, did not flinch from the small electroshocks. The original tomb-plan came and went: single peristyle original, this new triple corridor display, double peristyle, single, double, triple—they flashed and flickered, cycled from one to the other.

It wasn't his vision then—unless it was misinformation at the brain's visual centre.

And when he looked at the phantom's face, saw the smile under the black glass eyes, he understood her simple strategy.

"I can't be sure now can I?"

Again, Ramirez's words were there. Allow that the Stones have you.

Beni sighed as if in frustration and despair, closed his eyes, accessed, believed he accessed, the neural link Ramirez had given him, actually given him, a parting gift surgically implanted in the town clinic, a legacy from surrogate father to surrogate son.

The single peristyle configuration—classic Tastan grab—sat in the light of his mind's eye. He was in the second length of corridor, so close to the chamber. He dared not linger over it in case she suspected. Again he sighed as if in frustration.

"Your decision?" she said.

"Excuse me?" Feigning bafflement, exhaustion, loss of resolve. Let her read those. The battle had been joined in earnest.

"On or back? I still may let you go. Perhaps with a souvenir as a reminder. Or perhaps none, provided you promise to come back and talk to me again. Keep me entertained."

Was that a possibility he dared consider? This intercept—this tomb, to make the distinction—did seem different from all accounts, rhapsodising, showing whimsy, negotiating, pretending to, taunting like this, first one mode then another, just as Ramirez had told him she would be.

"I'm your little egg-stealer, remember. We continue."

"Hope is always beautiful," she said.

Beni didn't comment, strode on five, ten, twenty metres, surely into the tholos, but would not glance at his display now, nor at her, would not consult his link. He wanted her to court him, whatever came of it. This visit had to matter. But he was in the tholos, the skull chamber, he told himself. Had to be.

Finally she spoke, easily, losing no face by it, perhaps in a new mode, he couldn't tell, though her question suggested it.

"So, little hunter, have you ever wondered why there are only 85 tombs? The Tastan culture lasted seven centuries, at least 35 generations. Why only 85 tombs?"

He didn't understand all her words. Generations. "Tell me."

"Guess."

"No more games."

"Entertainment, remember? There really are only my games here. I'll reward you."

"How?"

"Trust that I will. I'll give you a clue. We were not necessarily royalty. Not rulers."

It did intrigue him. "Another caste in your society?"

"In a sense. Go on."

Beni fought to think, pressured by the changeless, vitreous dark, by the unchanging yellow fan of his lamp showing not the tholos but only more and more corridor, its glow whitened by the added glow of the figure floating, standing beside him, seeming to.

Tholos, maze, wherever he was, the intercept really did seem to want an answer.

"Our culture is five hundred years after yours," he said.

"Good. Yes?"

"But"—he hated saying it—"is debased by comparison. Technologically."

"Such finesse, little hunter."

"You belonged to a scientist caste."

"Wrong."

"A holy order. Priests. Sacerdotes."

"No."

"Criminals being punished."

"Fool!" She said it with incredible fury. The black eyes glittered. "Don't you know any history? What happened to our culture?"

Beni was stunned by her vehemence, the unconcealed contempt. It told him something he did not yet understand.

"You vanished," he said, and then, to show he did know some history, what Ramirez had told him, added: "Like the Mayans. The Anasazi. Your cities were abandoned, allowed to run down; most were reduced to slag by housekeeping programs—"

"So where did we go? Our millions? Our millions, Beni?"

What did she want him to say? And millions. The Tastan millions.

"Into these tombs?" The certainty of it amazed him. "All coded in. Immortal. You're the guardians of your race! Eighty-five repositories but housing millions."

Arasty's expression may have been the result of holistic psychonic printing or just some simulated response selected from a housekeeping menu, but Beni saw what looked like genuine scorn, genuine revulsion. If it were a deception then it was a subtle one, something naked, seeming spontaneous, well beyond the disapproval and impatience it resembled.

What am I missing? Beni asked himself, and with it felt a conviction. She needs me to guess. It really is important that I do. But what did she—it— want him to say? He wanted to shout the question. Didn't dare now. All he could think of was to show humility, self-effacement, and hope for patience.

"Please, Arasty, help me more. This is important." He hoped the compliment, his respectful tone, would do it.

The phantom watched him sidelong with her dark eyes just as a human would, as if in fact a discrete entity deciding, not a defence intercept scanning precedents, selecting options.

"You really have no idea, do you? A great culture, possibly the greatest the world has known, reaches a point where it dismantles itself, gives way to a simpler, let's say impoverished, less sophisticated successor. Why would they do it?"

"I can only think of two answers," he said quickly, honestly. "There was some enemy—"

"You could say that." The intercept's eyes flashed with interest. "Or?"

"You gained by it. It had to be progress. Something you saw as better." And he remembered what she'd said—impoverished— and barely dared utter the words. "You became *us!*" Remembered what else she'd said: less sophisticated. "You simplified your culture, someone did, something, some ruling elite maybe, and became us—"

"Yes." There was something like madness in the phantom's darkling bits of eyes, something reckless and fervent, but Beni dared not suggest the tombs housed what remained of the Tastan's dead insane. It was more. It had to be more. But he did not have to stumble over words to form a question. Arasty continued speaking.

"Some ruling elite, yes. An enemy, true, that culled our millions and our cultural heritage. Downgraded us all. To simple, immortal, happy folk like you—"

"Then—"

"Immortal. Happy ichneumon. But able to be maimed, killed by violence. With time to be curious, to ponder, to forget, to indulge. Happy, happy, happy ichneumon!"

"Then you're here—"

"Go on!" Madness spun in the darkness of the eyes.

"To cull us! Prey on us! To give purpose to immortal lives! They planned ahead. Saw we would need—"

"No!" The intercept had halted in blazing fury, actually flickered, flashed off and back again. The face was rigid with a rage and suffering held in such perfect suspension that Beni was faint with the involuntary numbing terror he felt welling up. The eyes, the black false eyes, held him.

"No, little hunter. No. See it our way. To give purpose to *our* thwarted lives. Some kind of revenge for those few among the elite, eighty-five out of all those many, to whom the genetic treatments did *not* bestow immortality. Who had helped cull and simplify, then found themselves without the intended blessing, left to die in the agony of exclusion from that. From you."

Beni saw the extent of the resolve, the old fierce hatred, that she would never let him go. He would never get to tell this story. Never even reach the central chamber. Or know he had.

"These aren't tombs. They're traps," he said, understanding, remembering the other meaning to her name for him, the insect leaving behind its offspring to feed.

"Yes, Beni. Traps to lure immortals curious in their long lives. A way of striking back at time."

And Beni felt the deep-down dread that Ramirez, some kind of Ramirez, tampered with, changed, or no—just allowed to go back unharmed—was acting as a lure out there in the bright summer days, giving hope, keeping the dream alive in others, but part of the trap, knowing or unknowing. Pray Destiny it was unknowing.

Such a small shrewd price to pay, letting one or two go free, letting others go back maimed. Let the tombs have a bad day and so keep them coming.

"Be merciful, Dormeuse. Arasty."

"I am, little hunter. With you I truly am. Normally I grant the beautiful lie, tell those I am about to rob of life, light and limb, beauty, eons of youth, of how normally death is what makes lives, cultures, ultimately defines civilisation. I remind them that it's right that immortals should reach a point of idle curiosity and need to be challenged, extended, tested. I tell them that whatever their fates individually, those I kill or hurt are helping maintain the tenor of life for all."

"But you're actually culling."

"Avenging. It's simpler."

"Out of envy."

"Bad enough in life. But when it's all there is, all that's left, it fills the largest cup, becomes a vast power. I phrase it so they think they will be spared somehow. That they are different and special. To some I even suggest that their personalities will join mine in the tomb matrix. Then, when there is hope, when vanity and optimism is there in hints and the absolute conviction of ego, then I cripple and kill, then I bring them to the worst of hells, to such terrible insurmountable despair. You I have spared this anguish, Beni."

"Spared me! By telling me the truth?"

"Yes."

"But I can't believe you, can I? Not after what you've just said."

"You really should. Look at your display."

Beni did, saw how simply, elegantly, the tomb's long-dead owner, this printing of her anyway, had expressed his dilemma.

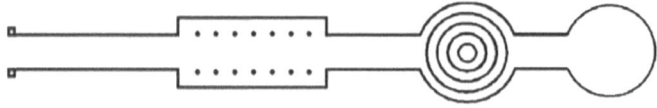

A maze. He was in a maze. He did not know what to say.

Arasty, the ghost of her, smiled. "Well?"

"Never be importunate, I was always told. Never beg."

"I've told you I'm being merciful. I might listen."

"All right. Don't kill me."

"I won't."

"Don't maim me."

"I won't."

"Let me return." As part of the trap, he didn't say, refusing to go so far.

"Earn it."

"I need to think. Concentrate."

"Shall I leave?"

"You'd still be here. You're in the walls."

"True. The tomb."

"The trap."

"The trap, yes. My personality is coded through all this. But it would be easier for you to concentrate." And the intercept vanished, took away her glow, left only dim yellow lamplight, tunnelling, vitreous, intimate darkness without her darkling eyes.

Beni stopped, pretended to think, triggered his implant, saw again the plan of her tomb picked out in light, saw that he was at the central chamber, the structural heart of what this thwarted, predatory, former woman had become. Out of despair.

"Oh, Dormeuse, Dormeuse," he murmured. "I am so sorry." Imagining how it had to be, the eighty-five labouring over the final secret plan, the hate and loss in their hearts as all the others sailed blissfully on, away, abandoning.

What choice then. What choice now. For them both.

"We can change this," he said, resolved, striding on to his goal, though he did believe he was already there. "We can make a start here. Try to be friends. Let me try to be that, Arasty. At least try to be that."

"Yes," the tomb said, the walls, the night, as he strode on in his cone of yellow light into the endlessness of the hill. "And that is why."

Outside the Nothing Stones pull and pull and will forever pull, drawing in the emptiness of infinity, the blackness of eyes made hard, so unforgivingly hard. She is punitive and spiteful and so so determined. It is all she will ever have.

Beni strides on with his young man's dreams—of success, of being different, better than the best, with his wonderful new dream of achieving something more, something new. He walks into night and does not see the final reading, does not know just how merciful she has been, that this time there is mercy, as much of it as there can ever be. He believes he can still be the greatest of them all. He still believes Ramirez is someone else.

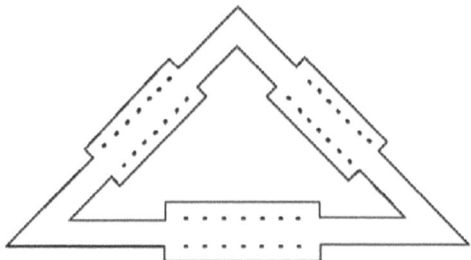

The Quiet Redemption of

Andy the House

Now all desires—even unknown ones—I had
Stand stript before me with their names writ under.
And will this make me really sane, I wonder,
Or only more intelligently mad?

— ERNEST G. MOLL

Welcome to Nefau

THE MEETING WAS quite an occasion for both men. Each had the opportunity to marvel at the absurdity of someone else's name for once. Small, round Pixie Rushbairn Todd, white-coated and aging stylishly (so his friends said), smiled and held out his hand.

"Doctor Balm. I am very pleased to meet you in person at last. Welcome to Nefau Clinic."

His guest, the tall, ascetic-looking, darkly dressed Frederick Balm, bowed slightly, though his narrow bespectacled head was angled back too far: courtesy, but with no indication of enjoying this, one of life's little jokes.

"Doctor Pixie Todd. It is an honour."

Pixie Rushbairn Todd could almost hear the heels click.

They shook hands, then Balm introduced his Bantu colleague, a fine-looking black woman almost as tall as himself, though clearly half his age. "This is Beris Abana, Doctor Todd. She helped me field-test the dream-gun."

"Of course. Welcome, Doctor Abana." Pixie shook hands again.

There was a bow from her as well (inherited, no doubt, from her days around the illustrious doctor of psychiatry), but at least her eyes twinkled. She was enjoying the circumstances far more than either psychotherapist could show. She smiled warmly, more from genuine pleasure, Pixie thought, than some need to keep his goodwill through this delicate business of testing their amazing new rehabilitation technique. The smile told him, as well, that she understood the authorities had given the Nefau trustees no choice in the matter. Nefau had Andy Bates, after all: the twenty-two-year-old patient who had spoken only fifty-thousand words in his lifetime, most of them unconnected, without apparent sense or purpose. Beris Abana's smile was both a thank-you and an apology. It did wonders for Pixie's peace of mind.

After Crafer had taken the bags and Gertrude had served tea in the front parlour of the old hospital, Pixie led them up to Andy's room on the first floor.

"You have seen our reports," he said as they mounted the stairs. "Andy does test out as schizoid. But for the one exception, which I will show you presently, he is a wonderfully neutral personality—if I can use that term positively.

"He is a personable, passive man; social, or rather, far from anti-social in any clinical sense. He will give you his attention—sometimes momentarily but enough to make you feel he is watching what goes on—then it will slip away. He feeds and cleans himself with minimum supervision, watches television, reads the books brought to him but requests nothing. He will not interact on any terms but his own. How does that sound to you, Doctor Balm?"

"Perfect for our purposes, Doctor Pixie Todd," Balm said, and Beris's eyes twinkled again.

Pixie raised his eyebrows in a silent question to her. Was that humour from the unbending Doctor Balm, this use of his full name? Pixie doubted it.

"I'm glad to hear it, Doctor Frederick Balm," Pixie said, and Beris Abana turned her sudden laugh into a polite cough.

Andrew Linton Bates was sitting in the middle of the floor when the three psychiatrists came in. He was examining the colour plates in a book on the Pre-Raphaelite and Symbolist painters, and did not so much as look up. The room was clean and well lit, with posters on the walls and some picture books, puzzles, even several toys scattered about. A television set and a radio were both going but with the sound turned low. Pixie switched these off, then got down on the floor next to the young man.

"Hello, Andy. This is Doctor Balm and Doctor Abana. They have come here to talk to you."

Andy looked up, but his gaze went between his visitors to a point on the far wall. Then he looked away.

"Tomorrow," Pixie continued, "Doctor Balm and Doctor Abana are going to use a wonderful new machine to help you talk with us. What do you think of that, Andy?"

Again the gaze came up, and this time swung across the two new faces before him before settling on the point beyond. Frederick Balm turned to follow that gaze, and when Beris and Pixie did the same, they found the focal point to be several books in the bookcase against the wall.

"He reads avidly," Pixie said, looking to see if Crafer had brought in any new titles from the Clinic library. No, the favourites were there. "He was taught at an early age with two of his brothers by a governess who could never make him talk coherently. Interesting choices, don't you think? That new book on the raising of the *Mary Rose*, Roland Auguet's *The Roman Games*, and Sagan's *Cosmos*."

"He reads these, you say?" Frederick Balm sounded sceptical.

"Seems to. A pupilometer shows the proper progressions and timings. The usual random saccades on the photographs and illustrations, but regular patterns otherwise. We assume he reads. But come." Pixie led his guests out of the room. As he closed the door, he held a single finger before his lips, urging them to listen.

"ABC," said Andy, beyond the door. "ABC."

Sitting in Pixie's cosy, wood-panelled office downstairs, Doctor Balm read *The Story of the House* for the third time. Beris Abana watched him as he did it; Pixie looked out through the french windows, watching as bands of sunlight and cloud-shadow marched across the well-kept grounds.

"Fascinating!" Balm said, and read it again.

Pixie glanced down at his own copy, though he did not need to. Every detail was pressed into his memory.

The Story of the House
by Andrew Linton Bates
(as dictated to Marjory Symon and Pixie Todd)

Once upon a time there was a house. The house hopped with people.

"I wonder if this is a New Year," said the man.

"This is an apple house, it skips along all the time-hop, hop, hop-a-hop."

"Hey, I don't know," said the Mummy. "Is it good or bad?"

"ABC, ABC," said the house.

"Cock-a-doodle-doo," said the rooster.

"Cock-a-doodle-dog," said the funny rooster.

The postman rang the doorbell. Ding dong.

The postman knocked at the door.

"Hello, I've got some mail," said the postman. "What a noisy house."

The night couldn't wait, but the morning came. But you watch the eyes.

That night the apple house was shattered with all kinds of colours. The colours were blue, green, light blue, brown, orange, pink, dark brown, and red.

But spirits came...pop pop. The spirits came along.

The spirits didn't know that the sky was dark. The sky was dark.

Ha-ha-ha-ha-ha-ha-ha, the house will be surprised.

Ha-ha-ha-ha-ha-ha-ha, the house will be surprised.

When the house comes home to eat his meal, he'll think we are not there. It will be easy to tear out his hair and spoil his meal.

Little Baby Jesus, cradled in the hay
Softly sang his mother ,Lula lula lay
Lula lula lula lay, Baby born on Christmas Day
Little Baby Jesus, cradled in the hay

The flowers were good. The people were in their beds. It was night-time. The sun had gone to bed. We had to go. If there was a poem I'll tell it to you.

"ABC, ABC," said the house very quietly.

"Nothing else like it?" Balm said when he had finished.

Pixie swung his chair around.

"Nothing before or since. He's been here seven years. We get signature phrases: 'ABC', sometimes 'Cock-a-doodle-dog', 'The spirits came along', and others—snatches of sentences related to the story. We've made keyword association tests, put direct questions to him, created visualisations. Specialists have visited us here at Nefau, tried hypnosis, drug therapies. Nothing. That story may be significant; it seems to be. But it may mean nothing at all. But tell me, Doctor Balm. I have read your published material, but this is so new I find I am the layman again. What do you do with this gun of yours?"

Balm passed the photocopy to his assistant so she could add it to their files.

"Well now. The gun lets us raid Andy's unconscious, quickly, very quickly, while Andy is in sedated sleep. His condition is measured against 8,216 recorded precedents, most of them sharing fundamental similarities. We establish parameters as far as we can, follow recommendations computed for those cases, then apply them, the three of us working together."

"Carl Jung—"

"Said the individual psyche must be treated on its own unique terms; yes, I know. And I agree absolutely, Doctor Todd. We will be imposing a dream on Andy, a control dream—a holding dream, we call it. Starting this afternoon, we will plant the first elements deep in his subconscious through our machine's own tracking-hypnosis method; elements of a thematic and causal template which will be repeated and reinforced. If you like, we are cramming his subconscious with orthodoxy, with relationships and responsibilities and extroversion—hundreds of psychic triggers and associations. It is done very quickly. In moments of maximum stress, he will return to the holding dream."

"Which will be what precisely?"

Doctor Balm smiled, but his head went back and spoilt any warmth his smile might have had. He looked indulgent.

"Simple things mostly. Nice things. I have chosen a seashore on a fine warm day. A small village full of people who know and love him. These are free elements, not exclusive. He can project on to these, tamper with them if he likes. Other factors will be more deep-seated, more impervious to interference."

"Like what?"

"Please, Doctor Todd. Observe the experiment for us. Be a true test-case observer. Let us have your objectivity a while longer. Just know that we will have placed a stasis-lock in Andy's world, a deeply subliminal construct to keep the holding dream in place while socialisation, rehabilitation, can occur. It has worked five times already with splendid results. The patients appear to be fully socialized—and after only very short periods of treatment."

"This is exciting news, Doctor Balm. But what of the allowances made for Andy's individuality, his special self ? Surely—"

"Allowances are made, naturally. Hence the room for improvisation. Trust us, Doctor Todd, please. Observe."

Day 2—Andy Under the Gun

At 9:30 the next morning, Andy was under the gun. He lay on a padded examination table in the dimly lit observation room, with the big cowl covering his head and shoulders and all the contacts in place. The drugs and the tracking-hypnosis had taken effect; he was in a deep sleep already.

Pixie Todd and Beris Abana watched through the control room window while Doctor Balm made the final adjustments.

"Let us begin, Beris," he said into his coat-mike, then faced Pixie through the glass. "We all contain the Mythmaker, Doctor Todd, the Storyteller of the Soul. Now we coax it to do openly what it does best in secret: tell us about this Self."

"We've got readings and we've got REM," Beris said in quiet voice.

"Excellent." Frederick Balm turned back to his patient and opened the remote channel on the large cowl.

"Tell us about where you are, Andy. Tell us what is happening."

It was startling how Andy's voice came out of the wall speakers, relayed from the throat mikes, the slurring and static eliminated.

"I am at the beach again," Andy said, his lips barely moving, but obeying the planted injunction to be the storyteller of dreams. "It's a hot fine day, and Hari and I are still allowed to mend the nets; such an honour. We are lucky. The villagers are down the beach, away from the huts, away from us. There's just Hari and me. And Ma Miller. Yes, Ma Miller's watching us. She smiles. We go on mending the nets."

"It's the holding dream," Balm said, nodding with approval.

"How do you know?" Pixie asked.

"The nets. One of our theme images. Our main one. Listen!"

"Then she's gone to join the others. Hari and I watch her go, then Hari says: 'I've been to see the fighters.'

"'You haven't! You wouldn't,' I cry, dropping my net, but I remember Ma Miller and pick it up again, glad she can't hear us any longer. The nets are important.

"'I told you I would one day,' Hari says to me.

"'I don't believe you.'

"Hari comes closer. We hunch down before the veils of the drying nets and speak of forbidden things, of the small beach to the north and the stone amphitheatre there.

"'I did, Andy. My rope is there, hanging on the wall. I cut notches in the beam I found in Sam Night's store and leaned it against the wall and climbed up it. I saw over the top. I did. I saw the fighters.'

"'Were there any changes?' I ask, full of awe and wonder. No one has ever climbed the Arena wall that I can remember, but there are the stories. People—Hoppy and Tuta—speak of it sometimes, in appropriate whispers, but never do anything about it.

"'No,' Hari says, and I am relieved. 'Just the breeze off the desert and the waves falling. Nothing has changed, I know it. The fighters never knew I was there.'

"'You're making this up,' I say, but know she isn't.

"Hari grips my arm in a pinch. Such spitefulness is unlike her, but she is trying to make me believe.

"'No!' she says again. 'Come and see. The rope's there. The beam's there. Climb up and see!'

"So we do. We leave the nets and creep out of the village, up through the long grass; run crouching over the dunes to the low headland, to the dry empty—almost empty—area where the desert comes to the sea.

"The Arena is there, a ring of stone close to the beach, its canted ashlar wall eight feet high—"

Beris: "These details are amazing. I would never have thought—"
Balm: "Listen!"

"I see the beam and the rope wedged in a crevice between two blocks at the top. I feel very afraid.

"'Hari!' I cry.

"'Come on, Andy,' she says. 'See the fighters!'

"I go on with Hari, caught between fear of Ma Miller, Samuel Night and the other adults—"

Balm: "Note that! Adults."

"—and my desire to see the armoured fighting men, this constant taboo motif of life on the shore."

Beris: "Whose language is this, Doctor Balm?"
Balm: "Listen!"

"At the base of the sloping wall, I listen for sounds. I imagine that I can hear the occasional distant ring of a single-edged sword against a heavy shield. I approach the rough-hewn, notched beam and look up. The rope is swaying in the hot, off-shore breeze.

"'Go on!' Hari says. 'You first.'

"I grip the rope and start climbing, positioning my feet and hauling myself up, determined now to do it. I reach the lip of the wall and reach over to hang on, then pull myself up on to the wide ashlar rim. There is tension on the rope and presently Hari is beside me, hauling herself up next to me.

"Together, we gaze down into the Arena. I feel good, somehow, when I do it.

"The fighting men are there on the hot sand in the very middle of the stone circle, blindly hitting out at one another, but rarely connecting. Their sightless, bronze helmets gleam dully in the hot sunlight.

"Blind gladiators. Their brown, oiled and sweating bodies shine more than their broad-brimmed, full-visored helmets, those fearsome eyeless helmets. They wear short heavy leather skirts, each man with one arm protected by a *manica* and a *galerus*, and the left leg covered by an *ocrea*. They carry heavy bronze swords with a single edge. As we watch, they move about one another in aimless circling movements, their shields in close, their sword-arms forever searching—"

Pixie: "He's got this from Auguet's book on the gladiatorial games."
Balm: "Doctor Todd, please!"

"—pity them at first, these hopeless blind warriors. They are like automatons. But I watch, fascinated, and become more and more afraid. Something is going to happen. Hari doesn't realize how dangerous this is. No one can really tell me why this Arena is here, who built it and when. But it is very important. I am so afraid, so very afraid—"

"Bring him out of it, Beris," said Balm.

"Yes, Doctor Balm." Beris adjusted the subliminals, imposed new lead images and slowly returned Andy to the beach and the nets. Presently, the holding dream was phased out altogether. Andy rested, calm now, left to free-form, to wake when he was ready.

Crafer served a late breakfast in the front parlour. Frederick Balm could scarcely conceal his excitement.

"A wonderful beginning. Just marvellous. I am so encouraged."

Pixie sipped his tea. "I take it the Arena and the gladiators is the stasis-lock for your controlled dream?"

Balm set down his cup.

"But no. Not at all. That's exactly the point, Doctor Todd. I used the mending of the nets for the stasis-lock, something far more simple. Andy should have returned to mending the nets the moment stress began, but he didn't. He has invented this Arena, focused all his anxieties on to it. It is the bugbear, the shadow, in this paradise. He chose to stay with it instead. I never thought he would show it to us so soon. That book, *The Roman Games*, must have had a powerful impact on his subconscious."

"What would have happened if Andy had been left on the wall?" Pixie asked.

"I cannot say, Doctor Todd. That is why I brought him back. This has not happened before and we can't risk too much. We don't have a full enough picture of his world. But the presence of mind, you agree, is startling."

"And our next step?"

Beris answered him. "Will be to take Andy back to the beach this afternoon. Frederick will strengthen the stasis-lock."

Day 2—Andy Under the Gun

"Hari comes to me while I am fixing nets and says the Elders want to see us. We go to Sam Night's store and there are many villagers there: Ma Miller, Sam, Tuta, Mary and Rose, the Arius brothers,

Lucky and Hoppy, even our best fisherman, Thrice Ian. We are worried but soon find it is routine business.

"They tell us we must take more care with the nets, but their words lack conviction somehow, as if that is not what they meant to talk about at all. All the same, we spend the rest of the morning making our best knots. It is a hot, fine day so we swim for a while at noon, then go back to the mending refreshed.

"No one will tell me any more about the Arena on the beach or about the fighters who spend their days endlessly circling one another, delivering their sudden expected-but-always-unexpected blows. I have only asked Bish and Carl; there's no one else I can trust—only Hoppy and Tuta, but they have to be drunk before they mention it.

"I watch Hari's brown back as she works. Beautiful Hari. I believe she thinks as I do—that the circular fighting ground inside the wall and the blind fighters are the stasis-lock for our world—"

Balm: "What!"
Pixie: "My God!"

"—liberation from the cycle of the nets—"

Balm: "What is this? Where did this knowledge come from?"
Beris: "Our coat-mikes were open during the setting-up. He listened—"
Pixie: "A reversal."

"—and sure of it. It is inherited knowledge, a certainty, a fact, like the wind, the sand, the waves falling, the gulls, the hot sun. Hari has this secret knowledge too because as I watch the small fine hairs on her arms, she turns to look at me and smiles—"

Beris: "Bring him out of it, Frederick!"
Balm: "We're losing it again!"
Pixie: "What is wrong?"

Day 2—Table Talk

After dinner that evening, Pixie and Frederick Balm finally argued.

It began naturally enough at the dinner table when Crafer had brought Andy down for a fifteen minute 'socialisation check' or, as Pixie preferred to call it, his 'meeting with the inquisitors'.

Gertrude has just cleared the plates away, more wine had been served, and Pixie had just finished telling Ramone and Michael, his two assistants at the Clinic, about Andy's unexpected resistance to the day's dream-therapy. Andy sat opposite Pixie at the far end of the table, with Beris, then Frederick Balm, on his right, and Ramone and Michael to his left. Crafer stood near the door, close by Andy.

The young patient was dressed in a loose shirt and jeans, and sipped at a glass of diluted chablis, looking alert and intelligent and for all the world like a junior colleague rather than an inmate.

It had been agreed that Balm would lead the discussion.

"I enjoyed your *Story of the House*, Andy," he said. "Very much."

Andy watched him, fleetingly, his eyes glancing at the other faces in front of him.

"It's a most interesting house," Balm continued, and sipped his wine. "A very remarkable place."

"ABC," Andy murmured, very softly, his lips close to the edge of his glass.

Balm nodded, as if Andy's reply made sense. He took another sip of wine, then tried again.

"Yes, indeed. ABC. A fine house. Does Hari live there too, Andy? Where does Hari live?"

There was no visible reaction to the name. Andy was watching the candles halfway down the table, using his wine as a lens.

Balm was not discouraged. "Tell me about the fighters, Andy. The gladiators in the Arena who cannot see."

"It skips along all the time," Andy said, and a frown narrowed his forehead. He stared at the wine.

"They trouble you, these gladiators, do they, Andy? They keep you from the nets. Distract you."

The frown remained. Andy set his glass down carefully on the white table cloth so the candles shone through it.

Frederick Balm exchanged looks with Pixie and Beris, then spoke again.

"These fighters, Andy. The blind fighters. You watch the eyes."

Andy looked straight down the table at Balm.

"ABC," he said again, very quietly, then pushed back his chair, got up, and left the room. Michael and Crafer went after him. Through the door they heard another "ABC", much fainter, then there was silence.

"Extraordinary," Balm said. "Most remarkable."

"There's tremendous power of the Self there, Doctor," Pixie said. "I cannot see how you will stop him reverting."

"Be patient, Doctor Todd. All his sleeping will be done under the gun now. We will reinforce the holding dream by the hour if necessary. It will balance out the conflict, minimise it. With proper diet and medication and stabilising treatments under the gun, Andy should not regress. We are aiming at homeostasis, nothing less. Eventually the whole thing will be completely self-regulating."

"Forgive me, Doctor Balm. I seem to be more the Jungian about Andy than I expected to be. We have here a unique Self, a unique madness, an apparently integrated, if elusive, perception-consciousness. I cannot easily accept these tactics you have devised."

"I understand such reservations, Doctor Todd. And you are being wonderfully patient with us—"

"Effectively coerced, shall we say?" And Pixie laughed.

Balm laughed also. "We will continue to monitor dream activity under the gun. Andy will speak to us more and more. The storyteller/mythmaker motif is well planted now. We should get a much higher order of presentation than he was capable of in his *Story of the House*. We will make sure his dreams contain the stasis-lock. We will strengthen that until he is stable. He will keep returning to the image of the nets, depending on how much he needs it. The Arena, the fighters, will go."

Pixie sighed. "This is what worries me. You make it sound as if Andy must fight to be free of your subliminal embeddings. That sounds wrong, against free will. Is it possible he might prefer psychosis?"

Doctor Balm looked at his assistant. Beris was carefully neutral.

"A curious notion, Doctor Todd."

"But a possibility, Doctor Balm, though you don't like my saying it."

"No, I certainly don't."

"Please. Let me say the obvious then. With schizophrenia, we may not be faced with just the notion of the divided personality. We know, by our conventional standards, that Andy is psychotic; he tests as schizoid. We ultimately do not know if his personality is integrated in that condition rather than divided and disturbed. Each case must be judged on its own merits."

Balm shook his head. "*The Story of the House* shows anxiety, stress, paranoia, morbid fascination—"

"The story does, agreed, but Andy doesn't. He is peaceful, without anxiety. His metabolism is in harmony; he *has* homeostasis! We call him mad because of his social conduct, his refusal to communicate apart from those House construct writings."

Doctor Balm stood. "No. We must try more. We are here—"

"Perhaps you should be here, Doctor Balm, to explore what madness is. I discover, all these years later, that I am here to work a cure only in terms of the patient, not of our preconceptions about what constitutes sanity."

"No! No! No!" Balm said, striking the table with each word. "That will not do. You cannot have such...non-participatory individuals judged subjectively sane. It is solipsism; you cannot justify it! And you cannot let such people operate in society. How could they operate?"

"Free Andy Bates and see. Observe him. Does he feed himself? Does he defecate without dirtying his clothes? Does he generally observe social customs?"

"I imagine he does, Doctor Todd."

"You know he does. That is the problem. Andy is not sociopathic, not misanthropic. He does fend for himself. In a forest, in a jungle, he would no doubt survive. As a solitary—"

"But only as a solitary! What is viable, Doctor Todd?"

"What is intrinsically wrong with his madness, Doctor Balm? Tell me."

"It is non-contiguous. It lacks any sense of cause and effect that we can relate to. It is—"

"Inaccessible! I said it before: Andy is a solitary. In any society, he could be left alone; a different proposition entirely to the village imbecile. He might even be acclaimed as a holy man, a mystic—"

"Hopelessly out of touch!"

"It would seem, though I question the word 'hopelessly'. That is what you should be exploring here, Doctor, with your wonderful machine. Will Andy accept our sanity or struggle to return to his? What does the Andrew Linton Bates personality want most? Socialisation—this exoteric re-alignment we are trying for—or subjective integration? We will observe the way he behaves with this holding dream of yours, the way he accepts or resists the stasis-lock."

"Yes," Doctor Balm said. "We will observe. But now I am very tired. I am up at 2 am to make adjustments to the gun. Goodnight."

Pixie and Beris watched him go, then sat looking into the fire Crafer had set to warm the room.

"It was difficult for you to tell Frederick how concerned you are, Doctor."

"You must call me Pixie, please. Yes, it was. And I should probably have waited. But it would be unfair not to express the balancing view from the outset. Our age suffers from too much literalism, from this pro-rational bias that lets reason account for everything so neatly. Frederick is a good man, Beris, but—"

"He gets results."

"He does, yes. And so seems to justify one approach over any other, changing unknown, totally subjective quantities, perceptions, value systems, into fixed quantities. I worry about that on principle. Are we restoring sanity, social viability—or conventionalising the subject? The 'or' is what concerns me, Beris. Not a belief, but a possibility of an alternative. Though I wonder how we are to explore such things. If I had your wonderful gun, I would set up situations, yes, plant key images, yes, but only so far. It seems important now, after such initial success, that Andy *can* choose the path he takes— our sanity or his. What irony if ethics and accepted norms should keep us from what might be true."

"Schizophrenia, psychopathology, and you suggest choices?"

"They are words, labels, handles, Beris. We really don't know enough."

Beris studied the flames curling up over the logs in the grate. "You feel Andy can choose? That he might turn the dream?"

"I suspect it is essential now, Beris, that he be allowed to, that it is built into his therapy somewhere. I believe he is already turning the dream anyway—as if his subconscious is indicating the need for a choice situation. It's a possibility."

Beris watched the flames a while longer, then yawned and stretched. "It's not going as easily as we'd expected," she said.

"It means a lot to hear you say so, Beris. What do you do next?"

"Tonight I start reading Auguet, if I can stay awake. Learning about gladiators."

Day 3—Where's Hari?

During the night, Frederick Balm intensified the stasis-lock element of the holding dream, and all the next day Andy responded well to the patterns. When he became the storyteller at mid-morning, he spoke of sitting among the nets under a fine blue sky, working away with great care and skill. Ma Miller, he told his audience, was very pleased, and twice Sam and Ian came to admire his handling of the nets. Some of the other village children even helped for a time.

"I think we have him at last," Balm said when Pixie came in at the end of his afternoon rounds.

"Yes?" Pixie said, then smiled at Beris who sat reading Auguet's book in the technician's chair, her long legs drawn up under her. He looked at the transcripts of the morning's dream-story.

"The images have firmed up and stabilised," Balm continued. "No mention of the Arena."

Pixie nodded, finished scanning the print-outs, then peered through the glass at the dimly lit observation room where Andy was asleep.

"So what do you think is happening now, Doctor?"

Frederick Balm seemed pleased by the question, as if it showed that Pixie Todd had finally reconsidered his position.

"The gladiatorial material was probably residual, a last-ditch and unusually strong resistance by the psyche, using anything Andy had assimilated. We've not encountered its like before. The psyche usually yields to the superimposed, reinforced templates. Beris has found correlatives for some of it."

"Oh?"

Beris uncurled her legs and sat up.

"Gladiator classifications," she said. "Samnite? Sam Night. Myrmillo? Ma Miller. Thracian? Thrice Ian. Different kinds of gladiators who fought in the Arena. I haven't finished it yet."

Balm continued. "Andy is fighting us, which we expect. He has used residues to build his own stasis-lock—"

"To protect his madness?" Pixie asked. "Is that possible?"

Balm's mouth tightened; he drew in a deep breath.

"Yes. Yes, of course. It is natural that he should do so. The sort of reasonable defence you would expect. We are the intruders, after all. His mind is sharp enough to know what we are doing. Heavens above, Doctor Todd! Crafer tells me Andy's even read books on psychology. This is not the usual situation. The Self is working with subliminal elements, symbols—important personal material enriched by association; it is formidable. We are opposing that, regularising that, imposing a system, a new, steady mould into which the personality can flow."

"Yes, I see that," Pixie said, more to calm the other psychotherapist than because he agreed. Too much was new here, too much was suspect, resembled tampering, brainwashing, aversion conditioning. Pixie said nothing about such things, and felt glad when Balm went out to get some fresh air.

"One point," Pixie said, scanning the transcripts again.

Beris looked up. "Yes, Pixie?"

"There's no mention of Hari here. He hasn't spoken of her today. Andy is alone on the beach."

Day 3—Table Talk

"You see it as a major issue?" Frederick Balm asked at dinner. There were only four of them this night; Michael and Crafer were out exercising Andy and some other patients. "Is this something especially Jungian, Doctor Todd? Hari as the female part of Andy's psyche?"

"It's highly possible, Doctor. He accepts her completely; she is certainly no threat. Why not his anima?"

"I can accept that. But does she have to be there?"

"No," Pixie said. "Not there necessarily. But to give her initial and vital presence, I would think she has to be somewhere relevant to our point-of-view storyteller. It is a related system—in some key areas a closed system, I should think—in spite of the gun's insertions. Why has Andy not reflected on where Hari is? If she is absent, she must be somewhere important. There may be a reason why the Andy-psyche does not disclose her whereabouts even to itself."

Balm turned to Beris Abana. "Is there a correlative in Auguet?"

"Not yet," Beris replied. "I haven't had time to finish it and monitor the transcripts as well."

"Show me where you are up to, Beris," Pixie said. "I don't sleep a great deal these days. Meanwhile, Doctor Balm, I would ask you to remember Hari's role in this scheme of things, her intimacy with Andy. It may just be a fantasy persona, an incidental dream-figure. But it may be his female self, working as comforter, a support, a mother figure or final protection."

"Her going may be a good sign," Beris said, diplomatically, as if to fend off another confrontation. "Like the phasing out of the Arena and the fighters."

"Yes," agreed Pixie, recognising what Beris was doing but unable to stop himself. "Or it may be a blind for what's really taking place. I must keep saying this."

Balm smiled. "Of course. So let's have Andy brought in. We may note some preliminary changes, and I want to improvise again."

Ramone got up and opened the door. Andy was waiting out in the hall, freshly cleaned and dressed. Crafer and Ramone led him in.

"Good evening, Andy," Balm said.

"ABC," Andy replied, meeting Frederick Balm's eyes directly with his own. "The man with the nets. *Retiarius. Habet! Hoc habet!*"

"I see," Balm said, and gave a significant look to Pixie and Beris. "You recognise me. The netman, I believe; the gladiator with the net and trident. I know that much. Tell us about the Arena, Andy."

Andy did not answer. He took his glass of wine and peered through it as he had before, watching the different lights in the room.

Balm lifted his own glass and looked through it the same way. "So, where is Hari? She was not with you today."

"*Habet! Hoc habet!*" Andy said, but not forcefully this time.

"It's a gladiatorial cry," Beris explained. "It translates as 'He's had it'."

Balm nodded. "I suspected I was Andy's opponent. He is resisting this— how did you say it: *retiarius?*—with the confounded nets."

Pixie repeated Balm's earlier question.

"Where is Hari today, Andy?"

"The postman knocks at the door. Knock! Knock! The house will be surprised. *Habet! Hoc habet!*" He finished his glass of wine and stood up.

Pixie also stood and led Andy to the door. "Thank you, Crafer. Andy is becoming excited."

As the door closed, Pixie held up his hand, bidding the others to listen. But no words came from the other side, and Pixie was left standing there with one hand raised and a frown on this face.

Day 5—Andy Under The Gun

Balm: "He's talking about her at last."

"—for three days now. No one has asked after her either, not yet. Most of the villagers are down on the beach at Sam's store, or building Lucky his new cottage back in one of the low sheltered hollows above the beach.

"I mend nets, hoping, hoping, hoping that Hari will not be found out. If Ma Miller or Thrice Ian catch her, something terrible will happen.

"Yes. I realise that is true. Something awful, terrible, will be done. I know it's silly, but as I work, I pretend to be talking with Hari, looking up and nodding sometimes in case Ma or Ian or Sam should glance back from the store and catch sight of me in the spaces between the cabins.

"It's all I can think of."

Beris: "There's deep stress."
Balm: "Continue. See if the lock holds."

"Then Hari appears from behind, jumps down in the sand beside me. She has been running and is very excited."

Balm: "Damn!"

"'Hari! Where have you been?' I cry.

"'Watching the fighters,' she says. 'Andy, the front of the helmets are pitted. Eyeslits are forming.'

"'What?' I jump up, dropping the net I've been mending."

Beris: "Doctor Balm?"
Balm: "Continue, Beris! Continue! We must have this!"

"—and Hari nods. 'Come look! Soon they will be able to see.'

"We run from the village, scurrying across the dunes down to the forbidden beach. This time we don't pause to look for Sam and Ian or the others. We scramble up to the stone wall and the beam, and haul on the rope.

"As I climb, I already sense something is wrong. There are no sounds coming from inside the Arena. We get on to the rim of the wall and lie there panting. Below us, the gladiators are no longer fighting. They stand several metres apart, their heads lifted slightly, their smooth, curving, full-visored faces watching the sun.

"Almost smooth faces.

"Where the eyes would be, the dully gleaming metal is scoured and pitted. Hari is right. Eyeslits *are* forming. The fighters stand, waiting for it to happen.

"I feel a thrill of terror, but of excitement too. Change has come to the beach. The stasis-lock is about to be broken, is breaking even as we watch— as soon as the eyeslits are done, as soon as the fighters can see.

"'Quickly!' Hari cries. 'Let's get down there before it happens.'

"Such a suggestion would normally be absurd, totally unthinkable. But now there is an urgency, a recklessness, a logic to the suggestion.

"We have to go down to the fighters. If we can bear to do it, we have to touch those nascent eyes; if possible, see what the fighters will see as their world becomes sighted at last."

Pixie: "Nascent? This vocabulary—"
Balm: "Sshhh!"

"Hari pulls up on the rope and throws it down inside the wall. She lowers herself to the floor of the Arena, and I follow, hand over hand.

"The perspective is altered dramatically. We are no longer in the world of the seashore. We can barely hear the waves falling or even feel the wind. Now we are in a strange world—of hot sand, a blazing blue sky, a relentless sun. Now there is only the wall— endless and enclosing, a rim to the world—and the fighters.

"I am terrified but fascinated. The gladiators have never ceased fighting, swinging and lunging in their blindness. I know they haven't. Now it seems that they watch us as surely as they do the sun, considering what to do.

"We can make out distinct slits now, becoming more deeply etched and perforated, making a grid really rather than a slit. Soon they will see us.

"Hari and I cross the hot sand. We watch the unmoving figures, the idle swords which have never been idle, note the fierce angles of their helmets and shields, their *ocreae* and dull *manicae*, their sweat-stained skirts, and we find we are no longer afraid.

"We approach those still figures, powerful-looking and almost twice our height, each of us going to a different gladiator. We reach up to touch the growing eye-openings. I feel hot metal, first the smoothness, then the uneven pitting in a definite groove. I feel a tingling sensation along my arm, through my whole being.

"Hari and I tear our hands away almost at the same instant, and look around us. We try to see what the figures will see when their eyes have come.

"It no longer seems to be just a ring of stone. It is as if we are in the centre of a colossal amphitheatre with tiers of seats stretching up into the bright sky, filled with row upon row of spectators staring down at us, watching the transformation, watching to see what we will do.

"Blinking, shading our eyes against the glare, we see the double image: one moment the hot, empty sky above the wall, and then, almost simultaneously, the rising sea of faces waiting there.

"'Who are they?' I ask Hari. My voice sounds as a harsh whisper in the silence.

"Hari shakes her head.

"'What do they want?' I ask.

"'We will know soon, Andy.'

"'What will we do?'

"'We watch the eyes! We watch them forming. We wait now.'"

Balm: "Too much stress! Bring him out! We'll take him back to the nets! I'll implant a Hari cipher. We'll control it."

Pixie: "No, Doctor Balm! Please!"

Beris: "No, Frederick! Pixie is right. This is a resolution."

Pixie: "Taking him back will only delay the process. He'll do it again. This is crucial for him. *His* solution."

Balm: "Listen then!"

"—to continue watching. It's almost done. The pitting is deep—"

Pixie: "There's something more, Doctor Balm. In Auguet. Blind gladiators are called *andabates*. You understand? Andy Bates! Those fighters may be Andy, gaining sight."

Balm: "Then we're coming to the end of it. He is helping us, providing his own more powerful stasis-lock. Our nets reminded him of a gladiator's nets. What did he call them? The retiarius' nets? He did the rest."

Pixie: "Or he's coming to a choice."

Balm: "We shall see, Doctor Todd. But I suggest he's doing the job for us, accelerating the process, using elements stronger than we could ever devise. The gladiators will see; you will get your Andy and Hari integrated at last—a pleasingly Jungian touch, I think. We need only take him back to the Arena in the final treatments, reinforce that part of the amended holding dream."

Beris: "What about the name Hari?"

Balm: "Doctor Todd? Anything in Auguet or the other books?"

Pixie: "Nothing gladiatorial. Possibly it's a form of *hara*—the Japanese for 'belly'; the centre of the Self. He's read Zen texts."

Balm: "Good. Let us listen."

"—with the slits. They seem to be done. Hari and I move towards the men again. I think I can see eyes glinting through the openings, watching us now. On all sides, the tiers rise into the sky; the silent faces peer down, still waiting to see what the fighters will do, what Hari and I will do.

"We stand between the fighters and are suddenly afraid—of their silence, of their lack of movement. Then the swords go up, a threatening action or a salute, with the half-hidden eyes, the faces on the tiers, all watching. Hari and I cling to each other and shut our eyes. We accept. We trust.

"The blows never come. When we open our eyes again, the fighters, the tiers, the Arena, are gone. There is only the quiet windswept beach, the waves falling, the hot sun, the dunes leading back into the desert.

"Hari and I do not speak. We do not need to speak. We go back to the nets; we go back to the mending."

Day 15—Farewell to Nefau

While Crafer loaded the luggage and equipment into the car, Pixie entertained Frederick Balm and Beris Abana in the main dining room. It was a special occasion. Michael and Ramone were there for a time before going off to do their rounds, and Andy had been given pride of place at the head of the table, where he still sat quietly finishing his lunch. He did not speak often, just a few encouraging words now and then, but over the past week his eyeline had stabilised. He made eye-contact much more frequently, and he seemed to be listening more attentively as well. As Frederick Balm had remarked several times during the meal, it was an auspicious beginning.

"When we come back next month, Andy, we will have many things to talk about, do you think?"

"Yes," Andy said, and looked directly at Doctor Balm.

"Good man. I'm very pleased. Now Doctor Abana and I must be going. We must make our flight. So, it's goodbye."

"Goodbye," Andy said.

They got up, all but Andy. Frederick Balm and Beris shook Andy's hand and headed for the front hall. As Pixie went to close the door, he stopped and looked in at the young man.

"Andy?"

The young man looked up. "Yes?"

"I'm very pleased too," Pixie said. "You have done very well." And as he closed the door, he remembered to lean in close and listen.

Frederick Balm and Beris watched him from the front door. They saw him smile.

"Anything, Doctor Pixie Todd?" Balm asked.

"Not a thing, Doctor Frederick Balm. Not a thing," Pixie said, and all the way to the car he prayed that Beris would understand what his smile meant.

With thanks to Kohan Ikin

The Maze Man

AT 8:30 AM ON Saturday 14 April, James Quinlan, a 35-year-old computer programmer living in an inner suburb of Sydney, awoke to find himself trapped in a maze.

At first, his discovery had all the pathetic buffoonery of a clown act, but fortunately he lived alone and Susan hadn't stayed the night, so it was a nightmare for one.

He got out of bed, went to cross the living-room of his first-floor apartment to the kitchen, and slammed into an invisible wall that now divided it.

Quinlan yelped in agony and surprise and fell backwards onto the floor, blood streaming from his nose.

He remained where he had fallen, supported by his arms, his legs out, blinking in utter amazement and staring across the room.

Then, with a curious but altogether natural pragmatism, absurdly inappropriate to the circumstances, he got up and went back to the bedroom to get a tissue for his nose.

He never got there. He slammed into another unseen wall and staggered back. His arms went up automatically, his blood-stained hands feeling above him. His eyes took on the cornered, hunted look small animals sometimes have.

He was in terror. His heart raced. But he found the wall, the unseeable wall, and felt the smooth, slightly soft then hard texture of it. He discovered, too, that it was impenetrable, a tough resisting barrier, neither hot nor cold.

Normally a somewhat stolid man, James Quinlan had a uniquely instantaneous indoctrination into a new reality. His normal world had ceased to be. His first impact with the wall was one thing, the "I must be dreaming!"— "Who left that sheet of glass here?" stage of his discovery. The second impact brought desperate cunning and an extraordinarily quick acceptance.

I don't want to hurt myself again, was his main thought, greater than the "What the hell!" and "Who's doing this?", greater than the bewilderment and the fear of insanity—a simple, deep-felt determination not to be hurt again. That fundamental acceptance would have surprised some psychologists.

In the space of six minutes, Quinlan learned to walk with his arms out in front of him and was tracing the wall. Its properties more than his predicament seemed the issue.

He came to a comer in the wall, followed its unseen ninety-degree turn around and found himself heading towards the wall overlooking Young Street. The invisible wall ended at the wall of his apartment, was blocked by plaster and brick, having missed the windows by less than a foot.

Quinlan leaned against the invisible barrier for a moment, then reached out his arms and took a step forward.

And touched it. Another invisible wall just over a meter away. He was in a corridor, a passage blocked at this end by the wall of his apartment, meeting a different passageway at the other end, so he surmised.

Quinlan went to find out.

Ten minutes later, he had established the pattern of his prison— a T-inter-section of two corridors in the middle of his living-room, one axial and running to the Young Street wall on the east; the other transverse and ending at the north and south walls.

By stacking things that he could reach, a coffee table, a chair that he could just touch and pull into his prison—he couldn't go to it but he could pull it in—he traced the wall upwards. No ceiling to it. Just an endless upward sweep, stopping at the plaster ceiling of his apartment. For all he knew it could go on to infinity up there, beyond the atmosphere, out into space.

It was as if someone had dropped a section of a gigantic rat's maze over him—a T-junction of corridors made of the most non-reflecting, non-refracting, hardest glass imaginable.

With no exit. Not to his bedroom, not down to Hanson Street. Just some fantastic junction, this set of two-metre-wide passageways.

Then it occurred to Quinlan—one more absurdity in all this—that the corridors were blocked only by the walls of his apartment, that they could well continue beyond. Already his process of logic had been suborned by his perception of a new reality.

He would have to wait for Susan or Twig—they both had keys. So he sat on the floor in the middle of his living-room, leaning (so bizarre to look at, he realised) against the wall of the "corridor".

Twig arrived an hour later. He knocked at the door first, then used his key to let himself in.

He smiled when he saw Quinlan in the middle of the room, then frowned and stared when he saw how Quinlan was sitting, as if his back were propped up by something.

"Hey, Quin, what's goin' on?"

"I can't get out, Twig. I'm trapped in a hallway."

"Sure you are, kid. Whatever you say. What did you do to your nose?"

And Twig walked through the very wall that his friend was leaning against.

"Do that again will you, Twig?" Quinlan said. "Go to the door and come back here to me."

"Sure, Quin," Twig said, looking at his friend oddly. "Then you can explain your nose, that leaning trick and what you're usin' to bring all this on."

"Do it, Twig! Then get me a tissue and a glass of juice from the fridge."

Twig did everything Quinlan asked, moving about the apartment with no trouble at all.

That was Quinlan's next discovery.

The maze was for him alone.

By the time Twig had phoned Susan and she and David had arrived, he was showing the first signs of shock. Though it was a Saturday, they got Dr Mell to come around. He heard the story from the others, gave Quinlan a shot to calm him, then considered the next step.

They had to get him out of the apartment, to a hospital, somewhere.

"We'll have to break down the wall or something," Twig said.

"Yeah," David explained to the doctor. "We can go to Jim but he can't come to us."

"It's true!" Twig added. "We nearly pulled his arm off trying to get him out of this hallway."

Dr Mell asked Quinlan about that. Quinlan indicated his sore nose, his bruised arms.

"At first it feels like it's going to give. It seems to soften. Then it starts hurting me, really hurting, all over. It's unbearable."

All the same, they tried it again, pulling on Quinlan's arms and legs until he was mashed up against the wall, sobbing with pain, and finally passed out. Even unconscious they couldn't move him through the walls.

A mattress was carried in, and bedclothes. Susan cooked him a meal. At 11.50, Dr Mell phoned the police. Twenty minutes after they arrived, they sent for the Rescue people. The unpleasant part of it was they all needed convincing the hard way for Quinlan—more of the pulling and tugging, more of the agony.

By three o'clock that afternoon, the owners of the apartment building had given permission for the Police Rescue crew to break open a small section of the Young Street wall of the apartment to get Quinlan out. At first this had been out of the question, but when the media teams and the curious started gathering, the couple who owned the building were only too glad to see the end of it.

The localised demolition was done neatly and efficiently, and Quinlan was helped down a near-vertical ladder to street level, whereupon he discovered the next corridor turning. One more in a network of the things. A maze.

It took them six weeks to get him to a private hospital on Grove Avenue; six weeks of Quinlan sleeping in a specially outfitted Police Rescue van parked across any corridor he was in, using a portable toilet and eating takeaway food, washing from an electric urn.

They didn't know which institution he would reach. At any moment, a corridor that had looked so promising would turn and take him forever out of the path of a likely sanctuary.

There were media releases during this time, all of them describing his condition as a purely mental one. Apart from ruining his career, these failed to account for the incredible delays in getting the poor man hospitalised and did nothing to stop the stream of requests from psychologists and university research departments all over the country.

The Rescue van already had four or five scientists and as many doctors on permanent duty during these weeks; five times that many when, after thousands of twists and turns, most of them in exasperatingly short distances, they got him into a specially prepared ground-floor bedroom at St Pat's.

Quinlan was on medication for most of the ordeal, and the police were marvellous, really, in getting him there. Once they realised it couldn't be a hoax, they cooperated fully. When the doctors brought Quinlan chalk, they even helped him chalk the lines of his labyrinth on roadways and sidewalks, whitewashing it on lawns and across gardens.

Every step of this pattern was painstakingly photographed and matched to wall maps all over the world. Five universities across Australia, learning the true story, allocated a portion of their annual research budgets in the science faculties to pay for damaged walls and property.

St Pat's was far from being an ideal place. Quinlan's room, it turned out, was in a particularly dense and intricate section of his maze, and while— incredibly—the toilet and shower cubicle in the narrow bathroom *were* accessible by a lucky right-angle turning in the corridor, it took Quinlan several minutes to get there—out through the french doors of what had once been a spacious patients' lounge and library area, back across the lawn, a dip into some former flower beds and back through a bay window.

At least at St Pat's the floor lines could be more or less permanent, though in the nearby suburbs that had been on Quinlan's route, some people had painted in the chalk lines of "Quinlan's Maze" for posterity, a bizarre and disturbing thing to see in the streets, and often short-lived. Even though the locals were free of its clutches, many felt uneasy at having an alien zone superimposed on their own world.

Within days of its bid for immortality, Quinlan's Maze was painted over with black bitumen paint in most thoroughfares, though portions of it remained in yards and back lanes and on the porches of the more curious and those who realised they couldn't afford to overlook this, to forget that— even for one person—the maze was there, contiguous with their own world.

From the first, the whole amazing phenomenon was an experience no-one knew quite what to do with. Circumstantially, it was virtually impossible to test the properties of the maze since it was available only to Quinlan's perceptions. Suggestions to explore the labyrinth's height, for instance, were ruled out. A balloon was fine until a strong wind blew it *out* of the corridor alignment while Quinlan remained behind, crushed within it. James Quinlan alone was the key; the man who now wore a thickly-padded jumpsuit and carried a cane and a pocketful of chalk.

On his 65th day in the labyrinth, a new line of thought occurred to him. It had been suggested many times already in the endless stream of questioning, but now it came as a premonition of his own, as a new refinement of his different and developing maze-faculties— like knowing walls or turnings were there before he got to them.

He realised the maze had an exit and a centre.

When he told the experts this, they gave him sidelong glances. It had been logical to them all along. *If* it was in fact a maze, then from all known precedents it would have a middle and an exit. That seemed a *sine qua non*. A lot of their observation-discussion sessions had included rapid-fire random questions like: "How large is the maze?", "What's at the centre?", "In which direction do you feel an exit can be found?", even "Who is watching you?" and "Who built the maze?"—all obvious enquiries based on maze-research in the mundane world. They hoped to surprise Quinlan into revealing something he did not know he knew.

So this latest revelation came as no surprise in itself, only in the way Quinlan now reacted to it, as if—in spite of their suggestions and questioning— the idea had never occurred to him.

The scientists were troubled. Some were even alarmed by what it could mean. More than anything else, it brought home the simple fact that the maze was not for them. They could only assume things. Quinlan *knew*.

But now they did have these two further correlations with earthly counterparts.

An Exit and a Centre. The terms were soon capitalised.

Where that Exit was and what was at that Centre, Quinlan couldn't say, but at least he had the certainty.

And because nothing else could be done by the scientists once their tests were made and duplicated and triplicated, they encouraged Quinlan to explore his surroundings in the maze-world, hoping for more of these sudden revelations.

The grounds at St Pat's became even more of a pegged-out mazeway, with small signs to direct Quinlan through its courses—though he had become very good at guessing the right paths too. He could go out to Marsden Road, even down to the local shops, if he had a mind, a bizarre obstacle course of sudden turns and switchbacks. It took him just over 14 minutes to do what was normally a three-minute walk.

During this period of exploration, some of the routines were relaxed, though there were still the daily question sessions, the medical check-ups and the endless cycle of psychological tests; everything that constituted what they referred to as routine surveillance.

On his 81st day, at one of the daily sessions, he revealed his next maze-conviction.

"There is something coming for me, Frank!"

As always, he directed his remark to Frank Bowen, the elderly scientist in charge of Quinlan's case. Bowen had directed all the studies from the start.

"What's that, Jim?" Bowen asked.

"There's something else in the maze with me. It knows I'm here and it's coming for me. I'm afraid."

The scientific and medical personnel exchanged more of their significant looks. Some of them had speculated on this very possibility, arguing that once you accepted the reality of the maze, you had to accept whatever related to the function and purpose of mazes.

For Frank Bowen there was a more fundamental and less dramatic concern. The maze-reality—the maze-world they were all calling it—was getting stronger, more dominant, was steadily taking over Quinlan's frames of reference. There had to be psychological repercussions from all that was happening, an alienation they could delay by normalising Quinlan's world but not stave off indefinitely. No number of expeditions to the Marsden Road shops could compete with the fact that something—someone?—was coming for him and him alone.

Already the pronounced schizoid aspects of Quinlan's personality had taken over, becoming stronger: an enforced duality of perception that was changing him, was inevitably changing even the most basic and trivial connections with the orthodox world.

He was becoming a Maze Man. In every sense of the word.

They were losing him.

It was an infuriating position. Here was the first clinically attested case of overlapping, simultaneous realities, their door into another level, and their one point of entry to it was becoming insane and inaccessible.

Already the media had phased down their attention, unable to make news out of the series of "No Change" reports that were being issued. Representatives from the scientific journals and the government departments remained on hand, unable to do otherwise under the circumstances, but all could see it was just a matter of time. Their mundane world was increasingly the alien landscape for Quinlan, the twists and turnings of the maze his more natural domain, with new and vital imperatives only he could appreciate.

He had long ago become a monomaniac, with life in the maze dominating almost all his thoughts. There was no logical plea they could make to persuade him to consider alternative priorities, no possible argument that could have relevance.

The one thing in their favour was that Quinlan had always had a good working relationship with Frank Bowen. The ageing scientist had been there practically from the first, and Quinlan would usually ask for him. Even in the most crowded sessions, Quinlan's eyeline would invariably go to the old man. His answers—even to questions posed by others—would be to Bowen. This made Bowen undisputed head of the surveillance team. All the other government departments had to deal through him.

In the carefully monitored sessions they had alone, Quinlan and Bowen would discuss the possibilities for how it would all end. They tried to anticipate every contingency.

At one extreme, Quinlan would wake up one morning and the maze would be gone. Just like that. Free. At the other, he would be found and slaughtered by whatever it was that was coming for him across the maze, by some invisible beast, by some other-dimensional minotaur. They had started calling this immanence the Dinner Guest, a private and bleak joke between them.

In the middle of the range of possibilities was a somehow even more tragic development to be considered: Quinlan, rejected and abandoned even by the scientific community when nothing more could be done, roaming the streets of Sydney, feeling his way along invisible walls, unable to cross some streets, but grimly determined, searching for the Exit or the Centre, whatever. Quinlan could see himself, speaking with interested passers-by about the maze, gratefully accepting food or a handout he could spend in one of the shops that rarely crossed his path, occasionally suffering the agony of having youths try to drag him through walls.

But despite their long conversations, even this peculiar bond with Bowen did not last. By the 110th day, Quinlan was showing definite signs of being misanthropic. He was hardly speaking, would only occasionally make eye contact with anyone, Bowen included. When he did speak, he revealed that his maze-sight was becoming better and better, that he could now choose whether he wanted the walls to be invisible or opaque.

"What!" Bowen said when he heard this news, but then changed his tone, afraid that Quinlan would go no further.

But Quinlan was quite open on the subject.

"Sometimes the walls are completely opaque, and I'm in corridors with shapes jutting into them, furniture and the corners of things, the architectural features of this place. Other times the walls are translucent, with a milky—no, more of a sepia light, and I can make out things. When I want, I can clear them altogether. It only takes a few minutes. But I can do it! I can shut out the outside world, Frank! I can shut it right out!"

Again, there was no easy way they could ultimately prove this new development in Quinlan's perceptions. Eye-tests and biopsies revealed nothing, and soon many of the scientists and medical people started feeling it was Quinlan's imagination—not saying as much and not believing it, but *feeling* it.

For, as from the start, the empirical evidence available to them began and ended with Quinlan's compulsory presence in the maze. That was both the one inarguable fact and the limiting factor. He couldn't leave it; they couldn't get him out. That remained the constant in all this. A clinical impasse.

And as stranded as he was at St Pat's, and as obsessed and antisocial as he'd become, Quinlan noticed the desensitisation setting in too. Re-sensitisation for him, to the maze-world; desensitisation for these observers, for the media, for the public—forced to accept the maze's reality but unable to in any meaningful way. Just as lines painted on doorsteps and in back lanes.

No change, but constant change.

Away from them.

It was Quinlan himself who brought enormous relief to everyone when he suggested leaving St Pat's and, in some incredible Thesean pilgrimage, making his way out of Sydney, in the hope that eventually he would reach a sufficiently remote spot where the Federal Government could arrange to buy some property to use as a sanctuary—a place more convenient in terms of national security, personal privacy and ease of observation.

This pilgrimage was a momentous one in every sense. Apart from the awesome security problems involved, the realities of placating then staving off the media and the curious, it was for Quinlan an attempt to explore the range of his maze, to find the geographical limits, to locate the Centre or the Exit.

Or the Dinner Guest.

Even with his new maze faculties, it was a 17-month journey, a nightmare of doubling-back, of days spent covering a few hundred metres.

On his slow progress, in the special van that was his moving rest-station, Quinlan became less remote for a time. He kept up reports to his supervisors after a fashion, though now the main topic of his comments was the Dinner Guest. It was still coming for him, was getting closer and closer, as certainly and inexorably as the sun rose in the outer world.

But—coincidence or not—Quinlan no longer feared the arrival of this fellow maze-dweller. He seemed preternaturally calm about its approach. After all, it belonged there as surely as he now did.

In the weeks that followed, they did reach an appropriate "safe house" location 80 kilometres out of Sydney, and once there in the specially built, prefab, double-storeyed house, all doors and large rooms and movable partitions, behind a high security fence, Quinlan was almost free at last.

The property—christened Escher Acres by Quinlan and Bowen—was purchased by the Federal Government and made Commonwealth land. Quinlan himself was proclaimed a security risk and kept very much out of the public eye.

Press meetings were fewer and fewer, so were the formal question and answer sessions and the check-ups. Quinlan's days were pretty much his own—ostensibly so he could spend long hours doing maze research behind self-opaqued walls, making his increasingly occasional reports to a resigned and philosophical Bowen and his staff.

A handy term that: maze research. It concealed so much. The real reason was so that Quinlan's almost total withdrawal from the conventional, shared reality was not noticed. For that's what it was. Only a matter of time.

In the observation control room late at night, Frank Bowen would watch Quinlan on the monitors, studying him asleep on his portable bed down in the house, down in his part of the labyrinth.

Bowen would consider what was happening out there. He would think of the thing coming for Quinlan through the maze, like some spectre leaping over rooftops, over back fences, scenting and sniffing and tracking him down, using whatever faculties it possessed to locate this man trapped in two worlds.

And then on the 624th day, the next surprise came.

Quinlan rarely spoke anymore, and then it was only when Bowen went to him in his maze, squatted in front of him and demanded answers.

But on this particular morning, Quinlan called for Bowen himself, actually shouting across the open-plan house.

The old scientist went downstairs and through the sliding partitions at his best speed.

"Yes, Jim? Yes? What is it?"

Quinlan was squatting on the floor in his padded suit, like some cross between a yogi and a spaceman. The position was called M-3 for Maze-3, the third most common physical configuration assumed by Quinlan in the maze and especially during opaqued maze-vision.

"I know what it is that's coming for me, Frank. It's very close now." Quinlan's voice had an edge of excitement once again, not fear, just excitement.

"What is it, Jim? What's coming for you?"

"It's the Exit!"

These days, Bowen doubted what he heard as a matter of course. The three words both did and did not register.

"What's that, Jim? You say the Exit is coming for you?"

Quinlan nodded, staring straight ahead, still in M-3.

Bowen pressed for more facts, fearful lest Quinlan would say no more, his own mind racing with thoughts of a maze with a shifting Exit and perhaps a movable centre.

"Are you saying there's a way out that moves through the maze and finally locates anyone trapped in it?"

A leading question. Always leading questions now. And a bad conventionalisation on Bowen's part. He was yet again acting as if someone were doing all this with a set purpose.

Quinlan stared at him and nodded slowly, thoughtfully, a look of intense concentration on his face.

The eyes shifted, became distracted.

Bowen knew the signs but pressed for more. "Does this mean we'll get you back, Jim? When the Exit reaches you? Is that what it means? It will free you?"

Quinlan surprised Bowen by looking at him again, and by speaking in a most odd tone of voice.

"There are two eventualities that will be unacceptable, Frank. To you. To the authorities. To your people. To everyone out there. The first is if the Exit frees me and the maze goes away. You realise that, don't you? You don't want the maze to go away. You'd all hate that. Even you, Frank. What a let-down!"

Frank Bowen was crouching in front of Quinlan, trying to keep his gaze, his legs aching with the strain of keeping such a position for so long.

"And what's the other unacceptable eventuality, Jim?" he said, half-knowing it already.

But Quinlan's eyes had shifted. He was staring out at the walls and turnings Bowen could not see, would never see, as if listening for the Dinner Guest coming closer, reading the maze.

"It's very near," was all Quinlan said.

And he went into Maze-1, a fetal position in the middle of the floor.

Bowen knew what that meant and left him alone. He made two hasty phone calls, then went to the playback room. There he waited, reviewing the conversation several times, then watching Quinlan's tightly curled-up form on the different monitors.

The next morning, Quinlan had vanished.

The hastily summoned experts and officials were shown his empty clothes, the locked and guarded rooms he'd occupied, but found no trace. They finally went to the monitors, activated playback, and reviewed the night's events.

On the screens, it showed Quinlan shortly after 4 am, waking from Maze-1, stretching, then assuming Maze-3 and looking ahead of him. There were no signs of distress, no anxiety of any kind.

"Frank," Quinlan said on the recording. But it wasn't shouted. It wasn't meant to rouse the old man who was sleeping then in the chair at his desk. It was the beginning of a quiet last statement spoken softly there in the early house.

For even as he spoke, Quinlan was starting to fade before their eyes, starting to discorporate somehow, like some trick of light, like a movie superimposition being faded out.

Quinlan was going.

"The maze is a staging point, Doctor," the fading shape murmured. "A half-way house. I'm crossing over now. Out of this place."

And that was it.

The other eventuality.

And Quinlan was right. It was totally unacceptable.

Bowen stared numbly at the deserted screens and realised he'd lost access to the maze, any access at all. He felt cheated. The authorities felt cheated. Everyone did. Disappointed, angry, resentful.

Then they did what people always do when they feel cheated and cut off, after an anticlimax, after they lose what they can never control.

They put it out of mind. They forgot about it.

And over the next few weeks, they painted over all the lines that were left.

Every single one.

One Thing About the Night

LIKE THE GOOD friend he was, Paul Vickrey had kept to our first rule. He'd told me nothing about the Janss place, hadn't dared mention that name in his email, but what precious few words there were brought me halfway around the world nineteen hours after it reached me.

Access to hexagonal prime natural. Owner missing. Come soonest.

Suitably vague, appropriately cautious in these spying, prying, hacker-cracker times, 'prime natural' would have been enough to do it. But hexagonal! Paul had *seen* this six-sided mirror room first-hand, had verified as far as anyone reasonably could that it was probably someone's personal, private, secret creation, and not the work of fakers, frauds, proven charlatans muddying the waters, salting the lode, exploiting both would-be experts and the gullible.

The complete professional, Paul had even arranged for an independent observer for us. Connie Peake stood with Paul Vickrey and me in the windy afternoon before 67 Ferry Street, the red-brick, suburban home overlooking the lawns and Moreton Bay Figs of Putney Park, which in turn looked out over the Parramatta River. She promised to be a natural in that other sense: someone with a healthy curiosity, an open and scientific mind, and a respected position in a local IT business, recommended to Paul by a mutual friend as someone unfamiliar with the whole notion of psychomantiums and willing to help.

And now Paul was briefing her, giving her much of what he'd given me on our way from the airport. The Janss place would have been an ordinary enough, single-storeyed house except that its missing owner had bricked up his windows a year ago. At least a year, Paul was telling her, because it was all behind window frames and venetian blinds before then. Finally one of those venetians had fallen, revealing an inner wall of grey brickwork beyond, making 67 Ferry Street an eyesore and its reclusive owner an increasingly mysterious and unpopular neighbour.

"Seems Janss was a nice enough guy at one time," Paul was saying. "Friendly, always obliging. When he lost his wife and kids in the car accident, he went funny. He bricked up the windows, never answered the door. He abandoned the shed he was building in the yard, though he moved his bed out there and prepared meals and slept in the finished half. The neighbours still saw him around the place until two months ago."

"Surely local authorities did something," Connie Peake said. "Contravening building ordinances like this." We hadn't known her long, but Connie definitely seemed the sort of person who used words like 'contravening'.

"They never knew," Paul told her. "Not till the blinds in the living room window there fell—in what used to be the living room anyway. Finally neighbours did phone it in. The council investigated, and my contact arranged for me to be there soon afterwards, as Janss's solicitor."

Which he wasn't, of course, but Paul was hardly going to tell Connie that. Who was to know that Janss hadn't had one since the inquest three years ago? Bringing me from the airport, Paul had explained that there was a sister in Perth who had come over for the funeral but seemed to have moved since then.

"A neighbour convinced them that they should break in in case Janss had had a stroke or something and was lying there. He wasn't. The place was abandoned. So they fitted a new lock and stuck an inspection notice on the back door. My contact told me about the room."

"And now you have a key." His sang froid had quite frankly astonished me.

"I do. If anyone challenges me on it, I'll say Janss and I had a verbal agreement. No paperwork yet."

"Provided he doesn't turn up."

"Provided that, though I'd just say someone phoned claiming to be him. Very thin, I know, but it's worth it. We have a window of opportunity here, Andy."

I could only agree. Hearing him talk to Connie now, I marvelled yet again at how my only contact in this part of the world, a middle-aged former lawyer normally busy running his antique business, just happened to learn of this particular house halfway across the city, not through his usual antique market channels but through an acquaintance who knew something about his interest in mirrored rooms.

"I'd like to see it," Connie Peake said, as if tracking my thoughts. "It's cool out here."

It was. A chill autumn wind was blowing across the river from the southwest. The big trees in the park across Ferry Street took most of the force, heaving and churning under a rapidly growing overcast, but screened off much of the lowering sun as well.

"Of course," Paul said. "We have to go round back. There's no front door anymore."

Connie frowned. "But—oh, it's bricked up too."

The comment brought a thrill. More than Paul's email, more than seeing the dull grey Besser bricks behind the window glass in the red brick wall where the living room used to be. There was a prime hexagonal in there, in all likelihood a genuine psychomantium and more.

Eric Janss had let the trees and bushes in his driveway and back yard grow tall. No curious neighbours could peer over their fences at us. Anyone seeing us arrive would be left with impressions of three well-dressed, professional-looking people talking out front, obviously there in some official capacity and driven inside because of the deteriorating weather.

Paul unlocked the sturdy back door and we stepped into an ordinary enough, combination laundry-bathroom. There was a washing machine, sink, drier and water heater to one side, a toilet and a shower stall to the other. What looked like a closed sliding door at the end led deeper into the house.

"It gets stranger from here," Paul said for Connie's benefit, closing and locking the back door behind us. "I'll have to go first."

At one time, the sliding door would have led into a kitchen. Now, as Paul drew it aside, it revealed a short dim passage of the same drab Besser brick we'd seen behind the front windows. At the end of its barely two-metre length was another door, made of wood, painted matt-black. Paul switched on his torch, waited till we were all in the passage, and slid the first door shut behind us.

"So most of the house is dead space or solid?" I asked, again for Connie's benefit.

"We can't know without demolition or soundings, Andy. Janss probably brought in the mirrors through the French windows facing the yard, then bricked them up behind the frames. None of this is the original house plan. He pulled down interior load-bearing walls, pulled up flooring and anchored the new construction in concrete."

"And the neighbours never knew?" I said. "Never saw him bringing in bricks or heard him doing renovations?"

"Apparently not. He was just the reclusive, recently bereaved neighbour. Maybe he brought in stuff late at night or waited till people went on holidays. Who would have known? You saw how overgrown the driveway and back yard are."

"Can we get on with this please, Mr Vickrey—Paul?" Connie said. "I'm supposed to be back at the office by five. You wanted me to see the room!"

She didn't mean it peevishly. She just had things to do; things no doubt set out very meticulously in a busily filled diary. In another life she might have been a relaxed, even pretty woman. But not here, not now, not this Connie.

"Of course," Paul said, and moved past us to push on the inner door. It opened with a spring-loaded snick.

Other torches shone back at us immediately, dozens, hundreds of them, in a sudden rush of stars. It was like walking onto a television set, that kind of dramatic, overlit intensity.

It was the single eye of Paul's torch, of course, thrown back at us a thousand-fold from the mirror walls of Eric Janss's secret room.

"Oh my!" Connie said. "It's all mirrors!"

Paul, bless him, had been right. This *was* a prime and, with any luck, a true prime natural.

We stood inside a hexagonal room at least five metres in diameter but seeming larger because of the floor-to-ceiling mirror walls on all six sides. Even the wall behind us was mirrored, the door set flush in it as a hairline rectangle and barely visible, spring-latched to open at the slightest touch from either side. The floor was dark varnished timber, but with little resilience to it: probably laid over concrete. The two-and-a-half-metre ceiling was matt black with a recessed light fitting at its centre. The only other features were an old-style bentwood chair and the reed-thin shaft of a candle stand next to it, a waist-high, wrought iron affair and empty now. Whatever candle it had last held had burned right down. The chair and stand were at the room's mid-point.

Paul crossed to where two mirror walls came together and pressed a tiny switch concealed in the join. Soft yellow light from the ceiling fixture confirmed the reality, sent images of us curving away on all sides. What had already been a moderately large room now went on forever, every wall the wall of another room just like it, then another and another and another, on and on. It was as if you stood in, yes, a maze, or on a plain, or at the junction of promenades like those on the space station in Kubrick's *2001*, arching and curving off. *Very large array* came to mind. It was startling, riveting, overwhelming, all those linked, hexagonal chambers, all those countless Pauls, Connies and Andys sweeping away in an infinite regress. You *knew* the room ended right there, hard and cold at silvered glass, yet that was nonsense now, impossible. We were at the centre of a universe.

"You see why I emailed you, Andy," Paul said.

Connie Peake had her diary out, checking the word Paul had given her earlier. "And this is a—psychomantium?"

"Probably is," Paul answered. "There are other theories."

"Psychomantium covers it," I said, trying to cue Paul to hold back, but it only made Connie more curious.

"No. Please, Mr Galt—Andy—you wanted me here as observer for this first entry. What is a psychomantium? What are these other theories?"

"It'll bias you, Connie. You're only meant to report on what you see today, what is actually here in case the site ever becomes—'

"I know. But you and Mr Vickrey both know I'm going to do a Net search the minute I get back to the office. You might as well tell me."

"All right. But help us here, please. Just observe. You can go verify whatever you want and bring questions later. Paul, best guess, how long have we got?"

Paul shook his head. "Can't say. It's not being treated as a crime scene. Janss has disappeared but there's no suggestion of foul play. He may have just gone off."

"But you don't think so," Connie said. "Look, I'm trying to be of use. Say I've done a Net search already. What's a psychomantium?"

Another time I might have resented the presence of this officious young woman, but not now. It was good to be challenged on the fundamentals, especially on the fundamentals. Instead of pleading jetlag and letting Paul deal with her questions, I kept my attention on the earnest face, not wanting her to see Paul and me exchange glances, and didn't hesitate.

"Okay. Psychomancy was originally telling fortunes by gazing into people's souls. Catoptromancy was scrying using mirrors. The Victorians were especially fond of combining the two: building mirrored rooms so they could contact spirits of the dead. Mirrors are traditionally meant to trap the souls of the departed and act as doorways to the other side; that's why they used to be covered or removed when someone died. A psychomantium is a mirrored room built for that purpose."

"You believe this?"

Again I didn't look at Paul. This was the way to go and I hoped he'd see that it was.

"That they existed and still exist today, yes. That they permit communication with the dead, no. But others believe it, and I've been collecting psychomantia, mainly the modern ones."

"What, as oddments? Curiosities?"

"As something humans habitually do, yes. As a constant; part of a fascinating social phenomenon."

"So not just as functioning psychomantiums," Connie Peake said. "You want the range of possibility behind them."

Now Paul and I did exchange looks. *Where did you find this woman?* mine said. *I had no idea!* said Paul's.

Again, I barely hesitated. Connie was surprising me, changing the preconceptions I had of her. "Exactly. It's the infinite regress that's the common factor, and Janss has created it here using a hexagon, what I consider the classic form. The reflections in the angling of two facing mirrors have to be as old as reflective surfaces: the first virtual reality. It must have always been profound, something people just naturally hooked things onto. The French have the perfect term for it: *mise-en-abîme*: plunged into the abyss."

We gazed into that abyss now, the endless rush of corridors taking the three of us off to infinity, doing it in long curves, sending us to the left in one mirror wall, to the right in the next, back to the left and so on. The ceiling light had seemed kind at first, pleasantly free of glare. Now my eyes had adjusted, and it lent a hard, almost clinical quality to the unending rooms and hallways, making me think of the oppressive cubicles in George Tooker's *The Waiting Room*. I couldn't prevent it.

"Have you seen many?" Connie asked, almost in a whisper. The *faux* cathedral space seemed to demand it.

"Not dedicated ones like this. Mostly you get full-length mirrors set opposite each other in drawing rooms and parlours that give the regression effect, or batwing dressing-tables with adjustable side mirrors set a certain way. Sometimes it's hard proving they were intended as psychomantiums at all. There are a lot of hoaxes; descendants staging the effect for tourism purposes, claiming all sorts of things. Paul and I are looking for prime naturals, dedicated set-ups like this with no trumped-up back-story to work through."

"And you've been lucky?"

"We've seen most of the famous ones," Paul said. "But it's the newer kind, the local ones we're after. I've found four naturals, none as fine as this. Andy's located five, including a dodecagonal room—twelve mirror walls marked out according to the hours of the clock—a splendid octagonal and two rather poor hexagonals."

"Using candlelight?" Connie indicated the candle stand.

"Almost always," Paul said. "It gives the most powerful—and traditional—effects."

"The most suggestive, I imagine. The most scary."

"No, powerful," I said, interrupting. "Look for yourself. This present lighting is effective. Janss knew to use a low-wattage, yellowish bulb, but it's like you get on mirror-wall escalators in malls and old department stores. It's not optimal, hence the candle stand. He wanted a controlled effect. So far as we can tell, all the naturals originally involved candles."

"Janss let his burn down," Connie said.

"And that's what we'll do," I said, letting Paul know that it was all right for Connie to know more. He'd accept the decision. "We'll sit here and let ours burn down."

"Turn about," Paul said.

"Turn about," I confirmed.

"You'll do it alone?" Connie actually gave a shudder. "It reminds me of that old skipping song we sang at school."

"I'm sorry. The what?" Paul asked.

"A skipping song." She gave an odd smile, part self-consciousness, part excitement, and recited it in the singsong rhythm of the schoolyard.

"One thing about the night,
One thing about the day,
You turn around and meet yourself
And go the other way."

She gave another little smile. "The rope would be going really fast and everyone kept singing it over and over till you had the nerve to turn around. If the rope was long enough you'd either move back to where you started and duck out, or you'd keep changing directions on the word 'way' until you were out. The one who turned the most times won." She gazed off into the regress. "I guess Janss did his sittings mostly at night."

Now she had me. "Why do you say that? The room is completely sealed. It shouldn't make a difference."

"I think it completes the effect. He's got infinite night in here, but the sense of corridors leading off would be completed at night."

"It's less virtual."

"That's it." Connie checked her watch, but instead of reminding us she had to go, she surprised me again. "Can I stay part of this? I won't intrude. I'd just like to—well—know more."

"We'll consider it, Connie," I said, the best refusal I could manage after a long flight and being awake for twenty hours.

"You hope to find Janss."

"We're doing this irrespective of Janss," I said too quickly, too harshly. "Excuse me."

"Can you explain that?" she asked. "Before I go?" Connie

Peake was proving to be a master at this, and her enthusiasm was infectious.

Paul came to my aid. "Janss left no journals, no papers, doesn't seem to have had a computer. We probably won't ever know what he was really doing. We'll have to go by what he made here."

"It's like archaeology," Connie said and turned to me again. "That other word you said about using mirrors. Catop—catop—something."

"Catoptromancy. Catoptrics is the branch of optics concerned with reflection, with forming images using mirrors. Catoptromancy is scrying by mirrors. A catoptromantium is an arrangement, sometimes a room, for doing this."

I hoped my tone would warn her off, remind her that I wanted to examine the room with Paul. She did begin to move to the door.

"So you can't know for certain if a room was meant as a psychomantium or not?"

"No, the distinction has been lost." My tone was even cooler. *Please go, Connie, go.* "It's more dramatic to talk of contacting the dead. It gets the media attention." Why was I encouraging her?

"I bet. And I guess you have lots of models at home. Miniature rooms made of mirror tiles."

She'd done it again. I had to laugh. "Yes I do. It's a hobby."

"It's more than that," she said. "You're trying to know something. Look, Andy, can I see you? Can we go for a coffee or a meal?" She was so direct it stunned me. It was as if Paul wasn't even standing there.

"Connie, ask me another time. I've just arrived. I'm jetlagged and there's a lot to do."

"Of course. But another time. Please."

"Another time," I said, and we saw her out, to discover that the weather had turned. Rain squalls blew in across the river and the park, keeping farewells to a minimum. We watched Connie drive off, then hurried inside. Paul locked the back door behind us.

"Sorry, Andy. She was more high maintenance than I expected."

"But valuable, Paul. We don't have a pedigree for this one and the chances of demolition are considerable. It's all we can do."

Another time, we'd have postponed our first session, allowing for my jetlag, or Paul would have done a solo sitting. But we really didn't know how long we'd have, and we'd been at so few sites together that we wanted to make a start: to log the room's properties and just enjoy being there. Tomorrow we'd alternate solo sittings, overlapping a half-hour or so to share information, and try another joint sitting later in the week, if we had that long.

Paul brought in a chair from Janss's makeshift bedroom out back and we sat with our camcorders and Pentaxes, taking footage and snapping dozens of shots, first by the overhead light, then using the new candle fitted in the stand.

It didn't matter that it was windy and rainy outside. In Janss's mirror room, it was lit as if for night. There were no windows for the rain to beat against, just blind brick. In a real sense, time had ceased to matter. We could have been anywhere, and in day or night for all the difference it made.

Though Connie had been right. It did make a difference. Of course it did. Doing this at night would complete something when the candle burned away. When darkness was restored.

We measured the room's dimensions next—smiling as we always did at the play on words—dividing the space into a clock face for easy reference. The door in its mirror wall was at six o'clock; that wall's juncture with the next, going clockwise, was seven; the centre of that face eight; the next juncture nine, and so on. Twelve o'clock was directly opposite the door; the concealed light switch was at eleven, a tiny, cunningly hidden press button, virtually invisible unless you knew where to look.

We didn't move the bentwood chair, of course. Its position to the left of the candle was as Janss had last had it, his back not to six o'clock but facing the full mirror wall at two, with the eight o'clock mirror wall behind. It had to be significant.

Paul and I were enjoying ourselves. His long-suffering wife, Cindy, had sent along a 'care package', as she called it, chicken sandwiches, blueberry muffins and a thermos of coffee, complete with a note: *Don't stay up too late.*

When we were finally settled in our chairs, we shared a modest candlelit meal with our myriad selves out along the ever-dwindling boulevards, remarking on whatever details of construction or effect caught our attention, even beginning to work out a timetable for the next day. Paul would do a four-hour morning watch before going in to the office. I'd do the late afternoon and evening, and he'd pick me up around nine.

Connie was right. I wanted to be there at night. Night did make a difference.

Inevitably we fell silent, looking off into the regress. As in other dedicated mirror rooms we'd logged, all the familiar things were there: the certainty of valid distance and genuine form, the sense of being watched, the uncanny stillness in which the smallest actions—gestures, sudden turns of head or body—sent immediate and startling motion across the lines, set crowds of ourselves gesturing, mimicking, almost urging stillness again by their manic imitation.

Paul and I knew the routine; nothing had to be said. We became utterly still, gazing into the deep, horizontal domains as Janss must have. In our sweaters and slacks, we made a dark knot at the heart of each chamber; faces and hands glowing in the candlelight like countless studies for Rembrandt's *Nightwatch*. The corridors and mirror rooms took that calm as far as the eye could see, into the impossibility of dimensions that couldn't exist, yet did: space wrested from illusion, imposed on perception, demanding to be real.

We managed nearly two hours before jetlag torpor made me call it quits. We hadn't let the candle burn away yet, but my journey across the world was already worth it. If Janss turned up right now, even if the police arrived and evicted us, we'd been in the Janss room at 67 Ferry Street. We were smiling as we went out into the rainy night and drove home.

I slept late, lulled by rain on the roof and wind around the eaves, and never saw Paul leave for his early sitting. An old friend of Cindy's dropped by and I didn't get to Ferry Street until after five. The rain had continued. The harsh autumn wind gusted in the trees, and the park and the river were reduced to so many inkwash veils in the chill afternoon.

I was glad to lock the back door behind me, to place my bag in the laundry and enter the mirror room again. Paul had left the ceiling light on, with a precisely measured candle in the stand so I could do a burn-down. It would take two hours. My mobile was off. My checklist and clipboard were on my lap, my Tai-Chi chime ball in my pocket. There was a penlight in case it was needed; my main torch, camcorder and camera were on the floor at my feet. Everything was ready.

At six sharp I lit the candle, switched off the overhead light and returned to the chair, sitting with my eyes closed for maybe a minute so they could adjust. Finally I opened them on the miracle of the mirror world.

I sat at the hub of an amazing wheel. Stretching away on all sides were corridors that existed only as reflection, arching off into replicated chambers of stars where other solitary watchers sat, eternally together, eternally alone. Each separate wall of the hexagon led into another hexagonal mirror room in which I was turned away, which then led into another where I was angled back, on and on, this way, that way, off to infinity, but with curves and archings according to counter-reflection and the imperfections and anomalies of the mirrors themselves.

In the ten o'clock wall, lines of Andy Galt made an infinite corridor to the right. In the nine o'clock wall, he arced to the left, then right, then left again in those puzzling alternations no-one could satisfactorily explain. If I looked near where two mirrors joined, there was a boulevard, the sense of a shadowed avenue between infinite lines of Andy.

Mesmerising didn't cover it. It was compelling, arresting, powerfully entrancing. I'd focus on a corridor, find myself staring at it, down it, across it, along all those curving lines of myself made into a string of honey-coloured moons, party lanterns strung out forever along drained midnight canals and antique avenues. Yes, I was at the centre of a universe. No other term came close. Janss had made himself a universe here, an orrery of realms in an arrangement few ever got to see, had brought endlessness into a red (and grey) brick suburban home, put eternity into grains of sand and silvered glass.

I logged the usual tricks when they came, the catoptric anomalies triggered in brains not intended to face things like infinite regress: the twelfth or seventeenth figure out behaving differently, the conviction of a light source not my own, the sense of rippling or of movements delayed or prefigured somewhere among the myriad forms, the constant game of Simon Says you played until you were sure one doppelganger was truly, even purposely, out of sync.

Complex mirror reflections like this had no precedent in nature, hadn't existed for the eye and brain to adapt to in the evolution equation. Perhaps mirrors were the most profound, the most dangerous, the very worst human invention. They suborned the integrity of the mind, couldn't do otherwise. We were never meant to have mirrors more elaborate than calm pools, clear ice walls, lightning-fused sand-glass and sandstorm-scoured sheets of metal or mica, dishes of water, blocks of obsidian, screens of iron pyrites or oddities like Dr Dee's lump of polished coal.

In the second hour, torpor took its toll, had me nodding off until—using the old Thomas Edison trick—I dropped the chime ball I was holding in my left hand and woke myself.

That was the cycle until 7:52, when the candle was barely a finger's width above the cup. The rooms were dimming on every side, readying themselves for night. It seemed as bright as ever, but that was an illusion. My eyes had adjusted to what light there was, had made an Indian summer noon out of a generous twilight. It was like the heat death of the universe out there, all that warmth and life being drawn away in subtle shifts, like some pattern of entropy replicated in an insect's eye. Janss had seen this, had been in *this* chair, seeing *these* gradations of night come.

Absurdly, I recalled the title of a Giacometti sculpture: *The Palace at 4 am*. It felt like that dead hour now.

Connie's song was there too, surprising me, the old schoolyard refrain about meeting yourself. That's what I'd been doing. Cued by the words I turned, swung round in my chair. There I was on every side: flickering, faltering selves out in what was left of the vast fading starwheel.

They trapped my eye, drew me image by image out into the regress. They were holding me there, fading, darkening. *Be easy now, easy. Be with us. Let it come.*

I felt a rush of dread, sudden and utter panic. The chime ball clanged against the floor; my clipboard clattered as I rushed for the switch, fumbled with it, brought up warm yellow light, saved us all.

Not tonight. No darkness tonight. I couldn't bear it. It was the jetlag, whatever. I'd do a burn-down at some other sitting. *We* would.

When Paul arrived at 8:53, he found me under the porch outside the bricked-up front door, sheltering from the rain.

Neither of us had managed a burn-down, it turned out. Perhaps it had to do with the room itself, the circumstances of Janss's disappearance, the unseasonal weather, even Connie's song. We agreed that it might be something best done together.

I did a nine till noon sitting the next day, taking dozens of photos and more video footage, this time using a tripod and automatic timer for PR shots, and adding a sporadic commentary, anything to keep me from pondering why I hadn't let the candle burn away. It had been a crazy thing last night; it was irrational now, but I couldn't help it.

When Paul arrived for his five-hour afternoon session, he brought a lunch invitation from Connie. There was a twinkle in his eye as he handed me the car keys and gave me directions. He knew how on-again, off-again my relationship with Pamela was back home. This would get me out of the loop, he said. It was good for me.

I felt trapped but pleased. I didn't try to consider motives. I'd keep it easy, light and professional and, with luck, get more of Connie's enthusiasm.

We met at a café in a rainy village court in Putney. Connie had her hair out and wore a shiny black raincoat too blatant to be calculated.

"I looked up the mancy words," she said, as I sat across from her. Her smile utterly transformed her face.

"The what? Oh, the mancy words. Right."

"I never realised people took it so seriously. Lithomancy: scrying by the reflection of candlelight off precious stones. Macharomancy, for heaven's sake: reading swords, daggers and knives. Imagine specialising in that. Clouds: nephelomancy. Things accidentally heard: transataumancy." She pronounced the word so carefully, as if relishing it. "It's like people made them up for the fun of it. Came up with wacky names like those collective nouns you get: a murder of crows, a parliament of owls."

"A loony of researchers!" I said. I wanted to see her laugh.

We ordered the lasagne with salad and coffee, then sat watching cars go by in the rain. I let Connie bring us back to it.

"Andy, if it's a natural like you say, Janss had probably never heard of catoptromancy. Never knew the word, never knew any variants."

"So the room is a psychomantium and all he was trying to do was reach his family. Maybe voices told him to do it; maybe he went quietly nuts."

"Surrounded by ordinary households and normal lives," she said. "Sat there while candles burned down. Did it again and again. Then probably sat in darkness, for who knows how long, without the reflections."

I couldn't help myself; I'd had a bad scare the night before. "Without reflections, but with the sense of all those rooms *still* there, those avenues filled with night. You can't help it."

Connie gave a shudder. "That's a chilling thought."

"It's part of the effect. Both Paul and I have let candles burn away." Not this time, I didn't add, and wondered why I didn't, why it mattered. "You feel the—pressure—of the rooms still out there, going on and on. You know there's nothing there, that reflections need light—"

"But the brain registers images for so long it can't give them up," she said, going to the heart of it. "A retinal after-image thing. Like a ghost arm effect."

"And you can restore it all so easily. The little switch is right there, and your torch and your Bic lighter and matches. But the feeling is that they're still there."

"That's creepy, Andy. You're the master of all those rooms. They exist because of you."

"And the mirrors."

"No, you. It's *your* perception. *Your* conviction that they're still there. *You're* the activating factor."

The food arrived but we let it sit a moment. "It gets stranger, Connie. Paul and I have confirmed it. When the candle finally does go out and you're in total darkness, it's as if your reflections, all the mirror versions you've been watching for hours, are pressing up against the glass. You even think you hear them moving in."

"That has to be hyperaesthesia. Anomalous perception. That's—"

"A mind thing, I know. It's exactly what it is. But it *feels* real."

We began eating, looking through the big window, watching cars in the rain.

"What if it's sciamancy?" she said between mouthfuls.

"It's what?"

"Sciamancy. What if it's a sciamantium: a place for making shadows, for reading shadows?"

I must have grinned in wonder for she smiled back. "Andy, what?"

"You've been busy."

"I mean it. What if Janss made a shadow place? Not to contact spirits or read reflections—"

"To scry the darkness." It was so close to my own catoptromancy fixations that I felt alarm, genuine delight, true fascination. It was so good to share this. "Connie, maybe it is a—sciamantium."

"Night has to be psychoactive for us, doesn't it? You reach a point where a perception, even a misperception, triggers something in the psyche. You haunt yourselves. Janss, Paul, all of us. Everyone who tries it."

"I hope so. I hope that's what it is." All it is, I didn't add, didn't need to.

We finished eating. The plates were cleared; second coffees brought.

"It does have to do with light, doesn't it?" she said.

"Darkness."

"You know what I mean."

"It's an important distinction. Light running out, darkness being restored, what you were saying. We've always feared night, responded to it dynamically. We made use of that fear, and did pretty well considering, but the primal response was to endure it, wait it out, worship and appease it."

"But mostly separate ourselves from it in sleep."

"Right. When we developed enough tribally, socially, to sleep safely. Then we modified the relationship over centuries, generations. Gas and electric light changed it, let night become romantic, a time for leisure and shift work."

"The brain does learn."

"It has to. But only to a point. It's a dual thing: the adjustment *and* the remembering. My relationship with darkness was probably determined by how it was presented to me as a kid. Maybe Janss sussed it out, was taking the appropriate next step of embracing the night for *all* it is, revisiting it as a conditioned mind liberated from fearing it."

"The throwback fear thing hardwired in, but the framing culture telling us it's okay. Maybe the energy behind that fear *can* be directed differently. We don't do an ordinary lunch do we, Andy?"

"We didn't want one."

Connie smiled. "So Janss is a creature of his time, one more solitary watcher responding to what night has become for us. What *else* it has become. Something to inhabit and colonise, something to avoid. Have you ever tried infrared cameras?"

There she was, blindsiding me again. "What, and night vision goggles?"

"Why not? It might give something."

"We've never been set up that way. We're more your boutique operation." Then it came out. "Connie, we haven't let candles burn down in the Janss room yet. Neither of us has."

There was kindness, instant understanding in her eyes. "So it might be sciamancy. The room could be a place for reading the form and nature of shadows, for creating intricate shadows, and both you and Paul sensed it."

It occurred to me then that if Connie was a natural too, I should let her be one. "Make an argument."

"What?"

"Make an argument. It's a sciamantium. Convince me."

"All right. It's what we said. Janss was calling up the night. Humans have that ancient—an atavistic connection with darkness, *and* with the subtleties."

Subtleties. One word glossed it all. "He was creating an *effect* of night," I said, daring to believe it again.

"An *effect* of shadows and night that only the mirrors bring."

"Trying to reach his wife and son."

"You don't believe that any more than I do. It was accentuation. No, intensification. It mightn't even be related to the deaths."

"Go on."

I expected her to say that she should accompany me.

"That's all. I just know that you have to be alone in there, Andy, like Janss was. It won't work with the two of you. It can't work. If it's psychoactive, it has to be just the individual enabling what happens with the mirrors, *your* mind reacting to the shadows. And keep Paul out of there. You should keep him out. He has a family."

"I'll do a burn-down tonight."

Despite what she'd said about being alone, I truly expected her to ask if she could be there. Part of me hoped.

"Just be careful," was all she said, and we sat watching cars in the rain.

I napped from three till five. After enduring Cindy's jibes about going on a date with Connie, I relieved Paul just after five. We sat in the warm calm of the Janss room for a half-hour or so, discussing everything but what Connie had suggested about sciamancy. One of us had to stay unbiased, and he didn't need to be burdened with additional labels and characteristics yet. That's what I told myself.

He finally left me to my evening shift, hurried out to the car and drove off through the bleak wet evening. This time we'd agreed to leave our mobiles on. We didn't need to say why.

I filmed, I photographed, I did more commentary into the pocket recorder. I reached 7 pm without dropping my chime ball once. Everything was the same. Everything was different. Just the names: sciamantium and sciamancy took it from a familiar candlelight vigil to something new and unsettling: a nightwatch for shadowforms out in the marches, the shadow-lands, a warding off of unproven enemies in the backwaters of forever.

By 8:10 pm I was exhausted, ready to call it quits. It was all too still, too constant, too laden with immanence. No, not constant, I kept reminding myself. Now and then the hot blade of the candle did stir, perhaps from something as simple and immediate as my breathing or a microzephyr sneaking around the cracks and door sills, finding a way in, and the lines of flames trembled, wavered, shook their points of light as if to catch my attention, as if to test me. *Did you notice? Did you notice?*

But mostly it was still, *we* were still, all of us in our articulated, nautilus chambers, our adjoining rooms.

The notion of a sciamantium kept me there, kept me resolved as the candle burned away, knowing that Janss had done this again and again, sat beside solitary flames made Legion, watching himself parcelled off into mirror chambers that gradually sank into night. He hadn't just been alone in a bricked-up, suburban house, not merely in a fabulous mirror world, but at the focus of rooms destined for darkness. He'd made waiting rooms, filled them with light then watched them empty out.

Waiting rooms, yes, where you waited for darkness to come, infinite, replicated darkness, growing, settling across all these real, unreal spaces. There could be no reflection, no possibility of rooms and boulevards when the flame died and the nautilus rooms emptied and slowly ceased to exist. Yet what if the opposite *was* true—if only in the mind? It was the old question of whether a tree falling in a forest made a sound if there was no-one to hear it.

I kept wondering about defaults in the brain. How was mine dealing with the idea of all those darkening rooms out there, the prospect of what might use those boulevards when the light was snatched away? What was it devising even now to protect Andy Galt from inconceivable, unprecedented threat?

Minutes felt like hours. I'd look at my watch to find the hands had barely moved. It was like being on detention at school, time cruelly stretched and distended. The thought sent Connie's schoolyard rhyme running through my mind. But I'd already turned, faced where I'd been, met as much of myself as I could, my selves, going this way, that way, mocking me, taunting shadowforms in the infinite regress. The song's words were an incantation, a maddening litany. What had Janss been doing?

Then something caught my attention.

Did I imagine it, or was there a shadowing off in the distance—the false distance at two o'clock where the images blurred into uncertainty? I blinked, took off my glasses and rubbed my eyes. There did seem to be something, a dimming, a shadowing out there.

I quickly looked about me. Behind and to the sides, the infinite rooms were as bright as ever, star chambers arcing off like settings for outdoor recitals. Carols by Candlelight. Madrigals by Mirrorlight. A Cappella in the Waiting Rooms. Nothing had changed. It was only ahead, in the mirror wall at two, that there seemed to be a darkening, like a storm at the edge of the world, spilling a little to the sides, but only a little, and way out in those real, unreal, never-real distances.

It was impossible, of course. Physically impossible. Any shadowing had to be replicated, shared, made part of all the reflection corridors and boulevards on every side. It was basic catoptrics.

Or selective self-delusion. Something served up by fatigue and an overstimulated mind.

My adrenaline rush was real. I went into automatic observer routines, questioning everything. If the candle flame had been down at the rim, close to guttering, I'd have accepted it more easily, but two centimetres of candle stood well clear of the cup.

It was me. It had to be. Some optical trickery, some effect of jetlag. I'd been sitting and staring too long. My bored brain was entertaining itself. Finding things. Making things.

Or it was the room!

I reminded myself that the imperfections of an average wall mirror enlarged to the size of the Gulf of Mexico became waves twenty metres high. Could it be the mirrors? Part of Janss's intended effect?

He had to have seen this, had to have been in this exact situation. That was why the chair was angled so. Checking the anomaly at two o'clock.

And he hadn't survived it.

Or he had simply gone away, seen something that drove him off.

Again I removed my glasses, rubbed my eyes. Again I checked the image field. It was there, definitely there, something was, something like swelling, burgeoning night, or perceptual trickery in the glass or in the vision centres of the brain. Defaults, yes, that was the word. What were the defaults set there?

Enough. I'd give it up for tonight.

As a way of withdrawing, anchoring myself in the reality of 67 Ferry Street once more, I located the tiniest black dot of the light switch where it sat in the join at eleven o'clock, looked over my right shoulder to confirm the barest hairline of the door in the mirror wall at six.

One more glimpse, one more try, I decided, as Janss must have.

The shadowing was there—the spreading 'darklands', whatever they were. I smiled at the fancy, a hopeless victim of autosuggestion now. It was crazy. Too much peering off into distances, making eyes track vistas rarely, if ever, seen in nature, never meant for eyes with a such a highly developed, reactive brain behind them. I simply wasn't sure what I was seeing.

I had my mobile. Now was the time to call Paul, to have him join me and verify what was happening.

Connie's words stopped me. I had to be alone with this, had to allow that the eye-brain link was overwhelmed, set to doing the only thing it could: imposing order, treating this as something real, even as crisis, but rigorously dealing with it. Of course there were shadows, optical tricks. Of course there was fear, feelings of disquiet and alarm. What we'd said about the night related to eyes and mirrors too. Just as we were completing our connection with night, so too we were changing what eyes, what brains, needed to do.

The darklands seemed to be growing, pushing from the two o'clock focus into the mirror rooms at one and three. Behind, everything remained as bright and steady as ever. It was in that two-o'clock spread that it was happening.

"Let it come!" I spoke the words to hear myself say them, aware of what an ominous line they would make on the audio track. I took more video footage, more photographs. I filled the time with deeds, filled the dying of the light.

The flame sank closer to the rim.

My mobile rang. Thank, God! Paul offering a reprieve!

But it was Connie.

"Andy, do you know what sciamachy is?"

Not now, not now, I wanted to tell her, but the word held me.

"Say again, Connie. What what is?"

"Scia*machy*. Not mancy, machy!"

"Not offhand. Something to do with shadows."

"Fighting shadows, Andy. The act of fighting shadows. Imagined enemies."

"Okay. Look, I'm nearly done—"

"Andy, what if it's a sciamachium?"

"Hey, look, thanks." I wanted her to go. I didn't want her to go. "Connie?"

"Yes?"

"Thanks. I mean it. I'm doing it. Alone. I'm doing it."

"I know. I know, Andy. But a sciamachium. Just call me when you're done, okay?"

"Promise." She had known, I realised as I put the phone away. She was a natural and she had known.

The shadowing beckoned, teased at two, flexed dark fingers. *Look at me, look at me!* Everywhere else the rooms were bright and constant, seemed to be. I sat watching the darklands, wondering how they could exist, finally convinced myself that they spread only when I glanced away. It was using my mind, my eyes to build itself.

I held the darkness with my eyes, daring it to slip into new rooms, consume new Andys. With all the bright rooms at my back,

I held it at bay with my eyes and Connie's words, Connie's skipping song running through my mind.

Urging me. Connie the natural urging me to turn around.

I did so, looked over my shoulder at the eight o'clock wall.

And there was dead black night filling the glass, night the hunter pressed to it like a face at a window. The shadowing at two had been the bait.

I tipped forward in shock, slammed hard against the floor, reached for the first thing I could find—the candle stand—meaning to angle it up, to fling it at the dead black wall of glass.

But stopped in time. Barely managed. Do that and I'd be in darkness when it shattered. Night would be everywhere, flowing out.

I scrambled to the eleven o'clock corner, reached for the tiny button.

Yellow light filled the rooms. Most of the rooms. The black wall held at eight like onyx, obsidian, a membrane about to burst. The darklands shadowed off at two, but just the lure, just the distraction.

Now I flung the candle stand. Now it struck the glass, crazed and shattered the wall. The pieces clashed down, left dead grey Besser brick beyond. At two o'clock the darklands were no more.

When Paul arrived fifteen minutes later, Connie was with him. They found me standing by the front gate in the wind and rain, cold and shivering. "Janss didn't know he had to turn around," I told them as I climbed into the back seat. "He didn't turn around."

Jenny Come to Play

WHEN DAN TRUSWELL learned from the activities coordinator soon after 2 pm that Wednesday afternoon that Julie Haniver was sitting catatonic in the hospital library, he took it as a routine shut-down by the slim, nervous, young woman, paged Hans and Carla, and left them to deal with it.

It was when Peter Rait knocked at his door less than two minutes later and said Dan had to come see Julie, talk to Julie, that Dan decided to check on her himself. Peter was one of Blackwater's star 'attractions', an amiable, likeable schizophrenic who had an uncanny knack for reading his fellow inmates. When Peter showed worry, it was usually worth worrying about.

Dan locked his office and accompanied Peter around to the library in the Prior Wing.

"What does Phil say?" Dan asked his frowning companion, knowing how Peter and his schizoid friend, Phillip Crow, made a fascinating double-act.

Peter shrugged, which was more exasperating than it ought to have been. Phil hadn't expressed an opinion this time. That meant Peter had reacted on his own, which was even more amazing. Then again, he'd shown Julie a lot of attention in the four months she'd been at Blackwater.

Dan trusted Peter's insights enough to let him be there when they entered the library. Hans and Carla were already with Denise, the activities coordinator, but hadn't yet approached the girl sitting by the corner window, looking out at the fine spring afternoon.

When Dan indicated Peter, they nodded and stayed at the desk. They knew Peter was good at getting through to Julie.

Dan crossed the room, sat near the petite, olive-skinned young woman with the short black hair and very pretty elfin features. Peter stood to one side.

"Julie?" Dan said gently. "Can you hear me, Julie?"

The young woman showed no sign of having heard. She sat absolutely still, gazing out the window, her eyes unfocussed, watching, yet watching nothing.

"Ask her who she's looking out for," Peter said, with uncommon directness.

"Peter, let me handle this."

But it was as if Peter hadn't heard. "Ask her, Doctor Dan. Ask who she's watching for!"

"Peter! That's enough!"

His tone at least made Julie blink.

"Ask her about Jackie!" Peter said, his parting shot because Carla was there then to lead him away.

But it was Peter suggesting it, and it was Julie—this withdrawn, shy, young woman who'd turned up one day back in June and signed herself in, without any identity but her name, no next of kin she could give, no family, no memories (she claimed) to help them build a past, the backgrounds of heredity and environment that had produced her.

"Julie, are you waiting for someone?"

Still the eyes gazed out at the grounds, broke into the emptiness and infinities of reverie before ever reaching the sunny lawns and trees.

"Julie, who is Jackie?"

Julie blinked once, twice. The eyes grabbed, locked into focus. She turned to face him, gave a nervous, embarrassed smile.

"Are you okay now?" Dan asked.

She nodded, ventured another tentative smile, noticed Peter and the others over by the desk.

Normally Dan would've left it to Carla at this point, but Peter going solo over this kept him there.

"Julie, who is Jackie?"

Julie frowned, sighed and looked directly at him.

"Jackie's my sister."

"Really? You never said you had a sister." Dan held back the rush of questions that were immediately there. There might be no sister at all, just an imaginary one, a convenient fiction. It hadn't surfaced during the hypnotherapy sessions. Nor did he want to move over to the armchairs or to an interview room. The view out the library window was probably part of it. She'd been watching for this 'sister' most likely.

"Tell me about Jackie."

"It's why I'm here."

"Jackie wanted you here?" Dan truly expected her to have forgotten how she came to be at Blackwater, to say that this sister had been the one who'd committed her, part of a familiar enough persecution and betrayal scenario. Julie's answer surprised him only by its opposite tack, not its content.

"No. I came here to escape Jackie. I thought she wouldn't be able to find me here."

"Ah, I see," Dan said, kindly. He'd heard this sequence of events many times too. Only the look of intense concern on Peter's face when Dan glanced round at the others kept him with her. "And have you seen her out there, Julie?"

"She's coming today. I thought it'd be last night but it will be today."

"How do you know?"

"Jackie always leaves things."

"Oh, like what? What sort of things?"

"Just things. Signs."

"You've seen these signs? What are they?"

When Julie didn't answer, Dan tried again. "But she wouldn't come from out there, would she, Julie? She'd come in by the front gate."

The young woman frowned, studied the grounds with renewed concentration. The emotion in her eyes could have been terror, panic, utter dread. (Phobos and Deimos, the twin moons of insanity—one of Peter's lines.) Not for a moment did Dan see it as guile, the sort of cunning so many paranoid schizophrenics affected. This woman seemed truly terrified.

"Julie?" he said, both to keep her with him and to comfort her.

"She won't give up. She'll keep looking."

"Yes, well, we'll keep an eye out for her too."

Dan almost fell off his chair when she turned and grabbed his arms.

"Don't tell her I'm here!" She spat the words at him, eyes wide, face twisted by fear.

"You're safe here, Julie," Dan managed, and by then Carla was there, soothing her, urging her up, Hans assisting, leading her off to her room, leaving Denise by the desk and Peter desperately wanting to follow, to do something. He came over to Dan.

"She's really scared of her sister," Peter said, as if it hadn't been obvious. "We have to protect her. Keep her hidden."

"There may not be a sister," Dan said, wondering as always why he bothered to tell Peter Rait these things.

"There is and there isn't," Peter said, frowning with what seemed to be both puzzlement and concern. "But Julie's right. Jackie does leave things."

This was where Peter Rait was his brilliant, entertainment-value best. It was just that Phillip Crow wasn't with him, making it unprecedented, almost as disturbing in a way as Julie's outburst.

"Oh, what sort of things?"

"Last week a piece of cloth tied to that pine over there." He pointed out the window. "Last night she would've put something closer to let Julie know she's coming."

"What sort of thing?"

Peter shrugged. "Something closer. Maybe not visible from the library window, but sharing a connection, yeah. Can I go sit with her?"

"She's resting now. You can see her later. Go wait for her in the Games Room."

Peter nodded, then smiled as if grasping some secret strategy Dan had suggested. "Right. The play's the thing, isn't it?"

Dan said nothing. From long experience he knew enough just to watch him go.

What Dan did do when he reached his office again was go over Julie Haniver's file, re-acquainting himself with what little they had. She'd admitted herself on June 4, uncertain of her age but probably around 22 to 24, had been diagnosed as stressed and exhausted, subject to unspecified feelings of persecution, anxiety attacks, even catatonic withdrawal, real or feigned. Though testing initially as a disorganised personality, she'd responded well to treatment and was usually calm and controlled. She could have been a case of nervous exhaustion following prolonged drug abuse, but her initial physical showed none of the attendant signs of that, no signs of harm at all apart from a nasty childhood or early adolescent scar above the hip on her right side. The distinctive double hand-sized patch of keloid ridges and welts may have been from an accident involving fire or acid, possibly was the result of extreme parental or sibling abuse. That might explain the disordered, dissociated behaviour—the anxiety of residual trauma. Someone named Jackie may have been responsible. Friend, relative or carer, who could say?

But nothing else in the file. Just ID shots and dated close-ups of the wound for the usual information, legal and insurance reasons. If it hadn't been for the scar and the memory loss (alleged, never proven), with its significant implications, Julie Haniver could have been discharged.

The more Dan considered it, the more she did seem like someone who might feign a mental disorder to be in a safe place. It certainly happened from time to time.

But the scar. Raw and brutal-looking. An acid burn? The result of a very clumsy, even amateur, medical procedure?

It was the photographs of the scar (and remembering Peter Rait's concern) that made Dan go out onto the terrace and walk round the outside of the building to the library windows in the Prior Wing. There was nothing tied to the low bushes or the pilasters of the terrace balustrade, but just below the window near where Julie had been sitting, there was a small stack of stones—maybe ten in all, just piled atop one another and collapsed in against the wall.

Dan immediately thought of Peter, yet knew that he would never knowingly interfere with a fellow inmate's treatment. There seemed to be only three explanations: it was coincidence—someone had just happened to leave a construct in that spot, or Peter had done it to confirm Jackie's existence for this newfound friend who desperately needed to believe she did exist, or that Jackie was indeed out there.

Dan left the stones where they were and returned to his office. No sooner had he put Julie's file away, then, like Fate on his heels, Angela phoned to say a Ms Jackie Haniver was waiting in Reception to see him about her sister.

Though Dan would have preferred to collect his thoughts, take time to consider the rush of events, he felt a real curiosity, even a sense of urgency about the whole business. He told Angela to have one of the staff bring Ms Haniver through at once. There were often days when Blackwater's well-established routines came undone in spectacular, sometimes alarming, usually comical ways, but this time Dan felt an uncommon pressure, as if the 'briars of unreason' (as Peter Rait and Phillip Crow put it) were indeed taking over the garden.

Less than ten minutes after discovering the pile of stones, he was sitting in his office across from what seemed to be Julie's identical twin. The young woman wore a smart blue suit, was well groomed and carefully made up, and appeared very composed about the whole matter, radiating a charm and poise well beyond her years.

"You understand, Dr Truswell, that I've been looking for Julie for quite some time. I can't make her come back with me, I know, even were you to allow it, but naturally I do feel responsible for her care and safety."

"And we're naturally very glad to see you, Ms Haniver. We've had so little to go on where Julie's concerned."

"Please. Call me Jackie. And it's Perfini, not Haniver. That's a name Julie's been using. I used it at Reception because I knew it would identify me to you. I have certified copies of Julie's birth documentation here. You can keep the photocopies." Dan scanned them when she passed them over, passed back the originals. "'Haniver' was a family *nom de guerre* or *nom de theatre*. Can I see my sister?"

"I'd like you to," Dan said, making notes on the writing pad in front of him. "But not right away. We have to deal with your appearance in terms of Julie's needs. She said she didn't *want* you to know she was here, and seems highly agitated at the thought of you finding her. Letting you see her could well seem like a betrayal. Forgive how this sounds, but Julie's well-being must come first. You can help us prepare her for meeting you. Help us to get her to ask for you."

"I have to take your word for all this, don't I? That she's agitated? That she doesn't want to see me?"

"I'm afraid so. If you have doubts, there are legal procedures we can suggest. You can bring legal representation to our next meeting. Outside experts can verify admission and diagnostic protocols."

Jackie Perfini smiled and raised a hand. "Unnecessary, Doctor. I accept what you're telling me. I'm just surprised and hurt about this. Of course I accept your professional judgement. But what are the chances of her being released into my care? The legalities?"

"Again that will depend on her recovery. You're probably aware that once someone is committed, or commits themselves as Julie has, they can only be discharged when a qualified person deems their condition satisfactory."

"Julie must be that, surely. She's dreamy and distracted and withdrawn, but hardly crazy. I'm surprised she's so upset and amazed to think she might have committed herself just to be away from us."

"Who is us, Jackie?"

"Our father died last year. I meant our sister, Jenny, and me."

"Your mother?"

"Died soon after Julie and Jenny were born."

"You and Julie look identical."

Jackie smiled. "Dr Truswell, I think you're interrogating me. In a moment you'll be asking if I have a scar of my left side just above the hip."

"Do you?"

"I'm afraid not. I'm eighteen months older than Julie and Jenny. We do look alike, I know, but Julie and Jenny were born conjoined. Congenitally united, as they say."

"Jackie, Siamese twins not sharing vital organs or major skeletal features are usually separated as soon after birth as safely possible. That's a nasty scar. A bad separation procedure."

"Bad 'procedure'! God, I love these terms! It was butchery! It's a wonder they survived. Dr Truswell, my family emigrated from Sicily. Lots of faith in the old ways. Lots of family honour. Lots of shame in having deformed children. Julie and Jenny were born there."

"It wasn't a hospital birth."

"Correct. But it's more complex, more tragic for them than that. Our father, the bastard, had more than a passing interest in teratology."

"Teratology? Monsters?"

"Don't look so amazed, Doctor. It's more common than most of us think. Alonzo was fascinated with the old *Wunderkammern*—

the 'wonder cabinets' and 'cases of curiosities' so famous and popular in the 16th and 17th centuries that became the private collections and eventually the public museums. He had a modest but growing collection of oddities, a museum of his own, a sort of travelling show."

Dan couldn't believe what he was hearing. "He *left* them joined."

Jackie Perfini nodded. "A shameful and hideous thing, I know. He had them wet-nursed by an aunt, then took them to be part of his own *Wunderkammer*. A living exhibit. But then Alonzo Perfini was a selfish and domineering man. A persuasive and charming man when he needed to be. An atheist and occultist. A would-be mystic and entrepreneur. His heroes were Giovanni Batista Belzoni, Elias Ashmole and the Dutchman, Dr Frederic Ruysch. These twins had caused his wife to die, he liked to believe, though it wasn't true. Maria was already very ill. Here he was with his great love of monsters, having become the father of two. Or one, depending on your viewpoint. It was destiny, something that suggested a mystical purpose. He was much taken with the notion of things being joined. The alchemical union of opposites."

"Hardly opposites, Jackie."

"Nevertheless, he left them joined to grow up like that."

"Until when?"

"Till just after puberty. They were barely thirteen. They persuaded a second cousin who was an intern to perform the 'procedure', as you call it."

"Without your father's consent?"

"Of course. He was furious."

Dan was still trying to follow the reality which had brought Julie, Jenny and Jackie to this point in their lives. "Where were you when this happened, Jackie?"

"I was with the show for a while as an infant, then Alonzo left me with some of Maria's relatives in a village outside Palermo before he took his troupe north. Eventually they sent me to Australia and I was raised by aunts in Melbourne. I was told my father had gone off travelling, grieving for the loss of his wife and baby."

"Baby?"

"No-one knew it was twins then. The story was that it was a stillborn boy. Maria was so sick, probably even she did not know the truth. They even had a funeral—it was all a mockery. When the girls were old enough, he added them to his show, had documents falsified saying they shared vital organs and had to stay joined. Even the girls grew up believing it. I didn't meet them until they came to Australia six years ago."

"Where's Jenny now?"

"Down in Sydney, safe and happy enough. Even more shy than Julie. But missing Julie terribly."

"Can you bring her here?"

"I tried to get her to come. She wouldn't. No offence, Dr Truswell, but she thought this place would be too much like the Perfini Chamber of Wonders and his travelling Wonder Show. She's had enough of imprisonment and disordered minds and being regarded as a curiosity. Part of one."

Dan understood her reservations. "Still, seeing her might help Julie's recovery considerably."

"My feelings exactly. But I've lived with this, Dr Truswell. I know only too well how Jenny feels. Until Julie went missing back in June, we all had a relatively quiet life together."

"A normal life, Jackie?"

"Normal enough. Jenny was seeing someone, a young man. I could give you his number next time I visit. Julie was starting to go out more."

Dan made a few more points on his notepad. "It's difficult to know what to do. Despite what you tell me, Julie was terrified at the prospect of your coming here."

Jackie Perfini smiled. "And she would've told you I leave things, signs that I'm following her. She's done that before. Left signs I mean."

"She does it herself?"

"I'm afraid so. It's something she did during their time in the show. At first it was just a book or a stone or a flower, but then she started making things out of folded paper, clay."

"Like piling up stones or tying strips of cloth to trees."

"That sort of thing, yes. But it's just a game. She'll still come into our rooms at home and leave things. It's not serious, is it?"

"Of course not. But in her stressed condition she's made it part of her perception of you, I'm afraid. She believes you're the one doing it."

Jackie frowned, then sighed and smiled. "Well, so long as she's safe. That's the main thing now. I respect her decision to come here, though I can hardly say I'm happy about it. I'd be grateful if you'd talk to Julie about all this. See if you can get her to come home. She's had a hard life."

"Jackie, how did you find her here?"

"I called hospitals, hostels, Lifeline, drop-in centres, places like that. Had the police looking for a while. You probably got a call here. Then Jenny suggested I try looking for her under the name 'Haniver', an alias they used in the show."

"I see. Well, I'd still like to meet Jenny. I think it's very important."

"Yes, well that's up to Julie and Jenny, isn't it?"

"I think it would probably be beneficial for both of them."

"I agree. So you speak to Julie and I'll speak to Jenny."

"How can we reach you?"

"Best I call you. I'm still deciding where to stay in the area. I can't be away from Jenny for too long."

"Can you give me a number where I can at least call Jenny?"

"Later, Dr Truswell. I'll need to clear this with Jenny first."

It was exasperating, even infuriating, though Dan was by no means a stranger to the byzantine nature of family affairs. Institutions like Blackwater attracted the end-products of crisis and despair, with the added pressures of inheritance complications and human rights issues. Jackie Perfini was giving him as much and as little as he was giving her.

"Then please call soon. We need to settle things for Julie's sake."

"All our sakes, Doctor. But Julie's and Jenny's most of all, yes. They had and still have a special connection. Jenny doesn't say much about it, but she's deeply troubled when Julie is away."

So how must she be feeling now? Dan wondered. *Who's minding her?*

Dan shook the young woman's hand when she stood and offered it, feeling more frustrated than he could remember. He wanted to ask more about her father's travelling show, where it went, what occurred during those crucial years, wanted to ask about her own life. But now it was *quid pro quo* and the smartly dressed young woman was heading to the door.

As soon as Jackie left him at Reception, Dan had Hans note the make and colour of her car, then placed an immediate call to Jay Wendt over in Everton.

"Jay? Dan Truswell. I need Wendt Investigations do me an urgent favour. There'll be a—" Hans said a few words from the front door. "—white 94 Laser coming down the highway towards town in about ten minutes. Victorian number plate. Young female driver. Blue suit, short black hair. I need a local destination for her."

To Dan's relief, Jay was able to oblige. He replaced the receiver and leaned back in his chair, told himself it was the most he could do other than talk to Julie, try to get her side of Jackie's story, find out more about Jenny from her. Later he'd phone Harry Badman down in Sydney, see if there was any background on the names Perfini or Haniver in the CIB database.

But now he had rounds to do, counselling to give, bits of his own fraying world to be brought to order. He was half an hour at it, busily trying his best to keep his thoughts off Julie's catatonia and Jackie Perfini's sudden appearance, the whole disturbing, strangely compelling sequence of events, when he was called to the phone.

"Dan, it's Jay. I'm halfway down the Putty Road. Your subject has left the Hunter Valley altogether."

"She didn't stay local?"

"She's heading for Sydney, I'd say. Flat out too. You want me to stay on this?"

"Jay, I really need you to. This woman is the sister of a patient. We might need a destination in a hurry."

"Then I'll call a pal of mine in Windsor. Stephanie Ashburn. She can pick it up there and I'll come back. She's good, Dan. Don't worry. If necessary, I'll get someone from Parramatta to get out there as well. There'll be other traffic but we might need to leap-frog the closer she gets to home."

"Sounds like quite an operation."

"Just like the big kids do. I'll do a trace on the registration too and call when I've got something, okay?"

"Thanks, Jay."

There was no way he could return to his rounds. At 3:50 he paged Carla and asked her to bring Julie Haniver to his office as soon as possible.

When the girl was ushered in and given an armchair opposite Dan's by the french doors, she looked calm enough, though she never took her eyes off Dan for a moment, obviously expecting some fears to be confirmed.

Dan thanked her for coming and opened his notepad. He'd already decided to play it straight with her. When Carla had gone, he didn't hesitate.

"Jackie was here, Julie."

"I know."

"How do you know?"

"Peter told me."

Dammit. Peter Rait had far too much liberty, Dan decided, then retracted it. Peter had never been the enemy before, probably wasn't now. Though he'd never acted on his own before either.

"She already knew you were here, Julie. We didn't tell her."

"Peter told me that too, Doctor Dan. It's okay. I shouldn't have used the name Haniver. It was an old show name."

Thank God. Dan settled back. Julie seemed uncommonly composed and alert now, very focused indeed.

"She told me about Jenny. About the Perfini Wonder Show. About your father and his interests."

Julie nodded slightly, as if expecting it. "He couldn't help himself. Jenny keeps saying it. He couldn't help the things he did."

"Well, maybe so, Julie. But we need to know more about it. What can you tell us?" *Now that Jackie's been here?* Dan didn't need to add.

"We didn't have to be joined. It was only cartilage and muscle. Alonzo knew some doctors interested in *Wunderkammern*. They faked X-rays of the Lugli twins from Padua. Alonzo showed the authorities false X-rays. Jenny and I never knew."

"How did you find out?"

"It just became too much. What he did. We kept away from Italy, certainly from Sicily. Our first names were changed. We used the name Haniver. It's an in-joke. But we found we had a cousin interning in Frankfurt when we were there. When Alonzo had food poisoning and was taken in for tests, Carlo came and got us from the carnival and took us to visit. We sometimes did go out with Papa and his friends. We could walk well enough to look like we were closely arm in arm. Carlo didn't take us straight to Papa's ward. He did some X-rays of us. We didn't have to stay joined."

"Did Carlo go to the authorities?"

"Not then. It was a family thing, you see. He got two friends to help. Alonzo was away. They did the operation in our wagon."

"They what? That's burn scarring you've got, Julie. Interns with access to X-ray equipment and hospital facilities would hardly use acid or resort to cauterising wounds with flame. Do you actually remember the operation?"

There seemed a dreamlike quality between them now, almost as if her words were being recited from some false memory. "No. Jenny told me about it. I've forgotten a lot of things."

"Jenny wouldn't lie to you." He had to be so careful.

"Never. Jenny is my dearest friend. She's in my song. I'm in hers."

"Your song? I don't follow."

There was much more animation in Julie's features now. She was smiling again. "When we were young, it was our private game. We'd sing it."

"Please sing it now, Julie. Would you?"

Julie smiled and did so, in a light clear voice.

"When will Jenny come to play?
When will Jenny come to stay?
Jenny's never somewhere else,
Jenny's here with me, myself."

"Thank you, Julie. I take it as an honour."

"Jenny would sing 'Julie'; I'd sing 'Jenny'. We thought we'd have one another forever. We didn't know we could be apart. We never expected it."

"You miss that, don't you, Julie?"

"Sometimes desperately, Doctor Dan. It was all there was. You made it your world every conscious moment. Washing. Going to the toilet. Even pretending to be alone by turning away from each other. Playing at separation. But I grew to hate it too. Because of Alonzo. What he did. And once Carlo showed us we were probably separable. It wasn't the same. It wasn't a necessity any longer. More like an oversight."

"So why don't you remember?"

"I was ill or something. Highly strung, they said. With bad headaches. I had to be sedated a lot. I remember that."

Dan leaned back in his chair, made himself lean back, stay calm. He could no longer be sure what was truth or fiction. Perhaps he did need Peter Rait's view on this.

"Julie, after the operation, what happened to Carlo?"

"Carlo? I've put so much out of my mind, Doctor Dan, I don't know. Carlo just disappeared. Alonzo was furious. Humiliated. He tried to convince us the separation *had* been riskier than Carlo said, that he never wanted to take the chance, even claimed that he'd been misled by unscrupulous members of his *Wunderkammer* group."

"Julie, what do you mean Carlo disappeared?"

"We never saw him again. I never did. Perhaps he ran away. Alonzo said what Carlo had done had shamed him, made him a laughing stock before his peers."

The story was changing again. "His peers, not his family. Who were they again?"

"Others who owned *Wunderkammern* and traded exhibits with him. We never went back to Palermo. Alonzo finally sold off his collection and brought us to Australia."

"Did he do that in a hurry?"

"Not for three years. But then it all happened so quickly."

"What name did you use in Melbourne?"

"The show name. Haniver. He didn't want to use Perfini. He preferred the Flemish name, said it advertised his field of interests better."

"Oh? How so?"

Julie shrugged. "I don't know. Perhaps others interested in wonder-cabinets would recognise the name."

"Right. Julie, you seem to be recalling quite a bit now. Can you give me your address and phone number in Sydney?"

"Didn't Jackie?"

"No, she didn't."

"She was protecting Jenny."

"But you trust me. Can you give me your home address or phone number?"

"Doctor Dan, please understand. I need to protect Jenny too."

Which possibly explained the lies. Dan studied the earnest face, lacking only make-up to be identical to Jackie's. Something *was* dramatically different now. If not for Jackie's visit to lend an element of credibility to the whole thing, Dan wouldn't have believed any of it. He still couldn't help but feel it was some kind of hoax, or at least that layers of deception were at work, being employed to conceal what little truth there was. It was almost as if Julie had done a quick change, had managed a conspiracy so she could play both parts. Yet more than ever he had to accept the prevailing situation, not fight it, not force it.

"Julie, you believe we're genuinely trying to help you? That we want you and Jenny to be safe?"

"Of course I do."

"You and Jackie both want to protect Jenny. Jackie says that she's with Jenny down in Sydney, is that correct?"

"Yes."

"Yet you didn't want Jackie to find you."

"That's right."

"Can you explain that? Knowing Jackie is living with Jenny, knowing that Jenny misses you terribly, why would you run away from them?"

"I don't know. I just don't know."

"Please try, Julie. Why did you run away from Jenny?"

"I ran away from Jackie!"

"Why? Why would you do that? Why would you do that to Jenny as well?"

"I just don't know."

"Do you want to know?"

"What?"

"Would you like me to help you find out why you're here?"

There were only frowns now, bewilderment and uncertainty crimping her forehead, her confusion drawing out into its inevitable edge of panic. He could see it pulling at her eyes.

"H-How?"

"You remember our hypnotherapy sessions, Julie. Now Jackie's found you, I'd like to use hypnosis again. See what we can learn."

What is true, Dan told himself.

"Hypnotise me? Now?"

"That's right. We did it before, remember? It might help a lot."

"You'll find out where Jenny is."

"Not if I promise *not* to ask you that, Julie. Do you trust me about that?"

Before she could answer, the phone rang. Dan excused himself, crossed to his desk and answered it.

"Hello?"

"Is that Dan Truswell?" a woman's voice asked.

"It is."

"Dr Truswell, I'm Stephanie Ashburn, a friend of Jay Wendt's. I've followed the subject to a Dalloway Road address in Horsley Park. That's outside Blacktown, near Fairfield. It's semi-rural. Lots of open fields and market gardens."

"I think I know it, Stephanie. Go on."

"I've just arrived. That's 72 Dalloway Road."

"Describe the location, please."

"Large enough property, maybe three hectares. Just an ordinary fibro cottage, a few big trees."

"Any sheds or garages?"

"There's a very large corrugated iron shed set away to the right of the house. It's seen better days but it's sturdy enough. I'd say about thirty metres by fifteen, about four metres high."

"Where did the car pull up?"

"Outside the shed."

"Not the house?"

"Right. No lights visible, but the shed has no windows on the two sides I can see. No signs of activity. What should I do?"

"You're not too obvious?"

"I'm quite a ways from the place."

"Okay. Stephanie, phone Jay and tell him where you are. I'd appreciate it if you could stay there till one of us calls."

"Let me give you my number here."

Dan wrote it down and hung up. Then, as he turned from the desk, he saw a small paper object sitting among his files. It was an origami figure of—what else?—two humans joined at back or front. But dropped there by which sister—Julie or Jackie? He couldn't know. When had either had the chance? Jackie as she left? Julie as she came in?

Without touching it, he turned back to the armchairs by the long windows, now golden with late afternoon light.

"The hypnosis, Julie. What do you say?"

She looked up at him, wide-eyed, clearly troubled by the prospect. "Can Peter be here?"

Dan didn't flinch, didn't blink or hesitate. "If you want. I know he'd like to be."

Julie nodded. Dan returned to his desk, paged Carla and asked her to send Peter round to his office. By the time he arrived, Dan had his recorder set up and a chair positioned slightly to the back of Julie's so their guest would be out of direct sight. Peter took it with a smile and a nod, for all the world like a colleague here to observe an interesting procedure. Dan couldn't help smiling back, then set the recorder going and began.

"Peter, Julie and I decided we'd try some more hypnotherapy and thought you'd like to join us. You'll observe the usual courtesies, I know."

Peter nodded. "As silent as the Moon," he said. "Not a bird, nor the mewings of the baby stoat."

Baby stoat? Was he quoting? Dan could never be sure. But Peter settled back quietly, his eyes fixed attentively on Julie for a moment, then closed in his usual contemplative manner.

Dan positioned himself, began the relaxation recital. Julie visibly settled in her chair, actually seemed glad to give in to Dan's suggestions. Within a few minutes she had lapsed into the trance.

"Julie, tell me about the Perfini Wonder Show."

"Wonder-cabinet," Julie murmured, plumbing the years.

"Yes, the Perfini wonder-cabinet. The *Wunderkammer*. Tell me about it."

"We travelled through Europe," Julie said. "Papa took us through so many different countries. Not the big cities all that often and not all the towns. He knew where to go. The special fairs. The right estates."

"I'm sure. When did he first start showing you and Jenny?"

Julie didn't hesitate. Jenny was such a powerful reality for her. "When we were five. We were the special exhibit. He saved us till last."

"Did you enjoy it?"

"We loved it. We loved the attention then."

"Then? Not later?"

"Later it was different."

"How much later?"

"When we had turned ten. It was different then."

"How was it different?"

Julie frowned and didn't answer. Her left cheek spasmed—a nervous tic. Behind her right shoulder, Peter Rait's eyes opened wide as if in some shared sympathetic alarm, then closed again. He was trying to behave.

"Julie," Dan repeated gently, "how was it different?"

Julie was resisting, was even shaking her head a little. There was conflict, something she didn't want to face. Dan was about to put a new question when Peter broke trust and, eyes still closed, asked a question of his own.

"All the best wonder shows have a secret room, Julie. A special room. What happened in the secret room?"

Dan was silently furious but said nothing. Like Jenny, Peter was a powerful force in Julie's life. *She* had wanted him there.

Tears were rolling down Julie's cheeks when she answered. "It was where Papa took us."

Dan stayed silent. Let Peter ask it.

"To do what? What happened there, Julie?"

"He showed us undressed. He let them touch us." Despair had tightened her throat. The words were pinched, broken with sobbing now.

"He molested you? Both of you?"

Dan found they were his questions, coarsely, heavy-handedly, almost cruelly put, as direct as Peter always was, though here he was, without Phillip, coherent and focused and helping *without* Phillip Crow! The briars of unreason were blooming indeed.

Julie blinked away more tears, nodded.

Dan might not have persisted. Peter did.

"But it was your father! How could it happen?"

"We resisted. They held us down. Sometimes they tied our hands. Put rags in our mouths. We had no choice."

Dan intervened. "What about your visit to the hospital? Carlo doing the X-rays? What about your separation?"

"Carlo didn't do the separation. Carlo became a fine pair of wings. We did some of it ourselves, Jenny and me."

"What?" Dan said and, unsure of what he had heard, went back. "Carlo became what?"

But Julie was locked onto Peter's earlier question. "Papa said it was what many collectors did. Became teratophiles. There were codes, passwords, that let them into the secret rooms all over Europe. They all had them—the travelling shows and respectable homes. There were special fairs. There still are. It isn't new. The practice has been going on for centuries."

Dan composed himself. "But Carlo tried to help."

"He tried. But Papa caught him. Made him into a fine pair of wings."

There it was again, but Dan didn't bring it up then. "So how were you separated? If Carlo didn't do it?"

"One of Papa's guests in Frankfurt was a surgeon. Papa let him visit us alone. He felt very guilty after he had been with us. He took pity on us, told Jenny and me it was just a lot of muscle joining us. No arteries, nothing vital. There'd be blood, he said, quite a lot, but he told us what he'd have to do, said he'd bring the necessary instruments and drugs."

Despite the bizarre experiences of Dan's own life, it all sounded like so much fabrication again, a tall tale growing larger and more improbable by the minute: first Carlo, now this Frankfurt surgeon, Carlo becoming a nice pair of wings.

But then, like a spectre at the feast, or more a mind-reader in a high-class nightclub act, Peter was there.

"Julie, this is very important. Doctor Dan and I are finding this hard to accept. You must help us. Your Papa let this surgeon bring a bag of things into the secret room?"

"A lot of them brought bags and cases. Teratophiles are like paraphiles everywhere. Some brought masks and hoods, special costumes and things to use on us. Their cameras. Papa trusted and liked this man. Xavier Pangborn was as great an admirer of Frederic Ruysch as Papa was. Only when the pain became too much and we were crying out, did Papa break in. He and Dr Pangborn had a terrible fight." Julie winced at the memory. Her cheek spasmed. "Jenny was in so much pain. She passed out. I had to finish the job before I passed out too."

Finish the job!

Dan made himself stay calm, focused. Things did happen violently, strangely, in life; people were capable of the most extraordinary things, acts of courage and strength, incredible perversion too, a mix of the courageous and the outrageous that did make it seem that orthodoxy and consensus were always somewhere else in human affairs.

"What happened to Xavier Pangborn?" Dan asked, warning Peter with a look.

"We awoke in a house with Dr Pangborn and women we didn't know tending to us. Alonzo was downstairs, furious, so very angry, but also very afraid that Pangborn would tell the authorities and so was trying to be civil. The same shame and guilt that had made Pangborn help us had also led him to destroy all incriminating papers and exhibits of his own. Now he was a pillar of belated virtue. He said he'd have contacts keep an eye on us. Alonzo would never be sure who he meant and so actually made the best of the situation. He eventually sold off his own collection and brought us down to Australia."

"So you were reunited with Jackie."

Julie frowned. "It was more like meeting her for the first time really. Jenny and I were too young to remember her with the show."

"She became very taken with Jenny. Why is that, Julie?"

"Jenny has always been shy and fragile. The trauma of what those men did, the results of the separation—she took it all so much harder than I did. One of us had to cope. One of us had to be stronger."

"But Jackie came looking for you, too, Julie. Jackie cares enough for you to have searched for you."

Julie's mouth was a grim line. Her frown crushed her brow with the intensity of suffering, not merely concentration.

They should stop soon. But there was still so much to learn and Julie was so responsive, so lucid like this. He'd never have expected it. Dan decided to avoid further mention of Jackie; that was the harming stressor here.

"How did Alonzo earn his living in Melbourne, Julie?"

The frown went away; her mouth softened. "He had contacts there—keepers of *Wunderkammern* like himself. One of them gave him a job as assistant curator in a local museum."

"With a secret room no doubt." Dan couldn't help himself.

Julie took it as a question. "I suppose. It was a large public museum. There are always parts the public doesn't see."

That the brotherhood of cabinet keepers kept secret, Dan decided.

"How did he treat you?"

"Well from then on. We were with family. He found his interests elsewhere. And Xavier Pangborn came to see us."

"Pangborn did?"

"He was in Australia lecturing at ANU and Monash. One evening he stopped by. That was before he went missing."

"Went missing?" It was going wild again.

"It was a terrible thing. His wife was with him. There was a big search. It was in all the papers."

Did Alonzo kill him? Dan wanted to ask, but somehow knew Julie would have no idea. If her story were true, this terrible, elaborate, improbable tale, she had every reason to want to put it out of mind. He was probably going too far now. But Jackie had disturbed him; the case of this mysterious young woman sitting before him had opened out, blossomed amazingly. There were too many facts but not enough certainties.

It didn't stop Peter.

"Julie, what did you mean Alonzo made Carlo into a nice pair of wings?"

"Peter!"

"She isn't under, Doctor Dan. She's pretending to be in a trance!"

Dan was affronted, amazed yet convinced all at once. He hadn't wanted to believe it, but of course she was pretending; it had let her deal with experiences too difficult to face otherwise. But the illusion had to be preserved. He had to try and save it.

"Peter, listen very carefully. Trust my professional judgement here. I know for a fact Julie *is* under, and she's going to answer your question right now to prove it. Julie, please answer Peter's question."

Dan again leaned forward slightly, urging the young woman with his body language to continue with the vital pretence.

And the words came in the same calm tone she had been using at the outset.

"Alonzo made monsters in the old way. Many keepers of *Wunderkammern* did. You know, fitting bat wings to the bodies of lizards, then carefully drying them to give dragons. Adding a human fetus's arms to the body of a skate. Sticking horns onto monkey skulls. The first platypus taken to Europe was regarded as such a fake. They tried to pull the beak off. Carlo was killed and dried, flayed and 'leathered'. His skin was used for wings."

Wilder and wilder, Dan thought. This can't go on. Julie improvising; Peter playing the role of a conspirator in some charade. Though Jackie *had* been real. She had been.

"Ask her about her surname," Peter prompted, leaning forward as well, playing his part, though he looked more concerned than ever. "Haniver."

"Haniver?" Dan echoed, but the phone rang. He crossed to his desk, grabbed the receiver. "Hello?"

"Dan, it's Jay. Stephanie's not answering her mobile. She was going to do a lost motorist routine. Knocking at the door, asking for directions, so she may have switched it off."

Dan kept him voice low and matter-of-fact. "Is there a problem?"

"Not necessarily. But it wasn't our arrangement. Whenever there's risk, what we call a 'nasty', we leave our mobiles on."

"What about your back-up from Parramatta?"

"Dan, there was enough traffic going into Horsley Park for Stephanie not to stand out. I called Rick and let him go. Oh, and incidentally, the Laser is registered to a Laura Barraclough in Melbourne and hasn't been reported stolen. I'd say it's on loan."

"Okay. Jay, I'm probably overreacting badly but there's an edge to this I don't like at all. If Stephanie's run up against Jackie she may be in trouble."

"But Jackie isn't the patient."

"Correct. Like I said, she's a patient's sister and seems pretty unstable. Let me know the moment Stephanie calls in."

"Done. What do we do in the meantime?"

"You've got the number in Dalloway Road?"

"Yes."

"Call in favours, Jay. See if you can get a local squad car round there."

"You really do suspect foul play?"

"They won't find anything," Julie said from her chair by the windows.

"Hold it a moment, Jay," Dan said, turning to face her. "What do you mean?"

Julie's face was like a golden mask in the last of the sunlight. "The house at 72 is a trap. It's what's called a 'false door' in Egyptology, what the teratophile cabinet owners call a blind to throw off undesirables. But it's a trap house. Jackie will have taken Stephanie to meet Alonzo and Xavier."

"But they're dead!"

"Yes. But she knows it'll bring me back."

More and more the briars were coiling up.

"Julie, you've got to help me. You've got to explain clearly what's going on!"

"Jackie's changed the rules. She's always been concerned with connection, bringing things together, but now she's harming Jenny."

That was Alonzo with the connection thing, not Jackie! Julie was changing her story again.

"We're going to bring the police in on this," Dan said. "Listen, Jay—"

But Julie's words brought him up short. "You'll never find the house if you do."

"What?"

"If you or your friend there call the police, Doctor Dan, I swear I'll go catatonic and you'll get nothing. Jackie will never call again. Jenny will die. Stephanie may already be dead."

"What then?"

"You get this Jay friend of yours to drive us down to Sydney. I'll take you to the house. Then you can call your police friends."

"I can't do that, Julie."

"But you know you will anyway. I've got to save Jenny, Doctor Dan. It has to be this way. I know Jackie."

Stephanie never called in; her phone remained switched off. The Fairfield police found her car outside 72, found the house deserted, its lights operated by timers, found the shed locked but empty inside when they forced the lock.

This came to them in Jay's Nissan Patrol as they plunged down the Putty Road, Jay driving, Julie next to him, Dan in the back waiting for Harry Badman to return his calls.

Neither Dan nor Jay were surprised when, at 6:20, they turned into Walgrove Road and headed for Horsley Park. Of course the trap house and the real one would be close enough for convenience.

"Tell us about Alonzo and Xavier Pangborn, Julie," Dan said. "How they can be involved."

"You'll see."

Dan refused to give up. "I think I might be a better friend to Jenny than you are right now."

Julie turned in her seat to look at him. "What do you mean?"

"You're doing this because you want to help Jenny."

"Yes! Save Jenny!" Still she faced him, half-turned, eyes glittering in the dim interior.

"Why am *I* doing it?"

"Because you want to know what's going on. Because of his friend." She indicated Jay. "Stephanie."

"More than that. You know it's more than that."

"What then?"

"You want to help Jenny. But I want to help Jenny *and* Julie. Because Jenny needs to have Julie safe too, doesn't she? It can't be all right unless you're both safe."

"Yes." It was a ghostly, feeling-charged affirmation, said with a new and different emotion. She believed him, was accepting what he said. Perhaps he was earning the truth from her.

"Tell me how Alonzo and Xavier are involved!"

And Julie told them as they sped along Walgrove Road.

"Both men were interested in joining opposites, in bringing things together, the old alchemical quest. Alonzo left us joined. Xavier used us because we were. The prize of Xavier's collection, probably genuine, were two joined bodies."

"Congenitally joined?"

"Oh no, Doctor Dan. An ancient Roman punishment was to tie the condemned to a corpse, back to back, face to face, then leave you. If you weren't lucky enough to die from shock, your body was poisoned by the rotting cadaver. Necrosis took over. Xavier had acquired the preserved remains of such a wretch left like this in a cell in ancient Syria long ago. Preserved by desert heat and aridity. The bodies were unearthed in the 1700s, reached Amsterdam in the 1830s, finally made it into Xavier's collection just before we were born. The same year."

Dan thought he understood. "Xavier acquired the double corpses. Alonzo then fathered conjoined daughters not long after. He couldn't resist. He left you like that as a gesture, a living symbol of Xavier's exhibit."

"Yes." It was breathed rather than said. "That was partly the reason. He also enjoyed the notion for itself."

"Then the separation—"

"Was motivated by genuine compassion from Xavier, we believe, by outrage at something they'd done as competitive, obsessive, heartless, younger men, not just to spite a rival."

"Then—" And again Dan understood. "When Xavier went missing—"

"Yes. Alonzo avenged himself in the appropriate way. Xavier ended his days in a cellar face to face with a corpse."

"How do you know this?"

"Jackie told me."

"*Jackie!* How does she know?"

"She became Alonzo's favourite when he came to Australia. He needed to gloat. He showed her what he'd done."

"Showed her! My God!"

They turned off Walgrove Road onto Horsley Drive, then Julie directed them right into Walworth and along the crests of the low hills, the road winding its way past isolated houses with cheerily lit windows, past long intervening outlooks and swales where the land rolled away in darkened vistas, marked only by occasional, far-off, twinkling points of light, touches of civilisation and sanity.

Enough touches. For other things were out there as well. The residues of madness and obsession.

"Lots of room out here, Doctor Dan," Julie said, as if answering him. "Lots of houses and sheds few people ever get to see inside of."

Lots of opportunities for secret lives, Dan thought. "What will Jackie do, Julie?"

"I don't know, Doctor Dan. But I think she wants to harm me and Jenny."

"She said she cared for Jenny. For you too."

"Sometimes she does. But she scared me. I had to leave."

You left Jenny! Dan couldn't accept that. "Julie, was Jenny already dead when you ran away?"

And is Jackie waiting to, Xavier-like, join the two of you back together? Face to face? To reunite you at last?

"Not when I left. But Jackie loves Jenny. She wouldn't harm her."

"She might to get at you. People do it all the time. Harm what they love."

"Not Jenny!" Julie said as if desperately needing to believe it. "Turn here!"

There was a street sign Dan didn't have time to read or even ask about because, almost immediately, Julie was telling Jay to pull over in front of a large open field. No, not a field—a drab fibro house sat at the end of a driveway, a single light showing dimly from what seemed to be the living room. To the right of the house was a large corrugated iron shed, just like the one Stephanie had described for the place on Dalloway Road, about thirty metres by fifteen, four metres or so high, with no visible windows and none of the double doors you'd expect for housing large vehicles in such a structure.

"There." Julie pointed, indicating the shed and the solitary door they could see on its northwestern corner.

Jay reached for his car-phone.

"Don't!" Julie said, in a voice that actually startled Dan, so different it was to anything he'd ever heard from her. "Please! She will harm Jenny! And Stephanie! She probably doesn't know we're here yet!"

Jay switched off the engine. "Lives are at risk, Julie."

"They certainly will be if we don't follow her system."

"System?" Jay asked before Dan could.

"That's a *Wunderkammer* there," Julie answered. "She will have prepared it for us."

Again Jay reached for the phone. "Someone has to know. No-one's going in there."

Dan gripped his shoulder. "Jay, it probably does have to be this way. What's the layout, Julie?"

"She will have changed it. It's the House of Iitoi most likely. From the Hopi legend. The maze pattern you see all over the Southwestern USA. The Arizonan labyrinth with Death at the centre. Your journey through the maze to Death at the centre is the journey through life."

"Julie!" Dan said, still gripping Jay's shoulder, knowing how carefully this had to be played. "Tell us what to expect."

"There's usually an entry corridor going round the perimeter, leading inwards. There'll be photographs, exhibits to arouse interest, *vanitas mundi* tableaux."

"*Vanitas* what?" Jay asked.

"Displays," Dan said. "Vitrines containing exhibits. Go on, Julie."

"Definitely a maze."

"With traps? Short-cuts? You've been in there. You've seen it."

"I can't say. She will have changed it, Doctor Dan. But she wants me in there with Jenny. She won't risk harming me."

"Give us the address here, Julie," Dan said. "As we go in, Jay phones the police. No-one goes anywhere till that's done."

"But *as* we go in," Julie said. "I have to be in there. Promise. Both of you."

Dan did at once. Jay hesitated, furious, then grudgingly did so, as if such oaths could hold true just by being given. There was danger here, and madness, though fortunately Jay, like Dan, recognised an essential process at work, saw that any show of force could not guarantee the safety of lives within. But a trail of crumbs had to be left for the cavalry, even if it was to be after the event. Everything on Jackie's terms, *if* they decided to go in.

"Lot 6, Jellicoe Road," Julie told them, opening her door and getting out, with Dan right behind her, determined to stay close.

Jay did too, slipping his gun into the inside pocket of his wind-jacket, his mobile in his left hand. "I want to check the address," he said, and rushed off into the night. They could hear his footsteps along the road.

"He'll call the police," Julie said, taking Dan's arm and leading him up the driveway, angling towards the shed. "We need to continue without him."

"We can't do that, Julie. His friend is in there. He deserves to be here too."

"Don't you see, Doctor Dan? If we make this difficult for Jackie, she'll make it difficult for us. He can follow. Please."

Dan tried to think it through, calculate what was to be lost or gained.

But the door was suddenly there and it opened easily when Julie turned the handle and, almost before he knew it, they were in the long 1.2 meter-wide passageway that stretched out before them, roofed and walled with sheet iron, wooden-floored, lit by single frosted bulbs every seven metres or so. The building's outer wall had been corrugated iron, but its interior was faced with sheet iron, suggesting a double wall, probably with insulating batts in between. On the inner wall of the passage were framed photographs—first, of the original eponymous twins, Chang and Eng, and of other famous conjoined siblings, then of a whole series of renowned 'freaks' and hoaxes. Hanging from the roofbeams, casting eerie shadows and set turning in the warm close air by Dan and Julie entering the corridor, were the shrivelled remains of false monsters. Dan saw a winged serpent-like thing the red of old blood, then a grimacing homunculus—no doubt a late-development fetus, its wizened features and oversized hands probably added by some experienced teratologist. Other dim shapes swung and spiralled further down the passageway.

From even further off, deeper within the structure, came music, the faintest strains of Prokofiev, if Dan wasn't mistaken, which lent a disturbing, too discordantly civilised edge to the whole thing, but also gave a sense of direction and destination, some kind of centre to all this.

Julie went on ahead, leaving Dan to follow. They had to complete the circuit, it seemed, follow the passage the length of the shed's long southern side, turn left along its eastern end. There were more sheet metal walls, naked bulbs, photos in dusty frames, shrivelled shapes turning overhead, then another turn left down the long northern side.

Now the photos were different. Now the pictures were of Julie and Jenny, their story told in graphic, pathetic detail: showing them first as infants, cute and normal-looking in matching outfits, then as happy little girls in identical smiling poses, then as pre-pubescent youngsters suddenly displayed naked and joined by their short 'bridge' of flesh, just the two of them alone initially, staring wide-eyed in confusion and alarm, then attended by as many as seven figures in dark business suits, though more often one or two and always male it seemed, all but the girls masked, appropriately, with dominoes or grotesque animal and demon masks, lacquered and snouted as if denisens from a Venetian Carnivale. Sometimes the girls were shackled; other times they simply huddled together, hiding their nude or half-dressed state.

Then it changed again. Dan saw images even more blatantly sexual, and more and more often, one of the twins was shown with her hands fastened behind her and her mouth taped, while the other received the attentions of some visitor or other with what seemed increasing abandon.

"Julie," Dan said, whispered in the close air, his first words in that terrible place. "You're the one restrained, aren't you?"

Julie nodded, not turning, sobbing. "She enjoyed it! The bitch actually enjoyed it, can you believe that? I was always raped, but she *liked* it!"

"Jenny did? But you said Jenny and you."

"Not Jenny!" she cried, sobbing bitterly now, still pressing ahead, still not looking round. "Not *Jenny*!"

"That's Jackie?" Dan's gaze flicked from image to image and knew it was. "But Jackie spoke of Jenny too."

He didn't need to go on, certainly didn't need to speak what Julie so painfully knew. It was what Peter Rait had said about there being a sister. *There is and there isn't.*

There was no Jenny.

They'd both lost a sister, had both changed too much to be what they once were for each other, yet both had vivid, profoundly affecting memories of a loved one who *was* another part of them, *was* the perfect friend and sibling.

Julie didn't see her in Jackie. Jackie couldn't find her in Julie.

They'd lost each other, couldn't be it for one another, had become too different, too definitely separate, yet out of trauma, betrayal, terrible loss, had invented the one point at which they *could* connect. Preserving something of the lost intimacy, some kind of way back.

As a schoolboy in Reardon, Dan remembered that his kindergarten teacher had made a Wendy House at the back of the classroom, named no doubt after Peter Pan and Wendy—a house where the children played at being grown-ups. This was a Jenny House—everything in it a shrine to what Julie and Jackie had made between them. But playing at grown-ups. What chance had they?

Dan saw how it was. Hurrying along after Julie, rushing past those frightful images, he understood the terrible dilemma. Jackie wanted to unite with her version of Jenny—which only Julie could provide. Of course she'd wanted her back. Julie wanted to unite with *her* version of Jenny as well, but *not* with Jackie! That paradox, that crisis of opposites, had made Julie flee; the opposite pendulum swing had brought her back again into the same irreconcilable crisis.

There was only one way the sisters could ever be joined that would let them *both* join with Jenny. Peter had probably known more about it in his incredible way, had wanted Dan to ask about their pseudonym. Haniver. Now there wasn't time. Now there was only the terrible danger.

"Julie, we go back!" he cried, grabbing at her arm, but she pulled away. Dan hurried forward, went to grab at her again, but then the lights went out and a tremendous snaring weight fell on him from above. He could hear a far-off pounding as he sank to the floor.

Perhaps he lost consciousness for a few moments, Dan couldn't be sure. He found himself trying to put the world back together, found himself fighting with the weight oppressing him when the lights came on again, showed he was wrestling with a coil of heavy rope triggered to drop from above. The driving beat he could hear was probably Jay pounding at the *locked* entry door (for Jackie would have locked it behind them).

Dan finally freed himself from the tangle and stood. There was no sign of Julie, of course, nothing ahead but the passage, the stuffy dimness and turning constructs, more pictures on the walls.

There *were* traps. There *were* short-cuts and secret panels. Julie had been snatched away.

The pounding stopped. The Prokofiev was back and other sounds, far-off scuffling, thumps against the iron, muffled cries.

Dan pounded the walls a moment, crying their names, then rushed along the corridor, his footsteps ringing on the wooden floor, his hands slapping the iron. He had to get to the centre, to wherever Jackie had Julie. And Stephanie, if she were even still alive.

There was a crash and the building shuddered. Dan ignored it, continued running, bringing wind to the dead air.

Again, the building shook to an impact, a shuddering crash, this time followed by a wrenching sound.

It was Jay! Jay was ramming his four-wheel drive into the building, trying to force a way in. And again the structure shook. Beams creaked. Pictures fell and iron sheets were sprung on their uprights.

Dan wrenched one sheet away, actually pried it free and brought it clattering down, then stepped into an inner part of the corridor. One stage closer.

Again Jay rammed the building. Beams groaned, dust settled, more metal sheeting warped out from the timber. Tearing his fingers, Dan wrenched another section of wall free, revealed another inner coil of the maze. There couldn't be many more. He ran on, slewing into the walls when Jay rammed the structure a fifth time, making headway surely.

Then Dan could hear voices raised in anger, accusation, women's voices shouting, made out actual words.

"Jenny doesn't love you!"

"Jenny doesn't love *you*!"

He stopped to listen.

"Do it! Go on! I dare you!"

"Not with you! With her!"

He ran, plunging round the circuit, trying to get into wherever it was. And again the building resounded to a blow, this time followed by a shuddering crash as more outer structural supports gave way.

Dan rounded the next corner, crashed into a locked door and went spinning back, stunned by the impact.

"Julie!" he cried. "Jackie, let me in!"

Again Jay rammed the building. It was solidly made, but never meant for this sort of battering. Something had to be giving.

"He'll do it!" a voice beyond the door cried, Julie or Jackie Dan couldn't tell. "He will!"

And dazed, bloodied, pushing against the door, Dan thought they meant Jay.

When the door gave way and Dan toppled into the large central room, he saw in a glance a host of disparate things: the old-style record player, the specimen tables and cases of exhibits, the clustering of shapes dangling from the roof-beams, saw the girls lying naked and joined in the shallow pit in the middle of the floor, yes, glued together front to front with the tubes of instant glue lying near them, Julie's hands tied behind her back, saw too what he had set in motion by pushing back the door, the big tub of acid even now tipping onto them.

He'll do it!

The screams and threshing about were hideous and mercifully short, and there was drumming, a relentless drumming that wasn't the blood rushing through Dan's heart and temples, that was suddenly Jay bursting into the room, eyes wide, gun drawn.

They stood in the dreadful quiet, in a near-silence of sizzling and dripping that faded even as they watched, faded to the lowest, faintest mewing of despair.

"Where's Steph?" Jay said.

"Listen!" Dan told him.

"Where is she?"

"Listen, dammit!"

And they heard it again, a dismal far-off wail, a dull thumping.

"Where's that coming from?" Jay demanded.

"There's always a secret room," Dan said, remembering what Peter had said to Julie. "Try over there, but stay clear of the pit. That's acid."

They circled the central depression where the bodies lay contorted and, yes, virtually indistinguishable now, went to one of the dimly lit corners. The mewing was louder, the dull thumping more distinct.

They discovered a catch near the ceiling, another sunk into the wooden floor, and fumbled at them, Dan with bloody fingers, Jay clumsy with desperation, but finally pulled back the panel to reveal a room lit by its single bulb.

Stephanie was on the floor, naked, gagged, strapped between the dried corpses of Alonzo and Xavier, their shrivelled heads and faces jammed against hers, their groins pressing close, front and back. Though clearly exhausted, she was jerking the hideous construct as best she could, eyes wide with sheer terror and a hysteria very close to madness.

Jackie had used false street signs, so it took the police and ambulances a while to find them at Lot 3 Dinsmoor Road, took hours of Dan and Jay answering questions at the local police station, explaining just what it was that had occurred and why. Thankfully Harry Badman phoned in at last and vouched for them, added his verifications to those already provided by Blackwater, but it wasn't until 2 am that Dan and Jay reached Everton again. Knowing how some things needed to be anchored in the mundane as soon as possible, Dan had Barbara, Mark and Carla 'debrief' them for almost another hour before sending Jay off home.

The next morning, Dan wasn't at all surprised to find Peter Rait sitting at the corner window in the library where he'd found Julie— could it be?—less than twenty-four hours before.

"I should've asked you about the name," Dan said. "Haniver."

Peter nodded and smiled. "You should have, yes. Though it couldn't have ended any other way."

"Tell me about it now."

"There used to be quite a thriving market in monsters. Many were made in Antwerp, a Flemish seaport on the Scheldt the French called Anvers. A 'Jenny Haniver' was the name they gave to such merchandise."

"These false monsters?"

"Yes, Doctor Dan. False dreams in a way. Imitations of wonder some needed to believe in so much. The sisters knew what they were making."

"They died for it, Peter."

"Yes, but it's closure, isn't it? They had already lost one another, were getting further and further apart."

"Their *Wunderkammer* was a death-trap."

"Ah, but then, Doctor Dan, that's like the world itself. The best of them always are."

.

Cheat Light

BRIAN GATES LOOKED up from the seven photographs on the café table in front of him.

"You took them, Mr Franklin?"

"Jeff. Call me Jeff," the little man said. "And no, Brian. They were in an old camera I bought at a pawnshop near Pauley Bay. An hour or so north of here, if you know it. An old Olympus 2N SLR with a roll of film in it. I was curious. How many people sell cameras with undeveloped films in them? There were these seven shots."

"All right. So how exactly can I help?" A television lighting technician doesn't get many off-the-job calls on his time. Brian was puzzled, flattered and intrigued that this short, middle-aged man had sought him out, phoned him at the studio in his lunch break, and asked for help with a professional matter. Paid help.

Now, four hours after the call, they sat across from each other on the veranda of the Blue Duck, with coffee cups in front of them and late afternoon sunlight flaring on the ocean swells.

"Like I said on the phone. I need someone who understands light. Lighting effects."

"Right. And these are in order?" Brian touched the photo furthest to the left.

"Yep. You can see Pauley Bay marked on that sign there."

Exactly what it was, Brian saw. The only thing visible in the blackness of the first photo: a local council signpost, metal pole, white metal sign and the blurred words *Pauley Bay 5 km*.

"You think whoever took them was chronicling a journey to somewhere near Pauley Bay?"

Jeff Franklin's small eyes glittered. "That's it. That's it exactly. Someone on a night shoot. Using fast film."

"This first one's a flash shot. Maybe the second one, too."

"Yes. Yes, I can see that. But it's the others. The later ones."

Brian had glanced at them all. Now he studied the progression again, deliberately made himself seem to be giving a professional appraisal.

The second shot was of a sealed road caught in the headlights of a stopped car, taken from the driver's side of the vehicle. Probably using a flash, or very fast film. And he saw the reason for the shot: the blur and shadow-sweep of a turn-off. Probably a dirt road leading away from the sealed road, off to the right.

"I can't make out the third one at all," Brian said. "It's just black with that tiny thread of light there."

The little man was nodding. "That's right. I figured whoever took it was too far away from what he was trying to shoot."

"He?"

"The pawnshop owner said a guy brought it in. The camera. I just automatically assumed he'd be the photographer."

"Photographs tend to be more important to females generally. On the other hand they're more inclined to part with undeveloped pics in a camera if a relationship has gone bad. Impulse purge. Small window of opportunity."

"Hey, that's right. That's exactly right. See, you're really helping, Brian. I'd have never thought of that. So if a guy brought it in, the camera could have been stolen."

"Certainly possible." Brian felt better. They'd agreed on fifty dollars for his time. He wanted to earn it. He began touching the photos again, making sure he had an appropriately thoughtful expression.

Franklin hunched forward. "So a camera found, maybe stolen, brought in by a he, but it might have been a she took them. I see that now. There's a lot of it going on. People needing drug money."

Brian looked up, saw the excitement in the little man's eyes, wondered what he should say next. "The pawnbroker must've seen some ID. Proof of ownership."

The little man shrugged. "Never asked. Never questioned it. I mean, you assume it's on the up and up, don't you? Don't the police check that sort of thing?"

"They do. They're meant to," Brian said. "Anyway, whoever took the third shot seems to be trying to catch an approach to something. The fourth shot is closer."

"Yeah. What *is* that?"

Brian hesitated, studying photo four again. It seemed to show the sides of trees picked out with dimmest moonlight, just the barest ghost edges showing, marking them as trees, the trunks of trees. Yet just from off to one side. Nothing in the higher foliage, so unless it was close to a full-phase moonrise, it wasn't the moon. It had to be something in low. The remaining three pictures showed similar hints of vertical light in darkness.

"Seems to be a light source back there," he said, stating the obvious.

"Exactly what I thought. That's why I called you, Brian. Why I needed an expert opinion. I was looking at the shots, really puzzled, you know? Disappointed. I figured they were trees."

"Right. Probably with houses back there. Yard light spill."

"Nope. I drove a lot of the road before I phoned you. The whole area seems undeveloped till you get back down to Pauley Bay itself."

"You drove the road? Saw the light?"

"Found the road. Started along it, but didn't want to go too far at night. I mean, I wanted to but, you know, it was pretty creepy. Not sealed or anything. Took me ages to find a place to turn around. But I saw the light on the trees. Like here." Franklin tapped the fourth photo. "Very dim. I thought it looked like moonlight, but I don't remember seeing the moon. Maybe it's phosphorescence."

"Or a cheat light."

"A what?"

"Like in film-making or night photography where there isn't enough available light. If you're not going to shoot day for night using filters, like most of the old movies did, you have to use cheats."

"Cheats?"

"You ever watch *The X-Files*?"

"Sure."

"Lots of cheats there. False light sources flaring up behind trees, behind rises and ridge lines where they shouldn't be."

Franklin was nodding. "You're right! I remember that. Torches and headlights always gave off too much light."

"That's part of it. But it's more like that CGI simulation in the Peter Jackson movie, *The Fellowship of the Ring*. Remember all those columns in the huge cavern where the dwarfs lived? There were cheats on the columns so you could see them, get the scale of the place."

"That was Dwarrowdelf," Franklin said, clearly pleased with himself for knowing the name and being able to say it. "It was vast. So it's like that here, you reckon?"

"Looks like it. You've got tree trunks highlighted on what's probably a moonless night."

"Why moonless? I didn't see one, but—"

"The light's too low. Too directional. Not on the tree-tops or the surrounding area. So unless it's a particularly striking moonrise, with the moon half-phase or more, what's the light source?"

"A cheat light." Franklin seemed pleased, seemed to feel he was getting his money's worth. "Could it be phosphorescence though? You know, luminous fungus or something?"

"Too strong for that. Too selective. You don't get reflected light from that, more localised point and patch effects."

"So someone was there!" Franklin was nodding again, as if his own suspicions had been confirmed.

"Seems like it."

"Car headlights?"

"Maybe. Is there a road in behind there?"

"That's the thing. Not that I could find."

"Then someone's rigged up Kleigs or something. Walked in and set up lights."

"But why, Brian? Who would do that? Could it be a night shoot? The habits of nocturnal animals, that sort of thing?"

Brian shrugged. "Maybe. But light like that would scare the animals away. They just use special film or sudden spots." He found he was becoming interested in spite of himself. Jeff Franklin's curiosity was catching. "Might be worth a look."

"Couldn't pay though," Franklin said.

"Call it professional interest. I do some lighting for independent films." He threw that in for extra clout. "If it's like what you say,

I'm curious, too."

"Right. That's good. But when could we do it?"

Brian glanced at his watch. It was five-thirty. "I'm free right now."

Franklin was delighted. "Hey, great! Can we? We'd be there by seven. Probably back by half-nine at the latest."

"Pity the pawnshop won't be open. We could've asked about the camera."

"It's a general store, gas-station set-up," Franklin said. "Second-hand stuff down at one end. It probably would be."

"Let's find out."

They took Jeff Franklin's Lexus and drove the coast highway north in the last of the daylight. As the sun slipped below the long ocean swells to their left, an orange glow filled the sky, fading slowly through purple to cobalt and indigo by the time they had left the last of the villas and housing developments behind.

Then it was ti-trees, banksias and other low coastal scrub to seaward, forests of eucalypts to their right, sparse at first, but becoming denser and taller the farther they went.

It wasn't as bad a drive as Brian had feared. Franklin wasn't quite the earnest, full-on nerd type he'd first seemed. He kept up the chatter, but left plenty of empty moments, too. He was clearly fascinated by Brian's profession.

"You make those film sets look so good. How do you know? Trial and error?"

"Experience. Years of trial and error," Brian said. "That's why set-ups can take ages to get right."

"What it's about, I guess. Light. Journeys in light. Like those rain-light and planet-light effect in *Solaris*. The Steven Soderbergh remake. So good. Did you see it?"

"I did." Brian hadn't but he wasn't about to spoil the mood. Then he thought he'd best add a comment of his own. "That worked. Not like those overkill waterlight effects in that remake of *Ghost Ship*."

"I saw that movie! Looked great though!"

"Yeah, but it was overdone. Seemed like every other interior shot had waterlight in it. Looked good but made you wonder at the light source. Like here."

Jeff Franklin was nodding behind the wheel. "Must drive you nuts, things like that! Most of us wouldn't care. We'd just go with it."

"I always try to. Like with that dwarf cavern." Brian didn't try to say the name.

But, of course, Franklin did. "Dwarrowdelf!"

They reached Pauley Bay just before seven. It was nothing like a bay really, just a curve of coastline that someone—a civic planner, a hopeful developer perhaps—had called one in the "name it and they will come" tradition so common on this part of the coast. There was no moon yet, and the little coastal community glowed under the three DMR sodium lights on its stretch of ocean highway like a handful of beads on a dull gold thread. It wasn't a township, nothing quite that substantial, just a small string of shops along the road with some houses tucked in behind.

"That's it there!" Jeff Franklin said. "Pauley Bay General Store."

Brian saw a sprawling, single-storeyed building with a long veranda facing the ocean and two gas pumps under the overhang out front. A large parking area, empty now, was marked out with painted white stones.

Franklin parked the Lexus and they both stepped out into a fresh onshore breeze, strong with the scent of brine, dry coastal vegetation and cooling sand. As they entered the store, a bell chimed. Brian saw the usual shelves of canned and packaged goods you found in these places, freezers and drink cabinets along the walls, hot food units up by the register. He could hear a television or radio playing through the curtained doorway at the rear. Down at one end of the main retail area stood a counter in front of shelves filled with boom-boxes, old game consoles, guitars, some well-used surfboards and wetsuits, clearly where Franklin had picked up his camera.

A middle-aged woman pushed through the curtain.

"Evening, gents. What can I get you?"

Jeff Franklin gave his biggest, sorry-to-bother-you smile. "Yes, look. I bought a second-hand camera here last weekend. An old Olympus."

"Yes?" The woman was both politely concerned and instantly wary. "If there's something wrong with it, you'll have to speak to my husband. He's out back if—"

"No. No, it's nothing like that," Franklin said. "It works fine." It was painful to see how tentative he was. "There was a film inside. An undeveloped roll of film."

Brian couldn't stand it. "He wants to return the film to the person who brought it in."

The woman smiled, brushed back some strands of hair. "Good of you. Guess you could leave it here. Can't promise anything, but if they come back in, I can pass it on."

"Don't have it with us, I'm afraid," Brian said. "Just happened to be passing through again and decided to mention it. If you could give us an address or a phone number—"

"How about you leave *your* number and I'll get them to call? They can tell you where to send it."

Brian noticed the neutral "they". Not a "he" or a "she". "Fine, fine. We'll do that. Probably forgot it was in there."

"Must happen all the time," the woman said, passing Franklin a notepad and pen. "A first for us though."

Franklin scribbled his number on the pad and returned it.

The woman glanced at what he'd written, then looked back. "Surprised you didn't get it developed. Couldn't resist something like that myself."

Brian decided there was nothing to be lost by telling the truth. "Fact is, that's actually what we did. Found just seven exposures. Nothing helpful. Nothing risqué or incriminating," he added with a grin.

The woman grinned back. Neither commented on his earlier version of events. A kind of mutuality had been reached. Brian often marvelled at the secret lives ordinary people lived, what they could accept, what was revealed, what was always held back. He found himself doing so now. How often did something like this happen?

"You have them with you?" she asked in a carefully off-hand way.

"We do." Brian turned to Franklin. "Jeff ?"

The little man brought the pictures from the inside pocket of his jacket, spread them on the counter.

"See anything you recognise?" Brian asked, keeping his voice as carefully relaxed as hers.

"Just the road sign. That's the one out by Junction Road. Other side of the Bay."

Brian nodded. "Anything out there?" He made it sound casual. "Houses?"

"Not that far out. Junction just leads down to Wattle Beach. Used to be a good surfing beach. Past ten years or so there've been bad rips at Wattle. Now even the surfers keep away."

Brian nodded again. "So no industry? No boat-building or council depots?"

"At Wattle? Nah?" The woman reached out, spread the photographs. "Just a fire-road really."

That might have been the end of it then, a sorry-I-can't-help-you closing silence from her, a nod and a sigh from Brian as he scooped up the pictures, but Jeff Franklin seemed oblivious to the usual social cues.

"Why would someone photograph darkness?" he said. "Or a road sign? The end of a road? It's just darkness." At least he didn't mention the light on the trees.

Brian decided to go with it. "Then sell the camera?"

The woman shook her head and stepped back from the pictures, distancing herself again. "Can't help you there, I'm afraid. We took the camera like we do any other sale."

"But the guy who sold it wasn't a regular? Maybe your husband can—"

"If he turns up again, I'll give him your number." The woman's tone was distinctly cool now. She was moving towards the curtain at the rear.

"But you'd have his details," Brian said.

"Have a good one, gents!" She was at the curtain.

"We'll need another torch!" Brian called to her. "You've got torches here?"

The woman turned, gestured to a side shelf. "Help yourself," she said, and frowned. "You're not going out there?"

"Thought we might take a look."

Brian selected a reasonably inexpensive fishing torch, found the right batteries for it and brought them to the counter. "Since we're here." He tried to keep it casual again. It seemed the only way to draw her out.

But the woman just shrugged and rang up the sale. "Nothing out there but bush." She put the torch and batteries in a bag, pushed it across the counter and bid them goodnight again.

And that was it. They stepped out into the windy spring evening and returned to the car.

Franklin started the engine, set the trip-meter, then pulled out onto the highway, turning right to follow the shallow curve of coast. "I've got torches!" he said.

"I know, Jeff. How did she seem to you?"

"I don't know. A bit wary at first. Understandable, I guess. Helpful enough."

"I mean about our going out here?"

"You think she doesn't want us to?"

"Not sure one way or the other. I just sensed something."

"I only met her husband last time. You don't think there's anything wrong?"

"Hard to say. Let's see what we find."

They had no trouble locating the highway sign in the first picture. Brian had Franklin continue past it for a kilometre or so while they checked for concealed driveways and any other back-road turn-offs that might indicate possible habitation. They didn't find any.

Franklin finally did a U-turn and brought them back to the sign, then took them twenty or so metres further on to the unmarked turn-off into Junction Road. They turned right into it, just as their unknown photographer must have done.

It was a different world then, the smooth openness of the main highway replaced by a narrow unsealed track flanked by banksias and melaleucas, with sudden clumps of eucalypts looming up in their headlights like ragged phantoms. They drove two k's without seeing much, just peering out at night burred and broken one minute by scrub, the next with indistinct sweeps out of gumtrees off in the gloom. Then they rounded a bend and there it was—more trees to their right standing back from the road, but with their trunks and lower branches picked out with lines of ghostly light, exactly as Franklin had said.

Brian was fascinated. There was no moon that he could tell, so there *had* to be a light source in there, a house, council facility, something, despite what the woman at the store had told them, despite the apparent absence of other access roads. Franklin had been right.

"Stop the car, Jeff!" Brian said.

Franklin had been expecting it. He brought the Lexus to a halt, switched off the headlights and the engine, no doubt what he'd done on his first time through.

Funny how it worked then. Too many Hollywood movies, too many television shows like *The X-Files*, too much day-for-night in countless old fifties westerns and Arabian Nights B-flicks.

Trees limned with lines of dim back-lighting, yet somehow it all looked perfectly normal. You had to remember to see it for what it was. Reality imitating art imitating nature. Simply wrong.

More than that. Impossible.

"Has to be something back there," Brian said as they sat listening to insect sounds and the engine cooling.

"What do we do?" Franklin asked.

Brian didn't answer right away. He smiled, but it was completely without humour. This could so easily become one of those bad Hollywood moments where curious people investigating odd phenomena ended up hunted by crazies, hanging from hooks.

"We go home. If you're up for it, we come back in daylight. Tomorrow's Saturday. I'm rostered on. But we could do it Sunday. Or wait till next week."

"Hey, Sunday's fine with me. But look, Brian—"

"Don't worry, Jeff. I'm doing this for me now, okay? A day search is my idea. So we get one of those empty drink cans from your trash bag there, jam it on a stick at the side of the road and mark our spot. Then we find somewhere to turn around, set our trip-meter back to the highway and go home."

"Good thinking, Brian. But you have to agree with what I said."

"About what exactly?"

"It's like Dwarrowdelf!"

"Oh, for pity's sake!"

They were through Pauley Bay and back at Junction Road by 1:40 on the following Sunday afternoon. Then it was nearly two and a half k's along the fire-road by the trip-meter till they reached the drink can glinting on its stick. They didn't stop this time, just kept going until they had passed their turnaround spot from two nights before and finally reached Wattle Beach.

The beach was deserted in the warm spring sunlight, just as the woman in the Pauley Bay General Store had said it would be. There were no surfers, no beachcombers, just lines of nearly identical blue-green breakers falling in tidy lines on the clean yellow sand. The only other movement came from seagulls picking over some clumps of kelp.

"Quite a spot!" Brian said. "You ever surf?"

"Do I look the type?" Franklin answered.

They chuckled at that, then set off on a quick walk along the beach. Forty minutes later, satisfied that there were no houses, no shacks tucked away in the scrub, certainly no council facilities or landfall groins for coaxial cables that they could see, they drove back along the fire-road to their marked spot. Franklin pulled off the road as much as he could. Then he locked the car and they headed into the bush to where they agreed the trees had been lit on the Friday evening.

It was tough going with the low scrub and the warmth of the early spring day, and they found nothing for their efforts, no obvious light source, no conceivable explanation for the effect they'd seen. No incriminating detritus either—the discarded drink cans, candy wrappers and old film packets that always seemed to turn up in the new rash of forensic television shows. Another instance of faked realities right there, Brian realised as he pushed through the scrub. Stylising behaviour. Forcing unrealistic time-frames and coincidences for the purposes of entertainment.

Brian had a thing about it. Back in the early '80s, he had called it the A-Team Syndrome after the old TV show with Hannibal Smith and Mr T. A generation of kids had been raised on that show, and Brian could only wonder at how many had proceeded to jump off rooftops and ridden their bikes off cliffs convinced that they only had to dust themselves off and go on fighting the bad guys. It had been reality without consequences. Cartoon reality.

Most forensic work was like this, doubling back and forth for an hour or so, going deeper and wider than they needed to, deliberately duplicating each other's routes just in case, and, yes, so often finding nothing, not a trace.

"Has to be done at night," Franklin said when they were back at the car. "So we can eyeball it."

Brian screwed the lid back on his water bottle. "Then we'll come back."

The little man looked hopeful again. "Can you do that?"

"Sure. My girlfriend's a travel agent. She's visiting relatives in San Francisco. You?"

"My wife will be glad when it's over and done with. She thinks I'm nuts."

"So what's it to be?" Brian said. "Another day, or do we stick around for four hours? Pity about the rips. We could always go back to that roadstop of yours and rent a surfboard. Teach you to surf."

"Nah. How about we just have some lunch and snooze under the trees for a bit?"

The four hours gave them plenty of time to verify their earlier findings. They tracked the shoreline well over a kilometre to the north and again found nothing. They also confirmed what the woman at the store had told them about no-one using Wattle anymore. It was a Sunday and, as far as they could tell, they were its only visitors. The reality of it struck Brian. Whole days must go by when no-one saw these waves or walked this clean white sand.

By 6:30, the last of the sunset had gone from the sky and it was sufficiently dark for them to try their tract of forest again.

Brian half-expected it to be a waste of time, but, sure enough, the ghostlight was there, easily a fifty, sixty-metre stretch of gums lit from a coherent source somewhere back in the bush. They pulled over near the middle of that stretch, locked the car, and stood watching the phenomenon.

Brian tested his flashlight, switched it off again. "Given how the light's breaking up, how thick the trees are in there, I'd say the source can't be more than forty metres back. Localised right there." He pointed ahead of them.

Franklin was testing his own torch, though as much as a nervous mannerism as anything. "So we just walk on in till we find it? Maybe we should've brought a compass."

"Jeff, it's right there. Shouldn't take long."

But that was the really odd thing. No sooner were they in under the trees, than the light began playing tricks. Again and again, Brian was sure they were close to where the source had to be, only to find that the light was off to the side, as if the source had moved. *Been* moved! Shifted to keep them from reaching it. Maybe they'd misjudged. Maybe Franklin had been right about bringing a compass, but no. Something was happening. There was *no* fixed source, not as Brian understood it.

"It's moving. Like a lure."

"It is."

Maybe it was how Franklin said it. Maybe Brian had seen too many processed movie and television realities, too many staged and stylised life situations. One moment he was studying the clump of trees they'd just left, then he just knew to look around, to look behind.

There was darkness there. Of course there was. But too much darkness, right there in a spot, a patch, a nugget of blackness in the black, as large as a tunnel mouth if it was at any kind of distance, as large as a black window if it was right there. It drew the eye and it was wrong. As wrong as ghostlight on the trees, or too much waterlight, or the columns of Dwarrowdelf.

Right there. He felt it pulling at him, drawing him out, pulling him in. Just relentlessly pulling.

"Jeff! What the hell—!" Pulling him away.

"The Old Dark," Franklin said, and Brian distinctly heard the capitals the little man put on the words. Heard them. Still could. "The light is how it hunts. Go with it, Brian."

"Hunts? But what—?"

"No surfers anymore. It just needed a bit of help. Being local and all, the wife and I thought, you know, we should bring people in. And a lighting expert! Not sure if there's a sense of irony at work, but, hey, it sweetens the deal."

"Deal?" It may have been a real word a not a cry, a genuine question formed by a coherent and lingering mind, but at that point through the window, down the tunnel, there was no way to know.

By the time Franklin was back at the car, the ghostlight had switched off, just like that, and the night was real again and dark and patient. And if you listened carefully, you could just make out the sound of waves falling along Wattle Beach.

Scaring the Train

"*Because for us, something might appear in the heart of the
day that would not be the day, something in an atmosphere
of light and limpidity that would represent the shiver of fear
out of which the day came?*"

—MAURICE BLANCHOT
The Infinite Conversation

1.
Portobello 1962

EVERY SUMMER DURING our childhood holidays at Portobello,
Maximillian and I would spend an hour every third day scaring the
train. Every third day meant twenty-one days before we'd duplicate
a day, which seemed clever at the time, neither of us realising that
it made its own pattern.

It never took more than a few exhilarating moments, of course,
the scaring itself, but the hour gave preparation time, let us prepare
our chosen section of track, the particular sheltered stretch or
cutting, never using the same one twice in a week unless that
became part of the strategy.

It gave us time to avoid the local constabulary (and, naturally,
the frightened drivers, firemen and concerned locals did get the
police onto us, though never with any luck). When Constables Pike
and Harlow came on their bicycles, or now and then with Sergeant

Jeffers in the district's single squad car, we were crouching down behind the long grass, peering through greenery, never seen, or were miles away with relatives and friends, secure in our alibis.

The scaring itself ? It was anything from running to a spot on the track moments before the locomotive reached it, to doing an oh-shock-horror!, freeze-frame, hands up, wide-eyed terror reaction or a classy matador flourish before leaping aside. Twice Max did his damsel-in-distress routine, lying across the line; we even did up a chicken wire and papier mâché boulder, though by then the engineers knew to call our bluff. With a scream of the steam whistle, the great engine plunged upon it, making us wish the boulder had been real.

We countered with the old dressed-up store dummy, its arm severed and painted with 'blood.' The engineers barely flinched. They had our measure right enough, had made their private decisions and adjustments. They would have driven through a massacre on that stretch of track after what we'd given them over four golden summers.

The whole thing entered a new phase when Sergeant Jeffers, rather belatedly, put two and two together and realised—at probably the same time we did—that since these "reckless and dangerous pranks" (as he had the *Portobello Weekly Mail* put it in one front-page write-up) happened only in the summer, it might well be the kids of families visiting from out of town.

Max and I weren't to be outdone. We made sure of our alibis, both with adults and the kids we hung out with, and took to using disguises more and more often—jumpers and caps, even wigs bought in home-town thrift shops and theatrical supply stores, taking pains to throw suspicion on local kids we didn't especially like.

Planning and timing became perfect; each scaring was a precisely calculated masterpiece and more exciting than ever. Of necessity, we had grown to be masters of those rare things in 13-year-old boys, restraint and patience. One evening, while I was conspicuously at a local party with my folks, Max put the first empty four-gallon drum on the left side of Hank's Creek cutting. It took him twenty-six minutes, there and back, riding without a light. Two nights later, I added the one on the right and linked them with multiple strands of heavy-gauge fishing-line souvenired from 15-year-old, ace-bully Rusty Cramer's fishing basket (an exploit in itself !).

Max and I didn't need to be there for the outcome but snatched thirty minutes from a Sunday family picnic to pedal furiously to Manton's Hill, there used our borrowed binoculars (birdwatching, right?) to observe the 10:58 from Madrigal plunging over the Hank's Creek bridge, the drums crashing down, bouncing off to the side—*kaboom! kaboom!*—clear as the bells of doom in the morning quiet (so we imagined; the train's own sound swallowed it all, perhaps even for the engineers, though they would have seen the drums plunging down; possibly did hear them pounding against the sides of the cab).

Max turned to me when it was over, eyes flashing. "We could've derailed that train if we'd wanted to, y'know, Paul." "Reckon. Or blown up the bridge. Stolen dynamite." "I'm serious."

He was, but on that hot quiet morning the talk went no further, for Max had his binoculars turned on the cutting.

"Hey, look!"

I raised Dad's glasses, swept my gaze in two big coins of dislocation suddenly made one across trees, fences and sunny fields till I found the place, saw the solitary figure standing by the tracks at this end of the cutting. Almost a mile away, no clear features, but someone in a thoughtful stance it seemed, not Jeffers or Pike or Harlow, no-one I knew, just some stranger drawn by Maximillian Sefti and Paul Danner's double booms of fate. He seemed to be looking down at the tracks, perhaps at the crumpled, dented drums and their trailing, incriminating lengths of line.

"Who is it?" I asked.

"No idea," Max said. But then, though it was a mile or more, though there were trees and fields and we were down on our bellies out of sight in the tree-shadow, our bikes back in the long grass so nothing glinted, nothing, the man looked directly out at us, directly at us. We couldn't see the smile or the nod though we imagined them well enough, but we both gasped when he raised an arm and waved, acknowledging us, someone, anyone who might be watching across all that bright sunny air.

We lowered our binoculars long enough, instinctively enough, to give each other a reassuring glance—we were both there, both seeing it—then looked back.

He was gone, of course, which completed the fright perfectly, had us scanning the intervening fields, noticing the pockets of shade like our own, patches of tree-shadow, the gloom in wind-dancing, sun-dappled copses, sockets of darkness where other watchers might be now watching us.

"Jeffers, I betcha!" Max cried as we scrambled down to our bikes, though we both knew it wasn't. "He's set us up."

But there was no-one else about and no interception as we pedalled back to the picnic grounds. All I could think of—and Max, too, I knew—was all that vast sunny space, the airy distances, the man waving, the sudden holes of black you just never noticed till you looked for them, then saw so suddenly, so nakedly.

Curiosity got the better of fear, of course. By the time we were cycling home at the end of the day, following the billowing dust of our parents' cars, we were no longer spooked. The mysterious stranger was no Bogeyman, just someone who had heard the racket and come down to investigate, who then seemed to be looking out at us, had seen a companion, an acquaintance, someone he knew, and simply waved in greeting. Nothing to do with Jeffers, nothing to do with vigilant local farmers setting a trap.

But enough of the fear remained, the mood of that morning hour, to power our curiosity. We were determined to stage another scaring on the Tuesday, breaking our third day ruling but needing to do something, needing to be sure.

By the time we reached Hayvenhurst Avenue we had our plan. The four rolls of three-inch grey masking tape from Bidder's barn were perfect and, as we weren't the only kids to take regular shortcuts across the Bidders property to get from Hayvenhurst to the creek, we judged the risk well worth it.

In thick woodland three miles out of town, close to the Manton cutting, we laid out seventeen by seventeen eight-foot strips of tape in a grid, carefully backed so we finally had a steel-gray portcullis, what looked like an iron grate to be fixed over the track on more of Rusty Cramer's fishing line.

We threaded line at the corners and sides, rolled up our grid, then did a few partial run-throughs, got the thing to the edge of the cutting and unrolled in less than four minutes. The hard part, scrambling down to get the end of the line hiked up and tethered to a tree on the other side, then weighting down the bottom lines with stones to get the tension needed, we figured would take another four to six, allowing for fumbles. We tossed a coin for the privilege and Max won.

We stored the grid in some bushes, rode back to town by a leisurely roundabout route, even stopped at the library to borrow a book on local bird-life, establishing our alibis there and justifying borrowing our folks' binoculars again.

On the Tuesday we were out at the Manton cutting twenty-four minutes ahead of the 12:10 freight. It was hot and very still in the cutting. Cicadas droned in the trees; only the slightest breeze stirred the dry grass stalks along the tracks. The rails gleamed like streaks of chrome in the noon heat.

In moments we had the grid unrolled, tethered and tossed down. Max scrambled after it, soon appeared on the other side, hauled the grid taut and fastened it, then weighted the trailing tethers with rocks. That done, he scrambled back and lay panting beside me, admiring our handiwork.

It was as if it had always been that way—a gated track, the lines like poured quicksilver coming and going, running off into the day, nothing else but insect song, dried grass stirring in the thermals off the rails, the barest flutter of breeze in the treetops.

"Let's go!" Max said, and we were up and on our way, cycling out to Byle's Lookout, using the long sweep of Salter's Hill to put us up the other side in a record six minutes. We were on our stomachs, panting, binoculars up and focused before our front wheels had finished turning.

We were a lot closer than at Hank's Creek and could make out the whole scene—the cutting exposed from this angle just before the tracks curved away towards Madrigal, everything as we'd left it, the scene deserted but for the grasses stirring and the improbable iron gate athwart the track. We could already hear the train approaching, a low sliding roar, building and building.

It was over in moments. The 12:10 was suddenly there, plunging at the grid like a demon. There was a scream of the steam whistle, oddly attenuated, it seemed, as if dampened by the cutting or the trees, then— *thwap!* (imagined not heard)—the grid was hit, carried away, and the eighteen bogies were clack-clacking their way off towards Madrigal.

But neither Max nor I jumped up to leave. Without having agreed on it, even mentioned it, we stayed where we lay, watching the tracks through our glasses.

And the man was there, just stepped into view from behind the embankment, seemed to be studying the rails where our gate had been.

Prickles of fear ran down my spine.

"Christ!" Max said. "Who is that guy?"

"Let's go, Max!" I spoke in a harsh whisper, not wanting to see him look out and wave, not again. I remembered all the dark places in the trees, saw them again right there.

"Wait, will ya!" Max said, feeling a need to wait, and I probably couldn't have left anyway. I needed it too somehow, this part of what we'd started.

And sure enough, the figure looked up, much closer than before, much closer, a man in his early 50s or thereabouts, in dark work shirt and drab workman's pants, wisps of grey hair stirring on his mostly bald head, deepset eyes peering out. And he smiled as if in understanding, possibly a grim smile, and nodded, yes, yes, I know, and not waving this time, just turned and stepped out of sight behind the embankment.

"Who is that guy?" Max asked again, but more to himself than to me.

Death, for my money, I wanted to shout. *Pavor diurnus*. Day terror. The Bogeyman.

"Has to be planted," Max continued. "They've been watching for us is what. Keeping an eye out. Listen, Paul." He turned on his side to face me. "That may not be the guy from the other day. They've got help. Guys from the railway maybe. Planted them at likely places. Maybe they're onto us, maybe not. So they wind us up by acting like they've seen us. He didn't see us just now, just knew we'd be watchin'. They're goosin' us, Paul. Rattlin' us."

It made sense. Blessed good sense.

"What do we do?" My voice was still broken by fear, embarrassingly querulous.

"We've got a week left. We can plan good stuff for next year. Real good stuff!"

"Lay low now, you reckon?"

"Not on your life. We get 'em a good one. One last scare."

"They could be watchin'. What do we do?"

"A night scare, Paul."

"They're not as good."

"No, so we do it where we never have before. Where they'd never expect."

"Like where?"

"In town."

"Town!"

"At night. Late at night. We rig up something at the end of the platform."

"But at night, Max. They just don't see enough."

"Yeah, so we rig something that uses that. We use the engine's head-lamp. Okay?"

"You got a plan?"

"Believe it, my man."

For the last scare of the last week of what was to be our final summer at Portobello, though we didn't know it then, we picked the Thursday, the 11:40 freight out of Madrigal, non-stop through Portobello at 12:16.

A monograph from the library—*Nightbirds* by George Lowry— furnished us with our alibi, while a coin toss gave me the privilege of the scare itself. Not something I actually wanted, but I wouldn't let Max know that for the world.

We sneaked out at 11:45, pedalled into town, hid our bikes and slid down to the station. It was deserted on this late-summer night, the air already cooling towards autumn, with crickets sounding and an occasional fragment of a night-bird's song to justify our visit if anyone found us.

The lights from Main Street and Hayvenhurst barely reached the platform; only the lights in the waiting room and the twin lamp-posts at either end showed where Portobello Station existed in the night.

We had minimal equipment just in case: a twenty-foot length of sturdy rope. Max's plan was simple. The rope would be tied round my waist and fixed to the lamp-post at the southern end. I would lean out at a bizarre 45 degrees from the platform's edge, giving the engineers enough time to see me before Max hauled me back.

It would be a dreadful sight for the engineers, a frantically waving figure leaning out—an impossible image to take with them as they plunged on through the darkness. So simple. So effective. Our bravura piece before we went our separate ways for another year, so we thought.

We rigged it up, did a few rehearsals so I could be sure of my footing and Max could get used to my weight. We agreed I would pull back myself if I wanted to—all we needed was for me to be glimpsed for a few seconds after all, and the approach was long enough. But leaving it to the last moment would make it the *pièce de résistance* of scarings.

At 12:05 we checked the knots, and Max took his place behind the post. I leaned out over the track, satisfied myself that there was ample visibility, and waited the few minutes, counting bits of the darkness like the worry beads Max's Mum used at mass, noticing it all: the dim lines made by fences, trees, cast-iron fittings, the soft lights of Main Street reaching out, striking into my eyes—look here! look here!—the red and green signal lights, the double tracks themselves, made into sliding sweeps of silver by a moon we couldn't see. There were just the crickets, the warble of a bird sounding far off, a few barks from a dog even further away.

"Get ready," Max said, needlessly.

I hung there, leaning out, sharp with anticipation and too much darkness, noticing it all, listening, straining for the slow sliding roar that would grow, edge up, come as both a wave of sound and a shiver underfoot, watched for the single eye, the shouts of steam. I strained for that unmistakable train rhythm—

locomotive! locomotive! locomotive!

There it was! Yes!

And there were words on that rush of sound as well.

"What do you two think you're doing?"

We froze in disbelief, Max gripping the rope, me leaning out.

And there was Rusty Cramer, fifteen, burly (fat), vindictive (blamed, implicated by the fishing line), and angry (dangerous).

"I said what do you two think you're doing?" He came towards us like a big block of night, something dislodged from the ordinary world and sent careening, spinning out wildly into all this calm.

"Wait and see!" Max cried, not wanting to lose our chance, not now.

"Yeah, well I knew I'd catch up with you arseholes sooner or later."

He was close and threatening, still improbable, but Max tried to keep him talking. "It's a joke we're pulling, see. Watch what happens now."

"You're both for it, you dumb shits! I'm gonna bust ya!"

"Watch the train first, okay. Here! Wow, look at that!"

"What?" Rusty Cramer said, and turned, saw the freight thundering on its run through the town, looked back, tried to figure exactly what it was we meant to do, turned again just as the light hit me and the whistle screamed in warning, terrifying me and keeping Rusty distracted. "What the hell!"

I remembered to wave my arms frantically, judged my own jump-back only to have Max haul me back first.

Actually I fell back, and the train was there, past, gone, leaving the steady thunder of bogies howling after it. And Max ran at Rusty, pushed him hard, sent him slamming into the iron sides of a bogey, where he sprang away again, slammed into the lamp-post, thud after sickening thud.

I was on my feet in seconds, staring, horrified, dangerously close to the track myself, saw Rusty Cramer pinball from bogey to post to the gravel, saw him flat, torn and dead. Saw Max wide-eyed, determined to have his alibi, his scapegoat, never for a moment saw the guard's van rushing up, dim and forgotten, or the bar or strap or trailing line, whatever it was that struck my skull and sent me flying, falling, and thinking as I fell: "I'm dead too!"

I didn't die. I spent three months in hospital with a fractured skull and got used to having a metal plate over the weak spot as a constant reminder of how lucky I was. Mum didn't say much about what happened, mostly: "There, there, Pauly, you just rest." But Dad gave me most of it.

"That damn fool Cramer kid!" he said on my second day out of a seventy-day coma. "What do you remember, son?"

I played dumb, frowned a lot, asked him to tell me more.

"Rusty Cramer's dead, you know, Paul?"

"What about Max?"

"Max. He phoned it in. Said you were after night birds, stumbled on the Cramer kid doing one of those pranks on the station."

"Right. That sounds right. Don't remember too much though."

"Course you don't. You startled him and he got hit, then something brained you good. You're very lucky, Paul."

"Seem to remember that. Where's Max?"

"Where do you think, son? School's been back nearly ten weeks. He said he'd write or call, keep in touch."

"Right. So Rusty Cramer did all those things."

"That's what the cops said. Blaming it on outatowners. Thug of a kid. I guess it's just as well he blew it."

"Why's that, Dad?"

"You remember he had a rope fixed to a post and was leaning out—how Max said you found him? Well, he scared the train drivers good this time. One had a heart attack from it, they reckon; died right there at the throttle. The other guy says Rusty must've scared him to death hanging out waving like that. You probably stopped other deaths happening, son. I'd try and look at it that way."

"I will, Dad. I will. I guess it's the only way."

Max and I did get to speak about it after a fashion, but on the phone, long-distance, three weeks later. I didn't ask him the most important question: *how* he could have done it, *how*, actually avoided it, convincing myself that it had been spur of the moment (though it hadn't been, of course, definitely hadn't been!), just something implicit in all our earlier games of death and mayhem, one more unreality, cartoon-like almost, not to be dwelt upon too much. And while we made our peace, alluded to his quick-thinking, run-to-the-phone-for-an-ambulance call, spoke of Rusty's death (murder!) guardedly, and that of the engineer (manslaughter), even mentioned the newspaper clipping from the *Mail* Dad had kept, about how the autopsies on Rusty Cramer and the driver were botched, we had to postpone the full weight of our discussion and debriefing, the reality of it, till our next meeting—other important things like the mysterious man at the cuttings, the botched autopsies, all the stuff that mattered all of a sudden.

"I'll write to you," Max said, far off across the country. "And we can talk about it in the summer."

Which didn't happen, of course. After the accident, Max's parents didn't choose Portobello that year, and with my sister dating, we didn't get there either. Two years after that, Dad's job took us down to Australia; I finished high school in Sydney, and in 1967 went on to do an Arts degree at Sydney University, and Max Sefti and my scaring the train became one more unresolved part of that ineffably dear, long, slow, blink-and-it's-gone, quickly stolen thing called childhood.

Imagine what it was like then towards the end of first term, sitting with nine other first-year students in our English tutorial, when the door opened and in came a student forced by part-time employment commitments to change tutorial groups, who turned out to be none other than Max Sefti—*here* in Australia, in Sydney, at *this* university, walking into *this* room.

It shattered the smooth consensual reality in a moment, was wonderful and utterly bizarre, even vaguely alarming. We had shared lectures in Wallace and Carslaw but hadn't spotted one another. There were no words to capture it, absolutely none. The tutor's remarks, the *Innocence and Experience* poetry of William Blake, stood no chance except as vivid counterpoint, but afterwards, over coffee in the Refectory, I found out about those missing parts of my life.

It wasn't an optimum spiel because Janice and Becky, two girls from our tutorial group, tagged along with a friend of theirs, an intense-looking, dark-haired young guy named Lucian. Consequently what might have been an incredible yet surprisingly natural bridging of days became the kind of narrative back-tracking I'm giving here. It was certainly interesting in itself since I was able to hear Max tell his version of it at last, filled with his forthright young adult confidence and my own self-conscious, artless lapses into cliché, an understandable refrain of: "My God, but you're here!"

The facts came out all the same, though as part of some incredible freak accident, certainly not as premeditated (however briefly) murder: Rusty lying dead, the unseen guard's van, my being struck hard enough to fracture my skull, send me into coma and require a long convalescence. That helped win back Janice and Becky's attention; they asked about the plate in my skull, exactly where it was, could they touch it, things like that. Dark-haired Lucian frowned and seemed clearly fascinated.

I heard how Max had given the police—the very ones we'd caused such trouble—an account of finding Rusty on the station, startling him in mid-scare, causing him to stumble and fall so he was hit and flung back into the lamp-post. He told how an unfastened strap or buckle flailing about had struck me on the side of the head, and how ready the authorities were to believe, actually believe, because Rusty had been such a swine of a kid all his young life and we did have our bird-watching book and all.

I learned, too, how Max had had the presence of mind to re-tie the rope from my waist around Rusty's, had got that done minutes before the police and the ambulance arrived so everyone believed, so no-one even for a moment thought to suggest we might have been in collusion with him, a local kid working with two outatowners.

That was the version he gave anyway: Rusty catching us at it, tripping during a scuffle, being hit; our arranging things so he was implicated, but all an accident. Just a terrible accident.

Max added a detail then that sent a chill through me in that sunny corner of the Refectory.

"Paul, something happened while I was re-tying the rope round Rusty's waist—"

"You saw the guy!" I blurted it out. The bits of fear had all connected up. The far-off reality was real again, finally, not pushed aside, not hidden away.

"No. No, I didn't." His tone gave me the 'but' before he said it. "But I looked for him, you know? I'd knelt on something sharp and just looked up. Expected to see the guy—like in that Charles Dickens story."

"But nothing?"

"Nothing. Just a feeling, you know. It was a really bad moment. I was fumbling with the rope, trying to get it under Rusty's body and tied before the cops arrived. I was breathless from running from the phone, my knee was hurting from whatever I'd knelt on, you were lying there covered in blood. I had Rusty's blood all over me. It was pretty awful."

I made myself ask it. "So what about the autopsy reports, Max? They were messed up you said."

"I did? Oh yes. Right. On the phone that night. The *Mail* had a bit on it. The train driver died of a heart attack, but the autopsy for cause of death said the blood had changed."

"Changed? What do you mean, changed?"

"Just that. Changed. Altered somehow. It didn't say. But the Cramer kid had the same thing. His blood had gone funny."

"But what does that mean?"

People at other tables were giving us looks.

"Paul, it didn't say. Just that the lab people had stuffed up."

I calmed myself. "But you sensed the guy?"

"Something. I went back to the station the next day. You were over in Madrigal, still on the critical list, still in a coma. They had already operated to relieve pressure on your brain, to get out the bone fragments too smashed up to leave there, they told us."

It was frustrating. He was talking for the others.

"See anything?"

"Just where it all happened. The post was actually bent where Rusty hit it. They hadn't sanded over the blood stains properly yet. I saw the nail I'd knelt on before getting the feeling. It was just—eerie, you know?"

"But no sign of the guy?"

"Uh-uh. But it was like he was there, you know? I kept looking up expecting to see him."

Lucian spoke then, the first words I'd heard him say that morning but for monosyllables.

"It's convergent energy. How you think of a thing makes a thing. How you name a thing defines a thing."

Thanks, Lucian, if that's your real name. I'd only known him by sight before today but that was his kind of patter, all Plato and Socrates, Sufis and Sophistry, Castanada and *Sergeant Pepper's*.

Max looked from him to me and back. "Say again."

"You probably haunted yourself," Lucian said. "We all do it. Set up expectations. Rope the unconscious into it—all that energy."

"Uh-uh," Max said. "I meant the other bit."

"Power of names. Naming gives shape. Summons. Bestows power. All part of primitive people's singing up the land, re-naming things, re-making things. The Navajo—"

"Yeah, right." Max had heard enough.

But Lucian continued, and just as well. "It's like these scarings. At what point did they become rituals?"

"Rituals?" I showed *my* annoyance now.

But Max was intrigued. "*Did* become?"

"All right. Do become, though I suspect they already have. And, yeah, rituals because we always do more than we know. Simple acts become metaphor, symbolic, representational as well as just themselves. We're left to find what they really mean."

Who's your friend? Max said in a look, but was interested in spite of himself.

Lucian probably read that look. "You have to admit it, Max. You were both pretty fixated. The blood and death and all. That man you saw. Lots of fertile stuff there. Of course there are going to be ramifications. All that emotion and psychic force; both of you looking for answers."

"Maybe." Max was yielding, plainly needed something of the reassurance that dark, assured Lucian seemed to be providing. "What do you suggest?"

"Suggest?" Lucian managed to look both surprised and confident all at once. "Why, re-stage the event—with us along as unbiased controls." He already had that good scientific word. "See what you get."

"A scaring? Here?"

Becky liked the idea. "Why not? It'd be fun."

"We've got trains," Janice said. "Lots of stations."

Now I was the one with the doubts. "Too crowded. Doesn't feel right."

"Okay," Lucian said. "I should be able to borrow a holiday house at Glenbrook. That's in the Blue Mountains if you don't know, about two hours away. Term vacation's, what, in two weeks? We could go up for a few days. Lots of little stations. Springwood. Blackheath. Medlow Bath. Hazelbrook. Wentworth Falls. Just pick one."

Max turned to me. "Paul? What do you think?"

"Yes," I said, connecting up the years, feeling relieved, reprieved somehow, giving all that had occurred its due place in my life, its correct perspective and proportion, getting another chance at—just something important. "Yes, I want to."

My certainty surprised me.

"What do you say?" Lucian asked Max diplomatically.

Max, so suddenly here, so dramatically in my life again just by being here, frowned, murmured: "Hmm", then said: "Yeah. Okay. Why not?"

I believe he thought he was doing it for me: allowing a psychotherapy, completing an equation, but deep down I knew he needed something out of this too: perhaps as elusive as redemption, expiation for harm done, control lost, perhaps as simple as nostalgia for what had been.

Our only days.

Late Monday afternoon was it. The five of us set out from the small wooden house in Glenbrook and drove through the Blue Mountains towns in Lucian's Holden. We had a rather tense and silent afternoon tea at the Paragon in Katoomba, then continued out to Mount Victoria, only to retrace our route, stopping and looking, stopping and looking, till we finally found a suitable station sufficiently hidden away from the road.

All things considered, we should have known better than to go ahead with it that particular evening; everything about the last hour of the day felt wrong. Rain was due and there was that low mean sideways light coming at us below an overcast, and a cool breeze hugging the land, moving the trees and grasses but leaving low clouds locked in place, wrinkled and bellying down.

Strange weather, the light sliding in from the edge of the world like that, giving us a disturbing overlit quality so we glowed like tricked-up idealisations of ourselves, figures in some garish Symbolist painting.

Even as we went down the steps into the shadow of the platform, something of that quality remained—a silvering, gilding, flaring in the sunset edges of the trees and waving grasses, each leaf and blade picked out, detailed, each whorl and valance of the locked and threatening sky.

"This is weird," Janice said, perfect bathos, typical Janice, and the rest of us laughed; it was so beyond words.

"Elemental, dear Janice," said Lucian, which she didn't get, but it was probably the right word: we were elemental on that lowering, fading, fateful evening, in one of those moments of incidental framing reality where every commonplace surprises you.

I know, I'm overdoing this, but that's how it was for me, and the others too, I felt. Some days, some evenings, night just happens as a background to other things, but here it was, being made, perceptibly forming out of cracks and corners, the blackness of the short tunnel pushing out, flowing up, as if prying itself loose, all of it heightened by the dramatic closing light we had just now left behind, shed from ourselves in return for discrete shadows, the self-same drab as the clouds overhead.

There were people, just a few, waiting for the next commuter train up from Sydney to take them on to nearby Mountains stops and beyond, or the express to take them down to the Emu Plains and out to the coast.

We stayed just long enough to work out the details, which side to use (lefthand facing west—the train would plunge straight into the quick darkness of the tunnel—blink, blink—did we imagine that?), how to make an easy getaway through the shallow tunnel itself. We stayed until the 5:50 from Sydney had dropped off its passengers and moved on, waited till they had vanished into the night and the lone ticket collector had gone back in out of the wind, then made our way to the car, headed back to Katoomba.

"I'm not sure about this," Max said as we were driving along.

Lucian must have expected it; he was clearly our motivating force now and still the perfect diplomat. "I know what you mean, Max. It's been a weird afternoon. What about you, Paul?"

Again I surprised myself. "Might as well go ahead with it now." Something about the quality of the light back at the station had fascinated me, given me a sense of imminence, something. But I didn't speak it, and must have even sounded a bit indifferent.

Lucian pulled over, turned to face us in the back seat. "Listen, you two," he said, but carefully, caringly. "Five years ago you got close to something really important for you. It affected you in all sorts of ways, I can tell. We don't have to do this. We can call it off. But it needs a bit of enthusiasm, okay? If we go ahead."

Janice grinned at him. "I'm enthusiastic."

"Right," Max said, to Janice or Lucian, you couldn't tell. "It was just so"—dramatic? frightening? vivid? I wondered what he'd say—"incomplete."

"So we're doing this now. Completing it." Lucian spoke as if he understood it completely, and maybe he did. "Next question. If we do it, your call, who leans out?"

I spoke first. "Me!"

"I will!" Max said.

"Toss for it!"

"My turn!"

Lucian, captain of the car, the whole night, decided. "Maybe it should be Paul, Max. He needs to do this. Okay?"

Max nodded. "You up to it, Paul?"

"I'm fine."

So we drove on, took in a movie in Katoomba, got back to our chosen spot at 11:02, in plenty of time for the 11:40 freight. Since we figured the train would probably sound its whistle when the scaring took place, we left the car half a mile from the station and walked there, not wanting disturbed locals to see us driving away afterwards. Our plan was to walk along the tracks and cut up to the highway.

The night had closed in, chill and windy, and though the overcast stole the starlight, the rain had held off. As we moved down to the platform, the wind soughed in the power lines, whistled round the stanchions, gusted in the trees. Grass bent low on the embankments. The dark hole of the tunnel seemed thicker, deeper, seemed to pull at us, pull then push in distinct night rhythms. I wasn't the only one to imagine it; the others made comments too, seemed to find it eerie, but then we were all oversensitive to such things.

The platform itself was deserted as we expected, with just a few lights showing in either direction, the four double lamp-posts, the two sets of signal lights showing their comforting red and green. The waiting room was lit too and cosily warm. A fire had been left in the generous hearth, with wood to one side. The honour system prevailed and, despite our mission, we fed it for anyone who might arrive during the long night that would follow.

It took moments to fasten the rope first to the westernmost lamp-post just before the tunnel, then to my waist, less than a minute or two to let me reprise my long-ago act of leaning out over the left-hand line, feet on the lip, Lucian and Max hauling me back a few times on Max's call. All straightforward, an anticlimax if anything after the build-up of our boyhood scarings, something almost pointless and foolish, stripped of context.

But Lucian was clearly excited and Max was becoming so. We were all on edge; any lingering sense of anticlimax was kept at bay by the night itself, so vivid and powerful, the constant, unsettling keening of the wind, the shuddering grasses above the cutting, the tossing trees, so many inexplicable sudden sounds. The darkness of the tunnel seemed even deeper—pushed, pulled, waiting.

This wasn't Portobello in the warm summer night of 1962. This was a small Australian mountain station racked by a chill, late-autumn sou'easter. This was a consummation somehow, a fitting resolve. Some kind of redemption.

Max knew it; dark-eyed Lucian did. Becky no doubt. Janice said she was cold and became in a moment persona non grata forevermore in all our minds.

The time drew near. The girls hid; I leaned out; Lucian and Max took their places, gripped the lifeline double-handed.

No-one came. No hint of the stranger. No Rusty Cramer this time (though, paradox, I did wish it could be so, generous in my need). The wind blew and blew; the rails shone by any light they could steal—found firelight, lamplight, stole light from our eyes to keep the silver there in that heaving autumn dark.

Train came impressed on that fragile darkness, a roar below, behind, above the wind, suddenly there in smouldering running lights, in the headlight beating out, a great diesel bearing down.

I stretched out my arms, waved, waved frantically, pinned in the hideous, devouring glare. The whistle screamed, screamed where it had never screamed before, at an hour when it never should.

I waved in the terror-rushing-darkness. How many heart attacks this time? How many? All fall down! Everyone!

Was hauled back, ricocheted as the raw and angry train ran by and was swallowed by the frame of the tunnel, swallowed whole, gulped in carriage by rachetting, sliding, angrily snapping bogey, vertebra by vertebra as its dark spine was sucked in, gone.

Max and Lucian had both caught me. There was a moment of exhilaration, of sheer delight at what we'd done, all our earlier fear turned into that. Becky was smiling, Janice too, though she still looked scared. Would we be caught? Would we?

But we didn't wait for some curious local to call in a complaint, or a lone patrol car wandering through these towns to investigate why a through freight would shatter sleep around midnight this way.

Max untied the rope and coiled it ready for throwing aside later, then we helped one another down onto the tracks and began our retreat, following the double lines to the shallow tunnel.

Max couldn't restrain his delight. "It worked, Paul! It worked!"

"Smooth as clockwork," Lucian said, sounding pleased too, then added: "We need to listen though. For vibrations in the rails."

"Could a train come?" Janice asked, first time of four or five.

Perversely I said, "Sure could." Scaring the Janice. Hating her insensitivity to this, her finding only the bogeyman when it was so much more.

The tunnel was only twenty or so paces long, and a train-wind pushed at us all the way, though it was just the sou'easter finding a way through. But when we came out the other side we noticed the changes at once. The trees still blew above us on the embankments, the grasses still leaned in waves; the wind was sounding, hitting at us, but it was as if stillness had been imposed on all that—those things drawn off, suspended somehow, changed.

And more. It was as if one of those heavily shadowed, cliff-locked, deep-tunnelled coastal stations south of Sydney—Otford, Stanwell Tops, Helensburg, I wasn't sure of the names—had been superimposed on this one. The tunnel had been too deep; now the sides of the cutting seemed way too high. Details were wrong, out of place.

Perhaps it was adrenaline rush, nerves firing with the excitement, all that noise and light replaced by the compressed dark of the tunnel and the windy silence, but we all noticed it, showed it by the looks we gave, though nothing was said, not even when we saw that there was fog in the cutting ahead.

Fog on a windy overcast night! It snatched the streetlight too, gave some to the tracks so they ran as quicksilver glint, drawn off and lost in the silvery pall.

But *fog.*

The next surprise: the line branched ahead. Branched! We were not even fifty metres from the tunnel and the left-hand westbound track we were following had a line running silver and fogbound into a cutting, steep-sided and not on any of the maps Lucian said he had studied.

This wasn't the stranger of summers gone, not Rusty Cramer bouncing pinball ricochet off the midnight freight to Madrigal. This was the world gone wrong.

"We go back now," Lucian said, and echoed that key word. "This is wrong."

"Something's there!" Janice cried.

locomotive!

We all heard it. A shuffle, snuffle, muttered, stolen back.

"Run!" Max said, and we did, not up, it was too steep, not ahead to cross that branch-line, but back.

locomotive! locomotive!

Unmistakable. Something waited in the old, new, different cutting. Something.

We ran on and on, entered the tunnel again, found it long, long, far longer, deeper than it had been moments ago, ran on, panting, breathing hard, Janice giving off a wail that never quite made it to a scream.

locomotive! locomotive! locomotive!

Pursued by the night, we fled, felt the train-wind at our backs, were pinned in headlight, light made from darkness, rail silver, stolen streetlamps, window-shine and eye glitter, dazzling, numbing, chilling light.

"Against the wall!" someone cried, Max, Lucian, I couldn't tell. "On the other side! On the other side!" And I ran with the others, trusting that someone had indeed calculated which track would carry the—*locomotive! locomotive!*—presently at the tunnel's mouth. *Train.* As if that covered it.

We rushed, clattered and stumbled to the tunnel wall, that wrong, south-coast tunnel wall, flattened ourselves against the slick, damp bricks, cold, so cold, too cold, tried to push into the hard wet surface, air coursing over us, smelling of train friction, metal on metal, ozone, dried blood, night-bitter, blood-bitter, *locomotive! locomotive!*

It ran past, whatever it was, going the wrong way on the wrong line at the wrong hour, in a tunnel that was wrong, wrong, with all of night and hell and angry disregard in its rush.

And we pulled back, peeled away, only when there was no sound (and no fog and no cutting, I was certain), no train wind or hint of its returning, no sign at all of that ultimate Night Train.

Janice was dead when we found her. All that carefully packed life bludgeoned—no—drawn out thin and gone, cut free, snatched away. No wound that we could tell in the meagre light, just wiped of life and light and fear, all in a moment, there in that space—a mere twenty or so paces deep. Normal again, hah! Never normal. Never again.

And when the police finally came and took us back to Katoomba and asked their hours of questions, it was left as heart attack and stupid uni students walking the tracks (apparently the engineers had not bothered to report the scaring). Sure, Lucian phoned around and word got back to us later that there was a glitch in the autopsy forensics; all the iron had been leached from her blood.

So that couldn't be the end of it for us.

We went back, three of us did, some months after the court hearing. Becky and Lucian were living together by this stage, but she decided not to go along. So Lucian, Max and I drove up one Saturday night, arriving late with our torches and memorial bunch of flowers (our excuse if anyone found us at it), and after entering the tunnel from the western end to make sure there was no extra line, no branch cutting beyond, we finally agreed on the spot where Janice had died.

There were no blood stains, of course, nothing on the hard round stones before that slick wall but moss, old cigarette packets, a candy bar wrapping, leaves and dried grass stalks, two bottle tops and a rusty nail.

Not quite knowing why I did so, I took the nail, put it in my pocket; it was something that was real, after all, part of it, part of the place and the time and the death. Of poor, brief, stupid Janice.

We left the flowers and drove away.

4.
Town Hall Station 1972–1994

There were four opening lines for this account I'm doing here, one for each version I've tried putting down, depending on which starting point I chose. One line you already have: "Every summer during our childhood holidays at Portobello, Maximillian and I would spend an hour every third day scaring the train." But I could just as easily have started *in media res*, as in an earlier attempt, with: "The train winds are the best in Sceptre City"—a good line: short, gripping, promising mysterious things—then worked back through it as Dr Day suggested I do.

Stealing a bit, really, because Sydney didn't get its third real skyline landmark—Bridge, Opera House, finally the Sydney Tower: God's Microphone, the Sceptre—until 1981, but as you discover as you get older in the eternal Now, you reach a point when it never seems otherwise, and you have to concentrate to remember how it really was then.

The line is as true for 1967 as today—tonight—and writing this down again, I do remember that name as part of that time.

Glancing back over what I've written, it seems that Lucian promised to be some sinister reincarnation of that stranger Max and I saw years ago. Sinister he was with his dark good looks and strange notions, but while Max and I remained in one another's lives after we graduated in 1970, we lost touch with Lucian and Becky who, last we heard, got married and mortgaged and snatched aside from the flow of life (or into it, depending on your view of such things).

Max got married too, to a young high-school teacher named Pauline. Me, why I'm Mr Popular, with relationships pretty well constantly, but have stayed single, communicating something unresolved in myself (I was told by one girlfriend who went away, vanished from my life, never answered the phone again), something tense and gripped too tightly. And I screamed during nightmares I never remembered. So, sure, I had ladies, partners, companions, in one-night, six-week, two-month lots, but never futures.

But Max stayed in touch and stayed interested (there was too much unresolved between us as well) and he was the one who phoned in May 1972 and asked me to meet him at Giovanni's Pizzeria at Town Hall Station to discuss train winds.

What he said. Train winds.

We'd tried Sydney's train winds before, back in '68 and '69, standing on Town Hall, Wynyard, St James and Museum, feeling the plunging piston push of air before trains arrived, the unmistakable slipstream, warm, redolent of oil, ozone, raw metal and dark places. It could delight you, thrill you or scare you silly, and we kept at it because we almost understood something every time, recognised or remembered something, though never quite what.

So began a decades-long series of infrequent, almost ritualistic meetings that usually started with a meal and ended with us going down onto the platforms and just experiencing the elusive telling-us-something quality of the train winds.

All routine until a week ago.

This time his voice on the phone had been troubled, urgent. Would I meet him? Yes. The usual place (now Alexander's Café). Sure.

I found him drinking coffee right there before the breathing stairwells of the Town Hall underground. He didn't say much, not then, but we bought City Circle tickets and went to the final level where there was the weight of the city and the lives, and the familiar twin tracks laid taut, silver and humming between their double gulps of darkness. Tunnels are like seashells; you hear impossible seas when you listen close.

We stood, toes to edge, peering off into one of those snatching gaps and then, then, we could talk, eyes on the dark in darkness, then we could.

"You know what Janice said that night, Paul?"

Janice? Janice? Years, moments, lives rammed together in an instant.

That Janice.

"What? When?"

"Before she died. Before we went up to Glenbrook that weekend."

"No. I didn't. No, I don't, Max. What did she say?"

Toes to the edge, we peered off into gloom, minds attuned to the faintest breath, listening, listening for the tiniest ghost-rush and whisper.

"She'd had dreams, she said. The same dream. Ever since we decided to do the scaring. She dreamt she'd die there."

I resisted the hard knot of guilt, fought shame and denial, emotion locking my gut. Bloody Janice! Bloody, changed-blood Janice!

"So?" Calm. Hard. Keeping it hard.

"Something sharp would take her. Something sharp."

Thanks a lot, Max. Bringing me this. "A train?"

There, I had named it, said it, peering into gloom. The Night Train.

locomotive!

And listened, watched the veins in the earth, those warm taut lines, worm lines, snail-slide of silver, watched the blocked black, ocean-shell darkness. For train. *Train.*

"Something sharp. I asked that too—a train?—before we set out that day."

"And? Come on, Max! And?"

"She asked if trains were sharp."

Ohmigod! Poor dizzy Janice. So brave, so driven. So changed.

"You never told me."

"Told no-one, mate. You didn't want to hear. You wouldn't have then, would you? Another death?"

"No." Small word. No. Remembering Janice. Years. Summers.

"I kept it from everyone."

"Lucian?"

"No way. He'd have gone off on one of his theories. We put it aside. Just like with Rusty Cramer."

"So why tell me now?" Though I knew what he'd say.

"I've had the dreams too, mate. Four of them. Something sharp. About trains."

We felt the faintest kiss of air, a hint, a flutter. It was. Oceans falling on midnight shores.

"So we don't do this anymore. We put it aside again, Max. It's just memory serving up old stuff. We've carried it with us too long."

We step back right now, Max, I wanted to say. We step back. No more scaring either way.

Feathers of air stroked our faces.

"I just had to tell you. Had to let you know."

"Down here?" What I didn't say was: Did the dreams scare Pauline away?

"Needed that too. Just did, you know? It's been too long."

The rush, the unmistakable smell of the pushing air, the smell. Metal on metal. Ozone. Electric fire in the underworld. Sharp fire deep down.

"It has." Step back now, Max. I took his arm; he let me draw him back with me, one step, two, another. "We should include Lucian. Let him know too. Talk it out."

"Already have."

"What? When?"

"He suggested this. Said I needed this."

The train was there, shattering, battering, squealing down to just a silver, ribbed 10:08 to Hornsby, modern and safe, harmless again.

We waited as people came and went, waited till the doors slid shut and it had pulled off into the undernight. I imagined it drawing the air from our lungs after it, pulling it into sighs, drawing it thin. Earth, fire, water and air.

Max did sigh. "I'm scared, Paul. Really scared, you know."

"So we keep away from places like this."

"Does no good. I see lines."

"You what?"

"I see lines everywhere. Just look down a street or an alley. There they are, clear and bright as anything."

Like the dark holes under trees. Black spaces in sunshine.

"You mean it?"

"Look again and they're gone. But it's not corner of the eye stuff, Paul. They're right there. I hear a noise at night, look out the window and see them going down the street. See them in the drive, going across backyards, running right through fences. I go out to the fridge. There are lines in the living room, Paul, just right there, you know."

I still had his arm, was gripping it hard. I made him listen to me, told him about my own visits to Dr Day, got him to quiz me on why I'd do such a thing. No, I wasn't having dreams or seeing lines. But I had anxieties, I said, problems relating, connecting. I had to write it out, I told him, which did seem to help. I said he hadn't done that, was all, hadn't sorted the coincidence of the deaths, hadn't worked through it. Been debriefed. Talked down. That's all.

We agreed: no more scarings. We'd meet with Lucian, patch up the ragged bits, talk it through, the three of us. Stay in touch this time. He was easier as we left the station; I was easier, having focused my own fear and edges through Max's own. He gave me Lucian's address, then we phoned, arranged to meet on the Friday night. Then I put Max in a cab and never saw him again.

5.

7:13 pm

Last night I found Lucian's nail.

Third opening of the four. This is the one I had before I decided to do it via internet, get it out as far and as fast as I could. It can't be everywhere at once. It can't look everywhere. There have to be gaps, ways through, yes, openings.

But time for this line anyway, bringing it nearly to the moment. One to go.

Last night I found Lucian's nail. Two inches long, flat round head, round body, the sort of short, dark, rusty nail you find by the dozens, hundreds, in the re-cycle bins of older hardware stores and in old paling fences.

But his. His.

Found it on the very night of the very day Lucian's package arrived with its ninety-minute TDK audio tape and the little cardboard box and the note—the package brought in by Tilly and used to weigh down her own goodbye note on the afternoon she too had had enough of remoteness, screams in the night, failure to commit, whatever she decoded it as.

Her note didn't surprise me. She'd tried; I'd tried, believed I had, believed I believed I had. I tried to wish her well.

But Lucian's note chilled me where I stood in the hall, the words scrawled in pencil, more disturbing somehow than if they had been in blood or purple ink.

Max's nail. Hide it. Tell no-one.
Look for mine. Hide them. Stop it here.

I resented the drama, the emotional grab on top of losing Tilly (with all the cumulative guilt of losing Louise and Jill, it just went on and on, back, back), but I was deeply and singly terrified too.

Max's nail. I opened the tiny box and saw it—just like Janice's, like Lucian's too I bet!—and knew Max was dead. Knew somehow, somewhere, he would be found with his blood changed, the iron gone to make this.

Nail.

I started to understand it then, you see. Standing in the hall, holding the small white box, with Tilly gone and the tape to play and the stupid note.

But not Lucian. Not Lucian dead too!

Two thoughts. Three. You've left me alone with this. Betrayed me. And: the Train was getting nearer.

Then the phone rang.

Standing there in front of it, compressed with loss, terror and disbelief, with too much unravelling of the ordinary world, I cried out and swore and would've shouted down the line except I thought: Tilly. Please, God, yes.

"Paul? It's Becky. Sorry to bother you but have you seen Lucian?"

"No. No, I haven't, Beck. What's happened?"

It went from there. Could I come over? Of course I would, left the tape waiting, unplayed, went to her place, heard how Lucian had gone with no word, no explanation. She'd waited the drunk-binge, affair-guilt, drug-down twenty-four hours (apparently he'd been hitting it hard in every sense of the word, goosed by ideas that wouldn't go away), made the appropriate calls to friends (well, closer friends), hospitals, the police, answered their questions: no, no sign of foul play, had finally, finally, two days on, phoned me on the off-chance.

Off-chance! *On*, more like it: the very day his package arrived.

The last time she'd seen him was as she'd left for work, sitting at the kitchen table, the morning after being out with Max till all hours. With Max.

I asked about that, heard they'd been seeing a lot of one another (without including me? So much for our meeting up again), allowed that the tape would tell me all about that.

I looked in the kitchen as surreptitiously as possible, looked there again while brewing Becky and me coffee, found it just sitting there on the bench top as if pushed to one side, that exact size and shape, would never have noticed it without looking for it.

His. It was.

"What's this?" I actually asked her when she came in to help.

She shrugged. "Don't know. Found it on the floor."

No real curiosity about such an ordinary thing. It's true when they say there is nothing more sinister than what we never suspect: teapots, cracks in sidewalks, the flutter of a curtain, the bang of a screen door, lawn sprinklers.

Where's the body then? I wondered. Thinking of Janice, the nail in the tunnel where she had died, the sharp thing Max had knelt on tying the rope around dead, changed Rusty. (I *was* putting it all together, you see.)

We ended up sitting at the kitchen table and I pocketed the nail when I went to pour us refills, then spent the next hour considering anything and everything, me trying to be calm and caring but frantic with the need to find Lucian's body, wanting more than anything to get out of there so I could play the tape. No police, no telling anyone till I'd played that.

But Becky's question brought me up short. Not the expected theories: the prospect of a clean break, running away with someone, not the improbabilities of an amnesia-inducing accident or even a thrill-kill, but words about our first days.

"It's all to do with Portobello, isn't it? That convergent energy thing."

How you think of a thing makes a thing. How you name a thing defines a thing.

I might have said No, gone on about how wrong it was to make Lucian's ideas the only handle on this. But Becky had had 27 more years of such talk. No doubt it did follow on, did connect up. She kept at it.

"That's when it all started, didn't it?"

I might have told her then, mentioned the nail—the nails—the tape, the scrawled note, but needed perspective, desperately needed detachment if I could get it.

"Let me think this over, Beck. Let me go through my old diaries, just think it through, you know, see what I come up with. I'll call you tomorrow."

Fortunately I'd been there long enough, sitting through the silences with her, that it didn't seem like I was abandoning her. We'd exhausted possibilities, gone from plausible to improbable, from rational to irrational. At last I could leave.

"There's nothing else, Paul. There's just nothing else," she said as we went to the front door.

I hated her certainty, feared it. "I'll call, I promise. The moment I have anything."

Then I drove home thinking, wondering, bringing it all back.

I could have started the account like that, you see, with finding the nail, then gone back to Portobello and 1962. But I needed to pace through it for myself, just to get it out, and I'm nearly done.

I went home and put Lucian's nail in the box with Max's, then slipped the tape into my sound system, pressed Play.

There was nothing. Nothing. Just the running noise of the capstans turning, a no-sound, like the vacuum of space against an open mike, a constant waiting changelessness.

Now that I've had words fade on the page in front of me, I know what to expect, but even then I wasn't the least surprised. Once you granted the nails, the changed blood, of course you allowed for tapes that erased. Allowed them all as parts of a system—something just being recognised.

I drank more scotch than I should have and slept, thank God, slept right through.

Not because I was brave, more that I missed Tilly and was lonely, I went out walking that cold windy Saturday morning (this morning), just went across to the park, loving the autumn chill, how the leaves blew in waves, scurried and rustled on the paths.

I had the nails in my pocket and had half a mind to drive up into the Blue Mountains, go to the tunnel where Janice had died, or easier, closer, to go down onto Town Hall's lowest level and just sit there, wait out the day—in case Lucian might come to me from some impossible cutting or out of some narrow squeezed-back, folded-in part the undernight.

I was halfway across the deserted park when the hallucinations began: the hint and glint of rails among the scattering leaves, the sense of a train wind: ozone, steel on steel, feather-flutter in the midst of the cold south-westerly, like a warm breath into chilled hands.

I kept waiting for the attendant sounds, imagined—*locomotive!*—yes, in the bending, shuddering trees.

And I knew. Just knew.

How Max had died. Rusty's death. Janice's.

Leaning out. Tethered. Lucian hauling, misjudging, some error. Max dead, a nail left from his changed blood, wrested out. Every adult human carried at least a two-inch nail's worth of iron in the blood. Carrying oxygen to the brain or something. What a death! Train pummelling through, laved in train wind, a kiss, a stroke, out goes the iron. The mind, the body, knowing what it lacked, stultified with the knowledge of the clean sweep. Something sharp. Bitter iron taste like blood in the mouth.

I kicked at the leaves, hands in pockets, walking, walking, catching hints of silver lines in the windy day, coming at me from under the trees, glinting in bushes, raw quicksilver, pared chrome, drawing off and off and away, treacherous as razors.

The lines. All the lines.

Somewhere, somewhere, I knew, as I turned out into Buckingham Street, passed sealed, windlocked houses, leaves scattering, blowing out of beleaguered trees, Max's body lay changed and dead, perhaps in a forgotten tunnel, overlooked in a culvert, someplace where Lucian had done—or not done—his deed.

But Lucian, where?

I turned from Buckingham into Wentworth, circled the park, crossed it again, expecting Lucian at any moment, sitting on a bench, standing under a tree, dead eyes looking straight out, face white, leached, starved. But no, nothing, and the hints of lines faded in the bleak afternoon, vanished altogether.

Yet had told me something. Accelerating affect. The lines leading out.

I phoned Becky from a payphone on the corner, meaning to be brutally direct ("Where did you leave the body, Beck?"), but there was no answer.

I caught a cab to her house, entered by the unlocked back door, and found her dead on the kitchen floor, plundered, changed, eyes wide, her own nail by her right hand, held but dropped in death.

I added it to the others in my pocket, wiped the door handle and left, went back into the windy afternoon and took a bus into the city, went down onto the lowest level of Town Hall Station. No tether for me, just a quick moment of agony, a small tragic ritual in this dead afternoon hour, only a few people about.

If you've gotten this far, get to see this much at all, then you know I didn't do it, of course.

As I waited, peering into darkness, I saw someone looking back at me. Standing on the track, barest hint of shadow in shadow, of eyeshine and pale, pale skin, someone.

Lucian, was my first thought, first certainty. Lucian, you bastard, my second. Not your nail in the kitchen. Some other poor bugger's to mislead us.

No-one else was watching. No-one else saw me jump down onto the line, stride into the warm, pulsing throat of the tunnel. No-one called after me. I went up to the figure standing in the middle of the track, was about to grab him by the front of his jacket, demand: What have you done? What you done, bastard? Had the words right there, but stopped short.

It was Lucian all right. I saw that in the glow of platform light over my shoulder, in the white of skin and the glitter of sightless, staring eyes. He was staring into light.

It's hard to say now what he looked like, what the loss of iron had done. What skin I could see was like marble, tight and cold. He just stood, dead, changed, scarecrow upright, arms dangling, but worse, worst of all, his mouth hung open, and through it, from it, came a wind, that wind, and the whisper—*locomotive!*—of barest noise-in-a-seashell words.

"Not yet, Paul." Named. Naming me. *It* did. The Night Train did. This Bogeyman. Bogie-man. "Not yet, little Paul."

I fled then, turned and ran out of the tunnel, clambered up onto the platform even as the sliding thunder came and—an unforgettable meat-slammed-on-a-table sound—dead Lucian was impaled, carried, dumped and rolled by the silver severed thread of a train—my sweet, unknowing, latest, alibi train.

I took out the box, opened it, saw that the nails were gone. And knew.

6.
7:38 pm

So, you've guessed. Well, I took longer than you, but I worked it out then, refined it tonight, writing this.

The plate in my skull: not plastic or stainless steel, no, not for me. If you looked, you'd find dead black iron. Intimate iron. I'm sure of it. A mirror curved onto thought, raw but never doing harm. Not to me.

How many lives, I wonder, for that piece of metal, just so this demon, this devil, can have its psychopomp, one who goes before? One of many, who knows? Successors, perhaps, to our man at Portobello so long ago.

How many of us, driven to silence? Needing to speak, drawn to tell, what do I do? Go on seeing the glint of rails across parks, in rainy avenues, flashing in the moonlight when there is no moon, twin lines of there, not there quicksilver, feeling the train wind in the tiniest breath and pulse, in the play of dust devils in an empty street?

Go on drawing others to me, those whose blood will be changed in the sharpened dark?

I don't expect you to believe any of this, if ever it does get out there. Just don't be surprised. That Becky died. That Dr Day didn't answer his phone tonight, will probably never answer it again. That I'm still alive.

We all like trains. We do. But how many of us did it take to build this train and its endless thundering bogies? (Bogies, oh yes!) And tracks that go on and on and spill into the ordinary world worn thin? How many nails? How many?

My final opening line? Easy now. Perfect ending.

Let me write it. Let me write it before the words fade again. You would have liked it.

Now I know what Death is.

There.

And here. The knock at the door. Someone—Sue or Carmen, maybe Tilly back again. Or maybe that new guy from the office. Gerry. He said he might drop by. Any old iron.

Even as I close this off, press send one more time, there are rails, hints of lines off down the hall, running into night, but not for me. Not for the Bogie-man.

There's the far-off sound, a warm familiar pressure in my skull, and the wind is already blowing.

Acknowledgements

"The Daemon Street Ghost-Trap" copyright © 1993 Terry Dowling. First published in *Terror Australis*, Leigh Blackmore (Ed.), Coronet 1993.

"Downloading" copyright © 1998 Terry Dowling. First published in *Event Horizon Online*, Ellen Datlow (Ed.) 14 September 1998.

"The Bullet That Grows in the Gun" copyright © 1985 Terry Dowling. First published in *Urban Fantasies*, David King & Russell Blackford (Eds.), Ebony Books 1985.

"The Gully" copyright © 1985 Terry Dowling. First published in *MJ*, Spring 1985.

"The Bone Ship" copyright © 2003 Terry Dowling. First published in *Gathering the Bones*, Ramsey Campbell, Jack Dann & Dennis Etchison (Eds.), Voyager, 2003.

"Beckoning Nightframe" copyright © 1996 Terry Dowling. First published in *Eidolon*, Spring 1996.

"Stitch" copyright © 2002 Terry Dowling. First published in *eidolon. net*, December 2002.

"La Profonde" copyright © 2006 Terry Dowling. First published in *Basic Black: Tales of Appropriate Fear*, Cemetery Dance Publications, 2006.

"The Saltimbanques" copyright © 2000 Terry Dowling. First published in *Blackwater Days*, Eidolon 2000.

"They Found The Angry Moon" copyright © 1993 Terry Dowling. First published in *Intimate Armageddons*, Bill Congreve (Ed.), Five Islands Press 1992.

"Clownette" copyright © 2004 Terry Dowling. First published in *SciFiction*, Ellen Datlow (Ed.), 16 December 2004.

"The Ichneumon and the Dormeuse" copyright © 1996 Terry Dowling. First published in *Interzone*, April 1996.

"The Quiet Redemption of Andy the House" copyright © 1989 Terry Dowling. First published in *Australian Short Stories* 26, Pascoe Publishing 1989.

"The Maze Man" copyright © 1984 Terry Dowling. First published in *MJ*, Summer 1984.

"One Thing About the Night" copyright © 2003 Terry Dowling. First published in *The Dark*, Ellen Datlow (Ed.), TOR, 2003.

"Jenny Come to Play" copyright © 1997 Terry Dowling. First published in *Eidolon*, Spring 1997.

"Cheat Light" copyright © 2006 Terry Dowling. First published in *Basic Black: Tales of Appropriate Fear*, Cemetery Dance Publications, 2006.

"Scaring the Train" copyright © 1994 Terry Dowling. First published in *The Man Who Lost Red*, MirrorDanse Books, 1994.

THANK YOU

The publisher would sincerely like to thank:

Elizabeth Grzyb, Terry Dowling, Jonathan Strahan, Ellen
Datlow, Grant Stone, Jeremy G. Byrne, Sean Williams, Simon
Brown, Garth Nix, David Cake, Simon Oxwell, Grant Watson,
Sue Manning, Steven Utley, Bill Congreve, Jack Dann, Stephen
Dedman, the Mt Lawley Mafia, the Nedlands Yakuza,
Shane Jiraiya Cummings, Angela Challis, Donna Maree Hanson,
Kate Williams, Kathryn Linge, Andrew Williams, Al Chan, Alisa
Krasnostein, everyone I've missed ...

... and *you*.